Mine

To

Avenge

The Douglas Files: Book Nine

Nathan Birr

Published by BEACON BOOKS, LLC

Cover Images Copyright ©
istock/abadonian
istock/AG-ChapelHill

THE HOLY BIBLE, NEW INTERNATIONAL VERSION®, NIV®
Copyright © 1973, 1978, 1984, 2011 by Biblica, Inc.®
Used by permission. All rights reserved worldwide.

The Holy Bible, King James Version. Cambridge Edition: 1769;
King James Bible Online, 2018.
www.kingjamesbibleonline.org.

ISBN: 978-1-7321373-5-6 (hc)
ISBN: 978-1-7321373-6-3 (sc)

www.nathanbirr.com

Also by Nathan Birr

The Douglas Files
Overnight Delivery
Three's a Crowd
All an Illusion
Shot List
Chasing the Wind
Blood and Treasure
One Life to Lose
Golden Key

Douglas Files Shorts
Black Male – Short
WinterKill – Short
Short Sail – Short

Last Resort Series
Fire & Ice
Broken Trust

God, Girls, Golf & the Gridiron
(Not Always in That Order) . . . A Love Story

All is Calm? – A Christmas Novella

The Book of Levi

To the true Avenger who will one day right every wrong . . .

Chapter One

Friday, June 14, 2013
3:43 p.m.

"I DON'T RECALL Republicans raising a stink when it was their guy at 1600 Pennsylvania Avenue," the blond female panelist said. She wore a bright pink three-quarter sleeve sheath dress, professional but appealing. Her hair and makeup were styled for a night on the town. A thin pair of glasses, likely cosmetic, added a touch of sophistication. They worked in tandem with her razor sharp wit and political acumen to dispel any sentiment that she was just a pretty face to grab ratings.

She shook her head, causing the strands of long, dangle earrings to tinkle together. "To do so now comes off as a little disingenuous."

"Since 'their guy' didn't abuse his authority, why would they?" the only male on the panel shot back. His defining feature was a salt and pepper goatee that perfectly—too perfectly to be natural—matched similarly tinged hair. He was her equal intellectually and superciliously, but his beige herringbone jacket and lack of tie gave him a casual, almost insolent appearance. Likely intentional.

"Please," the woman said. "Every time this president so much as uncaps his pen, Republicans in congress start sniveling about abuse of power."

"That's because every time this president uses said pen, he uses it to skirt Republican leadership in the House and a growing minority—and likely to be majority come next fall—in the Senate. This latest example, sanctioning what amounts to Hitler's *Einsatzgruppen*, is just another in a long line of presidential oversteps, and one that is incredibly dangerous."

1

"Oh my goodness!" the woman said, cutting off the moderator before he could interject. "This is absurd. They aren't death squads, and comparisons to Hitler . . ." Her eyeballs nearly rolled right onto the desk. "But if you want to talk about executive action, then let's talk about Ronald Reagan, who you Republicans worship as if he came from heaven, born of a virgin, proclaimed by angels in the field. Ronald Reagan issues 381 executive orders, everything from fighting AIDS to broadening the powers of the intelligence agencies to restricting access to presidential records. That's just fine. But let a left-leaning moderate 'Demon-crat' issue a few, and the sky is falling."

"Moderate?" He huffed. "You know, I really don't know where to start, whether with your apparent misunderstanding of the word 'few,' your absurd comparison between what we're seeing with our current president and the leadership of our fortieth president, or your almost slanderous disdain for Mr. Reagan."

This time the moderator did manage to insert himself into the conversation. "Let me interject a moment so we can hear from the third member of our panel."

"Hold on a second," the woman said. "This is such a common tactic. This president isn't doing anything any other president hasn't done in terms of executive orders, but because of the D in parentheses next to his name, every pen stroke is a sign of the apocalypse to those on the right."

"It's not the how, it's the what," the man countered. "These death squads—and that's exactly what they are—" he said, raising his voice to silence her rebuttal, "are a threat to our liberty. We're dealing with this right now, the HSGAC's investigation into Senator Nantz over his misappropriation of funds to support some unconstitutional black ops slush fund, and—'"

"We're getting off top—"

"Those are alleged and unproven accusations," the woman said, "and like all senate investigations, there will be a lot of bluster and bravado and posturing by Republicans out for blood, but nothing will come of it."

"I'm afraid we have to cut this off and give our third panelist some time," the moderator said forcefully.

On his couch in Pacific Palisades, Jackson Douglas sat up. He had virtually no interest in the sparring of political talking heads, nor was he familiar with the specifics of the executive action in question. He knew nothing of Hitler's death squads, other than to say the pronunciation of *Einsatzgruppen* seemed exaggerated, and he certainly had no idea what actions the current U.S. president had taken that were drawing comparisons—outlandish or otherwise—to *der Führer*. Nor did he know what the HSGAC was, why it was investigating Senator Nantz, or even who Senator Nantz was. The extent of his knowledge of world events was that the Dodgers were close to signing a Korean lefty with an unhittable slider, and he usually shied away from political back-and-forths. But the third panelist, despite his internal insistence that he was ambivalent, drew him to the TV.

Having been called on, she sat a little taller in her chair around the crescent-shaped table. "Thank you, Bret. First of all, I don't think the ultimate dissonance is between Republicans and Democrats or right and left," Maggie said, her gray-blue eyes gleaming as if she had been born for the spotlight. "Rather, I think we're seeing Americans in general becoming more and more disenfranchised with a government they feel is out of touch with their wishes and values. They are fed up with politicians on both sides of the aisle."

She spoke smoothly and calmly, as if this wasn't her first time on national television. Then again, it wasn't. Her exposé on corruption in the Mexican oil business the previous December had garnered Maggie national attention, including a one-on-one interview with CNN's Anderson Cooper. Several months later, after her newfound Christian faith had begun to infuse her columns, she'd been let go by the *Los Angeles Times*. A seeming setback to a promising career had quickly turned into a boom as she had been hired by an online news outlet to write a regular column, in addition to being sought by all the major players—CNN, Fox News, MSNBC—for her insight, practical wisdom, and charisma.

Jackson would have been incredibly proud had he not been so jealous. After several years of a very casual dating relationship, he and Maggie had "broken up" when she announced she had started dating the son of the pastor at Jackson's church. They'd had little interaction since, but she had still phoned him up to let him know she would be making her debut as a panelist on Fox News. Jackson had ignored her call, then listened to her voicemail with mixed feelings. He hadn't been sure he'd even tune in, but sadly, he had nothing else to do on a Friday afternoon.

"As for this current issue," Maggie continued, her wavy chestnut hair dancing as it fell over her shoulders and the edges of a sleeveless burgundy blouse, "with all due respect to my colleagues, I don't think it's a matter of Republican versus Democrat either. We're dealing with a question of constitutionality, which transcends party or preference." She glanced to them, then back to her host. "The framers were very specific in outlining the President's authority in the Constitution, and equally specific in limiting it. So the crux of the matter is not what one party or the other feels is appropriate, or even—frankly—what the people feel is appropriate. It's what the Constitution says is appropriate. Obviously, that's not always black and white, which is why there's so much room for debate and disagreement. And it's why I think this case will ultimately, like so many before it in the last few years, end up in front of the Supreme Court to determine just that."

Both the blond woman and the salt-and-pepper man were primed for more airtime, but the host looked instead to Maggie. "In your opinion, how do they rule?"

"Given the balance of the court right now, that's hard to say. But if they stick to strict, literal interpretation of the founders' intent, I'd have to say they find the President's actions, in this case, unconstitutional. Article I, Section 8 gives to Congress the power to, and I quote, '*provide for calling forth the Militia to execute the Laws of the Union, suppress Insurrections and repel Invasions.*' Now, the President's objectives in putting together these 'task forces' are ambiguous at best, but it would seem to me to fall under the suppression and repelling category, which in turn falls under the purview of Congress. Now, one could argue that the phrase '*he shall take Care that the Laws be faithfully executed*' from Article II, Section 3 would grant him the authority he seeks. I wouldn't dare to speak for the Justices," she added with a sly grin, "but, again, looking strictly at the Constitution and at the spirit in which it was written, I'd have to say this falls on the unconstitutional side."

As the host thanked his panelists and teased the next segment, Jackson reached for the remote and muted the TV. Maggie didn't give off any auras. She didn't flaunt her intellect, didn't dress up (except when appearing on Fox News) to impress anyone, didn't put much effort into being anything other than she was. Maybe it was that, or maybe it was because Jackson's relationship with her had been personal more than professional, but he often found himself surprised at how good she was at her job—whatever that job was.

Too bad she'd be coming home to L.A. to play kissy-face with Russell James.

Jackson sighed as he stood, wandering into the kitchen of his small, one-bedroom, split-level house overlooking the Pacific Ocean less than a mile away. Normally relaxing, the the view was uninspiring. The skies were low and gray, and the water beneath them was murky instead of shimmering. It fit the mood Jackson had been in for as long as he could remember.

He leaned on the deck, mulling his dinner options. It'd been a carousel of grilled burgers, frozen pizzas, and boxed noodle mixes with canned chicken for a few weeks. He was rescued from further contemplation by the ringing of his cell phone. He dug into his pocket and flipped open the cover of the outdated model. The number on the display was familiar, but he couldn't immediately place it. Why not?

"Jackson Douglas."

"Jackson, it's Ike Haywood. How you doing, brother?"

"I'm all right," Jackson said, the standard brush-off.

"Hey, I know it's really short notice, but Jules and I are in L.A. and wondered if you're free for dinner tonight."

"Tonight?"

"Yeah. There's actually something we want to talk to you about."

"Uh, yeah, sure. I guess."

"Great, man. Pick the place. It's our treat."

Jackson's old fallback was Cameron's, the bistro/beachside café owned by his best friend Reggie Cameron. But Cameron's had been his occasional alternate to burgers, frozen pizzas, and canned chicken, and he felt like a change.

"How about Rusty's? I'm in the mood for seafood."

"Shoot, we can do better than that, Jack. If you want seafood, how about Water Grill? An old favorite of ours."

"I won't argue with that."

"Seven?"

"I'll be there."

"Great. We'll see you in a bit."

Jackson closed his phone and frowned, wondering what the Haywoods could possibly want to talk to him about.

*   *   *

Two Years Ago . . .
Tuesday, May 10, 2011
4:04 p.m.

JACKSON MENTALLY patted himself on the back for a good decision. Schmoozing was very much not his thing, and when he'd heard about the Small Business Social put on by the Santa Monica Chamber of Commerce, his initial reaction had been to avoid it like the plague. He'd talked himself into going, however. As an entrepreneur and a freshly minted private investigator, he'd have to get used to such unpleasantries. Besides, he could use any and all local contacts and potential referrals to help get his business off the ground.

So far, he'd made little headway in that regard, although he had met the owner of a Chinese restaurant over on Colorado Avenue—an owner who had been offering samples—and it promised to be a profitable relationship. But the weather was glorious—sunny, seventies, an ocean breeze. The view from Palisades Park, which fronted Ocean Boulevard for 1.5 miles, was spectacular. And despite his disdain for "mixers," Jackson couldn't help but be excited about his new career. After years of jumping from job to job, putting in time and punching a clock, he'd finally found a vocation he could sink his teeth into. He could use his smarts, his natural knack for problem-solving, to do good, help people, make a real and practical difference. He couldn't wait to tell his family, after months and even years of keeping his true plans a secret.

As an added bonus to the day, the Chamber of Commerce had outdone itself with catering, serving a selection of hors d'oeuvres and samplers from several of Santa Monica's finest establishments. Jackson was on his second plate, casually making the rounds, when a high-pitched whistle reverberated off and through the tall, thin fan palms—A.K.A. "sky dusters"—that speckled the park.

Jackson turned his head to a small dais erected against the backdrop of the cliffs that towered over Highway 1 and the beach. A couple dozen business owners and other bigwigs—including the seven members of the city council—had assembled behind a small lectern. They were spiffed up—some of the men even wearing jackets—for the occasion. Jackson had traded a T-shirt for a plaid button-down, which put him on the casual—but not impolitely so—end of the spectrum. And that was just fine.

The whistle had been caused by a man in a full suit—even a tie—who stood behind the lectern. He tapped the microphone once, laughed nervously, then grinned. He introduced himself as "Arnie" Kendrick, the mayor of Santa Monica. He was honored with very light applause, as if he'd just hit a wedge shot to the middle of the green at a golf tournament.

He went into a rather lengthy introduction of the other members of the council, his daughter Hailey, selected business owners and entrepreneurs, and various people and organizations that had helped put this day together. It was boring, but it gave Jackson time to eat without having to balance a plate, a bottle of water, and the business cards he'd printed just that morning at The UPS Store. And time to give a second glance at Mayor Kendrick's daughter. She was maybe in her mid-twenties, with a cute face and long, wavy hair that was blondish brown. Smiling as she stood in the sunshine, wearing a three-quarter-sleeve jacket (Dodger blue) over a white blouse, a pink tiered miniskirt, and heels that made her appear roughly Jackson's height, she was definitely worth a second look.

The mayor transitioned to a brief outline of the council's mission for Santa Monica, a lot of corporate buzzwords and community admiration that Jackson let drift away on the breeze. When he concluded to more light applause, Jackson ditched his empty plate and drained bottle of water and set out to visit some more booths. More than a few local businesses had set up displays on everything from shared halves of tables to their own trade show pop-up stalls. Most were staffed by at least two smiling reps, usually a man and a woman, young and smartly dressed, if not terribly formal.

Jackson did not have a table, nor an attractive female second. Just the business cards. So he kept on the move, trading a few names while collecting pens, refrigerator magnets, and hard candy. Spotting a bowl of Tootsie Rolls on one of a trio of tables at the end of the cordoned off area, Jackson weaved through several small crowds of conversation and found the trio of tables belonged to a dentist (not offering the Tootsie Rolls), a chiropractor, and "Ad Astra Investigative Agency," according to the business cards on a small stand. Glancing around, he picked one up and studied the competition.

It appeared to be a husband and wife team, and their elegant business cards with engraved text claimed they specialized in confidential representation of celebrities, business execs, and other professionals who wanted their affairs kept out of the limelight. Jackson looked around again, but nobody seemed tethered to the table. Shooing away his initial petty proclivity toward potential rivals, he decided that his best option, professionally speaking, might be to make nice with his fellow sleuths. He had no ambition of representing the Hollywood elite. Who knew, maybe a friendship could lead to them funneling less exclusive clients his way?

"Hello there, can I help you?"

Jackson turned as a woman broke off from a conversation with another woman behind the Tootsie Roll table and moved to stand opposite him. She was young and pretty, with curly black hair drawn into a loose ponytail, several strands left loose at the side of an oval face. Her skin was caramel in color and seemingly in texture, and she didn't so much wear a sleeveless lime green top and black, yellow, and matching green skirt as she was draped by them. Her arms, muscular but still feminine, were adorned with a series of bracelets and bangles. Her earrings looked like something B.A. Baracus might wear, but on her, they were tasteful, not gaudy.

Jackson took in her entire appearance in a second while forming a reply. She waited with a beaming smile and narrow, brown eyes.

"Jackson Douglas," he said, extending a hand.

"Juliet Haywood." Her skin felt like caramel too.

He withdrew his hand and reached for a business card. "I saw your card, saw we were in the same line of work."

"Douglas," she said as she took the card. "Douglas? Name doesn't ring a bell. You new to the area?"

"I just hung out my shingle."

"Ah, that explains it."

"I take it you and—is it your husband?—are veterans of the investigative business?"

"Yes, my husband, Ike, and we actually just incorporated last month. But we did pretty thorough research of other firms and investigators in the area." She raised his business card as if it represented his brief tenure. "This would explain why we didn't find you." She leaned around Jackson and waved. "Ike, come here a sec."

Jackson turned as a tallish man in a gray sport coat and jeans approached. His head was slick, his skin a few shades darker than Juliet's. His eyes matched hers. So too did his smile. Like her, he wore his clothes as if they were his skin, and moved with grace and ease as he joined her behind the table.

"This is Jackson Douglas," she said. "A fellow private detective."

"All right," he said, offering a firm hand. "From here in Santa Monica?"

Jackson nodded.

"He just started, like us."

"Well, congratulations," Ike said. He seemed genuine. So did Juliet's perpetual smile. "How long have you been in the area?" he asked.

"Santa Monica, since January. Been in L.A. since '09."

"But not as a P.I.?"

"No, I worked at Bauer & Bauer for a year and a half."

"The big insurance company on Wilshire and Western?"

Jackson nodded again. "I was a claims adjustor, putting in hours toward my license."

"Well, that's certainly more practical than our approach," Juliet said.

"You could say that," Ike agreed. He nodded at Jackson. "I've spent the last five years since leaving the Army working part-time as a CPA and part-time as a talent agent for B-list actors, a few ball players, musicians."

Jackson felt his eyes widening.

"And Jules here got her break as a fashion model. She's also a motivational speaker, health and fitness guru, a life coach."

"I hate that term," she said with a crooked, closed-mouth grin. "It's so overused. Seriously, what is a life coach? It's almost . . . demeaning."

"Athletes need coaching. That's not demeaning."

"No, but that's in a specialized pursuit. How to hit a curve ball or tackle Adrian Peterson. Not how to live."

"You're the one who put it on your business card."

"Well, that's because it's a term people recognize. I still think it's a little weird."

"Forgive us," Ike said, turning to Jackson. "Been seven years—"

"Almost seven years."

"—but we're already like an old married couple."

Jackson only grinned in response.

"At any rate, Jules' success puts mine to shame. She's worked with Hollywood writers, actors, socialites, a regular who's who list."

Juliet waved her hand dismissively.

"That's impressive," Jackson said. "Both of you. How do you find time for another career?"

"We make time," Ike said. "No kids, no family in the area, so we throw ourselves into work."

"And we love what we do."

"This is really more of a hobby for us. It's why we picked a very specific niche of clientele."

"We've both got inroads through our current careers 'to the stars,'" Juliet said.

"To the stars?" Jackson asked.

"*Ad Astra*," Ike said. "It's Latin for 'to the stars.'"

Juliet's smile vanished. "You don't think that's too kitschy, do you?"

"You're asking the wrong guy. I haven't made it to thinking up a slogan."

Her smile returned.

"We're still figuring out the ropes ourselves," Ike said. "We're hoping we can make this work and still keep our other entrepreneurial ventures going too. And stay in love," he said, floating his arm around Juliet's waist, drawing her a step closer.

"Young, in-love entrepreneurs who solve crimes as a hobby," Jackson said. "You two are basically the black version of *Hart to Hart*."

For the first time, Juliet frowned, withdrawing from Ike's arm to stand up straight. "Who?"

"No, I know them," he said. "That was that old TV show with . . ." Ike snapped a few times. "Robert Blake and that lady from *Charlie's Angels*, right?"

"Robert Wagner," Jackson said.

"Right, right. *It Takes a Thief*. Classic. And the lady was Sabrina, right?"

"The teen-aged witch?"

"No, man, on *Charlie's Angels*."

"I don't know. Before my time."

"And *Hart to Hart* isn't?" Juliet asked. "How old are you, anyhow?"

"Twenty-nine on Saturday," Jackson answered. "My parents ate it up though."

"And what about you, Shaft? When did you become an expert on leading ladies of the 1970s?" she asked, causing her earrings and curls of hair to sway back and forth. Her indignation was fake, as evidenced by the smile burgeoning beneath the surface.

"Um, stammer . . . stammer . . . stall."

"Uh-huh."

Ike winked. "Jackson might be onto something here, Jules. Maybe we should change our slogan to Black *Hart to Hart*."

"Smooth change of subject."

"It's why you love me."

"Your scattershot thinking?"

"My smoothness."

"That must be it."

"Well, I don't want to take up any more of your time with potential customers," Jackson said. "It was nice to meet you both."

"You too," they echoed.

"Good luck," Juliet said.

Ike offered his hand again. "If we can ever be of any help, offer a professional courtesy, you need only ask."

"I'll do that," Jackson said, pocketing one of their cards. "Likewise."

He gave Juliet a second handshake, then turned to see if the food line was still serving or that Chinese guy had any samples left.

Chapter Two

A HOSTESS GUIDED Jackson to a booth in the back of the dimly lit Water Grill, where the Haywoods were waiting. They hadn't aged a bit. If anything, they looked younger than the last time he'd seen them.

Ike, as he had the first day they'd met, wore a sport coat (navy blue with elbow patches) with blue jeans, and made it look as if it was the most comfortable getup in the world. Juliet wore a yellow, knee-length dress under a denim jacket, also with the ease with which one might wear a pair of sweats. Her hair was a little longer, but everything else—right down to the toothy smile with which she greeted Jackson—was the same.

"How have you been, Jackson?" Ike asked. He'd stood to greet him, and clapped him on the back as they shook hands. "Busy, if the news is true."

"More or less it is," Jackson said, sitting down on the opposite side of the booth from the Haywoods. "Hi, Juliet."

"Hi, Jackson," she beamed.

A waiter arrived to introduce himself before anyone could say more. He passed out menus and took drink orders, after which Juliet immediately ordered an appetizer of steamed razor clams. The waiter scurried for the kitchen and Juliet leaned forward.

"So, you've become famous."

"More like infamous," Jackson said.

"Hardly," Ike said.

"Heroic is the word I keep hearing and reading," Juliet said.

"Now'd you just get back from the Middle East a few months ago?" Ike asked.

"Back in February, yeah."

"And the Greek Isles," Juliet added.

"And France," Jackson said. "Twice."

"Yeah, yeah, man, we read all about that in that article by the reporter who went with you, what was her name?"

"Maggie."

"Maggie," he repeated, as if that didn't sound right. But before he could say anything, Juliet started plying Jackson with questions about the trip. And for the next twenty minutes, while they perused their menus and sampled the clams once they arrived, Jackson caught the Haywoods up on his myriad adventures over the last year-plus. He left out the painful stuff—the suicide of his client the previous July, his bloody rampage at a decommissioned Air Force base in Nevada a few months subsequent, and his recent weeks-long trip to Florida, New Orleans, and the Bahamas. He'd originally ventured to the Sunshine State for some R&R and as a favor to an old friend. Only, that friend had been missing when Jackson arrived, and the authorities eventually concluded he'd been killed at sea. Jackson had teamed up with a local woman named Sawyer to track down the people responsible for his death and to find the long-lost pirate treasure Jackson's friend had been seeking. They had recouped over nine million dollars in gold and other valuables (after taxes), all of which was now in Jackson's possession. It was not something he advertised.

"And all in the span of a year's time?" Ike asked when Jackson had summed up his second most recent case. Their entrées had since arrived—wild Australian swordfish, pan sautéed halibut, and California Dungeness crab, along with sides of coleslaw, French fries, braised kale, and grilled carrots with Fresno chili. In short, it was a feast.

Jackson nodded. "Yep. Since my birthday last year."

"I don't know how you've had time to think," Juliet said, cutting into her halibut.

"Better if I don't sometimes."

The Haywoods looked at each other.

"So what's life been like for you two?" Jackson asked as he cracked a crab leg. "Ike said on the phone that you were in L.A., as if that's not normal anymore."

"It's not," Juliet said. "We've been working out of San Diego since last January."

"Really?"

"Business was actually getting too big," Ike said as he lifted a forkful of swordfish to his mouth. "Mm-mm." He swallowed. "We never anticipated being full-time, sixty or seventy or eighty hour a week P.I.s. And that's what we'd have been at had we kept up at the current pace."

"We also were less than bowled over by our clientele," Juliet said.

"Man, Hollywood people are messed up," Ike said.

"We naïvely thought we could provide a service to people who needed a delicate touch. You know, the high-profile writer who has his screenplay pirated or the ballplayer who has a personal problem or company who suspected an exec was embezzling. Real issues for real people who don't want the publicity."

"Instead it was petty love squabbles by wannabes, cocaine-sniffing rich kids fighting their parents for an early inheritance, and missing—read sold by his ex—movie memorabilia." Ike said.

"Not our cup of tea."

Jackson nodded along, fighting with a dead crab for its meat. It was at best a draw. He gave up on a small leg and looked up. "Don't tell me you're not Black *Hart to Hart* anymore."

"We re-strategized," Juliet said. "Narrowed our focus. Ike's idea," she said, nodding his way.

He nibbled on a fry. "If we were going to work this deal sort of like a hobby, we could afford to take fewer cases. And with Jules making good money as a speaker and me still doing well part-time as a CPA, we could financially afford the hit in business."

"He didn't ask for our budget," she said. "Tell him your idea already."

"It hit me one night while I was looking through some old correspondence with my Army C.O. who had just passed. We could make military members and their families our target market."

"That's not a bad idea," Jackson said.

"That's what I said," Juliet said. She scooped some more kale onto her plate, then extended it to Jackson.

"Pass. Thanks."

Ike continued. "With the naval base in San Diego, it made a lot more sense to live there."

"Our lease was up at the end of the year," Juliet said, "so we made the decision one night over Japanese takeout. We bought a condo in San Diego, closed our current cases, rebranded, and opened up the Freedom Detective Agency in January 2012."

"That's great," Jackson said.

"And it has been. We've seen so much good come from the cases we've taken. We love seeing that look of relief or joy on someone's face when we're able to solve a case. Knowing the sacrifice our military and their families make for us, that look and that joy are that much sweeter for us."

"Plus San Diego's a great city, and so much more laidback than L.A."

"Tell me about it," Jackson said, practically mutilating a leg to get a few morsels of tender crabmeat. He succeeded, then lost half his catch in the cup of drawn butter. He temporarily quit and reached for his iced tea. "So what brings you to L.A.?"

"A case, actually," Ike said. "It's a long story—"

"Which you can't tell him," Juliet interjected.

"I wasn't going to tell him."

"It sounded like you were, like you almost told Major Levering about you-know-what."

"I did—"

"You know how it goes," she said to Jackson.

"I do."

"A long story," Ike continued, "the short of which is that we had to interview a few family members in the city. We got in yesterday afternoon, in fact, and have been chasing around town ever since. We were about finished up when I called you."

Jackson took a second swig of tea, trying to dislodge a tendril of meat from the back of his mouth. The last swish succeeded. "So why did you call?" Jackson asked. "As much as I'm enjoying it, I don't think it was to catch up."

The Haywoods looked at each other again.

"No, it's not," Ike said.

Juliet wiped her hands on her napkin. "We don't want to open old wounds, Jackson. But we think there's something you should know."

"Okay."

"Last month, we were approached by a man named Aaron Rutledge, a San Diego attorney who represented a former Navy petty officer. Jackson, it was Shauna Grabel."

Jackson swallowed as his gut began to churn.

"He explained to us that Petty Officer Grabel had been sexually assaulted by a man named Joaquín Padilla back in 2011, when she was still in the Navy, and that Padilla had been convicted of the crime and given the maximum sentence—four years at Kern Valley State Prison—which I'm sure you know."

Jackson nodded mechanically.

"Mr. Rutledge informed us that the San Diego County D.A. had arranged to have Padilla released for time served in exchange for his testimony in another case. Petty Officer Grabel, through Mr. Rutledge, wanted to hire us to go over the case against Padilla with a fine-toothed comb to see if we could find anything that might persuade D.A. Moreno or the judge to quash the release."

Jackson somehow found his voice. "Did you?"

Juliet shook her head, hoop earrings bouncing off her cheeks. "But we did find something else."

He cleared his throat and nodded for her to continue.

"Grabel testified at the trial that she had arranged to meet Padilla at her apartment for drinks at seven before they went to dinner. However, he was late. She was unable to pinpoint the exact time of his arrival, likely because of trauma from the assault. She originally told officers and detectives at the scene that he had been fifteen to twenty minutes late. They also testified to this at the trial. Grabel, however, testified that Padilla had been approximately thirty minutes late. Padilla's attorney jumped on the discrepancy, and it was the biggest hole in the

17

prosecution's case. Fortunately for the prosecution, Grabel cut a very sympathetic figure to the jury, Padilla had a litany of previous charges and convictions against him, and they were able to pass the discrepancy off as 'fog of war,' according to her attorney."

Jackson was aware of everything Juliet said, but it was as if he was in a fog himself. His brain was flooded with images and memories he had worked to suppress for over two years. As they all rushed to the surface, he felt his chest constricting, his ears humming as if bombs had just gone off. He forced himself to focus as Juliet continued to recite facts painfully familiar to Jackson.

"The prosecution also had the testimony of one of Grabel's neighbors, a man named Tim Van Vleck. He was adamant in his claim that he saw Padilla's Dodge Dakota arrive at precisely 7:23 p.m. That was close enough to the fifteen to twenty minutes Grabel initially told the detectives, and not that far off from the half hour she said on the witness stand. Van Vleck's testimony pretty much erased whatever doubt the defense had created, and Padilla was promptly convicted. Again, you probably know all this, but I wanted to provide context."

While Jackson's brain pushed the question of "context for what" aside, it also bombarded him with knife-like fragments of recollection. Joaquín Padilla's assault of Petty Officer Grabel had occurred on the same evening as the explosion at a San Diego restaurant that had killed Jackson's parents and brother. Padilla had initially been a suspect in the explosion, due to a number of factors, including his past convictions and suspicions of arson and his one-time friendship with the restaurant owner's son. But when he was arrested for sexually assaulting Grabel—and once the timeline proved he couldn't have been at the restaurant and at Grabel's apartment—investigators turned their attention elsewhere. Eventually—and primarily because of lack of evidence—they ruled the explosion an accident, a ruling that had never settled terribly well with Jackson.

"We wanted to be thorough," Juliet said, "so we talked to Grabel, who was still fuzzy on the time of Padilla's arrival. According to her memory, he arrived 'between 7:20 and 7:30.'"

Ike interjected for the first time. "She's living in Mississippi, so it was a phone call. But you could hear in her voice the whole time this uneasiness and uncertainty."

"Not surprising after the ordeal she went through," Juliet said. She paused to take a drink. "We also went to the Van Vleck's apartment. Tim Van Vleck wasn't there, but his ex-wife, Mira Austin, was. She told us that she and Tim had since divorced, and he had moved. We asked for his contact information, but she said not to bother. When we asked why, she said because he had been wrong about Padilla's arrival."

Jackson's stomach was no longer churning. It was a roiling cauldron.

"Tim Van Vleck had dyslexia," she said. "It was something only a very few people knew, but it caused him to mix up numbers. For example, he would look at his watch and see 7:23 when it was really 7:32. Tim Van Vleck, according to his ex-wife, was also something of a bully and a chauvinist. Apparently, when the police arrived to question them, he took over and spoke for both of them, insisting that Padilla had arrived at 7:23 because that's when he truly believed it had been. But Mira told us Padilla didn't actually arrive until about ten minutes later, likely 7:32."

Jackson again found a way to ask a question. "Likely?"

"She knows it was after 7:30 because she was working out and listening to a Padres game on the radio, and the visiting team . . ."

"The Rockies," Ike said. "We checked."

"The Rockies scored five runs in the first inning and when it finally ended, she looked up and saw that it had lasted for twenty-five minutes, till 7:30. According to Mira, it was a few minutes later that Padilla's Dodge Dakota 'whipped'—her words—into the parking lot. She didn't look at the clock then, so she couldn't provide a precise time, other than that it was after the top of the first inning. But given Tim's insistence that Padilla arrived at 7:23, she told us it was very likely 7:32, which fits the timing of the game and would make sense with his dyslexia."

Jackson reached for his tea and took a drink. He needed to wet a suddenly dry mouth, and if he didn't put something down into his stomach, he feared something would come up.

He'd done the math hundreds of times. He'd even dug up San Diego traffic reports from the day of his family's death. Even had Padilla driven like a madman, there was no way he could have made it from Carmel Valley to Grabel's apartment in La Playa by 7:23. The explosion and ensuing fire had been so hot and severe that it had burned most of the evidence—and David, Hannah, and Grant Douglas's bodies—but investigators had somehow been able to exclude any sort of remote detonation. Given his presence at Grabel's apartment at 7:23, Padilla couldn't have blown up the restaurant.

But add nine minutes, accounting for Tim Van Vleck's dyslexia—even adding seven in accordance with Mira's statement that it was after seven-thirty and . . . Jackson almost subconsciously did the math, computing miles per hour, compensating for traffic, for stoplights—it was tight, but Padilla could have made it. He could have been at the restaurant at 7:11 when the explosion occurred and at Grabel's apartment nineteen to twenty-one minutes later.

Ike and Juliet Haywood's expressions indicated they too had done the math and reached the same conclusion.

"The rest of our investigation didn't turn up anything one way or the other," Juliet said. "Suffice to say, our findings didn't influence the judge and he okayed the deal." She looked down and lowered her voice. "Padilla was released from Kern Valley two days ago."

Jackson managed to swallow, but it wasn't easy.

"It doesn't prove anything," Ike said. "But we know Padilla was a suspect in your family's death, and we know that suspicion went away because he had an alibi."

"And now he doesn't," Jackson said.

"It's at least inconclusive," Juliet said.

Jackson sat back and inhaled deeply through his nose.

"Jackson, we're so sorry. The last thing we wanted to do was bring this to the surface again after all this time . . ."

"But we figured you would want to know the truth, whatever that may be," Ike said.

Jackson nodded, not bothering to tell them "this" hadn't been all that far beneath the surface to begin with.

He swallowed again, took another drink of tea. "Why, uh, why didn't Mira speak up earlier?"

"She was afraid of her husband," Ike said. "He had a hair trigger for his temper, especially if anyone brought up his dyslexia. She also said she didn't think it mattered. Padilla had clearly assaulted Grabel, and she didn't want to do anything that might hinder his conviction."

Jackson nodded.

Ike reached into his jacket pocket and came out with a business card. He slid it around plates and cups to Jackson. "On the back is the cell number of Special Agent Dion Collier, a friend of ours with the FBI. He works out of the San Diego office and has helped us on a number of cases, including this one. He's the guy to talk to if you need the particulars on an investigation, especially with Padilla. If you have any questions, he said to give him a call."

Jackson nodded again—it was about all he could manage at the time—and took the card.

Juliet reached across the table and put her hand on his. "And if there's anything we can do . . ."

"Anything," Ike said.

"I . . ." Jackson cleared his throat. Twice. "Yeah, I um . . . I appreciate it. And thanks for letting me know."

"I know you've got a lot to think about," Ike said. "And we should be getting back home too. What do you say we call it a night?"

Jackson nodded again.

Ike caught the waiter's eye and a few minutes later had settled the check. The trio walked out to the sidewalk, where they said goodbyes. Ike offered another firm handshake and again promised any help he and Juliet could provide. She gave Jackson a hug. "I'm sorry about the circumstances, but it was good to see you again."

"It was," he said.

"Don't be a stranger, okay," Ike said.

"I won't."

"Take care of yourself."

"Yeah. You too."

They turned and started down the sidewalk toward their car. Ike put his arm around Juliet's shoulders and she leaned into him as they walked.

Jackson watched until they turned the corner, at which point he realized he was obstructing the flow of traffic on the sidewalk.

He turned and strode for his car, parked on the next street over. The night was cool, the wind biting. Even so, the streets of Santa Monica were packed with festive diners, shoppers, and clubbers. Jackson still felt as if the edges of his vision were blurry, his senses all dulled by the hammering in his head and heart. It was a sensation he'd grown used to in recent months, but one that hadn't been this intense since the moments just after the "accident."

Chapter Three

BUOYED BY HIS meeting with the Haywoods, Jackson made the rounds through Palisades Park with a little more eagerness. He passed out a few dozen business cards, with several of the recipients seeming genuinely interested and one—an attorney—asking for a small stack to hand out to clients. Jackson wasn't sure they would generate the type of leads he was hoping for, but he couldn't afford to be choosy.

He lingered for a few minutes at a local bathroom fixtures provider's display table, flipping through a brochure. He had begun renovating his new house, purchased that January. The previous owners, druggies, had—as he liked to tell people with pun intended—let the place go to pot. In addition to repairing and updating it, he also had plans to merge two small upstairs bedrooms into one "master" bedroom/office. That included remodeling much of the bathroom, a project he had just completed. Well, almost completed.

"It's just not like him," a female voice said. He cast a quick glance to his right, spotting a trio of girls and a guy standing in front of an unmanned table. He had to stop himself from doing a double take when he realized one of them was the mayor's daughter.

"Have you texted him?" another female voice asked.

"Like fourteen times."

Jackson hid a smirk at what he assumed was romantic angst. Back in the day, he had watched a few episodes of *The O.C.*, finding its melodramatic portrayal of SoCal life to be ridiculous. Having lived in L.A. for twenty months, he was changing his tune. It was spot on. He tried to ignore the babble while doing math on fixture prices in his head.

"Have you tried actually calling him?"

"Yeah. No answer."

"You don't really think something happened to him, do you?" It was the guy, kind of a nasally voice, and his question furrowed Jackson's eyebrow.

"No." It was unconvincing. "I mean, I don't think so."

"What would have happened to Connor?"

"Nothing."

"But?"

"He's been missing for several days."

Jackson took another casual glance at the group. His detective brain observed several things. One, the mayor's daughter seemed to be the one expressing concern over a missing guy, as evident by the frown on her face, moderately slouched posture, and nervous nibbling on her fingernails. Two, all three women were from well-off families, based on their clothing and accessories. Jackson didn't exactly follow women's fashion, but he could tell the difference between a purchase from Kohl's and from Dolce & Gabbana or Prada. Three, the guy and one of the girls were dating, seeing as how his arm was around her lower back. Over the shoulders could be a casual friend thing, but not lower back, and not with her leaning his way. Four, the mayor's daughter was really quite cute up close.

"I am sure he will totally show up."

"Yeah, don't worry, Kenny."

Jackson frowned and sneaked a peek. It was not the guy but the mayor's daughter who nodded in response to the name Kenny. She then lowered her hand as Jackson returned the brochure to the table and grabbed one for toilets. His was in okay shape, but he was stalling.

"You have to be going?"

"Yeah. Rowan's parents are taking us sailing."

"And I have to work."

"Thanks for coming."

"You should blow, K."

"I promised Dad I'd meet some friends of his, so I'd better not leave early."

Out the side of his eye, Jackson saw the group split up. He waited a quarter of a minute, then put down the toilet brochure and stepped away from the table. He spotted the two girls and guy headed toward the street. Sweeping his vision to the right, he found the mayor's daughter as she approached the food line.

An idea had popped into his mind, and he wasn't sure if it was brilliant or brash. He took several steps toward her while trying to sort it out. He also tried to tell himself the idea had nothing to do with a girl's good looks, but he was a twenty-eight-year-old single man—everything had to do with a girl's good looks.

She had stopped just short of the food table, in the shade of a fan palm, and withdrawn her phone from her purse. She stood with it low in front of her, using the shade to make out what was on the screen.

Feeling good about the progress he'd made at the social and ready to bolt if his venture went south, Jackson chased away the butterflies and approached her. He hovered for just a second, until she looked up.

"I'm sorry to interrupt," he said, "and I didn't mean to listen in, but I couldn't help hearing your conversation a minute ago."

The girl squinted at him, not saying anything.

"I only heard a little, so if I've got the wrong idea, let me know, but it sounded like a friend of yours is missing."

She maintained the squint, but with one eye. "I'm sorry, you are?"

"Jackson Douglas. I'm a private investigator, and I thought, if there's any way I—"

Her squint turned to incredulity. "You're a private eye?"

Jackson nodded as he drew a business card from his pocket. He handed it to her, and she scanned it for a second.

"This is for real? This isn't some pickup line?"

"I'd like to think I could do better than that for a pickup line."

"I didn't know private eyes still existed. I thought you went out with fedoras and trench coats."

"Trench coats are in this spring, I hear."

That actually drew a smile, or at least an upturn of the corner of her mouth. The more Jackson looked at her, the more he realized how pretty she was. In all fairness, that might have had something to do with copious makeup, including lip gloss that sparkled in the sunlight, and meticulously curled hair, no doubt aimed to look natural.

"Why do you want to help me?" she asked.

That was indeed the question. Telling her that ever since he'd decided to become a private investigator he'd fantasized about working cases for beautiful women was out. And it probably wasn't a real good idea to tell her that he'd already considered the potential benefit to his new business that helping the mayor's daughter might create. So he gave her his third reason.

"Because that's why I became a P.I.—to help people."

"So how many people have you helped?"

Jackson grinned. "You'd be the first. I just got my license last week."

"At least you're honest."

"Yes, ma'am."

"Ugh, not ma'am." Her countenance transformed to a smile. "Hailey."

"It's nice to meet you, Hailey."

They shook hands.

"Well, Hailey, if you are in need of help, and if you're interested, I'd be happy to talk with you further."

"I don't know . . . How much do you charge?"

He'd had no idea what to charge. Top-rate firms billed hourly, outrageous sums. His former employer, MTR Investigative Services in San Diego—where he'd sharpened his teeth as an administrative assistant for two years—had used a complex fee structure he never quite understood. Jim Rockford had charged $250 per day, plus expenses. Jackson couldn't remember anyone ever balking at the fee, but that had been back in the '70s. He'd doubled it for inflation and set his rate at $500 per day, plus expenses.

"I'll tell you what, you get the first-case discount. It's on the house."

Hailey huffed in disbelief. "What, are you some rich kid trying to be philanthropic?"

"Do I look like a rich kid?"

Another smile.

He shrugged. "I figure the good publicity will make up for it."

"You're pretty confident."

"I'm optimistic. And I've got nothing to lose by offering."

She scrunched her face. It wasn't unattractive.

"Let me make you a deal," Jackson said. "Do you have a boyfriend?"

A frown turned to an amused smile and a shake of her head. "No."

Jackson was momentarily distracted by loose curls of hair tumbling across her shoulders, but quickly recovered. "Let me buy you dinner. You can tell me what's going on and I'll try to earn your trust. If you like what you hear, I'll work the case, for free. If not, all you're out is dinner on me."

"Dinner?" she said. "And what if I said I did have a boyfriend?"

"I'd tell you to bring him along. I'm not running game, Hailey."

She studied him with eyes the same color as the ocean behind him. Slowly she nodded. "Okay. Drinks. Copa d'Oro. Six o'clock. You have to earn dinner," she said with a flirtatious smirk.

"Fair enough."

"You should know that my dad is Arnold Kendrick, Mayor of Santa Monica, so if you are 'running game' and using this P.I. thing as some ploy to ask me out, any hope you have of working in this city will be history."

"I know who your father is, and you have my word, no tricks."

"Copa d'Oro at six," she repeated.

"I'll be there."

She shot him another lopsided smile before turning and walking away.

*   *   *

6:10 p.m.

HAILEY HAD not changed since the park. Jackson had. Having returned home and Googled Copa d'Oro, he'd decided a fresh shirt and a reapplication of deodorant and cologne might be in order. With nothing else to do, he'd arrived early and procured a table near the bar. Seated on a padded stool at the two-person bistro table, he had an eye on the front door as Hailey walked in.

He'd spent the better part of eighty minutes mulling his judgment. His decision to approach a complete stranger, based on a few snatches of eavesdropped conversation, surprised even him. He wondered, had Hailey been shaped like a football with the face of a Cabbage Patch Kid, would he have been so eager to take her case? Probably not, although being the mayor's daughter made her a hard opportunity to pass up. Perhaps not the most altruistic of motives, but hey.

Several times on the drive over, he'd shushed that irritating inner voice telling him to be careful. He wasn't sure if it was the Holy Spirit or too many '80s TV series about private investigators, but it had been warning him against mixing business with pleasure. He wasn't worried. He had never been the type to rush into anything with a girl, no matter how cute. Hailey was no exception. A little flirting aside, he had no intentions of her becoming anything more than a client. And he was getting ahead of himself; so far all she had agreed to was drinks.

Hailey spotted him and strode over, flicking hair off her shoulders with a slight nod of her head. "Sorry I'm late," she said with a demure smile, sliding onto a stool adjacent to him.

If that client happened to be a head-turner, so be it.

"No problem," Jackson said.

She set her purse on the table. "I almost wasn't going to come."

"Oh?"

"But despite my doubts, I had to give you credit for audacity. I figured I owed you this much."

"I'm glad you came. What can I do to ease your mind?"

"First, let's order."

"Okay."

There were no waiters on a Tuesday, so Jackson ordered at the bar, a Moon Goddess—a combination of elderflower liqueur, grapefruit, and sparkling wine according to the menu—for Hailey and a soft drink for himself. As he returned to the table, Hailey frowned at him.

"I don't drink," he said, taking a seat.

"What? Ever?"

He shook his head.

"You're not just being cheap, are you?"

"Nope."

She shrugged, took a drink, and settled into her stool. "Okay, tell me about yourself. Who is Jackson Douglas and how did he become a private investigator?"

Jackson took a deep breath, then looked Hailey straight in the baby blues. "I grew up in San Diego, mostly, with my parents and brother. Dad's a Navy man and Grant, my brother, is one of L.A.'s finest, a calling he's had since before I can remember. My mom is very active in our church and the community and as a mom. I've never known any of them not to be rock-solid in their purpose. Then there's me."

Hailey was hanging on every word. Around them, Copa d'Oro was bustling, especially for a Tuesday night. It was easy to let his eyes drift to the busy bartenders or the building's unique architecture, or his mind to other conversations or the background music. But he focused on the vision that had sparked his career change, and on the first person to ask him about it.

"I drifted for a decade—college, odd jobs, a few months in the Army, college again, more jobs. None of it was the right fit. I was happy hanging with family and friends, enjoying SoCal and the beach, but it started to gnaw at me that I didn't have a real purpose. Ever since I was little, my mom and dad told me that God had made me for a specific reason. And I believed that; I just didn't know what it was."

He took a break and cleared his throat. She took another drink.

"A couple of years ago, I worked as an assistant at a P.I. firm in San Diego. I did grunt work—research, typing up reports, running errands. But a couple of times I actually got my feet wet as an investigator. After the place closed, an idea hit me. Maybe I could become a private eye." He smiled. "My initial reaction was the same as yours. Are there really still private eyes out pounding the pavement, peeking through keyholes, chain-smoking, hitting on beautiful blond secretaries? I let the idea simmer on the back burner for a while, and it started to take root. I spent a year and a half working as a claims adjustor here in L.A., earning enough investigative hours to get my license. I passed the exam in March, and here I am."

Hailey nodded. "So why is this different? Why is this not just another job? Why is this your purpose?"

"Truthfully, it might not be. But I hope I can do good. Help people who really need it. Solve cases that matter. Do something with meaning."

"That's impressive," she said, taking another sip.

Jackson shrugged and did likewise.

"Most guys don't care if they have a purpose."

"I've never been most guys, in any number of ways, good and bad."

She smiled, the way a girl might smile at a guy she was starting to find attractive. It changed to a challenging smile. "So how do you know you'll be able to do it?"

"I don't. But I've always been a problem-solver. Good at figuring out mysteries and riddles. I totally saw the ending to *Sixth Sense* coming."

"Everybody saw that coming."

"Okay, what about *Unbreakable*?"

"Huh?"

"Bruce Willis, Samuel L. Jackson. He had the Frederick Douglass haircut, always wore purple."

Hailey shook her head and took another drink. Jackson reached for his soda.

"Anyhow, I seem to have a knack for it. We'll see if it pans out."

"If not?"

"I've still got the business cards, so I can try hitting on random women in the park and see if the title impresses them."

She smirked at him.

"So who's Hailey Kendrick? And why do they call you Kenny?"

"They don't," Hailey said, her face turning red. "Only Sabina does, and I've told her it's totally lame."

"I wasn't going to say anything."

She giggled, then played with the edge of her napkin. "What do you want to know?" she asked, looking up with her head still down.

"Well, since we're here on business, why don't you tell me about that?"

"Potential business."

"Potential business," he said. "Tell you what," he said, reaching for his wallet. He pulled out a twenty and set it on the table. "Since it's happy hour, that covers your drink and mine, a second for you if you want it, and a tip. So here's my deal: All I heard was that someone named Connor

30

has been missing for several days and isn't answering calls or texts. You fill in the details for me, as much as you're comfortable, and I'll tell you my plan of attack. You think I'm credible, we go forward. If not . . ." He nodded at the twenty. ". . . Drinks are on me and it was nice meeting you."

With her tongue in her cheek, Hailey thought for a minute. Then she leaned forward. "Connor is my brother—stepbrother, actually. He didn't show up for work yesterday or today, and this after not saying anything all weekend. That's not all that strange, but to miss work is. All my calls go straight to voicemail. He won't answer texts. It's one thing for him to be quiet, but for him not to respond when I contact him is weird. I can't help but think something's happened to him."

"Have you contacted the police?" Jackson asked as she took a drink.

"No. I don't actually know that he's missing yet. I mean, I went to his apartment and nobody answered the door, but that doesn't prove anything, right? He could have been shopping or on a walk or sleeping. And I'm the mayor's daughter. It's not like Dad's the governor, but still, to call the cops over a missing person is kind of a big deal. If it turns out to be nothing . . ."

"Is your dad aware that Connor's missing?"

She nodded.

Jackson waited, sensing there was more.

"He doesn't think there's anything to be worried about. Says it's just Connor being Connor."

"What does he mean by that?"

Hailey sighed. "Connor's . . . an introvert. He's not a big people person. He likes to 'lay low.'"

"Any chance that's all this is, him laying low?"

"Maybe, which is why I'm hesitant to go to the cops. But he wouldn't miss work without a really good reason, and he wouldn't ignore me either."

"The two of you are close?"

"Yeah. There's no 'step' between us."

"When was the last time you saw or talked to him?"

"Friday morning. I texted him about the finale of *30 Rock* and he texted back."

"Did he sound normal?"

"It was just a short text, but yeah, it was typical."

"What about before that? Anything he's said or done recently that was suspicious."

"Nothing. I've thought about that a dozen times, and there's nothing."

Jackson sat back, stroked his jaw, like his dad did when thinking. "How many times have you called him?"

"Three, maybe four."

"When?"

Hailey frowned. "Monday afternoon, Monday night, and again this morning. Three I guess."

"And they all went straight to voicemail?"

"Yeah." She lifted her glass. "Why?"

"Maybe nothing. But normally a phone rings a few times first. It goes straight to voicemail if they're on another call, maybe if their phone's off or the battery's dead. It may be nothing," he said again. "I'm just thinking aloud."

She leaned forward. "Jackson, you should know, Connor can be a space cadet. He zones out. You asked if maybe he's just laying low, and I could actually see him getting so into something that he lost track of time and his phone is turned off and between couch cushions or something."

"But?"

"But, missing work is just not his style. He's responsible. I can't believe he would do that."

Jackson nodded. He took a drink. "Okay. Okay," he said a second time. "Here's what I'm thinking. First, I'll need to—"

Hailey held up her hand. "You can tell me over dinner."

"Dinner?"

"I can tell by the questions you're asking you know what you're doing."

Jackson didn't tell her he was winging it, not sure himself.

"And I trust you that this isn't some game. I can see it in your eyes."

He nodded.

"So yes, dinner. You're hired."

Chapter Four

Saturday, June 15, 2013
9:27 a.m.

FOG—TECHNICALLY MARINE layer—blanketed Jackson's Pacific Palisades neighborhood when he got up Saturday morning. It was late, but that had become typical. Over the last few weeks—ever since returning from Florida—he'd found himself staying up later and later at night (and thus sleeping in later and later the next morning), mostly because he wanted to postpone another day. Life had become empty, void of happiness, void of meaning.

Last night had been no exception. He had returned home after his dinner with the Haywoods in a fog that matched that outside. For two years now—two years, one month, and one day—he'd been living with a gaping wound, with part of himself missing. Life had been little more than coping, looking for one escape after another. His lifelong faith and good friends had kept him anchored—barely. He'd still slipped, spending a night in jail after being busted for marijuana possession. Mostly, his escapes had been his friends and his virtual USC Trojans and L.A. Rams, or taking out video-game baddies with his friend Mouse. He'd given up on justice for his family, concluding there was none to be had this side of eternity. The explosion had been deemed an accident. It was plausible, but Jackson had never been comfortable with it, for a number of reasons.

Joaquín Padilla had been one of them. Even when his alibi, such as it was, had negated him as a suspect, too many of the pieces had seemed to fit for the authorities to chalk it up to a huge oops. Restaurants didn't just explode, particularly in a way that totally scorched a private dining area in seconds while providing the rest of the patrons in the main dining room time to escape. Not in an explosion that wasn't instigated in the kitchen by an overheated stove or a grease fire or a gas line being ruptured. Not in an explosion triggered at just the right moment, when no kitchen or wait staff were in the hallway, when no patrons were headed to or from the restrooms. (Only one other person had died, a waiter in just his third day on the job.) No, this felt like a precise, targeted attack, right up until the part where there was no suspect, no motive, and no concrete evidence to prove it one way or the other.

Now, in lieu of the Haywoods' revelations, that was possibly changing. Jackson had lain awake well into the early morning hours, re-running the facts of the case as he knew them, double- and triple- and quadruple-checking timelines. Could Padilla have been at the restaurant and made it to Petty Officer Grabel's apartment by 7:32? Could he have committed both crimes? Could he be charged and convicted without more evidence?

And what did it matter?

David, Hannah, and Grant Douglas were still dead.

Jackson mindlessly went through his morning routine, showering and dressing. He skipped a shave. When he trudged downstairs a little before ten, he saw that it was not only foggy, but drizzling. He set a pot of coffee brewing and sat down at the table to wait for it, hungry but not in the mood for anything he could think of for breakfast.

He reached into his pocket, pulling out the business card Ike had given him. "Special Agent Dion Collier," he said to himself. He stared at the card until the number was burned into his memory, then flicked it across the table. He got up, poured a cup of coffee, and took it into the living room, where he'd left his laptop.

While it booted, he clicked on the TV. It was still on Fox News from the night before, and he switched to ESPN to catch baseball scores. The Dodgers were floundering around .500, way behind the Giants again. He muted way-too-early NFL hype and logged onto the internet.

For almost two years now, he'd been meeting with a therapist. Originally, it had been part of the court order that got him off with no other penalty for his marijuana possession. The order had expired, but he still saw Dr. Furman T. Zachary once a month. They'd had something of a breakthrough a year ago, when "Zach" had encouraged Jackson to let some water through the dam, so to speak—let some of the painful emotions out, in an effort to heal. Jackson had feared drowning but, as of yet, had kept his head above water. As he began searching online, he feared that was about to change.

Jackson was not the stereotypical burdened detective with a hidden away casefile, the cold case he couldn't solve or the personal vendetta he wouldn't let die. He didn't need such a casefile, because everything relevant was in his head, rattling around, trying to fit together a puzzle with too few pieces. Or so he thought. But, after two years (and a month and a day), he admitted it was possible there was something he'd missed or forgotten, something that might suddenly make sense of it all now that Padilla's alibi was shaky.

It didn't take long to dig up old newspaper articles, TV news accounts, and fire investigation and crime scene reports. As Jackson read and watched, suppressed memories erupted like a once-dormant volcano. Each one was like a fresh prick of fire, like lava on his flesh.

Channel 7 in San Diego had led their coverage with news of the explosion, speculating it was a kitchen accident, a grease fire that had spread to the gas line. By the time the morning papers came out and *Wake Up San Diego Weekend* aired, it was confirmed that four persons had been killed and one injured (it turned out to be a minor burn and a few scrapes to a cook). Investigators were considering the possibility that the explosion had been intentionally triggered. David, Hannah, and Grant's names—along with that of the waiter killed with them—had been made public later that day.

By Monday, the stories were split. Half of them probed the specifics of the explosion and the ensuing investigation. There were unconfirmed rumors SDPD had a suspect, or at least a person of interest. NCIS and the FBI were also investigating. The words "domestic terrorism" were used. Arson experts, criminal profilers, and various pundits were interviewed and opined at length, while the actual investigators kept mum on their progress.

The other half of the stories studied the victims. David's career with Naval Intelligence made him a hero in the public's eye, while also giving rise to conspiracy theories pertaining to potential motive. Grant's ties to

LAPD brought the matter to the attention of the *Los Angeles Times*, the *Los Angeles Daily News*, and several local TV news programs, all of which painted him sympathetically too. The *San Diego Union-Tribune* ran a very flattering piece on Hannah, highlighting her service as a Sunday school teacher, AWANA leader, and volunteer with various area charities and causes.

San Diego seemed to mourn as one, right up until the funeral. Then, with the investigation petering out, with no more theories to posit, experts to interview, or slices of life to celebrate, the media and the public—as always—moved on. The joint SDPD, San Diego County Sheriff's Department Bomb/Arson Unit, and FBI's ruling that the fire had been an accident got moderate coverage. Padilla's conviction for sexual assault was reported with a note that he had at one point in time, according to a source, been a person of interest in the "death of the entire Douglas Family . . . back in May." Jackson hadn't been offended by the slight to him. At the time, he'd felt the report had been entirely accurate. Aside from a mention in the May 14, 2012, *Union-Tribune* that marked the one-year anniversary of the explosion, that had been it.

Jackson spent several hours and multiple cups of coffee reading and re-reading, until he was sure he'd exhausted the news coverage he would be able to find on his own. His stomach growling, he got up and ransacked his fridge to make a sandwich. As he ate while watching the muted TV, he thought about calling Maggie. Back in the day, she was his first contact when he needed info, such as any missing news articles, a post by a credible blogger, or any other intel her newspaper connections could ferret out. But three things stopped him.

One, none of the articles he'd read had done anything more than dredge pain to the surface.

Two, Maggie no longer worked for the *Times*, and he didn't know what resources she had as a whatever it was she was.

Three, he just couldn't bring himself to call her up. They'd never "gone steady" or committed to any serious relationship. But she had now, with someone else. And Jackson couldn't—and wouldn't—bring himself to looking past that and "still being friends." It just didn't work that way.

*　　　　*　　　　*

3:40 p.m.

JACKSON KILLED a couple hours fast-tracking his way through USC's non-conference schedule. Fresno State gave him some guff, but he rebuffed them with a strong third quarter. He was sleep-walking.

Putting away the Xbox, he Googled Joaquín Padilla. His search pulled up a dozen news stories and a mugshot of an ugly, scowling Latino man with thinning hair and a scraggly beard. Jackson dug for half an hour and found that Padilla's record was longer than an L.A. commute. In addition to the sexual assault of Petty Officer Grabel, he had been convicted or pled guilty or *nolo contendere* (no contest) to a DUI, a second DUI and leaving the scene, simple battery, disturbing the peace, misdemeanor burglary, a third DUI, and a juvenile charge of arson. That was all small potatoes. He'd also been cited, arrested, charged, and/or tried for underage drinking, indecent exposure, assault and battery, domestic violence, assault with a deadly weapon, robbery, and a second assault with a deadly weapon. He escaped serving time for any of the charges due to lack of evidence, in exchange for testimony, thanks to a contaminated crime scene, and as a result of a combination of a good lawyer and a quirky hung jury. There were also numerous times when he was a suspect or person of interest in cases, ranging from arson to murder, none of which had led to an arrest or any charges being filed.

In short, Joaquín Padilla was a crappy excuse for a human being, a boil on the backside of humanity. He was just the kind of sleaze who would blow up a restaurant and then sexually assault a petty officer half an hour later. Only question was why?

Jackson was considering calling Special Agent Collier when his doorbell rang. Probably Connie, his rotund, flamboyant neighbor needing her lawn mowed, her Pomeranian puppy-sat, or some other favor. Just how he wanted to finish his drizzly Saturday.

He opened his door, ready to trot out an excuse, and was surprised to see an eye-catching brunette standing there.

"Maggie?"

"Hey, Jack," she said, her smile wide. As stunning as she'd looked the day before on TV, Maggie was just as beautiful in jeans and a New York Yankees T-shirt, her wavy hair drawn back into a ponytail.

"Hey. Thought you were in Washington."

"Just got back."

He looked past her to the Chevy Avalanche parked across the street. "Where's your bike?"

"Russell let me take his truck to the airport. He's gone for a long weekend with Teen Challenge."

Jackson nodded.

"Okay if I come in?"

"Yeah, I guess."

Maggie stepped into the living room and turned back toward him. "You don't look so good."

"Yeah, well . . ."

She paused a moment. Then her smile flickered back onto her face. "Did you see it?"

"I did."

"And?"

"You were great, Maggie. You ate the other panelists' lunch." He'd done a little more Googling that afternoon, and learned that the president had authorized an interagency task force to fight domestic terror threats, and there had been several raids that had—depending on the news source—effectively neutralized a clear and present danger or egregiously encroached on civil liberties. He had also learned that a Senator Charles Nantz was being investigated by the United States Senate Committee on Homeland Security and Governmental Affairs—more specifically, its Permanent Subcommittee on Investigations—for a variety of infractions—namely, gross misappropriation of government funds. It was a sordid mess, and he didn't dig too deep. Nor did he bother telling Maggie what he did or didn't know about any of the political goings on.

"Thanks," she said, "but you might be overstating it a little."

He shrugged. "So they fly you all the way out there for one segment?"

"I also shot a couple sound bites for a few weekend shows. And," she said, beaming wider, "it sounds like it could morph into a semi-regular gig."

"That's great. A lot of Sky Miles."

"They have a studio here in L.A."

"That's great," he said again.

"Wow, that was heartfelt."

He shrugged again.

"Jack, what's wrong?"

"Relatively, not much."

She eyed him for a few seconds, but didn't probe. "Have you eaten yet?"

"You'd have to specify which meal."

"Sorry, I'm still on D.C. time."

"Been there, done that."

"You want to grab something to eat? I'm starved."

Jackson frowned. "Maggie, don't you think you're taking this open dating thing a little too far?"

"I'm not talking about open dating. I'm talking about two people having dinner."

"I can get my dictionary out, but pretty sure that's under date."

"Is that what this is about?"

"Is that what what is about?"

"You in a funk."

"Maggie, I'm sorry that I'm not giddy with happiness right now for you, but it's kind of hard when my life is falling apart."

"Why? What's wrong?"

"It's a long story."

"So tell me about it," she said, taking a step closer. She put her hand on his arm. "I'm your friend, Jack. I'm here for you."

He huffed out a laugh. "Yeah, until Monday morning."

She withdrew her hand, and for the first time, her gray-blue eyes clouded. "What's that supposed to mean?"

"It means, I don't hear boo from you for weeks because you're playing young-and-in-love with Russell, but as soon as he's gone, you want to kick it like old times. It doesn't work that way, Mags."

"That is not what this is."

"And yet here you are."

She shot him a death glare. "I came over because I thought we were friends and you might want to share in my happiness. I guess I was wrong." She walked past him toward the door.

"I am happy for you, Maggie."

"You've got a funny way of showing it," she said over her shoulder as she reached for the doorknob. She appeared to reconsider and stopped. "You know, I thought you were mature enough that my dating someone wouldn't ruin our friendship. I guess I was wrong on that count too."

"You are wrong, Maggie, because it has nothing to do with maturity."

"No?"

"No. How would you feel if I stopped over at your place to tell you about my hot new girlfriend and, oh, by the way, she's busy saving the whales so wanna grab some cheeseburgers, Mags?"

Maggie's face showed almost as much pity as contempt. Instead of responding, she just shook her head. "Goodbye, Jack."

He said nothing, letting her go. The door thudded to a close behind her, and he watched through the window as she, without looking back, drove away in Russell's Chevy Avalanche.

He took out his frustrations on Oregon State, 73-10.

Chapter Five

Tuesday, May 10, 2011
7:27 p.m.

"START BY TELLING me about Connor," Jackson said. He and Hailey had just ordered at Chez Jay, an iconic steakhouse on Ocean Avenue. One wouldn't know it to look at it, but Chez Jay was a favorite of celebrities past and present, a Santa Monica Landmark. Outside, it looked like an old, seedy lounge, with neon signs advertising cocktails and the fare of seafood and steak, in addition to the restaurant's name. Inside, checkered tablecloths, dim lighting, and odd knickknacks—like a ship's wheel and a canopy made from a sail—made it resemble any other dive bar in L.A. It looked ripe for a stakeout on an episode of *NCIS: Los Angeles*. But the food was delicious and the atmosphere friendly and inviting. And on short notice, it had a table for two.

Hailey took a sip of her ice water before answering. "When I was twelve, my mother died in an accident on the 805."

"I'm sorry."

She nodded. "Dad remarried Connor's mom, Christine. I was sixteen, he was fourteen. It was horribly awkward for about the first six months, but then we became really close. So when Dad and Christine divorced four years ago, we remained close. Like I said, there's no step between us. We're brother and sister."

Jackson's turn to nod and reach for his glass of water.

"I mentioned that he's an introvert. It's not like he has some sort of phobia or something where he's scared of people or hates them or anything. He just is perfectly content by himself. He's a math genius. He can do long division in his head, aced calculus in high school. I was

41

literally crying doing my homework and he finished it for me in like five minutes, and he hadn't even studied at that level yet."

"Does he work in the field?" Jackson asked.

"Sort of. He's a data analyst for a big commercial real estate company, but he's so underused. He also works for Dad's new girlfriend's company. It's an online dating service called MatchStick. Their tag is that they light a fire that will last, as opposed to some of these other dating sites that just plop people together based on shared love of puppies or something."

"You sound skeptical."

"I just don't know that love can be strategized for and determined based on some algorithm," she said, sitting back as a waitress brought their salads.

"Thank you," Jackson said. "Is that what Connor does, create the algorithms?"

"Yeah." She picked the onions out of her salad and stirred the dressing as she talked. "The whole idea behind MatchStick is that they profile at such a deep level that they can use their state-of-the-art formula—which Connor created—to find a match that will stick. Corny, right?"

"A little."

"The whole thing comes off as clinical to me. I mean, where's the romance in a computer telling you who to date?"

"I'm with you."

She stabbed the first bite of her salad. "Even all . . ." She covered her mouth with the tips of her fingers as she finished chewing. ". . . the data in the world isn't going to guarantee anything, no matter whose algorithm computes it."

Jackson concentrated on sticking a crouton with his fork, a near impossibility.

"But business is good. And they claim a success rate that beats most of the big-name sites and services. And I'm here with you instead of a boyfriend, so who am I to talk?"

Jackson grinned.

"Sorry, that didn't come out very nice."

"I know what you mean."

"Where was I?" she asked.

"Does Connor still work for MatchStick?"

"Here and there. He continues to tweak the algorithm, improve it as they collect new types of data or add questions to their form. In fact, I think he was working on it this weekend. He's full time for the real estate company, so he works for MatchStick on nights and weekends." She looked down to get a good mix of salad on her fork. "It was one of the reasons I thought maybe he'd gone down a rabbit hole for the weekend," she said before ingesting it.

"What does he like to do apart from work?"

"Anything that will challenge him mathematically. He went to a trade school out of high school, but even after graduating, he still takes online classes for the fun of it. Crazy, right? He's a voracious reader. Technical manuals and applied mathematical concepts. Oh, and spy thrillers. He loves Tom Clancy."

"Does he have a lot of friends?"

"No. Hardly any."

"Anyone you can think of to contact?"

"Most of his friends aren't flesh-and-blood friends. I mean, they are, but not here. They're old school friends or people he's met at math seminars, or online. He never really hangs out or socializes."

Jackson nodded and ground on a stalky piece of lettuce. "What about the two of you? You hang out ever?"

"Once in a while. I'll have him over or go to his apartment and cook dinner and watch a movie. I'm not much of a cook, but Connor struggles with box macaroni and cheese. As close as we were growing up—as close as we are—we don't really have a lot in common, so we don't do much together. If anything, we just talk."

"What about calls, texts? How often are you in contact?"

"Most days we text, and it all depends. We'll go back and forth all day some days, and some days we don't get past 'How's it going?'" She reached for her water. "Calls," she said, setting it back down, "maybe a few times a week."

"You said you texted him Friday morning?"

Hailey nodded.

"When was the last time you saw him in person?"

"Oh my gosh, it's been a while . . . Last weekend—No, weekend before that. I was slammed at work last weekend."

"Where's that?"

"My work? I'm a hostess at O'Bannon's."

Jackson nodded. He spent the time until their entrées arrived asking about Connor's likes and dislikes, looking for behavioral trends in recent months, gathering as much intel as he could in the hopes his brain would sort through it and find something.

"I have to ask," he said as she sawed into her steak. Jackson had been somewhat surprised when she'd said back at Copa d'Oro that she was in the mood for a steak. He'd expected her to be one of those people who didn't eat anything with a face. He'd considered the possibility that she was testing him by asking to be taken to a steakhouse, but the first look on her face after biting into the medium rare coulette steak convinced him otherwise.

"Mmm," she said, her eyes closed. She opened them, licking a spot of demi-glace off her lip. "Sorry," she said, dabbing with a napkin. "Ask what?"

"I can hardly bring myself to say it," Jackson said. "It's so prosaic. Does Connor have any enemies? Anyone with whom there's bad blood? An old high school rival? Someone he beat out for a job? A cantankerous coworker?"

Hailey had started shaking her head and continued as she spoke. "No. No. No, there's no one. Connor doesn't make a lot of friends because of his personality, but he doesn't alienate anyone either. Nobody dislikes him. And he'd never start a fight with anybody."

Jackson spent a few moments savoring his top sirloin and shrimp. He tried not to think about his finances. Bauer & Bauer had paid well, but buying a house and committing money to renovations had left him without a whole lot of liquidity. If he could generate some paying clients, he'd be fine, and this dinner would be a worthwhile investment. If not, there wouldn't be much more Chez Jay in his future.

Instead he mulled Connor's apparent disappearance. Years of watching the news—and police procedural dramas—told him there were three likely scenarios. A, Connor had overdosed and was lying dead in his bed. Jackson had hinted at drug use in his questioning, and Hailey had said Connor rarely even drank beer, so he doubted that was it. B, he'd been kidnapped, but the why and by whom were gaping black holes. C, he'd run away, but the why was just as gaping there. Okay, so Jackson wasn't Sherlock Holmes, able to make a few clever deductions and solve the case by simply hearing his client's problem.

"I'd ask how your steak is, but I think I know," Jackson said.

"It is delicious." She reached for her water. "None of my friends will touch red meat, so when I get a chance, I'm afraid I get a little bit wide-eyed." She took a long gulp. "Okay, what else do you want to know?"

That was a good question. He couldn't think of anything else to ask about Connor, although he was sure he was missing something. It was, after all, his first official case. But there was no need to keep pointing that out.

"For now, I think that's it," Jackson said as he swallowed a shrimp.

"So what's next?"

"Do you have access to Connor's apartment?"

"I know where he keeps the spare." Her countenance fell. "I should have checked his apartment."

"Yes and no. If he pulled an all-nighter working on algorithms, then went into a sugar coma from too many cherry mashes, we've jumped through a lot of hoops for nothing. But if there is something more sinister at play, then it probably would be best that you didn't enter what could be a crime scene."

"It's hard to think of it being a crime scene."

"We have no reason to believe it is," Jackson said. "I'm speaking hypothetically."

"So is that the plan, check out his apartment?"

Jackson nodded. "You look at somebody's house, you can get a pretty good idea about them. You can also, if you know what to look for, find clues as to what they had been doing or were about to do."

"And you know what to look for?" she asked, looking up at him from under her furrowed brow.

"I do."

45

Hailey broke off her gaze first, sawing into her steak.

Jackson stabbed an already cut bite of his sirloin. "Then, I talk to neighbors, coworkers, family—anyone who might have seen or heard something, whom he might have confided in. One way or the other, that should give us some leads."

"When? Tonight?"

"It's getting kind of late to go knocking on neighbors' doors."

"What about checking out his apartment? Can we go tonight?"

He shrugged. "I don't see why not."

"You don't mind me going with you, do you?"

"No, it'd actually probably be helpful. In case I have any more questions."

She nodded and resumed eating.

Jackson surreptitiously watched her. Not like a creep, and not like he'd caught a couple other guys at Copa d'Oro or here at Chez Jay doing. He was studying his client. Her blond-brown hair was originally brown, judging by the roots, with blond highlights, so well done that the blend looked natural. Her mascara trended toward heavy, not in a Kardashian way, but more than was necessary to draw attention to almond-shaped eyes. She wore abundant jewelry in all the normal places. It didn't come off as tacky, but it certainly flashed in the sunlight—or the strands of Christmas lights dangling over the bar and booths at Chez Jay—and caught his attention.

It all was part of what Jackson called the California Condition, that materialistic desire to be famous, to be noticed, to be *it*. He'd known too many girls—and guys—who worked so hard to check all the boxes but still got a failing grade. He'd also known people who truly had *it*— whatever *it* was—people who were naturally beautiful, full of charisma, smart and savvy and at ease in the limelight. The trouble was, too many of them spent so much time shouting when they already had everyone's attention. Looking at Hailey—her clothes, her jewelry, her makeup and hair—he wondered which group she fell into.

Then again, he'd known her for all of three hours, so maybe he was rushing into judgment. He'd read a short story once, by Sir Arthur Conan Doyle, the creator of Sherlock Holmes. In it, Holmes' famous assistant

Watson had made a number of deductions, just as Holmes always did so brilliantly. Only all of Watson's deductions, while plausible, were incorrect. It had been written, Jackson had once heard, as a mockery of Holmes, whom Doyle didn't consider to be the epic literary character he had become in the public's eye. At any rate, was Jackson Holmes or Watson?

"You're staring."

"Guilty," he said with a grin. "I was analyzing my client."

"Uh-huh."

"Honest."

"And what is your professional analysis?"

He picked up a shrimp. "For starters, you probably don't mind my staring."

"And what gives you that impression?"

"You wear four-inch heels and a mini-skirt, with salon-quality hair, to an event you only went to because you were doing your dad a solid."

"For the record, I often dress like this."

"Not sure you're not making my point for me."

Hailey regarded him through a half squint as she reached for her water. "What else?"

"I take it you do okay financially. Betting that's a designer purse, name-brand clothes, and your bangles probably cost more than everything I've got on."

"You notice my looks and my money? Isn't that kind of shallow?"

"Just observations. I also notice your loyalty to your father trumps your loyalty to your friends, which isn't shallow. You're close to your brother, who by your own admission, isn't exactly Mr. Popular. Not shallow. And you're concerned enough about him to take a stranger up on his offer to help."

Jackson smiled to himself, realizing he may have just answered his earlier question about which category of person Hailey fit into.

"So how do you know how to do all this stuff?" she asked.

"What stuff?"

"Observe and analyze people, put clues together. How do you know what to do to find a missing person?"

"Some of it's just natural. And I told you, I worked for a P.I. firm for a few years, then as a claims adjustor."

"You said you did grunt work. And you didn't learn all this as a claims adjustor."

"I also watched a lot of *Magnum* and *Rockford. Columbo.*"

"Who are they?"

Jackson raised his eyebrows.

"Did they work for that firm you were at?"

He raised them farther.

"What? Who are they?"

"Finish your steak, Kenny."

Chapter Six

8:44 p.m.

CONNOR NOVAK LIVED in a 1970s-era apartment complex in Mar Vista, a few blocks south of Venice Boulevard. It was about a twenty-minute drive from Chez Jay. Since the restaurant wasn't that far from Hailey's apartment, they agreed to drive together. After taking one look—and a long laugh—at Jackson's 1976 Ford Granada, Hailey had offered to drive. They careened across town in her BMW convertible, while listening to the latest pop on her satellite radio. At least she didn't sing along.

The complex boasted four long buildings side by side, with a parking lot on one end and "green space" in between the buildings. Nothing had been updated since original construction. The paint was faded and chipped. The windows looked ready to fall out of their jambs. The sidewalks were cracked and slanted. Politeness would have kept Jackson from asking, were he not working a case, "Why here?"

"He's cheap," Hailey said as she varoomed into a parking spot between two turn-of-the-century automobiles. Her 3 Series 335i would stand out almost as much as she would. She slammed the gearshift into park. "Back when he moved in, he worked at an insurance company not far from here, so it was convenient. And if you don't mind the noise, it's a good place to be a loner."

Jackson nodded, and they got out. The night air was chilly, but only in comparison to the gorgeous afternoon.

"There's his car," she said, pointing to the end of the row at a red Ford Taurus from years—if not decades—ago. "That's a good sign, right?"

"Maybe," he said, again looking around. He'd been in worse neighborhoods, but they weren't places he frequented. Half expecting

49

some slinky dope dealer to approach and hit on Hailey, he kept his eyes on a swivel as she led the way between the middle two buildings. Aside from an old man in a wife-beater smoking on his front stoop, the place was quiet.

Connor's apartment was third on the left, on the second story. His door, however, was on the ground level, and Hailey stopped in front of it and looked around. Then she reached up to the channel above the door that the siding slid into. From it, she extricated a key. She was about to turn it in the knob of a weathered brown door with a gold C203 hanging crooked on it, but stopped. "Should we knock first?"

He shrugged, then banged on the door with his fist. They waited a minute, listening to crickets and the distant beat of rap music.

"Go for it," Jackson said.

Hailey turned the key and opened the door.

"I'll go first," Jackson said.

Hailey flicked on a light, revealing thinly carpeted stairs. Jackson climbed them and turned to face a counter. It separated a galley kitchen from a living room that faced one of two windows in the apartment. Around to the left, off the kitchen, a door led presumably to a utility closet. A dark hallway extended off the living room. Everything was retro, from the wood paneling that ran halfway up the living room walls to the wood spindles on either ends of the counter to the yellow sink, refrigerator, and oven. The carpet was threadbare, and the linoleum scuffed and scratched. Even so, the apartment wasn't messy.

"Connor!" Hailey shouted. "Connor!"

Her shoulders dropped when no answer came.

"I'll check the bed and bathroom," Jackson said. "In the meantime, don't touch anything."

She nodded, and he headed for the hall. It was just a stub, with a bathroom at the end and a bedroom to the right. Jackson located the light switches and was relieved not to find Connor with wrists slit in the bathtub or prostrate beside a bottle of pills in his bed. He hadn't expected either, but one never knew.

"Not here," Jackson said, returning to the living room.

"Great." Another shoulder sag.

"Where does he keep his car keys?"

"Right here," she said, pointing at a small hook and shelf to the side of the door. It was empty. "Wallet's gone too."

"Okay. He didn't drive anywhere, but he has his keys and his wallet."

"Meaning?"

"Not sure yet. Let's see what else we can find."

"What are we looking for?"

"It's not so much what we're looking for, but what we're looking at."

Hailey frowned.

"I'm observing," Jackson said. "Everything. Every detail. You never know what might be relevant."

"Can I help?"

"You said you come and cook for him now and again?"

"Yeah. Why?"

"Look for anything that has changed. Anything moved? Anything missing? Anything added? Any change could be significant."

"Can I touch stuff?"

"Best if you don't, just in case. If you have to, try to do so as minimally invasively as possible. We don't have to worry about leaving prints, because we're here legally. But we don't want to potentially contaminate anything."

She nodded and headed into the living room. Jackson started in the kitchen. He remembered an episode of *Psych* where a guy who supposedly had committed suicide had a steak marinating in the refrigerator, and it didn't take a psychic to wonder why a guy about to off himself would make preparations for a fancy meal. Connor's refrigerator was pretty bland. A half-gallon of milk, half gone but not yet expired, sat beside a bottle of cranberry juice in similar condition and a six-pack of bottled Dr. Pepper. The next shelf contained a pizza box with a few leftover slices of pepperoni and black olive, hard as a rock. Eggs, butter, mayo, ketchup and mustard, ranch dressing, chocolate syrup, and a box of baking soda were in the door, some fruit and veggies in the crisper. That was it. No marinating steak.

The freezer had two kinds of ice cream, a variety of frozen dinners, a half-empty ice cube tray, and a Tupperware of what looked like lasagna.

No clues there either. The sink contained a few dishes—a plate with dried pizza sauce, a bowl and spoon, and a glass with residue of cranberry juice in the bottom. Several more plates, bowls, cups, and utensils were drying in a rack in the other half of the sink.

Jackson came around the far end of the counter and stopped at a computer desk in what was theoretically the dining area. There was no table and chairs, just a trio of plain, wooden barstools at the counter. It made sense. There was no reason for a bachelor without a social life to have a family-sized seating area.

Saving the computer for later, Jackson scouted the living room. It was standard. A sofa, a mismatched end chair, a cheap coffee table with an old edition of *TIME* and what looked like a math textbook on top of it, and a flat TV console were the only items of furniture. The TV was a flat panel, a small, older model. A cable box sat atop a DVD player on the shelf below. No gaming console. No stereo or advanced sound system. A meager selection of DVDs and a few VHS tapes on another shelf.

There were no plants, very few decorations, just blinds in the window.

"He's a minimalist," Hailey said.

"Yeah."

"What are you seeing?"

"Nothing that looks out of order. He keeps a pretty clean house," he added, running a finger across the TV's baseplate. It drew just a few particles of dust.

"Yeah, Christine was—is something of a neat freak. She taught him to clean, and he does regularly."

"I saw a few dishes in the sink. Is that abnormal?"

"He usually does them at the end of the day."

"Religiously?"

She shrugged.

"There's what looks like a pizza plate in there, along with a bowl and spoon."

"So?"

"So, if he did the dishes every night, it would mean the last day he was here, he was here for at least two meals."

"I guess so. Everything looks in place."

Jackson headed for the bedroom, and Hailey followed. It too was standard—a bed, made; a nightstand with the usual items like an alarm clock, lip balm, and an eye mask; a bookshelf with a mix of spy novels and books about math and physics. Jackson picked out a title—*Fermat's Enigma*—and flipped through it.

"He actually reads this stuff?"

"I thought we weren't supposed to touch things."

"Yeah," Jackson said, putting it back.

They checked his closet, a small unit accessible by folding doors. Jackson used the sides of his fingers to pinch the knob and pull it open. "You know if he has luggage?"

"Luggage?"

"A suitcase, a duffel bag?"

Hailey shook her head.

"If you could identify one as missing, it would tell us he left on his own."

"Sorry."

"Forget it. I only ask because my brother has this ridiculous San Diego Padres duffel bag he got at some all-fan giveaway as a kid. Ugly brown, the logo's all faded. Never mind," he said, seeing Hailey's eyes glossing over.

They moved to the bathroom, where nothing drew either Jackson or Hailey's attention. Connor's apartment was thoroughly run-of-the-mill, with no signs that its occupant was anything but out for the evening. Or maybe the rookie P.I. just didn't know what to look for.

They returned to the living room and Jackson sat down in a sleek, comfortable office chair. He studied Connor's desk. A closed laptop, wireless mouse on a mousepad depicting a tropical sunset, a second flat-screen monitor, a notepad, a pencil, and a small desktop organizer occupied the dust-free surface.

"I think the second screen is for work," Hailey said. "It lets him see more data."

"Makes sense." Using his pinky, Jackson lifted the laptop. "You happen to know his password?"

"No," she said, leaning on the back of his chair. "And knowing Connor, it's some complicated math formula or something."

Jackson booted the computer, using a knuckle instead of a fingertip to turn it on. "You ever use this computer?" he asked, looking over his shoulder.

"I have before."

"Have a seat." He stood. "See if you can guess the password."

"Me?"

"Try names of family members, pets, important dates, cities where you've gone on vacation. It's easier for you to type them than tell me, and your fingerprints won't raise any red flags."

She sat down and began entering passwords. Jackson surveyed the room again, begging his eyes to see something out of place. So far, he had nothing to go on.

They settled on a pair of picture frames mounted above the desk. One showed a toddler between a man and a woman. It was faded and the fashions were from the '80s or early '90s. The other was a candid photo of Hailey and presumably Connor on what looked like a yacht out at sea. She wore a red and white polka dot sundress, her hair swept around her head and butterfly sunglasses propped on top of it. She held a champagne glass in one hand. Her other was looped around the guy's waist. His was over her shoulders. He wore a shirt and tie and was squinting a little. Both were grinning from ear to ear.

"This Connor?" Jackson asked, reaching up for the frame.

"Yeah," Hailey said, a smile similar to the one in the photo gracing her face. She sat back. "That was Christine's wedding to Shane, her new husband. About a year ago."

Jackson looked down at her. "You went to your dad's ex-wife's wedding?"

"I went for Connor, so he wouldn't be alone. This was the after-party on Shane's boat. It was all their friends and we were the only two people each other knew. It was a beautiful day, and we had a blast being together, talking, laughing. It was . . . one of the best days of my life. I have the same picture on the wall in my house."

Jackson nodded and re-hung it. "This him too?"

"Yeah. With Christine and his father."

"Divorced?"

"He died of brain cancer when Connor was six."

"Wow."

"Yeah."

She went back to guessing passwords and he ransacked the drawers on the side of the desk. They contained software CDs, operating manuals, a couple of floppy disks from way back, an old mouse, adapters, spare cords and other junk. He moved an empty garbage can to the side and peeked behind and under the desk, just in case something was taped to it or hidden in some way. It wasn't.

"You mind?" Jackson asked, pointing at the drawer under the desk. Hailey scooted her chair back and to the side, and Jackson opened it far enough to peek inside. He spotted sheaves of loose paper, along with a ruler, a protractor, a stubby eraser, and partially used pencils of various length. He lifted out the sheaves of paper and stepped back. He took a moment to sort them so they were facing the right way, then scanned them. They were equations, formulas, strings of numbers, notes about the same.

"I give up," Hailey said, sitting back.

"Don't worry about it; it was a Hail Mary anyhow. Any of this mean anything to you?"

She took the sheaf of papers from him and studied them for less than a minute. She huffed. "No. I barely can figure out algebra. I have no idea what this is."

"Maybe for work? The MatchStick algorithm?"

"Maybe. Knowing Connor, it could just be fun on a Friday night." She got out of the chair, and Jackson replaced the papers in the desk drawer. He closed the laptop and swept his eyes over everything again. He stopped, staring intently at the scene. "What is it?" Hailey asked.

"I don't know. Something's . . . off."

"Off how? What do you mean?"

He didn't answer, instead focusing on the desk, the pictures above it, the garbage can beside it, the floor and chair. He reran the contents of the drawers through his head. Something he'd seen? A number or formula on one of the papers in the drawer? He slowly sat down.

"Jackson?"

He suddenly stood up.

"Jackson?"

He ignored her and entered the kitchen. He reached for the cupboard door beneath the sink.

"What are you doing?"

"The garbage can by the desk is empty. So's this one," he said, pulling it out from under the sink. "Completely."

"He takes out the trash."

"When?"

"I don't know."

Jackson went to the bathroom and found its garbage can also completely empty. "You texted him Friday," he said when he returned to the living room.

"Yes."

"And he texted you back?"

"Yes."

"Did he usually eat breakfast here, on the go, at work?"

"Um, here, I think. I don't know. Jackson, what does this have to do with garbage?"

"The bowl in the sink smelled like milk. I'm guessing cereal. If he does dishes at the end of the day, then we can assume the last day he was here, he ate breakfast and at least one other meal, pizza by the looks of it. Since he texted you back on Friday, and went to work on Friday . . ."

"Yeah, I assume so."

"Then we can also assume he came back home on Friday to use the plate."

"Okay. I think I follow. But so what?"

"So, the garbage men don't come on Saturday or Sunday. So why are all his garbage cans empty?"

"I don't know."

"Let's assume the dishes are from Sunday, that he was here through the weekend."

"Okay."

"If his garbage is collected on Monday morning, he could have conceivably rounded it up Sunday night, then disappeared before doing his dishes."

"He'd do them right after dinner. It's when he always does."

"Then that doesn't wash, pun not intended."

"Jackson, I'm getting a headache. Where is all this going?"

"I think somebody else searched his place."

"What? Why?"

"Private Eye 101," Jackson said. "The best way to learn about somebody is to dig through their garbage."

"And you think somebody dug through his garbage?"

"Otherwise, where is it?"

She shrugged.

"And look at the notepad," he said, returning to the desk. "See that little piece right there? A page has been torn out."

"Okay? That's what people do with notepads."

"You have a quarter?"

"What?"

"Or a nickel, a dime?"

"Uh, yeah, probably." She reached into her purse and dug for a few seconds. Then she handed Jackson a quarter. "What are you going to do with that?"

He took it and sat down at the desk. "If what he wrote on the previous page made an imprint in this one, we can see it," he said, placing the quarter on the pad and rubbing it back and forth. He glanced up at her. "It may not be relevant, but it's worth a try."

Hailey stared at him, a dubious look on her face. He couldn't blame her. This theory that someone had gone through his garbage was circumstantial at best. And there was no guarantee that the last thing written on the notepad would shine any light on Connor's whereabouts. But, like he'd told her, it was worth a try.

"It's working," Hailey said, peering over his shoulder. A few curls of hair fell on his shoulder until she brushed them away. "Where did you learn this?"

"*Magnum, P.I.*"

"Who?"

"You ever heard of Tom Selleck?"

"Sounds familiar."

"Unbelievable. You have Netflix or Hulu or something?"

"Yeah."

"Go home tonight and watch *Magnum, P.I.* It's the episode with the Admiral's son and the lady who's really an FBI agent or something. And Dennis Haysbert, before he was President Palmer."

"What are you—Are you telling me you learned this on TV?"

Jackson nodded and held up the pad. "A. Maystadt?"

"Magstadt," she said, taking it from him.

He tipped it in her hand. "G. I'll buy that."

"And this has to be a phone number."

"Else a Swiss bank account."

"He could have written this a month ago."

"Could have." He sighed. "It's getting late, so I'll call A. Magstadt in the morning, see if he or she knows anything. It could be a lead, could be a dead end. I'll also come back and talk to the neighbors. I should also talk to other family members—your dad, Connor's mom. Your dad's girlfriend and his mom's husband wouldn't hurt."

"I can get you their numbers. Maybe even give them a heads up."

"Might be a good idea."

"So is that it here?" Hailey asked.

"Unfortunately, for now." He stood. "I didn't see a phone anywhere."

"He just uses a cell."

"I didn't see that either."

"He probably has it on him."

"So why isn't he answering it?"

Hailey frowned. "I don't know. This is so weird."

"His car's here but not his keys. House key on the same chain?"

She nodded.

"So maybe he went out for a walk."

"With his wallet?"

"Yeah, that's odd too. But the good news is, there's no sign of foul play."

"So where does that leave us?"

Jackson sighed. "With work to do."

Chapter Seven

Sunday, June 16, 2013
12:59 p.m.

THE SANDWICH SHOP was straight out of a *Law & Order* episode, the type of place where Paul Sorvino or Jerry Orbach would eat, grouse about the lack of progress in the case, and spill mustard on his tie. It was small, off the beaten path, a little dark and a little dirty. But the sandwiches were huge, full of meat and cheese, and aromatic. They were, of course, served on white butcher paper.

Jackson had left L.A. right after church, which he had attended only out of duty. He was getting tired of Pastor James' sermons of late. He was doing a series entitled "Where is God . . ." Where is God When I'm Afraid? Where is God When I'm Angry? Where is God When I'm Confused? Today's sermon had been entitled "Where is God When Life Doesn't Make Sense?" In theory, it should have been perfect for Jackson's situation. But it was just more of the same Sunday school answers that didn't seem to provide much help. Yeah, it was all true. But how did that truth fit with the crap of life? Why couldn't anybody ever connect the dots? Worse yet, why did people seem to leave the service each week bubbly and excited and humming some lame chorus as if all their problems had been erased?

Then again, maybe Jackson was just bitter because Pastor James was Maggie's boyfriend Russell's dad.

Traffic had been light on I-5, considering it was L.A., and he'd made decent time to San Diego. The forecast had called for the sun to break through the clouds, but it hadn't. Not really. Instead the sky was a burning white mess of high-level clouds and haze, and the usually pleasant San

Diego temperature had spiked into the 80s. The sandwich shop was not air-conditioned, so Jackson had picked a booth under a massive ceiling fan that was, so far, doing the trick.

"Are you Douglas?"

Jackson looked up at Tiger Woods. White cap with a pink Nike swoosh to match his golf shirt, khaki pants, and two-toned FootJoy shoes that clacked as he took the last few steps to the booth. He was on the short side, five-seven, maybe five-eight, with eyes a few shades darker than his skin. He wore a small gold cross around his neck, a little odd since he'd apparently spent his Sunday morning on the links. Then again, Jackson wasn't in position to judge.

"Yeah."

"Special Agent Dion Collier. Excuse the threads," he said as he set a small laptop case in the booth opposite Jackson. "Just played eighteen with my boss."

"You win?"

Collier only grinned in reply. "Give me a few to order and we'll talk."

Jackson nodded and returned his attention to his sub.

He'd made the decision to call Collier after Maggie had left the day before. He'd spent a while in a funk, wanting to blame her for their fight but knowing he couldn't. Then he'd realized there wasn't really a choice to be made; he wouldn't be able to rest until he had pursued the Padilla Possibility (as his supposedly humorous brain kept referring to it) to its full extent. He'd called the number the Haywoods had given him, and Collier had agreed to meet him on short notice. Given that, making a trip to San Diego seemed more than fair.

Collier returned with a foot-long sub bursting with meat, cheese, and veggies and dripping with several types of sauce, along with two bags of chips and a thirty-two-ounce cup of something. He dropped into the booth with a small grimace.

"Thanks for meeting with me," Jackson said.

"My pleasure, my pleasure. When Ike mentioned you might be calling, he didn't tell me much about you. I looked you up last night. You've got an impressive record."

"I guess you could call it that."

"Anyhow, he said you might have questions about Joaquín Padilla and how it related to your family's death?" he asked as he took the first bite of his sub. Mayonnaise and lettuce shot out onto the butcher paper.

"Yeah," Jackson said, briefly explaining—while Collier inhaled the end of his sub—about Ike and Juliet's conversation with Mira Austin that altered Padilla's timeline.

"You want to know if he could have been responsible for the explosion?"

"I have to know."

Collier nodded as he pulled a fragment of roast beef into his mouth with his tongue. "Well . . ." He reached into his case and withdrew a thick manila folder. Since there wasn't much room on the table with their sub wrappers, he handed it to Jackson. "This is Padilla's file, everything the Bureau has on him. It's a lot, so I'll hit the high points for you."

"Thanks."

Collier must not have had breakfast the way he was gulping down his sub. He took another mammoth bite, chewing a little more graciously before speaking. "Joaquín Padilla is a dirtbag. I'm cleaning that up because my wife doesn't like it when I curse."

Jackson nodded, studying the photo of Padilla attached to the inside of the file. With dark eyes, a broken nose, a scar on one cheek, an unkempt mess of a beard outdone only by the dead animal atop his head, and a scowl that would—as Jackson's grandpa liked to say—make a freight train take a dirt road, it was a face only a mother could love. A blind mother at that.

"I don't know how much you know about his record, but it's all in there. As it relates to your family, the important stuff is as follows. In August of 1992, Padilla burned down a horse barn on a farm in Lancaster belonging to his extended family. He was fifteen. He pled guilty to arson, was sentenced to a year in juvie and probation until he was eighteen. The sentence was a little heavy, but he'd already had two prior instances of underage drinking for which he was fined and sentenced to community service, and a ranch hand was injured—some minor burns—and two horses died in the fire."

Collier returned to his sandwich like a swimmer gasping for air. "The kicker is, when he was asked at trial why he did it, he said with almost a glint in his eye, 'Because I wanted to see it burn.'"

Jackson was quiet.

"Padilla served his year at VYCF, finished his probation clean, and then went on to be a repeat offender. A lot of his crimes were alcohol related—underage drinking, DUIs, fights at bars. Nothing related to arson." He paused for another bite of the sandwich. It was two-thirds gone, and he'd yet to touch the chips or the drink. "August 2002, just after ten years to the day after he torched the barn in Lancaster, an abandoned warehouse in San Clemente goes up in flames. Padilla was never charged, but he was on the investigators' radar because he spent the night in the company of a woman named Adelle Garcia at her place just outside San Clemente. A horse farm, oddly enough. She said he was with her the whole night, and there was nothing else to tie him to the crime."

"They catch the perp?" Jackson asked.

"No." Another bite. "The following June, he was questioned twice by the cops in regard to a warehouse fire in Encinitas."

"Let me guess, he was shacking up with a lady forklift driver?"

"No. He was working part-time at a bar in town, having just been released after serving four months of a six-month battery charge stemming from an incident in Huntington Beach. Now get this: a week before the fire, several witnesses saw him get into an altercation with the bar's owner. Cooler heads prevailed and nothing happened, until the fire."

"But no arrest?"

"No evidence."

"You know, I looked at a lot of his record yesterday," Jackson said. "I see he was accused of a lot more than he was charged of and charged with a lot more than he was convicted. Is he good or just lucky?"

"There's nothing good about this guy. In December of 2008, he nearly killed a guy with a baseball bat outside a bar in East Village. The trial was a mess, the jury hung itself, and the D.A. moved on and didn't mess around with a retrial. But he was guilty as sin. In 2010, the cops had him in about some gang murders, just asking questions. Wouldn't surprise me if he had his hand in that too. Like I said, a real piece of crud."

"That was my assessment too."

Collier went to work on his sandwich for a minute, and Jackson cleaned up some stray pieces of meat and lettuce from his. Half of it was left, but he'd lost his appetite.

"What can you tell me about the Grabel case?" he asked.

Collier finished a mouthful. "It was pretty open and shut. Combined with her testimony, the neighbor who saw him arrive, other neighbors who heard sounds of the struggle from the apartment, the fact that his DNA was at the scene and he had her blood on his hands—not to mention his lengthy rap sheet—it was an easy conviction."

"Even though Grabel was inconsistent on the time of his arrival?"

"Even so. It was clear he was there and what he did—what he tried to do. She apparently fought him off before he could actually rape her. Still, the judge sentenced him to the max, four years at Kern Valley."

"So why's he out?"

"Remember those gang murders I mentioned?" Collier said, wiping a dab of mustard from his lower lip. "No arrests were ever made. But earlier this spring, SDPD raided a coke 'warehouse' in Barrio Logan, hauled in about eight members of the Logan Heights Gang. A few of them sang. They didn't know who'd committed the killings, but they knew who did know."

"Padilla?"

Collier pointed at Jackson and clicked with his mouth. Then he took another bite, down to the end of his sub. "The D.A. initiated talks with him, commutation of the rest of his sentence in exchange for tabbing the killer or killers. Personally, I'm surprised he took the deal."

"Why's that?"

Jackson had to wait for the FBI agent to finish chewing the final bite of his sub. He wiped his mouth, then his hands as he spoke. "He had roughly two years left on a sentence. This is a guy who's been in and out of prison his whole life. It's not like he was a lifer who got paroled. And now he's probably got a price on his head for ratting out a murderer." He tore open a bag of chips. "Of course, once word leaked that he knew, he'd be a marked man anyhow."

"So he cuts a deal and gets out for time served?"

"That's it." Collier crunched on a chip. He turned the bag to Jackson. "Want some?"

"No, thanks. Doesn't Petty Officer Grabel get a say in this?"

"Sadly, no. The judge can weigh her testimony if he wants, but it's at his discretion." He munched a few more chips. "It's the age-old story. There's always a bigger fish to fry."

"And I hear he was released Wednesday?"

Collier nodded as he chewed. Finally, he reached for his drink and took a huge slurp through the straw.

"Is Grabel in danger?"

"In theory, but last I heard, she had moved to somewhere in Mississippi. Biloxi, I think it was."

Jackson frowned. Ike and Juliet had mentioned she lived in Mississippi, but somewhere in his head, he'd made a connection that she was still in the area. Maybe because the attorney was local?

Collier had resumed eating chips. "What else can I answer for you?"

Jackson glanced at Padilla's file, which he'd set on the booth beside him. "One more question. Do you think Joaquín Padilla killed my family?"

Collier stopped eating. He set the chip bag down and sat back. He took a deep breath. "I don't know all the details of that investigation. I know the basics, but I haven't done what you'd call due diligence in investigating it. All I know is Padilla. And from what I know of that . . . slime ball, what I know of his history . . . Yeah, it'd be my guess that he's responsible."

Jackson nodded.

"If I study it in detail, maybe I change my mind. Maybe I become more convinced of it. But at first blush, so to speak, yeah."

Jackson thanked Special Agent Collier for his time and assistance, and the two said goodbye. Jackson walked back to his Granada, tossing his wrapped up half a sandwich onto the leather passenger seat, where it would no doubt spoil on the two-plus hour drive back to Los Angeles.

Chapter Eight

JACKSON PULLED OUT his phone as he sat in Santa Monica traffic. He had opted to avoid the freeways on his way back to Connor's apartment complex to question his neighbors. On TV, the cops and detectives always found a nosy little old lady or a grumpy guy in his underwear who had seen something suspicious. Jackson wasn't sure that one could count on finding such clues in reality. But aside from the name and number he'd found on the notepad on Connor's desk, he didn't have much else to go on.

After they had searched Connor's place the night before, Hailey had driven Jackson back to his car, parked on the street adjacent to Chez Jay. He'd promised to be in touch, and had driven home to do a little research. He'd browsed to MatchStick's website and debated filling out a profile, but he couldn't see what for. He'd Googled a few names—Mayor Arnold Kendrick, Christine Kendrick-Stoeckl, her new husband Shane Stoeckl—just to see if any of them happened to pop, say with a headline about a prior indictment for kidnapping or mob connections or something. No such luck.

Then he'd searched the white pages for A. Magstadts. Turned out there were four in the Greater Los Angeles area. Adrian, Alton, Amy, and Anne. It was the latter, Anne Magstadt, whose white pages number matched the one on the pad. Jackson had deemed it too late to call her, but had plugged her name into his search engine. He'd discovered she was a reporter, and his brain had started to make possible connections. Unless Connor had pulled her name and number out of MatchStick and had been working up the courage to ask her out, the only other reason Jackson could think of to call a reporter was if you had a tip on a story.

Instead of speculating further, he'd gone to sleep. Wednesday had dawned sunny and clear, and as Jackson left home, he found himself glad he didn't have a job that tethered him to an office or a cubicle. That happiness lasted until traffic ensnared him, and he concluded it was as good a time as ever to give Anne Magstadt a call.

Three chirps, then a second of dead air as someone came on the line. "Hello?"

"Anne Magstadt?"

"Yeah. Who's calling?"

"My name is Jackson Douglas, I'm a private investigator," he said, half expecting her to hang up right there. "I'm working a case and your name came up."

She didn't answer immediately, and when she did, it sounded as if she had a frog in her throat. "Came up how?"

"I'm looking for a man by the name of Connor Novak. He's been missing since the weekend, and he had your name written down at his apartment."

"How'd you get into his apartment?"

"His sister knows where the spare key is."

Another pause. Jackson realized traffic was moving again and accelerated.

"What's the sister's name?"

"Are you fact-checking me?"

"Can't be too careful. I get a lot of crank calls."

"And I sound like a crank call?"

"The jury's out."

"Hailey," Jackson answered.

"Novak?"

"No. Kendrick. Technically his stepsister."

"Did she hire you?"

"I can't tell you that."

"Guessing she did, or why else would she have let you into his apartment?"

"I never said she let me, just that she knew where the spare key was."

"Sure you're not a lawyer?"

"Heaven forbid."

Anne may or may not have chuckled. "You say my name was in his apartment?"

"Written on a notepad. Actually just A. Magstadt. But it had a number, and—"

"You're a competent P.I."

"Well, I was going to say proficient with a phonebook, but let's go with your version."

"Look, Mr. Douglas, I've got a meeting in just a few minutes, and interviews scheduled through most of the day."

"I can call back another time. When works for you?"

"Four o'clock, La Brea Tar Pits."

"Is there a particular payphone you'd like me—"

"I like to meet with people face to face, look them in the eye."

"Fair enough. Four o'clock at the La Brea Tar Pits."

"Maybe four-thirty. If I get crunched, I'll give you a call."

"Works for me. How will I recognize you?"

"Find a copy of yesterday's paper. Page B6. I'll meet you by the circle out front of the museum, next to the Lake Pit."

"Okay, sounds good. I will see you then."

He collapsed his phone and nearly rear-ended a sedan at another stoplight. As he waited, he replayed their conversation, trying to picture Anne. She was definitely a flirt. He wavered between blond and brunette, picturing each with the voice. It had been a little strained. Did she have the sultry voice of Scarlett Johansson, or was she suffering from a head cold? And was she really the young, attractive reporter he was picturing or an old chain-smoker with an attitude who looked like Hot Lips toward the end? He could just see that, finding her hand-feeding birds a stale piece of bread when he arrived. Better take her up on that idea of finding a newspaper, so as to be prepared.

Connor's apartment complex was quiet when Jackson arrived, with quite a few less cars in the lot than the night before. He'd thought about dressing up a little bit, instead of his blue jeans and the Switchfoot T-shirt he'd thoughtlessly selected that morning. But the last thing he wanted to do was give off a Jehovah's Witness vibe. Besides, he had his P.I. license if anyone questioned his identity.

He started with Connor's building, and the first three doors he knocked on—two uppers and a lower—were unanswered. The fourth, a lower unit, was answered by a woman with a baby in her arms. The baby had a face like a bulldog, which it—the gender was a guess—had inherited from it's mother. Brown hair tinged with pink was wadded up behind her head, half of it loose over a white tank top stained with what Jackson guessed were mashed carrots. More of the same caked the baby's chin and cheeks. From somewhere back in the apartment, Jackson heard the sound of crying. Seeing what he could of the messy living room through the open door, Jackson couldn't blame the child.

"Ma'am, I won't take up much of your time," he said, reaching for his wallet. He opened it to his private investigator's license. "I'm a private investigator looking for Connor Novak."

The woman shook her head. "I don't know him," she said with a Southern accent.

"He lives just above you and over, in C203."

"I don't get much chance to meet the neighbors. Now, if you'll excuse me."

"Uh, one more question, please. You didn't happen to see or hear anything unusual this weekend, did you?"

She huffed. "I don't hear much of anything but crying children. I'm sorry, I can't help you."

She closed the door while Jackson smiled professionally. When the door latched, he wiped the smile off. The next door was to the apartment beneath Connor's, and his knock again went unanswered. After two more unanswered knocks from the apartments on the other side of Connor's, Jackson decided to cross "the quad" to Building B. It was more likely someone with a window facing Connor's apartment would have seen something than someone farther down in his building. That was, if Jackson could get anyone to answer the door.

He started with apartment B113, directly across from the last door he'd tried. It got him nowhere, so he moved to B213, the upper above it.

He knocked and was about to give up when he heard footfalls on the interior steps. A moment later, the door swung inward.

"Hey, man."

The guy was high. Jackson could tell because he was still smoking a joint. The glazed eyes were a giveaway too.

"Hey," Jackson said. He started reaching for his ID but decided to forget it. "You know Connor Novak across the way. Apartment C203?"

The guy took a drag. "No, man."

Jackson briefly described him.

The guy shook his head and tugged a strand of greasy hair back behind his ear. "Why?"

"He's missing. I'm a P.I. and I'm—"

"No way," he said, drawing it out. "Dude, you're a . . . No way."

"And you have a good day," Jackson said, turning away. He'd never smoked weed, never intended to, so he wasn't positive on the impact of a joint when you were already higher than Mount Whitney. But it seemed to him like overkill. Why not pound some Doritos and save the rest of your hash for when the high wore off?

The next two doors went unanswered, and he was cussed out and possibly hexed by a tattoo-laden chick with a mascara addiction in apartment B115. He was considering retiring when his phone chirped. Stepping off the sidewalk and into the grass he flipped it open.

"Yeah?"

"Jackson? It's Hailey."

"Hey, what's up?"

"Are you busy this morning?"

"I'm at Connor's complex right now, canvassing the neighbors."

"Any luck?"

"Not yet."

"Oh. Say, last night you said you wanted to talk to family."

"Yeah. You made contact?"

"Turns out Christine and Shane—her husband—are in Spain through the end of the month. A second honeymoon."

"Nothing quite as a romantic as a bullfight."

"Right? But I'm calling because I arranged a meeting with Dad. At ten-thirty, if you can make it."

"Yeah. Where?"

"His office on Marguerita Avenue." She gave him the address. "I'll meet you there?"

"Okay, sounds like a plan."

"Great. See you."

He closed his phone, mulled for a moment why people found Spain so romantic, and returned to knocking on doors. The occupants of B215 and B216 weren't home or weren't in the mood. The last door, B116, was opened by a young Indian woman in a gray maxi dress with full-length sleeves.

"Yes? Can I help you?"

"My name is Jackson Douglas, I'm a private investigator." He flashed his license. "I'm looking for Connor Novak, who lives in C203."

"Yes, I know Mr. Novak. He is a very nice man."

"Do you know him well?"

"No, not at all. But I see him coming and going. He is very friendly. Would you like to come in?"

"I don't want to take up much of your time."

"It is no trouble. Please."

She stepped back and he entered the apartment. It was drab. He'd expected lots of rugs and tapestries, which probably spoke to some insensitive, culturally-deprived, stereotyped view of Indians. Or the one time he'd gone with Grant to his college roommate Ajith's home in Canoga Park. But the woman's apartment had plain walls, nothing but blinds on the windows, and the simplest of furniture. Being a lower and a corner unit, it was shaped a little differently than Connor's, but not much.

"You are looking for Mr. Novak," the woman said as Jackson's eyes scanned the living room. Lots of books, no TV, a laptop on the coffee table. Probably a tea table, in this case. "Why?"

"He's missing," Jackson said.

"Oh dear."

"He didn't show up for work yesterday or Monday, and no one has heard from him since the weekend."

"Oh dear."

"I'm just canvassing the neighbors, seeing if anyone happened to see anything out of the usual, noticed anything suspicious. It's a long shot."

The woman put her hand over her mouth. "You do not think they did it, do you?"

"They who?"

"The government."

"N-no. No, I don't think so."

"They hound so many of us."

Jackson was ready to go see if the stoner could maybe help after all. But he pressed on. "Us who?"

"Foreigners. I have a green card, but I am constantly watched."

He had no idea what she meant, but wasn't all that interested in finding out. "Con—Mr. Novak isn't a foreigner."

"Oh, is that so? I assumed with a name like Novak. I have a sister in Anaheim who lives next door to a man named Dvorak. He is from Czechoslovakia."

Jackson wanted to tell her there hadn't been a country named Czechoslovakia since the early '90s, but didn't.

"Have you heard or seen anything unusual lately?" he asked instead. "Maybe a visitor to Mr. Novak's apartment, or maybe a stranger hanging around?"

"No. We had gang trouble here last summer. There was a shooting. They say it was another gang." She leaned slightly forward. "I do not think so."

He didn't bite.

"But nothing like that since."

"Do you know when the last time you saw Mr. Novak was?"

"Thursday night. I am a night-janitor at Venice High and was leaving as he was arriving home from work. He is very nice."

"Yes, ma'am."

She put her hand to her mouth again.

"Yes?"

"There was a truck Saturday night."

"A truck?"

"A black, big truck. An SUV. Like the government agents drive."

"Where was this truck?"

"In the parking lot," she said as if answering the stupidest question ever. "I saw two men get in and drive away in hurry."

"Saturday night?"

"I called in sick. I have been battling mono for quite a while."

"I'm very sorry."

"Thank you." She smiled at him until it was awkward. "The truck," she said, as if suddenly remembering.

"Yes. Two men got in?"

"Yes. They were white, dressed like department store salesmen."

"Do you know where they came from?"

"No. I saw them out that window," she said, pointing to one on the end of the building. "As I was making a late-night snack."

"Could one of them have been Mr. Novak?"

"I really could not say. Yes, I suppose so. I did not get a good enough look. They were in the truck very fast."

"Do you know what time this was?"

"Nine-thirty. Approximately."

"Anything else?"

"No. I do hope you find him. He is very nice."

"Thank you, I hope so too. Thanks for your help."

She showed him to the door, then stood watching as he walked to his car.

Jackson shook his head. A stressed out mom with pink highlights in her hair, a pothead, a white Voodoo Mambo, and an Indian conspiracy theorist. Right now, his working theory was that Connor had run away to someplace sane.

Chapter Nine

Monday, June 17, 2013
12:11 p.m.

LUCY'S TACO SHOP was a tiny little place on West C Street, a block north and east of the Central Courthouse in downtown San Diego, wedged between a criminal defense firm and a bail bondsman. It offered a couple of sidewalk tables on a small "patio" cordoned off by a wrought-iron fence, but San Diego County District Attorney Daniela Moreno had arranged to meet with Jackson inside. She had already been eating at a table by the corner when he arrived. Not overly hungry, he'd passed on ordering and taken a seat opposite her.

"You're not eating?" Moreno asked.

"Late breakfast," he said. That was sort of true. He'd grabbed a couple McMuffins as he'd left home around nine, wanting to make sure to have enough time to deal with traffic, navigate downtown San Diego, and find a parking place. He'd arrived one minute before their scheduled meeting time of ten after noon.

It was his second trip in as many days to America's Finest City. His drive back the day before after meeting with Special Agent Collier had been a drag. It was a lazy Sunday afternoon, and in the good old days, he could have called Sam to watch a movie or Maggie to grab a pizza. But those options were no longer on the table, so he'd vegged in front of the TV alone, watching nothing, avoiding thoughts about Padilla and his family and what it all meant.

They hadn't gone away, reconfirming his conviction that he had to get to the bottom of things. He'd called Moreno that morning and asked if she could carve out a few minutes for him. She happened to have a free lunch hour—technically forty-five minutes before a deposition—and he'd told her to pick the time and place. Now, here they were.

Moreno was attractive. She was tall, he could tell even though she was sitting, with jet black hair that was short and flared—almost fluffy, although Jackson guessed it was shellacked in place by enough hairspray to combat a gray, windy day. Her tan skin denoted her Latina heritage, and brown eyes were warm yet penetrating. She wore a shirred navy blouse and slacks. Attractive but not flaunting it and not—save for the hair—wasting time on her appearance.

That fit with the little bit of research Jackson had done before leaving. Moreno was just thirty-two, young to be a D.A., never mind just the second woman to hold the office in San Diego's history. She was known for her no-nonsense attitude and her brevity, in the courtroom and out. Her record—four years as A.D.A. and just over thirteen months as district attorney—was spotless. Colleagues, opponents, judges, and past jurors all spoke well of her. And Jackson had to hand it to her—she could eat hard-shell tacos without looking unprofessional.

"Thanks for making time to see me," he said.

"Certainly. You have questions about the Joaquín Padilla deal?"

"Yes and no."

Moreno frowned. "How so?"

"I am curious about the deal, but I actually wanted to talk to you about the Carmel Valley Investigation from a couple of years ago."

"Of course, Douglas. I'm sorry, I didn't make the connection this morning."

Jackson explained about his visit from the Haywoods, and how they had learned of the discrepancy in Padilla's timeline the night he had assaulted Petty Officer Grabel. He then summed up his conversation with Special Agent Collier the day before.

"So what is it specifically I can help you with?" Moreno asked when he was done. She had finished her tacos and now sipped what was undoubtedly a diet cola through a straw.

"You were the A.D.A. in 2011, right?"

"That's right."

"Were you privy to the investigation into my family's death?"

"I was this office's liaison with the investigators on the case," she answered.

"So you're familiar with the particulars of the case."

"Intimately. It still sticks in my craw."

"How so?"

"Because I think Joaquín Padilla committed the crime."

"You do?"

"Yes. I always have. I pushed to investigate him more fully."

"Didn't the supposed timeline of Grabel's assault rule him out?"

"I was never convinced," she said, leaning forward. "Petty Officer Grabel herself was uncertain of the time, and her statements never matched those of her neighbors. I was frankly surprised Padilla's attorney wasn't able to make a bigger deal of it at trial, but there was so much physical evidence against him. Plus, it didn't get much attention, but although the Sheriff's Department's investigator ruled out a remote trigger, he did state it was possible some sort of delay-action fuse could have been used."

"I never heard that."

"It could have delayed the explosion by several minutes. With the confusion as to when Padilla actually arrived at Grabel's house, it wasn't a leap for me to connect him. And he has the past to warrant such suspicion."

"Then I have to ask, why didn't you bring charges against Padilla?"

"Because we couldn't then, nor could I now, prove his guilt. It's not a matter of guilt or innocence, but whether guilt can be proven beyond a reasonable doubt. I'll spare you some eloquent speech about our legal system, but for better or worse, it is what it is. And I've seen my share of trials. Trust me, I know when I won't stand a chance with a jury, and there's no sense wasting time and taxpayer money when you don't have a case. Sadly, in this instance, I didn't have a case."

Jackson sighed.

"Sorry, I know that's cold."

"It's fine."

"There is another consideration," Moreno continued after a pull on her soda, "the double jeopardy provision of the Fifth Amendment. If we go after someone half-cocked and can't get a conviction, we lose any chance of ever trying him or her again in the future, should that evidence present itself at a later date."

"And this gap in his alibi created by Mira Austin's testimony doesn't provide that evidence?"

She shook her head, sympathy played out on her taut face. "If the shoe was on the other foot, if you had to prove innocence beyond a reasonable belief, it'd cost you the case. That's it. That's how far we are from having enough proof to go forward. I'm sorry."

Jackson sighed again.

"I know it must be a blow seeing him released. Please believe me when I tell you I don't take something like this lightly. I've sat across the table or across the room from a lot of victims and their families and had to explain why the person who had brought them so much pain wasn't going to prison or wasn't facing full punishment or was getting out early. As much sense as it makes in the grand scheme of things, I know how hard it is to swallow. And I'm sorry for that too."

"I get it," Jackson said. "I do. You know, I've always talked about the explosion as an accident, because that's what it was ruled and for all I know, that's what it really was. But part of me has always questioned that, and part of me has always attached Padilla's name to the case, because he was the only suspect they ever had. And it always consoled me that if it wasn't an accident—if he was responsible—at least he was in prison."

"And now he's not."

"Yeah."

"I won't insult you by feeding you a line about the greater good then, because, like I said, what makes very practical sense to a district attorney doesn't ring true with someone who has been personally impacted by the crime."

"I appreciate your candor, Ms. Moreno."

"The way I see it, people deserve nothing less," she said with a smile.

"Can I ask you something else?"

"Can you walk with me? I could use a few extra minutes of prep before my deposition."

"Sure."

She reached for her purse and a briefcase from the chair beside her, and he took the opening to grab her tray. He dumped the contents in the trash and followed her outside. The wind was steady off the ocean at fifteen to twenty miles per hour. It was tempered somewhat by all the buildings, but also funneled down the east-west streets. When they turned the corner, it slackened considerably.

"What's on your mind?" she asked.

"Like you said, you've got a lot of experience with criminal cases. In your experience, what percentage of the time when someone's guilty does sufficient evidence exist to prove it?"

"That's a tricky question. I'm convinced the evidence is always there. It's impossible to commit a crime without leaving evidence of some kind. But knowing where to look, having the capability to look and access the evidence, recognizing it, processing it—that's where criminals fall through the cracks in the system."

"So with Padilla, if he did it like you think, then there must be proof."

"In theory, yes."

"So someone just needs to find it."

She looked at him, her brown eyes piercing. "Mr. Douglas, the case was closed."

"I'll open it. I am, after all, a private investigator."

"With all due respect, because I looked you up too, and your record is impressive, the FBI, SDPD, SDSO, and NCIS all investigated this case. Do you really think you'll find something they didn't? And after two years? Even if they did miss something, some key piece of evidence, there's no guarantee it will still be there or be viable."

"It's a risk I'm willing to take, Ms. Moreno. You said this case sticks in your craw, and with all due respect to you, it sticks in mine a whole lot worse."

She nodded. "I imagine so."

"You said earlier you pushed to investigate Padilla further at the time. Why didn't they?"

"A number of reasons. If you want the full scoop, talk with Special Agent Lance Kilpatrick."

"FBI?"

Moreno nodded. "He had the lead on the investigation. He can give you more details than I could."

"All right. Thanks. I won't keep you any longer. Thank you for your time."

"Give you a piece of advice?"

"Of course."

"I've talked to a lot of people who've been where you are, experiencing our justice system when it doesn't seem to work. I'd like to tell you that it ultimately works out, that justice is ultimately served. But the sad part of this line of work is that sometimes it isn't. I bust my tail to try to make it so, but I know my success rate is less than one hundred percent. The advice is this: You can't let it consume you. As much as it pains you, as wrong as it feels, you have to find some way to make peace with life that isn't always just. I've seen firsthand how it destroys people who don't."

He nodded. "Thank you, Ms. Moreno."

"You have my number. If you need anything else, give me a call."

"I will, thanks."

He peeled off and headed back toward his car, hands in his pockets. Talking with Moreno had only frustrated him further. He'd sparred with Grant's fiancée Hillary, a defense attorney, numerous times about the flaws in the justice system that allowed criminals to get off. This wasn't exactly that, and yet, it felt quite a bit like it. When a D.A. was convinced a career criminal was guilty of murder but could do nothing about it, something was wrong.

Two other things she said bugged him too as he walked back to his car. The first was about finding peace. As a Christian, Jackson knew he was supposed to have "the peace of God, which transcends all understanding" in the midst of the chaos of life. So why didn't he? What was he missing? What was he doing wrong?

The second was her statement about commuting Padilla's sentence being done for the greater good. A guy who had sexually assaulted a naval officer and possibly murdered four people was being let out of prison early. How could that be good?

But that wasn't what really bugged him. What really bugged him was that the idea of "the greater good" had been one he'd operated by as a P.I. time and time again. And now it was coming back to bite him in the butt.

Chapter Ten

Wednesday, May 11, 2011
10:27 a.m.

KENDRICK INVESTMENTS LEASED space in a multipurpose office building just off Marguerita Avenue. The building, which also housed an attorney, a small accounting firm, and a psychiatric partnership according to its marquee, was situated in the heart of a residential neighborhood. With its olive green siding and beige brick façade, the single-level structure fit in well.

Being an ace detective, Jackson noted the fresh asphalt and crisp lines in the parking lot and the trees that were little more than saplings shading the front lawn, and concluded the building was new to the neighborhood. It was nothing terribly insightful, the type of observation he'd made all his life. But now that he was making observations for a living, he felt a little bit of pride in them.

A silver Beemer was parked out front, and instead of turning into the parking lot, Jackson coasted to a stop behind it. As he did, the driver-side door opened and Hailey got out. She cut a rather nice figure in a Kelly green sundress, her hair as pristine and perfect as the night before, and silver jewelry everywhere sparkling in the morning sun.

"Good morning," she said as Jackson got out.

"Morning."

She frowned, looking at his shirt. "What's a Bro-Am?"

"It's a surf contest and beach concert put on by Switchfoot each year in San Diego. Lot of food, fun, obviously music. All for charity."

"Sounds fun. What's Switchfoot?"

"Check 'em out on iTunes. You ready?"

She nodded and walked beside him up the walk. It really was a beautiful morning, and the sunlight did wonderful things as it caught Hailey's blond-brown hair and the bright green dress. Jackson got the door for her and the air-conditioning engulfed them. Sky lights in a vaulted ceiling shone abundantly on the wide entry and main lobby. A young receptionist sat behind a semi-circle desk, and greeted them with a formal smile.

"Hailey Kendrick, to see Mayor Kendrick."

"I'm with her," Jackson said as the receptionist glanced at him. Then her eyes went to a computer screen, only for a second.

"Of course, Miss Kendrick. Go ahead."

The various offices were situated around the square lobby. Kendrick Investments occupied the entire back of the building. Hailey pushed open a glass door and they entered a second lobby, this one carpeted, a touch warmer, and without the soft pop streaming from speakers in the ceiling. A water cooler and a display rack of brochures and pamphlets flanked a doorway on the left. A short couch next to an end table stacked high with magazines was under a window straight ahead. Another receptionist—this one older and without the smile—sat behind a desk on the right.

"Good morning, Miss Kendrick," she said.

"Good morning, Veronica. Can I go on in?"

Veronica nodded, raked her eyes over Jackson, and went back to work. Hailey led the way around her desk and through a closed doorway beside a bank of filing cabinets. "Knock, knock," she announced as she entered the room. Jackson followed, quickly taking it all in.

Three men were seated on a sectional sofa in the left corner, under a pair of windows. A polished, gleaming desk was in the opposite corner beneath a series of magnificent photos of various Santa Monica landmarks. To Jackson's immediate right, a conference table was flanked by a wet bar. In the middle of the room, looking like the lobster tank at a seafood restaurant, was a circular aquarium full of tropical fish. It reached almost to the ceiling, with seaweed or kelp floating in the large tank, giving the fish something to navigate in their endless circle of swimming.

"Hello, Hailey," the mayor said, rising from his seat against the far wall. The two other men, sitting under the window, rose as well. Mayor

Kendrick looked like the dad from *Growing Pains*, only with all gray hair. He wore a suit, the jacket of which hung over the back of the chair behind the desk. His collar and cuffs were crisp, his pants wrinkle-free. Before Hailey had returned the greeting and had the chance to introduce Jackson, the mayor was already giving him—and his apparel—a hard glare.

"It's nice to meet you," he forced.

"You as well, sir," Jackson said.

Mayor Kendrick turned to the two other men. "My head of security, Luke Tyler."

"Mr. Douglas," he said with what could have been interpreted as disdain. His grip was like iron, and his arms strained the sleeves of his slate dress shirt, no tie.

"And you know Hailey."

Tyler nodded. "Ma'am."

"Luke."

"Vincent Diaz, my associate," Tyler said, and the other man offered a handshake to both Jackson and Hailey. His light blue sleeves contained his arms, but barely.

"Can I offer you something to drink?" Kendrick asked, perfunctorily.

"I'm fine," Jackson said.

"I'll grab a water," Hailey said, and turned toward the wet bar.

"Please, have a seat," Kendrick said. Jackson took a plush armchair across a spacious, square coffee table from the two security guys. Diaz carried a leather notepad folder, and unclicked a pen as he sat. Kendrick crossed his legs and smoothed his tie. He waited until Hailey returned with a bottle of water, then said, "I understand my daughter has hired you to find my stepson."

"Yes, sir."

"Any luck?"

"A few possible leads."

The mayor nodded. "I have to admit, I was a little surprised when she informed me of her decision."

"So was I," Jackson said with a grin. It was not reciprocated.

"You don't seem to take this very seriously."

"On the contrary, sir. Finding Connor is my top priority right now."

"Ahead of wining and dining my daughter?"

"Excuse me?"

"Dad," Hailey said.

"She told me you took her for drinks, then dinner. Is that standard procedure with your clients?"

Jackson couldn't help but grin again. "Well, so far."

Kendrick nodded, settling his eyes on Hailey for a moment. They contained disapproval. "I didn't tell my daughter this, but yesterday afternoon I asked Luke to look into things."

"We searched Mr. Novak's apartment," Tyler said as if bored. "There was nothing amiss, nothing to suspect foul play. In fact, it appeared as if Mr. Novak could have been at work."

"Except his car was there," Jackson said.

Tyler nearly nailed Jackson to the far wall with his eyes. "We also spoke with his employer, who advised us that he hadn't come in. But he said Mr. Novak's work had been typical of late. There was nothing out of the ordinary."

"You didn't also happen to speak to his crazy neighbor who thinks the government's out to get us all, did you?" Jackson asked. He wasn't sure why, but for his entire life, whenever he encountered someone who was overly uptight or cranky, it brought out even more of his smart-aleck attitude.

"We did not. In fact, we found nothing to suggest anything had happened to Mr. Novak."

"So that's it?" Hailey asked, looking at her dad. "You're giving up?"

"You heard Luke, dear. There's no indication whatsoever that anything has happened to him."

"But he's missing. He hasn't come in to work."

"That could be voluntary."

"So where is he?"

"Have you considered calling the police?" Jackson asked.

"No," Kendrick said flatly.

"This is a rather non-critical situation," Tyler said. "As I said, there are no signs of foul play, nothing to indicate anything has happened to Mr. Novak, no evidence of any sort at his apartment."

"It doesn't warrant their involvement," Kendrick said.

"You found no evidence at all?" Jackson asked.

"That's correct."

He turned from Tyler to Kendrick. "We found a name."

"A name?" Tyler asked.

"Written on notepad on Connor's desk," Jackson said, still looking at the mayor. His return gaze was stone-like.

"When was this?" Tyler asked.

"Last night, about nine-thirty."

"We were there in the afternoon, and there was no name on the notepad. We took photos that will prove—"

"It was an imprint from the previous page," Hailey said.

"What?"

"Somebody had written a name and a number on the pad, then torn off the page," Jackson explained, "but there was an imprint on the page underneath."

"And how did you find this?" Kendrick asked. "I doubt you have the type of equipment necessary to read such an imprint."

"I used a quarter."

"A quarter?"

"Rubbed it over the page," Jackson said, demonstrating with his fingers in the air. "Saw Magnum do the same thing once."

Tyler snorted under his breath.

"And what was this name?" Kendrick asked.

"A. Magstadt."

"Who is A. Magstadt?" Tyler asked.

"That's what I intend to find out," Jackson said, not feeling like divulging anything further.

The mayor cleared his throat. "Mr. Douglas, I don't know who this person is or what connection—if any—they have to Connor, but I'm sure Luke and Vincent can figure it out. We won't be requiring your services any further."

"With all due respect, sir, I'm not working for you. I'm working for Hailey. It's her call whether or not I continue."

Four sets of eyes turned her way.

Hailey looked at Jackson before turning her attention to her father. "He found clues your guys couldn't."

Before the mayor could retort, a knock sounded on his door, and it swung inward. A woman walked through and all four men rose, Jackson last.

"I'm sorry, am I interrupting?" she asked. She was pretty if not beautiful, maybe thirty. Her hair was blond, golden really, and hung just low enough that it splashed onto her shoulders. She wore a white skirt suit with an orange ruffled blouse. Neither the blouse nor the skirt did a terribly thorough job of concealing her figure, nor did she, practically strutting into the room. Jackson was laying even odds among mistress, second stepchild, and the attorney from next door.

"Not at all," Kendrick said. "You know Luke and Vincent and of course Hailey. This is Jackson Douglas," he said with minimal disgust. "Mr. Douglas—"

"Jenn White," she said coolly, offering a dutiful handshake. It was like shaking an icepack. "Hailey, I didn't know you were seeing anyone."

"Mr. Douglas is a private eye," Kendrick said, nearly sneering. "Hailey has hired him to attempt to locate Connor."

"Has he still not shown up to work?"

"No."

"I'm sorry, I should have called," she said, looking to the mayor as if no one else was in the room, "but I was out this way, and I have those quotes we talked about." She held up a small clear presentation folder. "Do you have a minute?"

"Of course," Kendrick said. "Excuse us a moment," he added, then gestured toward his desk. White peacocked past Jackson, receiving a gentle, guiding hand on her back from the mayor.

"This name," Tyler said, starting to sit down.

"I'm sorry, I'm just gonna grab a water," Jackson said. He looked down at Hailey.

"Second door on the left," she said, and he walked to the wet bar, trying to hear the mayor's conversation with Jenn White. But they spoke in hushed tones on the far side of his desk as Jackson retrieved a bottle of water. He took a sip and watched them out the corner of his eye as he returned to his seat. He ruled out stepchild when he saw her place a hand on his arm as they talked and giggle when he made some comment with a mirthful smirk. Still fifty-fifty on mistress or lady neighbor attorney.

"The name," Tyler said as Jackson sat down. "Was that the only thing you found?"

"So to speak."

"What's that mean?"

"You said you were in Connor's apartment yesterday afternoon?"

"That's right."

"Did you look through his garbage?"

Tyler shook his head. "No, we did not."

"Was there garbage?"

"Why wouldn't there have been?"

"Because there wasn't when we searched it last night. Not a scrap."

"Connor's something of a neat freak, isn't he?"

Jackson looked to his left at White. She and Kendrick had returned to the seating area.

"He'd surely have some trash," Hailey said.

White shrugged. "I have to be going. It was nice meeting you, Mr. Douglas."

"Uh, yeah, you too."

"Arnold, I'll see you later."

"I look forward to it."

They briefly squeezed hands, and Jackson settled on mistress. Technically girlfriend, since Arnold wasn't married. But she had to be twenty years his junior.

"Hailey, Luke, Vincent."

They all said some form of goodbye, and she strode toward the door. She stopped just past the aquarium. "Oh, Arnie, you should call Alan today about CenTel."

"I'll do that."

She smiled, turned on her four-inch heel, and exited the room. Jackson was first to have his head back around. Kendrick retook his seat on the sectional, sitting forward with elbows on his knees. "Mr. Douglas, let me be candid with you."

"Please."

"If something has indeed happened to Connor, I am confident Luke and Vincent will be able to ascertain what that is. I would be most grateful if you didn't take any more of my daughter's money working a case when your involvement is redundant."

"I can appreciate that, Mr. Mayor."

"Good."

"But I'm not taking any money from your daughter."

"How's that?"

"I'm working the case for free."

Tyler huffed.

"Free?" Kendrick asked.

"Yes, sir. Sort of a 'grand opening' discount."

"I see."

"And if you don't mind, I do have a few questions."

Kendrick appeared to bite his tongue. "Go ahead."

"How would you define your relationship with Connor?"

"I beg your pardon?"

"He's your ex-wife's son, correct? Are you two still close?"

"I don't see what business that is of yours."

"I don't mean to pry, but I'm curious when the last time you spoke with him was, had you noticed anything unusual in his life, that sort of thing?"

"I considered Connor like my own son. I still do. I spoke with him weekend before last and he seemed fine."

"He was fourteen when you married his mother, correct?"

"Yes."

"Did you ever have any disciplinary problems with him? Was there any trouble at school, any issues with drugs or alcohol?"

"Just what are you implying?"

"Nothing. I'm looking for anything that could hint at why he's missing."

"And you think it stems from an incident when he was a teenager?"

"I have to consider all possibilities."

"Mr. Kendrick," Tyler said, "I really think we should get back to business. This isn't going anywhere."

"I concur. Mr. Douglas, I appreciate what you're attempting to do here, but I think we'd be better off leaving this to professionals."

"Dad."

"I am a professional, Mr. Mayor. And like I told you, that decision is Hailey's."

"And I've made it," she said.

"Then I think we're through here."

"Yes, sir," Jackson said, standing as Kendrick did. "Thank you for your time. Mr. Tyler, Mr. Diaz."

Hailey stood as well and turned to follow Jackson out.

"Hailey, might I have a word with you, please?"

She and Jackson both stopped.

"Alone."

"I'll be out in a minute," she said, and Jackson nodded and headed for the waiting room.

Jenn White was leaning on Veronica's desk as the two of them talked in quiet tones, holding in laughter. When Jackson emerged, they both straightened up like busted schoolgirls.

"I'll see you later, Veronica."

"Good day, Miss White."

Veronica's smile vanished as she looked Jackson's way, and he wandered over to the rack of brochures. It didn't take a "professional" detective to know that Kendrick and Tyler didn't approve. What he couldn't figure out was why they seemed borderline hostile. For that matter, dismissive. What had Hailey said, that the mayor had referred to Connor's absence as "Connor being Connor." Tyler had talked almost flippantly about the search of Connor's apartment, and Kendrick seemed more intent on Jackson quitting than in finding Connor. To that end, Jackson wondered if Hailey would emerge from this meeting with her father and fire him by fiat of the mayor.

Father and Daughter Kendrick's lack of desire to go to the police was also a little unusual. Hailey's reasons—being unsure if anything was truly wrong and not wanting to drag the mayor's office through the public relations hassle calling the cops would cause—made sense. Jackson could especially see why Hailey wouldn't involve the police without her father's say-so. But Mayor Kendrick, for all his indifference, had sent Tyler to check Connor's apartment. So why not call the police?

Jackson wandered over to the magazines on the table, absentmindedly checking covers—*Sports Illustrated, Good Housekeeping, Field & Stream, Redbook*. The way he saw it, the mayor's dismissive response about contacting the police had three possible motivations. One, he just didn't care, and any actions otherwise were for appearances' sake. Two, he knew something about Connor's disappearance and didn't need or want the cops involved. Three, he had something to hide and involving the police might bring it to light. It was all speculation and conjecture, and Jackson brushed it aside as the door to the mayor's office opened.

Hailey marched out, on the verge of tears or epithets. She forced a thin-lipped smile at Veronica, then said a quick, "Come on," to Jackson. He followed her out into the main lobby. Her low—compared to Jenn White's—heels clicked extra loudly on the tile as she marched toward the front door. Only when they were both outside did she stop. She turned to face Jackson, and he expected her to vent.

"I am so sorry," she said.

"Don't worry about it."

"That was unacceptable behavior. He can be so bull-headed."

He placed a hand on her elbow. "Hailey, it's all right."

"That crack about professionalism."

"He's sort of got a point. I mean, I've yet to make a profit in this line of work."

That drew a thin smile.

"You okay?"

"Yeah, I'm fine." She blew out a final angry breath. "Are you hungry?"

"Yeah, kind of."

"You want to grab something to eat, my treat?"

"Sure. Just don't tell your dad that you're now wining and dining me."

The dam broke, and a smile spread across Hailey's face.

Chapter Eleven

Monday, June 17, 2013
5:15 p.m.

FBI SPECIAL AGENT Lance Kilpatrick had the disposition of a Soviet bureaucrat. Sunken eyes, no expression on his face, and pale skin. His suit was neither sharp nor rumpled—it was just there. His tie knot was tight and small. Maybe that explained it—maybe the pressure was squeezing the life out of his face.

Jackson vaguely remembered him from the initial investigation. Back then, he'd been torn between following every detail, trying to be kept in the loop at every point, and wanting to run from all thoughts of it, from all memories. He'd met with the local cops and the FBI at least twice, but was having trouble assigning more than a dour face with the name Kilpatrick. Then again, so much of that time was a blur anyhow.

After meeting with District Attorney Moreno, Jackson had called Kilpatrick's office and left a voicemail. Then he had called the San Diego Police Department, hoping to speak with either of the detectives who had worked the case along with Kilpatrick. One had since retired, and had not returned Jackson's call, and the other had moved out of state and then moved again, no longer a police officer, pretty much off the grid. And the lead investigator with the Sheriff's Department's Bomb/Arson Unit had died of colon cancer, Jackson had learned when trying to track him down. That left Kilpatrick, who had called back while Jackson sat in the Granada at Sunset Cliffs Park, watching the endless waves mindlessly.

Now they were sitting across the table from each other at a Starbucks in a strip mall just off San Diego's I-805. The weather had not improved, with the wind howling outside the window, accompanied by a slate gray sky. The San Diego Chamber of Commerce owed Jackson a refund.

"What exactly can I do for you, Mr. Douglas?" Kilpatrick asked in a voice to match his expression. Ben Stein without the perkiness. "There's no new information. No change in status."

"Did you hear about Joaquín Padilla's early release?"

"Yeah, so?"

"Did you also hear that Petty Officer Grabel's neighbor testified that Padilla had not arrived at her apartment at 7:23 as originally believed, but approximately ten minutes later?"

"I hadn't, but I don't see how that changes anything." He took a long pull on his Venti coffee.

"It means Padilla could theoretically have triggered the explosion and made it to La Playa."

Kilpatrick shrugged. "Wouldn't change much of anything. He's still not good for the murders."

Jackson tried to be patient with Kilpatrick's humdrum attitude, but every dispassionate response made him want to reach across the table and finish the tie's job in strangling the guy, just to get some answers.

"Would you mind going through the investigation with me again anyhow? For my own edification?"

Kilpatrick sighed as he took another drink. When he lowered his cup, he said, "What do you want to know?"

"For starters, how did the FBI get primary jurisdiction?"

"We didn't. SDPD had it. Given the nature of the potential crime, we worked with them and the SDSO."

"What about NCIS? My father was working for ONI at the time. Why wasn't this their case?"

"They released it to us."

"You, not SDPD or SDSO?"

"Us collective." He took another drink. "What are you getting at?"

"Just trying to figure this all out. Why'd they not pursue it?"

"You'd have to ask them."

"Okay, so Padilla was originally a suspect, right?"

"He was a person of interest."

"Why?"

"A number of reasons," Kilpatrick said through a sigh. "For starters, he had a long rap sheet, including an arrest for arson as a juvenile. We found a cell phone at the scene, mostly burned. We couldn't pull any prints off it, but our lab tech was able to discover the list of recent calls. All to one number, an Oscar Martinez. We're not sure, but we believe it may be the same Oscar Martinez who supplied Padilla with the black powder he used back in '92 when he burned the family horse barn in Lancaster."

"You think it was a burner and he dropped it?"

"It was a theory."

"Not a trigger of some sort?"

"No."

"You said you believe it was the same Oscar Martinez. How do you not know?"

Another sigh. "The number on the phone was to an Oscar Martinez who lives in Escondido. The old Oscar Martinez's last-known whereabouts were in San Marcos, just up the road. We didn't get any closer before Padilla was off our radar."

Jackson now sighed at what he considered sloppy investigative work. Talk about letting loose ends dangle in the wind.

"What else?" he asked.

"Padilla's finances were in the tank. He'd been working odd jobs, some legal, some not, but was still about six grand in debt."

"Debt to who?"

"Owed loans to two banks, one in San Diego, the other in L.A."

"Okay, so how's that connect? How does burning a restaurant in Carmel Valley ease his debt?"

"If it's a job for somebody else . . ."

Jackson nodded, having not considered Padilla may have just been a hired torch, so to speak.

"Padilla also had a relationship with the owner, Carlos Gomez. He worked with his son Jake at a restaurant in San Diego for about a year in '04 and early '05."

"Was there bad blood?"

"No. We made no connection, but it was coincidental, we thought."

"Anything else?"

Kilpatrick shook his head and took another drink. Jackson lifted his Tall coffee to his mouth. Still scalding.

"Okay, so why'd you come off Padilla?"

"Mostly the timeline. Never mind how unusual it would be for a guy to blow up a restaurant, then make a mad dash across town to sexually assault a Navy officer, but once the investigator ruled out any sort of remote detonation, the timeline made it impossible."

"Okay, but you just said a stretched timeline wouldn't matter. Why not?"

"Because there's nothing besides some circumstantial, coincidental evidence. No eyewitnesses to place him at the scene, no motive besides conjecture. Absolutely no DNA on scene."

Jackson mulled for a minute. "What about Grabel? Do we have any idea how he knew her?"

"They met in a bar, from what I remember of his trial."

"She's in the Navy, he goes after another Navy officer?"

"He didn't go after anyone that we know of."

"Hypothetically. I know his record, but was there anything at all that would hint at why he might have done this?"

"Nothing."

"Any potential employer you could track down?"

"No. He's a dead end."

Jackson sighed. He couldn't accept that. There was too much smoke for there to be no fire, the awful pun not intended.

"I suppose you never talked to Jake Gomez?"

"No. He was living in Mexico at the time."

"What about Carlos?"

"Of course we spoke to him. He didn't even know Padilla."

Jackson took a frustrated gulp of coffee and paid for it when he swallowed.

"I get you're mad, Mr. Douglas. But there's nothing to tie Padilla to this. Nothing at all. Even if he did it, which I doubt, you'll never prove it."

Jackson thanked Special Agent Kilpatrick for his time and remained at the table after he left. Assuming the restaurant didn't just explode by itself, someone was responsible. There were zero leads, other than Padilla, a career criminal with a history of arson, debt, ties to the owner, and no alibi. Plus a phone with the name of a previous supplier of his had been found at the scene. He could see D.A. Moreno's point; no jury would or should convict on that evidence. But to say there was nothing seemed a little harsh too.

So how, Jackson asked himself, did he find the dirt that would incriminate Joaquín Padilla? Or therein failing, how could he ever silence the hunch that Padilla was indeed responsible for murdering his family?

Chapter Twelve

Wednesday, May 11, 2011
11:40 a.m.

JACKSON AND HAILEY drove separately to Venice City Beach. They parked and walked south along the Ocean Front Walk, a pedestrian-only promenade crowded with street vendors, artists, performers, svelte bodies of both sexes, and plenty of weirdos. Unlike every TV or movie scene ever shot in Venice, there were no bikini-clad babes on roller blades darting in and out of foot-traffic.

Hailey led the way to a hole-in-the-wall sandwich shop between a beachwear store and a souvenir emporium. It offered wraps and paninis and sandwiches with the freshest of local, sustainable, humanely harvested (whatever that meant), organic ingredients. Jackson had never given a Flying Wallenda where his food had been grown as long as it tasted good, but that was becoming a big thing, especially on the Left Coast. And since Hailey was treating, he didn't complain.

Lunch in tow, they resumed walking. Nearing noon on a weekday, the promenade was busy but not crowded. A part of Jackson wished he and Hailey were just out for a carefree jaunt. But he made sure to focus on their true purpose in being together, especially after Mayor Kendrick's criticisms.

"So thanks for sticking up for me with your dad," Jackson said before taking a bite of his club sandwich. That was something of a misnomer. A good club had ham, turkey, bacon, tomato, lettuce for roughage, a little mayo, and was served on white bread with fries. This one was on chewy whole wheat bread, and he had to hunt for meat amidst a garden of lettuce, spinach leaves, tomatoes, cucumbers, and something else he couldn't identify. Even so, it had been the best option on the menu.

"Ugh, my father," Hailey said. "I really am sorry for his behavior."

"It's all right."

She looked his way, and the breeze that had been blowing her hair over her shoulder now carried tendrils of it across her face and under her chin. She extended a few fingers holding her one-hundred-percent made-from-recyclables cup to also hold her veggie wrap, then used her free hand to guide the hair back in place. "Are you close with your parents?" she asked.

"Yeah."

"But do they ever drive you crazy?"

"Sure. My mom can be a bit of an organizer, try to coordinate everything. Like my birthday, for example. It's Saturday, and she is scheduling this dinner like the President's coming. She's already made reservations . . ."

"What?"

"She said something about a private dining room." He shook his head. "I really hope this isn't a surprise party. I hate surprise parties."

"Seriously?" Hailey said.

"Yeah."

"I mean, seriously, that's the extent of your parents driving you crazy?"

He squinted. "Off the top of my head."

A skateboarder with a green Mohawk zipped past them.

"I love my dad," Hailey said, "but when he gets like this . . ."

"What'd he want to talk to you about, if I may pry?"

"He told me in not so many words to drop you."

"I see."

"I told him I was twenty-three years old and could hire or fire whomever I wanted for whatever reason I wanted."

"I'm guessing that didn't play well."

"I don't know. I walked out of his office before he could respond." This time she shook her head to dislodge windblown strands of hair, and they eventually trailed behind her with the rest of her tresses.

"Sorry to come between you."

"You didn't. It's Connor. It's almost like he doesn't care."

"So it wasn't just me picking up on that."

She looked his way. "You thought so too?"

He nodded. "How well do you know Tyler and Diaz?"

Hailey shrugged. "I've seen Luke around. I know his name. I recognized Vincent but wouldn't have known his name had Luke not said it."

"Your dad said Luke was head of security?"

"Yeah, why?"

"You know what that usually entails?"

"The mayor of Santa Monica doesn't warrant a protective detail, but Luke and his firm provide any personal security as necessary. They coordinate with the city or police for events like yesterday, handle security at Dad's home and office. It's a pretty vague job description."

"So he's not an investigator, per se?"

Hailey had taken a bite of her wrap, and she shook her head as she swallowed. "I don't think so."

They had reached an open expanse of grass that intruded onto the beach. The Marvin Braude Bike Trail ran along the other side of it, at the edge of the beach. The grass itself was interspersed with more "sky duster" palms, and with people reading in the sun, bathing in the sun, and probably worshipping the sun. Hailey nodded toward the grass and away from some knife jugglers ahead on the promenade, and they cut over.

"Ask you something, Hailey?"

Her eyes tracked a Frisbee in front of them, then looked his way. "Of course."

"When we first talked, you said you didn't want to call the cops because you weren't sure Connor was truly missing, and you didn't want to make a scene if there was nothing going on."

"But now we're pretty sure he's missing."

"More so."

"And you want to know if we should call the cops?"

"I'm not begging off the case. But they admittedly have more firepower than I do."

"Remember what you said to my dad when he said you weren't taking things very seriously?"

Jackson nodded. "I said finding Connor was my number one priority."

"You think LAPD will feel the same way?"

"No."

"Then I want you."

"You can have both."

"You think it would do any good?"

"I think it can't hurt."

"Unless Dad found out. He'd have a bird."

"There is that."

"But I'll think about it."

He nodded.

They reached the bike path, opposite which was a large skate park and then a wide beach. Technically for bikers, 'boarders, and 'bladers, the path was also used by a lot of pedestrians. Given the lack of bicycle traffic, Jackson and Hailey resumed southward on the path. It veered around a scrap-metal sculpture and a playground before approaching Venice Beach's famous handball and basketball courts.

"Your dad said he and Connor were still close. Would you agree?"

"Mmm, yes and no."

He stuffed the last of his sandwich into his mouth while waiting for her to explain.

"They never were the palling around kind of father and son, and they certainly aren't now. But there's no bad blood between them either."

Jackson decided against giving Hailey his three potential motivations for Mayor Kendrick to not involve the cops. She was on his side in this thing, and there was no reason to potentially shift power. And yet, something wasn't quite right about the mayor's reaction to Connor's disappearance.

"Who's Jenn White?"

Hailey looked at him. "Isn't it obvious? Dad's girlfriend."

"You don't approve?"

"She's six years older than me, Jackson."

"I thought she seemed a little young. It serious?"

"Ish. They've been dating for about a year. But I don't think Dad's in any hurry to get married again." She sipped her drink.

"What's Connor's relationship with her?"

"Odd."

"Because she's taking the place of his mother with your dad?"

"And because she's his boss."

"What?"

"MatchStick is Jenn's baby."

Jackson stopped, waiting for Hailey to turn around. "Kinda buried the lede there, Kenny."

"Don't call me that," she said with a playful whap to the arm.

"So when he was working all weekend on MatchStick algorithms, he was working for her?"

"Yeah. What's that mean?"

"I don't know. Maybe nothing. But it's interesting." They resumed walking. "So describe odd."

Hailey shrugged. "I didn't mean anything. Just that his boss turned out to be his stepdad's new girlfriend."

"If you don't mind me saying so, your family is very '90s."

"I know, right?"

They had reached a span of sand volleyball courts, a few of which were occupied. They found a bench beside the bike path and sat down.

"One more question."

"Go for it."

"Any idea why your dad, his head of security, and Jenn—his girlfriend and Connor's boss—would all seem to think there's nothing to Connor's disappearance, why they would all sweep it under the rug?"

Hailey shook her head. "None." Her eyes settled on Jackson. "Do you?"

"No, but . . ."

"But what?"

He sighed. "It's almost as if they're hiding something."

"Hiding something? Like what?"

"I don't know. That's just it, it's nothing more than a feeling, a hunch. But they were dismissive about the police, downplayed our evidence, even downplayed his being gone in the first place."

"But Dad did send Luke to check it out, so he isn't being totally dismissive."

"Right, which is what makes it odd."

Hailey sighed. "Jackson, my dad can be all-business, can be a little gruff sometimes, and you're not the first guy I've introduced him to that he's treated with condescension. But he's an honest man, a good man. He's not involved in something shady, if that's what you think."

"I'll take your word for that, Hailey. And I didn't mean to imply otherwise. It's just that something's off here."

She sat back. "I know." A half minute passed, the breeze carrying the shouts from the volleyball courts and the swimmers at the water's edge toward them. Hailey rolled her head toward Jackson. "So I never asked. What did you find out about A. Magstadt? Did you call the number?"

"Yeah. A woman named Anne. She's a reporter. I'm meeting her at four."

"Can I come?"

"Don't you have to work?"

"I work a lot of weekends," she said, shrugging. "I had off yesterday and took off today. I thought I might be able to help you."

Jackson couldn't help but smile.

"What?" she asked.

"Nothing."

"No come on, what is it?"

Every TV private investigator Jackson had ever watched—Thomas Magnum, Jim Rockford, Rick and A.J. Simon, Spenser—always had a moment when the pretty female client got to them. Sometimes they fell for her romantically over a candlelight dinner. Sometimes she struck a nerve of protection with them the way a little sister would. Sometimes they fought and fought until their passion turned to romance. It wasn't always easy to define, but you could always see it in the investigator's eyes. And now, from inside, Jackson could recognize it inside him.

He wasn't falling for Hailey romantically. He'd known her less than twenty-four hours, and although she was attractive, he couldn't see himself with her. Besides, she was a client, and the unwritten rule about not dating clients was one he intended to stick to. Nor did she strike him as a damsel in distress who needed him to be a big, strong knight in shining armor. On the contrary, really. And that's what hit him.

He'd misjudged her. He'd seen the styled hair, make-up, bangles clanging together, designer clothes and shoes, the Beemer, and pegged her as another L.A. socialite, spending Daddy's money and frittering away her life in shopping sprees, mani-pedis, and yoga classes. But the innocent and vulnerable way in which she'd simultaneously offered and asked to help revealed an authenticity inside her, a depth of character he'd assumed wasn't there.

But how to tell her that?

"How about you and I go back to Connor's apartment? We can try to talk to some of the neighbors I missed earlier."

"Okay. And you're going to tell me what that look was about on our walk back to the cars."

* * *

1:58 p.m.

HAILEY LOST Jackson in traffic—she drove like it was Daddy's Beemer—and was waiting in the parking lot at Connor's complex when Jackson pulled in.

"I thought maybe that old thing had conked out on you," she said with a nod at the Granada.

"It's like a good woman or a good wine; it only gets better with age."

"You don't drink."

"Nor do I date old women, but it sounded good."

"So how do we do this?" she asked as they walked toward Connor's building.

"Well, I prefer the traditional knuckles, but some people use the side of their fist," he said, demonstrating against the air.

"Shut up," she said backhanding his arm. Her smile was worth the momentary sting.

"Straight up," Jackson said, his grin gone. "Tell them who we are and what we're doing."

"Sounds easy enough."

Just like that morning, the first three doors they knocked on got no answer. The fourth, C102, was home to the baby lady, and Jackson practically tiptoed past it. The next door, the apartment beneath Connor's, belonged to a middle-aged woman who answered the door in an Albertson's shirt, a cigarette in her mouth. She spoke with them just long enough to tell them that she didn't have time to talk with them, and even if she did, she "didn't know nuthin'."

"I don't doubt it," Jackson muttered as the door clicked.

A frail, old black man wearing a cardigan sweater over a Lakers T-shirt opened the door to C204. "I help you folks?" he asked.

"My name is Jackson Douglas, and I'm a private investigator. This is Hailey Kendrick. We're looking for her brother, Connor, who lives in the apartment next door."

The man nodded. "Yes, I know Connor." He leaned out his open door, looking to the side. "He not home?"

"He's been missing for several days," Hailey said.

"We're talking to all the neighbors, trying to see if anyone spoke to him recently, if anyone saw or heard something that might give us a clue where he's gone."

"Missing, you say?"

"Yes, sir."

"Since when?"

"The last anyone heard from him was Friday morning."

"Friday? Naw, he was here Saturday."

"Are you sure about that?"

"I am. I saw his car drive away about ten o'clock."

"You're sure it was his car?" Jackson asked.

"Only red Taurus I've ever seen in the lot. Yes, sir."

"Ten a.m. or ten p.m.?"

"Ten in the morning."

"Did you see it come back?"

"No, but it was in the lot when I went to church Sunday morning."

Hailey looked at Jackson. He mulled. Connor hadn't officially been missing until Monday when he didn't show up for work. His dirty dishes in the sink suggested he'd been home at least Friday, and now his car had been seen leaving Saturday morning, and had obviously come back sometime after that. Assuming it had been Connor driving it, that still left an approximately forty-eight-hour window.

"For that matter, I heard him Saturday night."

"You heard him?" Hailey asked.

"Well, I heard somebody in his apartment. Making all sorts of ruckus."

"What specifically?" Jackson asked.

"Sounded like somebody was moving furniture around—dragging it on the floor and banging it into the walls. I thought it was the TV at first, but it went on for a good ten minutes."

"Do you remember when this was?"

"Let's see now . . . I'd say about nine o'clock, maybe quarter after. I know I was about to turn in and I was afraid it'd keep up all night."

"But it didn't?"

"No, sir."

"Anything else?" Jackson asked. "Anything you saw or heard that was out of the ordinary Saturday or Sunday?"

The man thought for a moment, then shook his head. "Naw, naw can't say as there was."

"Thank you for your time," Jackson said.

"Thank you," Hailey echoed as they turned to leave. "What do you make of that?" she asked when the door was closed.

"I don't know. The lady on the corner over there, who I think is crazy, said she saw a black SUV tear out of here about nine-thirty."

"You think . . . you think he was kidnapped?"

"Let's not rush to conclusions. It could have been someone searching his place. It could have been a coincidence. For all we know, since he was apparently still here Saturday morning, he might have been trying out a new living room arrangement he didn't like."

"Jackson, I'm getting worried. I never . . . I never thought anything truly bad had happened to him."

"We don't know that it has," he said, placing a hand on her shoulder. "Let's see if we can learn anything else."

They crossed over to B building, avoided the weed-eater, the witch, and the wacko. They spoke to single guy in B114 who appeared to have just woken up. He was friendly enough but unhelpful.

Hailey still seemed shaken as they walked back to their cars. "Jackson, I've been thinking."

"Yeah."

"Maybe you should go meet with Anne by yourself."

"Why? What are you going to do?"

"I think I'm going to go to the police and fill out a missing persons report."

Chapter Thirteen

Tuesday, June 18, 2013
9:59 a.m.

SPECIAL AGENT HIRAM Nicks bore a slight resemblance to Michael Jordan, sans earring. He was tall and bald, muscular, with eyes—Jackson knew from experience—capable of nailing another person to the wall. He wore khakis and a blue polo emblazoned with the letters NCIS in white above the left breast. And while he didn't smile, his mouth at least slackened as he extended a hand to Jackson.

"Mr. Douglas."

"Special Agent Nicks, thank you for seeing me."

"Please come with me."

He led Jackson down an open hallway that provided a view out glass panels of a dreary, rainy, chilly San Diego morning. From its location south of downtown at Naval Base San Diego, the NCIS Southwest Field Office could have provided magnificent views of the city's skyline, the Coronado Bridge as it spanned San Diego Bay, and Point Loma. But there was nothing magnificent about today's views.

Jackson had spent the night at a Motel 6 off the interstate and called first thing in the morning to schedule a meeting with Nicks. According to the FBI's Special Agent Lance Kilpatrick, NCIS would have had claim to jurisdiction over the investigation of David, Hannah, and Grant's death due to David's tenure with the Navy. But Kilpatrick said they had released jurisdiction to the FBI, and while it may not have had anything to do with finding out the truth as to why and how they were killed, Jackson didn't feel like leaving any loose ends. Besides, anything he could learn from NCIS might lead to something.

On the TV show *NCIS*, the conference room featured a prominent wood table, a window overlooking the naval yard, phones and fax machines, clocks showing the time at various worldwide locations, a plasma screen, and a few lamps for decoration. On *NCIS: Los Angeles*, conferences were conducted at a lunch table in a boatshed. The Southwest Field Office's conference room was painted blue like a typical San Diego sky, with a long oval table whose black surface was polished to a shine. Comfortable swivel reclining office chairs were spaced around it, all vacant except for one at the end. Seated beneath a large framed photo of an aircraft carrier at sea was woman wearing a blazer over a red blouse. Her hair was drawn back into a tight ponytail, stretching an already taut face. Her expression made Nicks' seem jovial by comparison.

"Mr. Douglas, this is Special Agent Dobraska. Lil, Jackson Douglas."

She grimaced out a smile and Jackson nodded.

"Have a seat," Nicks said. "Coffee, water, soft drink?"

"No, thanks."

He nodded, bypassed a small built-in counter/refrigerator/brewing station and sat opposite Jackson, with Special Agent Dobraska between them on the end.

"You said when you called you had questions about the investigation into your family's death," Nicks said. He shook his head. "I didn't work that case."

"I know, sir, but you are the only contact I have at NCIS. I know we didn't part on the best of terms last time—"

"That's putting it mildly."

"I'm hoping a sincere apology could smooth the waters. It was never my attention to ruffle feathers or cause trouble. I was simply seeking the best interest of my client."

"Who turned out to be a spy."

"Traitor to the highest bidder, perhaps. But I was unaware of that at the time, so—"

"What do you want, Mr. Douglas?"

"I spoke with Agent Kilpatrick of the FBI yesterday," Jackson said. "He told me that NCIS didn't pursue the investigation, even though Dad was a career Navy man. They passed custody of the case to the FBI and SDPD. I'm wondering why."

Nicks nodded at Dobraska, who flipped open a navy blue folder. She slid out several sheets of paper. When she spoke, her voice was like the whir of a saw slicing through wood. "NCIS conducted a preliminary investigation into the deaths of Captain Douglas, Hannah Douglas, and Grant Douglas, in conjunction with the FBI, San Diego Police Department, and San Diego Sheriff's Office. We were unable to find any evidence that Captain Douglas was targeted because of his position in the United States Navy, or that the crime had any connection to it or his service."

"That's it?" Jackson asked when she didn't continue. "A preliminary investigation didn't reveal a connection, and you dropped it?"

"We didn't drop it," she answered. "We left it in the very capable hands of the FBI and the local authorities. Given the nature of the alleged crime—arson—the investigation was better suited for them anyhow."

Jackson didn't buy that NCIS wasn't competent to investigate fires, but he didn't push that.

"Did you agree with their ruling, that the explosion was an accident?"

"Not being privy to the extent of their evidence or their investigation, NCIS isn't in position to agree or disagree," Dobraska said. "But there is absolutely no reason to question their judgment in this or any matter."

"How long did you investigate?"

"As I said, we conducted a prelimin—"

"Right, but how long did that take?"

Dobraska consulted her notes, sliding one sheet to the side to read another. "NCIS was notified of the incident at 8:47 p.m. on Saturday the fourteenth, and we officially withdrew from the investigation Monday morning the sixteenth."

"May I ask who led NCIS's investigation?"

Dobraska turned her eyes to Nicks, who nodded.

"Special Agent Webb."

"Would it be possible for me to speak with Special Agent Webb? I'm not suggesting you're holding anything back, bu—"

"Special Agent Webb was transferred to CAFO last fall."

"CAFO?"

"Carolinas Field Office, at Camp Lejeune."

"Well, could we arrange a phone call or FaceTime or something—whatever you guys do in MTAC and Ops?"

Dobraska sighed and again looked to Nicks.

He again nodded. "I'll set something up."

"Thank you," Jackson said, sitting back so that his chair creaked. Good grief, these guys made Leroy Jethro Gibbs look like an old softie.

*　　　　*　　　　*

11:04 a.m.

JACKSON HAD never been accused of being overly savvy, technology-wise. He could type with both hands, navigate the web just fine, and didn't have to call Geek Squad every time an unfamiliar dialogue box popped up on his computer. But he still used an old flip phone that did little more than make phone calls, wasn't on Facebook or Twitter or Instagram or Snapchat, and wasn't sure that his laptop even had a webcam. So it would be a little strange to be talking to a computer screen that was both transmitting his voice and his image across the continent.

They had not taken him to some upstairs room accessible only via retina scan, but had merely delivered a laptop to the conference room. A tech had set it up and run a sound check, then left Jackson alone in the room with Agent Dobraska. Nicks had other business to attend to, which was fine by Jackson.

"Hello?"

Instead of a wait screen, Jackson now saw a young, smooth-faced man in a drab, olive green shirt sitting in front of a window. It was hard to tell, given the light streaming in through it, but the ocean appeared to be in the background. Whatever it was, it was clearly bathed in sunshine.

"Special Agent Webb?" Jackson asked, looking from the screen to Dobraska and back. She was no help, sitting scribbling into a notepad.

"Yes, sir. Mr. Douglas, I presume."

"You can call me Jackson."

"Bryson."

"Yes, sir."

"I understand you have questions about an old investigation."

"I do." Jackson briefly explained that he was looking into the death of his family, and mentioned his conversations with Special Agents Collier and Kilpatrick of the FBI, District Attorney Moreno, and now NCIS. When he was finished, Webb started by offering his condolences for Jackson's loss and then asking, with what Jackson deemed genuine sincerity, what he could to do help.

"I understand you spearheaded NCIS's investigation?"

"There wasn't really that much of a spear. Just myself and a probationary agent."

"Was that typical?"

"It wasn't atypical. Resources were a little stretched at the time, and we didn't have any proof that Captain Douglas—sorry, your father's— death was or wasn't tied to his service. In fact, our initial investigation didn't turn up anything to conclude that he had been targeted, or even that the explosion had been anything other than an accident."

"Did you investigate a man named Joaquín Padilla at all?"

"Not directly. His name came up, but by then, he had already been arrested for the sexual assault of a Navy petty officer. From my understanding, that gave him an alibi for any potential involvement in the explosion."

"Special Agent Webb—"

"Bryson," he said amicably.

"Right, Bryson. What if I told you that alibi was gone?"

"Come again?"

"I've just learned that the timeline that placed Padilla at Petty Officer Grabel's apartment a dozen minutes after the explosion was inaccurate. He actually arrived about ten minutes later. He could have been at both places."

Webb exhaled. "Well, I don't recall all the details of the case off the top of my head, but if I remember correctly, there was nothing concrete tying Padilla to the explosion. In fact, the investigation ultimately ruled it an accident, correct?"

"That's right."

"You don't buy that?" Webb asked.

Dobraska looked up from her shopping list or love letter or whatever. She said nothing.

"No, I don't. Not anymore."

Webb took another deep breath. "Jackson, I'll put in a request to review NCIS's evidence. I'll see if there's something we missed, something that stands out in light of this new timeline you mentioned. If I may, how did you learn about the discrepancy?"

Jackson recapped his talk with the Haywoods and Mira Austin's testimony to them.

"Hmm. Well, I'll see what I can find out, like I said. But I'd caution you against getting your hopes up. Even without any alibi, I don't know that we'd have had enough to tie Padilla to the explosion. It was a major contributing factor to why we didn't pursue our investigation further."

"Contributing factor. Was there more?"

Dobraska again raised her head.

"Like I said earlier, there was no evidence that your father was targeted, that—even if the explosion was intentional—it had anything to do with the Navy."

Webb seemed poised to say more, and when he didn't, Jackson asked, "Is that it?"

Dobraska was now at full attention.

Webb opened and closed his mouth before speaking. "We, uh . . . we were also advised not to pursue the investigation any further."

Jackson flicked his eyes to Dobraska. Her face had, if possible, tightened even more.

"Advised by whom?"

Webb sighed. "Admiral Sullivan."

Jackson sat forward. "Admiral Francis Sullivan?"

"Yes, sir."

"He told you to stand down?"

"Not in so many words. He advised our office to turn over the investigation to the FBI and SDPD."

"Why?"

"I don't know. I don't believe he said."

"He didn't speak with you directly?"

"No, to Assistant Director Harding."

"Do you know where he is, how I can speak with him?"

"He passed away last Christmas. Lung cancer."

Jackson sighed. "And you have no idea, no clue, what motivated the order?"

"I do not. I'm sorry."

"Thank you very much for your time, Bryson. I appreciate it."

"You're welcome. I wish you the best, and I'll get your information from Special Agent Nicks. I'll be in touch if I find anything."

"Thank you."

The screen went black, then returned to the wait screen.

Jackson sat back in his chair. "Excuse me," he said, then stood and exited the room, out into the hallway. He watched the raindrops streak down the side of the glass, watched the gloom blanket the naval yard. Why had Admiral Sullivan, his dad's old C.O. at the Office of Naval Intelligence, given NCIS a stand down order in the investigation?

Jackson had no idea, but he knew one thing. His mom, dad, and brother's death had been no accident.

Chapter Fourteen

Wednesday, May 11, 2011
4:34 p.m.

SCIENCE HAD NEVER been Jackson's thing. He didn't really care how plants stayed alive or how old somebody speculated a rock was or what the laws of thermodynamics proved. As long as the earth's gravity didn't someday release him into the void of space and assuming his body could continue to intake oxygen, he was content to let other people—most of them likely without girlfriends—figure out the hows and whys. Nor was he particularly fond of the smell of rotten eggs. So he had never in his time in L.A. or Southern California ventured to the La Brea Tar Pits. Besides, he'd had enough lectures on how the earth was 80 bajillion years old and he was a product of fish turned birds turned monkeys or whatever. He'd much prefer an afternoon at Chavez Ravine, where the only application of science was by opposing batters trying to connect with a Jonathan Broxton fastball.

But Anne Magstadt had chosen the Tar Pits as the meeting place, and had called just after he left Hailey at Connor's apartment to tell him she was running late and they'd better make it 4:30. He'd arrived at the famous Hancock Park on Wilshire Boulevard early (for a change) and made a lap around the twenty-three-acre park to find the parking lot on its north side, where he'd promptly been charged twelve bucks for parking. Jackson wondered if he could bill expenses to a client he wasn't charging in the first place.

He walked around the museum, a largely subterranean building with a blocky square canopy and through the open, grassy center of the park. A few oaks, lanky palms, and walnut trees helped create an isolated atmosphere amidst the hustle and bustle of Los Angeles. The thirty-two-story *Variety Building* just across the street quickly wiped it away. At least the air was fresh and not tainted with sulfur.

Once south of the museum, he cut across the grass to a paved circle that fronted the entrance to the museum and overlooked the famous Lake Pit, a bubbling asphalt seep with life-sized mammoth and mastodon statues in the lake. Jackson caught a whiff of rotten eggs, but the scent was carried away on the afternoon breeze.

He'd used the extra time to scrounge for a day-old copy of the *Times*, which he'd found at a newsstand. Page B6 had contained a story about water conservation efforts by various non-profits, penned by Anne Magstadt. It included a thumbnail photo in black and white that didn't help much in identifying her. And yet, as he came around to the front of the circle, he saw a woman he assumed was her.

She was not what he had expected. All day, Jackson had been picturing a lady reporter in a V-neck blouse cut just high enough to remain professional, slacks, and heels that came to a point at the toe. Else with hair in a ponytail, a shoulder satchel over one shoulder, wearing a dusty leather jacket, and ready to ride with guerillas against some corrupt South American government. One too many '80s TV shows.

Anne was neither. She wore jeans and an orange knit pullover, sleeves up to the elbows. Sneakers. She was tall, just a few inches shorter than Jackson, with an attractive face despite a lack of any obvious effort. No lavish makeup or excessive jewelry like Hailey. Her brown hair wasn't painstakingly styled, just naturally curvy, like her. She leaned against the trunk of a palm tree, hands in her pockets, seemingly content to people watch, catch some rays, and let the breeze play with her past-the-shoulders hair.

Jackson hid a grin. Definitely not the old, crusty battleax he'd feared.

"Anne?" Jackson asked as he approached.

She stood. "Jackson?" So it wasn't the phone connection that had made her voice a trace husky.

He nodded and they shook hands, her grip firmer than a lot of guys' from Southern California.

"Call me Maggie," she said.

"Maggie?"

"Only the IRS, DMV, and our copy editor call me Anne."

"All right. Thanks for meeting me, Maggie."

She nodded.

"So, you a big fan of wooly animals or do you dig asphalt?"

"Neither. The park's close enough to home that I can walk."

"Aha."

"Plus I figure the hassle of finding parking or the fee to pay in the lot is a good way to weed out the cranks. If you're willing to jump through a few hoops, I figure you might be legit."

"So does that mean I'm legit?"

"I don't know. You got a license?"

"Several, in fact. Driver's license, a P.I. license, a license to carry. Still working on a license to kill, but then again I am new."

Maggie hid—mostly—a smirk.

Jackson reached into his pocket, drew out his wallet, and flipped it open to show his California private investigator license. "Here."

She looked at it for a moment, then said with a wink, "How do I know you didn't make this at Kinko's?"

"Because I don't even know the state's motto."

"You're not what I expected," she said. "You sounded so . . . proper on the phone."

"I think I'm offended."

"At being accused of sounding proper or at not meeting that expectation?"

"Maybe a little of each."

"Walk and talk?" she asked.

He nodded, and they started along the Lake Pit, enclosed by an eight-foot-high wire fence.

"So what's this about my name being on a notepad of a missing person?" Maggie asked.

Jackson briefly recapped his search of Connor's place and finding her name on a notepad. He left out his quarter-rubbing technique. It seemed so . . . improper.

"So you're wondering if he ever made the call," Maggie said.

"I am."

She hesitated briefly before answering. "I think so."

"You think so?"

"I got a call Saturday afternoon, but he didn't want to give me a name. I told him as a reporter it would remain confidential, and he identified himself as Connor. No last name."

"So either him or a remarkable coincidence."

"Or an imposter."

Jackson frowned.

She explained. "He asked if we could meet, to talk in person."

"Right up your alley."

She formed a playful glare. "I asked him what it was about, and he said he didn't want to divulge anything over the phone. He sounded scared."

"Did you agree to meet with him?"

"I did. I get calls like this a couple of times a month, cloak-and-daggery, usually offering me some juicy scoop and unwilling to speak over the phone. My experience is they're one-third stalkers, one-third conspiracy wackos, and one-third semi-legit. It's why I arrange to meet in public places, or pass altogether."

"So what made you think Connor was 'semi-legit'?"

"I don't know. You can just tell sometimes. Like I said, he sounded paranoid or scared, but not creepy or crazy." She shrugged. "I'm still making my bones in this town, so I figured it was worth a chance."

"So you met with him?"

They had passed the Lake Pit and curved around the entrance to the Los Angeles County Museum of Art, heading through a small grove of trees toward more exhibits and bubbling tar pits.

"We agreed to meet Sunday morning, ten o'clock, here," Maggie said. "He didn't show."

Jackson slowed for an instant, wondering if the timeline of Connor's disappearance had narrowed.

"I gave him till ten-thirty, then gave him a call. No answer, and I never heard back from him."

"And he didn't give you any indication of what was on his mind?"

Maggie shook her head. "But that's not all. Sunday afternoon, about two maybe, somebody knocks on my door."

"They actually knocked? They didn't ring the bell."

"Easy, Sherlock, just an expression."

"My bad."

"There's a man and a woman there, look like feds, and yet they didn't. They asked if they could come in, I said no. They didn't identify themselves, and when I asked for IDs or badges or something, they just said they were representing Connor Novak and wanted to know if he and I had spoken."

"What'd you tell them?"

"That I had no idea who that was." She shrugged. "Which is true. I told them that I saw he'd called and I returned the call but never spoke to him."

They had curved back around, nearing the Pleistocene Garden, a supposed recreation of Ice Age-era flora.

"Did you leave him a voicemail when you called?" Jackson asked.

"No. I figured he was the one who arranged the meeting and wanted to talk, so he could call me. I have better things to do on a Sunday than chase around a no-show."

"Fair enough. What'd the non-feds do?"

"Pressed me a little, and when they saw I wasn't going to give them anything, they left."

"You hear from them again?"

"Nope. Went out with some friends Sunday night, went to work Monday, and mostly forgot about it until you called."

"Hmm."

"Sorry I don't have more for you."

"Not your fault. I'm just trying to figure this out. Somebody must have Connor's phone—or at least access to it—or they'd have no way of knowing who you are."

"You don't think those two really represent him, huh?"

"No."

"Yeah, me either."

"What'd they look like?"

"Average, about your height. He had dark hair, chin dimple. Good-looking but not great. She was a few inches shorter, light brown hair, a few pounds overweight. Very buttoned-up."

"Sunglasses?"

She frowned for a moment. "No."

"Then definitely not feds."

"Basing that off what, all the times you've watched *Men in Black*?"

"I only watched *Men in Black* once. Mildly amusing, but very disappointing. I mean, Will Smith and Tommy Lee Jones and we get that? So much wasted potential . . ."

She raised an eyebrow.

"So, two questions," he said. "A, who were those people and who were they really representing, and B, why did Connor call you?"

Maggie shrugged. "He didn't say, but I assume he had a story—or at least, what he thought was a story. That's why most of them call."

"Right, but I mean why *you*? Forget the *Times*, there have to be a lot of good-looking lady reporters in L.A."

"Now I think I'm offended."

"My off-handed compliment not strong enough? Knockout lady reporters?"

"Maybe it had less to do with my looks or my sex than my writing."

"How is your writing?"

"You didn't pick up yesterday's paper?"

"I did, but I got caught up in the comics."

"Read it when you get home and let me know."

He nodded. "In all seriousness, you break any big stories lately? Forgive me for not knowing, but are you a famous, better-than-good-looking lady reporter?"

"No, to the big stories or fame. But your 'better-than-good-looking' might be the finest compliment a man has ever paid me."

"I seriously doubt that."

She smiled and this time it wasn't a smirk.

They were almost back to the museum, and Jackson felt a twinge of sadness that he had no more legitimate questions for Maggie. So he floated a balloon. "Well, I can cut over to the parking lot here. I would offer to buy you dinner as a thank you for indulging me, but I have a better-than-good-looking lady client to check in with."

"That's okay. I've got a Rangers-Islanders game on the DVR and a couple of meh-looking guys on speed dial for just such an occasion."

Jackson couldn't help but grin. "Well played." He nodded and extended his hand. "Thank you, Maggie."

"Any time," she said with a smile.

As he turned and walked toward his car, he couldn't help wonder if she'd been referring to helping on a case or to dinner.

*   *   *

5:52 p.m.

"JACKSON!"

He turned from his deck, knowing already that the shrill voice belonged to his neighbor, Connie. She was bustling (there really was no other word for it) down off her deck and toward him. Her deck, like her house, was much larger than his. Then again, Connie was quite large too, a fact she did nothing to hide with garish red hair, layers of makeup and lipstick, and gaudy apparel. Today, a lime green and black chevron blouse, a green skort, and flip-flops. Not to mention gold rings and bangles to outdo Hailey. Speaking of . . .

Jackson had called her as he'd left the parking lot at Hancock Park. Hailey had just finished meeting with an LAPD detective, and Jackson had asked if she was interested in catching up over dinner. They could order pizza, grab some take-out, or he could throw some burgers on the grill. She had liked the idea of burgers, and he had swung by a Safeway on the way home.

"Hi, Connie."

"My goodness, you're not going to eat all those yourself, are you?" she asked, looking at eight hamburger patties he had placed and was placing on his grill.

"Well, they do reheat. But no, I'm having company, and she should be here soon."

Hint, hint.

Connie wasn't big on subtleties.

"Say, I have a favor to ask you," she said. "I'm visiting Adriana this weekend, and she's allergic to dogs. I was wondering if you wouldn't mind doggy-sitting Fluffy."

Fluffy was Connie's new Pomeranian puppy, and already he/she/it and Jackson were at odds—mostly because of incessant barking and ankle-nipping.

"I'm sorry, Connie, but I'm headed down to San Diego this weekend."

"Oh? What's in San Diego?" She asked as if no viable reason could exist for Jackson to go there.

"Birthday celebration."

"Whose birthday?"

He smiled.

"Oh, congratulations! How exciting."

Wasn't it though?

"Look, Connie, I do have to get dinner ready. My client will be here soon."

"Client? Oh, right. You're a private—ahem, ahem—investigator."

He had no idea what the "ahem, ahem" meant, nor did he care.

"Yeah. Sorry about Fluffy," he said, although he wasn't. "Have fun with Adriana."

This time Connie took the hint, waddling back toward her place as Jackson took the burger packaging back inside. He'd just washed his hands when he heard a knock on the door, and he hurried through the living room to the front door.

Hailey had changed into a navy blue T-shirt with an orange 34 stamped on it—likely an expensive, designer T-shirt made of some exclusive fabric blend while designed to look casual. Jackson was sure Hailey had no idea what a 34 in Chicago Bears colors represented, but it looked good on her, and that was indeed the point. She wore distressed blue jeans with holes in the knees and thigh (not, he gathered, from too many hours of manual labor) and sneakers. Her hair was in a ponytail, a fringe swept to the side. Minimal makeup, and no jewelry but for medium-sized silver hoop earrings. Very collegial.

Apologizing for and briefly explaining why the house looked like, well, a drug lair, he led her back to the deck.

"Wow, this is quite a view."

"I can't complain. You thirsty? I've got tea, water, soda."

"Ice water's fine."

He fetched the water, along with a few of the fixings for burgers and a few bags of chips, and returned to the deck. "So what'd the cops say?"

Hailey sat down with her water. "Not much. They took all my info, listened attentively, but there isn't much to go on." She took a drink as Jackson flipped burgers. "They weren't real thrilled when I told them two different groups had already gone over his apartment."

"Do they plan to?"

"I told them where the spare key was. I don't know."

Jackson shrugged as he hung up his spatula. "It was worth a try." He ducked back inside to grab plates, napkins, and condiments. Back outside, he sliced a tomato, pulled apart a few leaves of lettuce, and set his small table.

"Is this typical?" Hailey asked.

"Is what?"

"P.I.'s making dinner for their clients?"

"Well, I can't see Sam Spade or Philip Marlowe grilling with a pretty dame, but we've got to eat."

She frowned. "Who?"

"Never mind." He held up as of yet un-split buns. "One or two?"

"One."

He sliced into the buns with a steak knife.

"What'd Anne have to say?"

"First of all, that her name was Maggie."

"Maggie?"

"Magstadt, Maggie." He shrugged. Then, as he finished tending the burgers, plated them, and sat down opposite Hailey, he recapped his conversation with Maggie. When he was finished, Hailey had the same questions he did. For both of their benefits, Jackson summed up what they knew so far.

"It would seem Connor disappeared sometime between Saturday morning when his neighbor saw him drive off and Sunday morning when he didn't show up for his meeting with Maggie."

"When did she say he called her?"

"Saturday afternoon."

"So wouldn't it be after that?" She lifted her burger to her mouth and took a big bite. Jackson paused a moment, thinking how a girl who dressed and looked like Hailey shouldn't crave red meat the way she did. Maybe he just knew too many of the wrong kind of California girls.

"Wouldn't it?" she asked again.

"Maybe, but he could have called after 'disappearing,' if he disappeared on his own."

"As opposed to being taken?"

"If we're considering all possibilities, that is on the table."

She sighed.

"Then you have the ruckus the same neighbor heard from Connor's house Saturday night, at approximately the same time the crazy Indian lady saw an SUV race off. The two could be connected, or not. But again, if somebody did kidnap him, maybe we're looking at Saturday night as the time when it happened."

"This doesn't make sense," Hailey said. "Why would anyone kidnap Connor? He's a statistician, for goodness' sake."

"Unfortunately, Connor didn't tell Maggie what he wanted to talk to her about, but there had to be some reason he picked a newspaper reporter. Either he thought he could sell her a story or he wanted to use her position to expose something. Either way, whatever that is becomes our best guess as to a potential motive for someone to kidnap him or for him to want to disappear and lay low."

"You mean if he thought someone was after him?"

Jackson had taken a massive bite of a perfectly grilled burger, and he nodded as he chewed.

Hailey's posture slumped.

"We'll figure it out," Jackson said after gulping the bite down.

"How?"

"I'm going to talk to Connor's employer, what was it, some real estate company?"

"Yeah, The Foreman Group, over in West Hollywood."

"I also want to talk to Jenn about his work for her."

"You think he found something at work?"

"I don't know. It could be that, or somebody at work might know something that could clue us in. Who knows, maybe I'll run into the guy and gal that showed up at Maggie's place. That's how it'd work on TV."

"Is everything you do based off of TV?"

He shrugged. "It has to be. I don't have any other P.I. experience yet."

Hailey reached for a few baby carrots. He'd picked them up at the store on the way home, figuring he'd better provide a female dinner companion something besides chips or pretzels to go with her burger.

"And speaking of those guys," he said, "I'm trying to figure out who they're working for. Not Connor, and not your dad's guy Luke."

"How do you know?"

"Because they knew about Maggie, and the look on Luke's face when we announced finding her name at Connor's wasn't the look of a man hiding something. He was genuinely surprised."

"You can really tell?"

"I think so."

They ate for a few minutes, Jackson trying not to concentrate on the way the breeze stirred loose strands of Hailey's hair.

"So tell me about Jenn," he said.

"What about her?"

"When I asked about her earlier, you didn't exactly seem smitten with her."

"She's fine," Hailey sighed. "It's just really weird seeing your dad date somebody who feels more like your big sister. But, it's not like we hang out or anything, or if she and Dad get married she'll be my new mom. Christine wasn't really my mom. A true mom is irreplaceable."

Jackson had no idea, so he only nodded.

"The thing with Jenn is, she's just very driven. She has her way of doing things, whether it's her business or giving Dad stock tips."

"Yeah, I noticed he seemed pretty keen on her advice."

"He's keen on everything she does. He's totally in the tank for her."

"Oh?"

"Whipped, I think guys call it."

Jackson grinned as Hailey took a drink.

"How'd they meet, anyhow?" he asked.

"She moved down here from Northern California a few years back, just as MatchStick was getting up and running. I can't remember if she first met Dad through Connor or his involvement on city council. But they were acquaintances, and then about a year ago, she actually asked him to dinner."

"She asked him out?"

"What, are you one of those old-fashioned guys that thinks the guy always has to ask and pay and hold the door?"

"Ask, no. Pay, definitely not," he said with a grin. "And door-holding is just good policy regardless of gender."

She nodded.

"You know how she found Connor?"

"He told me that she said he came recommended by someone." She reached for her water with a shrug. "I don't remember who, but Connor does a lot of odd side jobs."

"How many people does MatchStick employ?"

"Three or four in the office. Most of it's automated, using Connor's algorithm."

"Hmm."

"Hmm what?"

"Nothing. Just trying to put the pieces together."

The truth was, he was developing a hunch. There was nothing to it, but something about Jenn bugged him. She was young, she had apparently initiated a romance with an influential man, she now had him "whipped." She also seemed cool to indifferent—admittedly judging by a very small sample—toward the disappearance of her employee and boyfriend's stepson. It was all just a hunch. But hunches and little voices always worked for Magnum.

Hailey helped Jackson clean up after dinner, then said she should be heading home. Jackson wasn't sure if that was an aversion to spending time in pre-remodeled house or to fraternization between an investigator and client. But he didn't dissuade her.

"I work from noon until nine or ten tomorrow," she said at the doorway. "But if you find out anything, give me a call."

"I will."

"Thanks for dinner."

"You're welcome."

"And thanks for all you're doing, Jackson. I really appreciate it."

"You're welcome for that too. I just hope we can make some progress."

With a smile, Hailey headed for her car. Jackson locked up behind her and returned to his deck to watch the sunset and mull.

And, it turned out, to receive a deck-to-deck thumbs-up from Connie.

Chapter Fifteen

Thursday, May 12, 2011
9:37 a.m.

"SORRY I'M LATE," Jackson said as he followed J.H. Hahn into his office on the seventh floor of The Foreman Group's building just off Santa Monica Boulevard in West Hollywood. "Traffic."

"Please, tell me about it," Hahn said, walking around a very modern, glass-topped desk. "Have a seat."

Jackson sat in one of two straight-backed office chairs.

"How can I help you, Mr. Douglas?"

Jackson had to draw his attention from a series of photographs on the wall behind Hahn, as well as the two windows overlooking the Santa Monica Mountains on either side of the photos. They showed impressive architectural marvels, most perched in scenic locations around the world. The pictures on his desk showed Hahn with a trio of children, all under the age of five or six.

"Like I said on the phone, I'm a private investigator looking for one of your employees, Connor Novak."

Hahn's congenial smile faded. "Yes, Connor has not shown up for work all week."

"Has that ever happened before?"

"Once, about six months ago. He called that evening and said he had been passed out on the bathroom floor with the flu. But four days with no contact . . . No, that has not happened before."

"When was the last time you heard from Connor?"

"He was in the office Friday, but I didn't see him. We exchanged a few e-mails."

"Had he said or done anything that made you think he was in any kind of trouble, maybe was preoccupied, was worried about something?"

"No, nothing."

"Had his work suffered, had he said or done anything suspicious?"

Hahn laughed. "I am sorry, but Connor is a data analyst, and a very introverted person. It is rare that he says anything that isn't work related. And his work has been top-notch since the day we hired him. I cannot think of an exception."

"What exactly does he do for you as a data analyst?"

"Researches and compares market trends, runs CBA's on proposed and actual transactions."

"CBA?"

"Cost-benefit analysis."

"Aha."

"Basically, any number or figure or stat related to commercial real estate, Connor finds and parses so our sales team, other analysts, marketing department—really everyone—are working with the most accurate and up-to-date information."

"A competitive field, I imagine?"

"Of course," Hahn answered. "But not a cutthroat one."

Jackson nodded. Seeing no reasonable tie to Connor's disappearance, he changed gears. "Did he have many friends here at the office?"

"I cannot say for sure, but no, I do not think so. He mostly kept to himself." Hahn continued before Jackson could ask his next question. "Tuesday, when he failed to show for the second day in a row, I spoke with several of his colleagues, people who might know where he was. No one had heard from him. You are welcome to speak with them, if you like, but I fear it will be a dead end."

"Yeah, I fear so too. Is there anything at all that sticks out to you?"

Hahn steepled his fingers and put them to his lips. A moment later, he lowered them. "I have to say no. I cannot think of anything."

"All right, thanks," Jackson said. "Thank you for your time."

"Of course. Let me walk you to the elevator."

Hahn led Jackson out of his office and through several corridors to the small seventh-floor lobby. Having pressed the call button, he turned to Jackson. "Mr. Douglas, I doubt very much that Connor has simply abandoned his job and his life. I am sure something . . . unexpected has happened to him. I hope very much you find him, and when you do, if . . . if he is all right, please have him contact me. He is welcome back here."

"I'll do that, Mr. Hahn. Thank you again."

The elevator dinged, and they shook hands. Wondering if this was going to be par for the course—looking for needles in haystacks and turning over rock after rock in an effort to find a clue—Jackson rode down to the ground level. If so, maybe he'd chosen the wrong profession after all.

He'd caught a weather report on the drive across town, and it had referenced a dip in the jet stream that had caused an area of high pressure to stall over southern California and Nevada. There was no end in sight to the string of warm, sunny days and the absence of "May Gray."

The one downside to such weather was the interior of the Granada, with its roasting leather seats and scalding metal seatbelt buckles. In no time, however, Jackson was cruising back toward the coast on the four-lane Santa Monica Boulevard, the breeze pouring in through the windows. He found some Bon Jovi on the radio and sat back, mulling some more.

Good at problem-solving, his brain didn't particularly like to be goaded. It preferred to load up on data, ruminate on its own, and spit out a solution when it arrived at one. Over the years, Jackson had learned to adapt to such a procedure, but every once in a while, he felt the need to stir the pot a little.

Gradually, as he neared Santa Monica, his mulling turned to ways to get information from Jenn White. He had been somewhat surprised that she had even taken his call that morning, even more that she had agreed to meet with him. He couldn't figure out any way she could be tied to Connor's disappearance, but something about her didn't sit right with him. Maybe it was just a bad first impression, or maybe he secretly disapproved of her and the mayor's May-December romance. Whatever the case, he hoped a talk with her would provide some resolution.

He hadn't known how long his talk with Hahn would take, nor what L.A. traffic might be like, and had scheduled the meeting for eleven o'clock. He arrived at the downtown office building that housed

MatchStick's office twenty minutes early, and figured the best place to wait in terms of possibly advancing his case was inside.

The building was old and a little outdated, not exactly the chic, hip, urban-loft complex one usually associated with Santa Monica commerce. But that changed when Jackson entered MatchStick's fourth-floor office. A non-descript wood door opened to a room decorated almost exclusively in white—walls, ceiling, carpet, furniture. Touches of color in the form of throw pillows, flowers, exotic accent pieces, and the company logo gave it some panache. The latter was emblazoned in large, flowing letters on the far wall. The word "Match" was pink; the word "Stick" was blue. The exception was a flame symbol dotting the "i." Jackson still wasn't sure if the brand was original or cheesy.

He turned toward a small reception desk, manned by a woman with spiky black hair and studs in her nose and eyebrow, to go with a bevy of rings in her ears. She wore a Bluetooth headpiece as she tapped on a keyboard off to her side. As Jackson approached, she raised a finger and resumed typing. He stood patiently and studied a bank of eight-by-ten and five-by-seven photos framed on the wall to his left. All showed men and women draped over and around each other, smiles plastered across their faces. On each frame was a small gold placard with first names. Successful matches, Jackson assumed. Else MatchStick shared space with a dentist's office.

After a couple of minutes, the receptionist quit typing and tapped the side of her earpiece. "Sorry. I'm Kara. Can I help you?"

She uptalked. It was a trait Jackson had expected of, frankly, Hailey.

"I have an eleven o'clock with Miss White."

"Your name?"

"Jackson Douglas."

Kara checked the computer, smiled perfunctorily, and offered him a seat. He took it while she went back to typing. The magazines scattered across a pair of tables were all variations of a theme—offering beauty tips, ways to make a fashion statement this summer, and secrets to better sex. Jackson sat back and listened to the edgy pop music instead, surmising that MatchStick's walk-in clients were mostly of the female variety.

Then again, he kind of surmised most dating service clients were women. After all, what kind of self-respecting, man-card-carrying, red-blooded male would use an online service to meet girls? For the love of John Wayne and Steve McQueen, where were the real dudes anymore? But, the wall of love showed heterosexual matches, so the proof was in the pudding. Welcome to the twenty-first century, Jack.

Jenn emerged from a door beside the reception desk five minutes late. She wore a tight, knee-length skirt and a sleeveless blouse that accentuated every curve while still falling under the tent of professionalism. Her hair was clipped in a loose ponytail, and she guided a stray strand off her brow with the back of one hand while offering the other to Jackson.

"Mr. Douglas."

"Please, Jackson."

She formed a thin smile. "Come with me."

Jenn led him through the same door and down a short hallway with doors left and right. She entered the last door on the right, stepping aside to hold it for him. Color infused Jenn's corner office via windows on two sides of the room. They looked out at downtown, the mountains, and between buildings, the ocean. There was no desk, but rather a pair of firm-looking couches on opposite sides of a wide glass coffee table. On the other side of the office was a small polished-wood conference table with half a dozen chairs around it. A wet bar, a large bookcase, and a small entertainment console were arranged around the perimeter of the room. So too was a large aquarium, and Jackson wondered if Jenn had passed her love of fish on to the mayor or vice versa. Or maybe it had been an initial shared interest.

"Please, have a seat," Jenn said, motioning toward the dual couches. "I hope you don't mind if I have lunch while we talk."

Jackson looked back to see her retrieving a clear plastic container from a mini-fridge under the bar. "Lunch, already?"

"It's our busy season. I've been up since four."

Jackson sat down, and Jenn did so as well. She shook a bottle of some colored liquid and set it on the table, then opened her container and began stabbing various undressed greens. "I'll be honest with you," she said before he could speak. "I don't fancy your chances of finding

Connor." She ingested the first bite of dry salad. Jackson almost gagged at the thought.

"Oh, why's that?"

"Because Mayor Kendrick's own team hasn't turned up a clue. With all due respect, how do you as a rookie private investigator expect to?"

"With all due respect right back, with the exception of my client, no one in the mayor's circle seems all that concerned with finding him."

Jenn took another bite, eyeing him all the while. She washed it down with a drink of her mysterious liquid. "What is it you want to ask me?"

"I talked to a Mr. Hahn at The Foreman Group earlier. Since Connor also worked for you, I was hoping you could tell me a little bit about MatchStick and Connor's role here."

"The concept behind MatchStick is simple," Jenn said as if she were reciting from a company pamphlet. "People are drawn to each other based on a number of factors—appearance, personality type, religion, cultural background, political ideology, financial status and strategy, hundreds of likes and dislikes, and so forth. We compile massive personality profiles addressing everything from their favorite physical feature in the opposite sex to methods of handling stress or fear to hobbies and favorite past times. Using an incredibly complex algorithm, designed and maintained by Connor, we match clients based on those profiles, targeting those our research indicates are more likely to lead to long-term success—to make a match 'stick' over time."

"And Hailey says you've done that—matched clients successfully?"

"No system is perfect," Jenn said coolly, "but we do generally achieve anywhere from five to twelve-percent better results than our national competitors."

"That's impressive."

Jenn smiled civilly.

"So is your success attributed to your in-depth profiles or a state-of-the-art algorithm?"

"Both. Plus our aforementioned research, which is second to none."

"How long has Connor worked for you?"

"Since 2009, when I started the company."

"And he created the algorithm?"

"Yes."

"From scratch."

She stabbed another bite. "More or less. He pulled formulas from some other sources, but the complete algorithms are entirely property of MatchStick."

"Not Connor?"

"Part of his contract."

"And you said he also maintains the algorithm?"

"From time to time as we get new data, he makes tweaks."

"What kind of tweaks?"

"For example, he searches through successful and unsuccessful matches to see which profile pairings proved accurate, which didn't, with what degree of success, and so forth. Plus, the times are constantly changing, so we're continually updating our profiles, which of course necessitates him tweaking his formulas. What sustained a relationship fifty—or five—years ago, may not be what does today. We have to factor that in."

"Is he the only one who has access to the algorithm?"

"Access, no. Ability to manipulate, yes."

Jackson nodded and let Jenn consume a bite of salad in peace. "Hailey said Connor was working on the algorithm this weekend?"

"Yes. I asked him to conduct a quarterly review, and he scheduled it for this weekend."

"Does that mean he'd be working here?"

"No, Connor always works remotely."

"Does he have access to a mainframe or a server or something?"

"Yes, for coding purposes. The data is kept in closest confidence, accessible only locally and only by myself, Destiny, or Meredith."

"They are?"

"Our matchmakers."

"I thought the algorithm was the matchmaker."

"It largely is. But there are aspects of the process that need a human touch. Plus, people prefer a face-to-face interaction. Destiny and Meredith provide that human component and also help walk clients through the process."

Jackson nodded. "So how does Connor review the data and tweak his algorithm without access to it?"

"I downloaded a redacted version of the data, which gave him all profile data but no names, no addresses, no social security numbers. I gave it to him Thursday evening."

"Was that the last time you saw him?"

"Saw him, yes. But he called Friday night and said he was missing some of the data. He asked if I could send it to him again, which I did via a secure FTP site."

"What time was that?"

"Maybe eight, eight-thirty. I was having dinner at the time, and sent it to him approximately an hour later."

"And you never heard back from him?"

"No."

"I take it he didn't finish his work?"

"If he did, he didn't upload it to the server. The old algorithm was still in use as of yesterday morning."

Jackson nodded, pausing before his segue. "Do you have much interaction with Connor?"

"Aside from work, virtually none."

"What about at work?"

"We speak maybe a couple of times per month. Mostly touching base on schedules, updates, that sort of thing."

"So you wouldn't really notice a change in his behavior, if something was bothering him, if anything seemed suspicious?"

"Not really. But I do have to say, the last few times I've seen him he's seemed . . ." She winced. "Sort of fidgety."

"Fidgety?"

"Connor is never the most relaxed person, but he seemed on edge, as if he was meeting a pretty girl for the first time."

"Thursday?"

She thought for a moment, setting her salad container on the table. "Yes. More of the same. And his data request was odd. He'd been asking a lot of questions lately about the data."

"What sort of questions?"

"What I made of certain responses, why we'd added this or that field, why we'd paired questions the way we had. I couldn't tell if it was just nervous chatter or if he was going somewhere with it."

"Going somewhere?"

"Figure of speech. I have no idea."

Jackson frowned, not sure what any of this meant. "Is there anything else?"

"Anything else what?"

"Anything you can think of that might shed a light on what happened to Connor."

Jenn pursed her lips and shook her head. "No."

Jackson leaned forward. "Gut feeling, do you think he disappeared on his own or someone caused him to disappear?"

"I don't have a clue, other than I can't imagine any reason anyone would have for doing something to him."

"Yeah, so I keep hearing. Thanks for your time, Miss White."

Her smile was perfunctory. "Of course."

"I'll see myself out."

She smiled again and Jackson stood to leave.

"Mr. Douglas," she said, also standing.

"Yes?"

Jenn took a half step toward him, around the end of the coffee table. "I don't know what you're thinking might have happened to Connor, what ideas may have popped into your head."

"But?"

"But, I know you spoke to the mayor yesterday."

"I did."

"I would hate to think you in any way thought he was involved in Connor's disappearance."

"I'll be honest with you, as you were with me. I have no idea what to think."

Jenn nodded and smiled again. But as Jackson exited her office and made his way back down to his car, he couldn't shake the very subtle warning conveyed by her eyes.

Chapter Sixteen

Tuesday, June 18, 2013
11:34 a.m.

JACKSON DIDN'T HAVE long to ponder why his dad's former commanding officer would have told NCIS to cease investigating the Douglas family's death. He sat in the Granada in the NCIS parking lot, listening to the rain strum down on the vinyl roof as he dialed on his flip phone.

He and Dr. Zachary had always met on the third Tuesday of the month, until recently, when they'd switched to the first. But the doctor had started June on a two-week "reconnect with nature" junket to the fog and forest of the Oregon coast, and they had rescheduled June's appointment for the third Tuesday. At the time, Jackson had been hesitant and thought about skipping, given the tenor of their talks—and his life—of late. But it was on the docket, a fact that had slipped his mind until that morning.

Dr. Zachary's overly perky receptionist seemed to have it in for Jackson, and he'd had to beg and beseech her that morning to check if the doctor would be amenable to conducting their session by phone. He'd pled extenuating circumstances, and Zachary had capitulated. Now, as Jackson called in for his session, Alaina was again less than friendly. But she patched him through.

"Jackson, how are we today?"

"Confused and frustrated."

"Oh?"

"Been quite a weekend, Doc."

"Let's explore 'confused and frustrated,'" Zachary said, no doubt tracing his eyebrow with his finger.

Jackson laid his head back against the seat and walked Zachary through his conversation with Ike and Juliet Haywood and his subsequent investigation into Joaquín Padilla and his family's death. It took him the better part of twenty minutes, bringing Zachary right up to his conversation with Special Agent Bryson Webb earlier that hour.

"So that's why you're in San Diego."

"It is."

"Let me ask you something, Jackson."

"Shoot."

"What is it you're seeking? What are you hoping to accomplish with this investigation?"

"I want to find the truth."

"To what end?"

Jackson frowned into his phone. "Does truth need an end? *'The truth will set you free.'*"

"Aha."

"Aha what?"

"*'The truth will set you free.'* Freedom, then, is the end. Is that what you're seeking, freedom?"

Jackson sighed. "Of sorts, I guess. More like justice."

"Let's explore 'justice.'"

"Not much to explore, Zach."

"On the contrary, Jackson. I'll repeat my earlier question. To what end do you want justice?"

Jackson frowned again. Dr. Zachary—who insisted his patients refer to him by the informal nickname—was a little strange, but Jackson generally liked the guy. However, there were times when Zachary absolutely drove him nuts. Like this, when he psychoanalyzed every word and phrase. Then again, that was his job.

"Jackson?"

"Yeah, sorry. Why wouldn't I want justice?"

"We all claim we want justice, but true justice would mean receiving punishment for everything we've ever done wrong."

"Sure, but sin and eternal judgment is a little over my pay grade on this one. I just want the man responsible for killing my family to pay."

134

"Sounds more like vengeance than justice."

"Don't they pretty much go hand in hand?"

"Mmm, yes and no. The Bible says *'vengeance is mine; I will repay, saith the Lord.'*"

"Right, but He also uses man as the instrument of His vengeance."

"Yes, but appointed men and women. Specifically, governing authorities."

"Yeah, well, I think the governing authorities may have dropped the ball on this one."

"Jackson, I won't pretend this isn't a sticky situation, that it's perfectly cut and dried. But I do want to caution you. Before you go after this man, make sure your motives are correct. Make sure this is indeed about justice and not a personal vendetta. One pursuit is admirable. The other is not."

"I don't even know if he's the guy. I suspect so. That's why I'm investigating."

Zachary paused, and Jackson could almost hear him switching gears.

"What else is going on in your life?" he asked.

"Nothing."

"You just got back from Florida, did you not?"

"And the Bahamas. NOLA."

"How was that?"

"Startling similar."

"Oh?"

"More people died and the girl got away."

"Would you like to talk about that?"

"Not particularly."

"What would you like to talk about?"

"Can I run something past you?"

"I suppose so."

"June 30, 1999, Dad retires from the Navy and his position with ONI. He's served for two decades, achieved the rank of captain, and has himself a nice pension and a chance to watch his boys graduate, go to college, whatever. And to be a full-time husband to his wife."

"Sounds very nice."

"Yeah. Ten years later, as we're about to sit down to lunch on Memorial Day, Admiral Francis Sullivan, his old C.O., calls him up. Just to chat, he says. To pick his brain. But a month later, Dad reenlists and rejoins ONI. The world has changed—9/11, a pair of wars in the Middle East, Saddam toppled, North Korea gets the bomb, Iran's raising a stink. So he goes back, helping fight the ongoing War on Terror. He works for almost two years until one night, as he's having dinner with his family, an explosion rips through the restaurant and incinerates him."

Jackson took a moment to swallow the lump in his throat. "And after a day and half turns up nothing in the way of concrete evidence on a suspect, that old C.O. who is still Dad's C.O., calls off NCIS. They claim there wasn't any evidence Dad was targeted, after a day and a half. And so my question for you, Doc, is, how in the name of John Paul Jones can the United States Navy conclude this explosion had nothing to do with Dad? How can they possibly be so sure that all his work tracking Al-Qaeda operatives and jihadis and rousting sleeper cells didn't motivate some piece of crap Islamist to put out a fatwa on him? How can they be so sure somebody wasn't trying to settle a score, that this wasn't an act of retribution? So sure that they call off the investigation? How? His own C.O.?"

Zachary was quiet for a moment, letting Jackson finish his rant. Then he said softly, "I don't know."

"Neither do I. But there's one person who does."

"Jackson."

"Yeah?"

"What are you thinking?"

"I'm thinking it's time I have a talk with Admiral Sullivan."

"Tread carefully."

"Yeah, I know."

"And keep this in mind. A few minutes ago, you were ready to be God's instrument of meting out justice on this man Padilla. Now you're convinced Islamic terrorists are responsible."

"I said it was possible."

"So how do those two tie together?"

"I don't know," Jackson said as he exhaled a breath. "But that's what I need to find out."

"Can I give you one more piece of advice?" Zachary asked.

"Yeah, sure."

"Pray."

"Pray? That's it."

"No. Pray long and hard before you take any action. '*A fool uttereth all his mind: but a wise man keepeth it in till afterwards.*' Proverbs 29:11."

"Yeah, Doc."

"That doesn't sound too sincere."

"No, I'm just tired."

"Hotel beds can do that to you."

"Not that kind of tired."

"We still have time. Let's talk about tired."

"You ever watch *M*A*S*H*, Zach?"

"Of course."

"I know it's just TV, nothing like real war. But they did such a good job of portraying the hopelessness of these guys like Hawkeye and Trapper and B.J. being stuck over there, drafted doctors, in some stupid war they wanted no part of. Missing their families, missing births, missing everything. Alan Alda in particular, he was so good, his facial expressions were incredible, portraying that emptiness, that utter hopelessness, that they would never get out of there—that they would never get home."

Jackson winced as a rumble of thunder interrupted him. He sighed before continuing. "And that's where I am, Doc. I'm beat. I'm gassed. I've just gone through twenty-four hours of 'meatball surgery.' I've saved some lives and I've lost a few. And all I want to do is collapse onto my crappy Army cot in my crappy Army tent and sleep and forget it all. But I can't, because Radar just announced choppers incoming, with more wounded, with more surgery, with more death ensuing. And it never ends. Day after day after day after freaking day. And I hate it and I complain and sometimes I put on a happy face and distract myself and I just keep ending up right back here, wondering if I'm ever going to get out of Korea."

Zachary was quiet. Jackson couldn't blame him. In the long history of unusual metaphors, this was perhaps his most unusual. And yet, so perfectly apropos.

"I'm a millionaire, Zach."

"Excuse me."

"Sawyer—the girl I mentioned? She and I found fourteen million dollars' worth of gold buried in the Keys. She gave it all to me, said she didn't want any of it."

More silence. Then, "Are you serious?"

"Yeah. It's sitting in a trio of bank accounts right now. I'm rich beyond my wildest dreams, Zach. But instead of spending any of my money, instead of enjoying it with the few people left on this earth I care about, instead of giving it away to church or a charity or finding some noble cause to benefit, I'm sitting in my thirty-seven-year-old car in a rainy parking lot chasing down some ghost evidence that will prove my parents and brother were murdered. And to answer your question from before, to what end, I have no idea. Because I know it won't ultimately make a difference. But I have to know, Zach. I have to pursue this. I cannot let this rest. It's like ever since I talked to Ike and Juliet, a gnawing awakened inside of me. I'm like Frodo, drawn to Mordor, the ring is calling out. And it might consume me, it might kill me, but I have to see this through. And that, Zach, is why I'm tired."

Almost a minute of dead air passed between them. Only the constant strumming of rain on the Granada's roof and windows made any noise.

"I can tell you're in pain, beyond what you're even capable of describing," Zachary said at last.

"Probably true."

"Maybe even beyond what you recognize."

Jackson only nodded.

"And certainly beyond a few platitudes or trite admonishments. So let me just say this, Jackson. I will pray for you."

"Thanks."

"In fact, let's pray right now."

Zachary began praying, and sitting in the parking lot a hundred miles away, Jackson closed his eyes out of respect. Zachary wasn't the only one praying for him. His grandpa, Reggie, Sam at one time—and probably still—had all vowed to pray for him. He appreciated it. He believed there was power in prayer. And yet, a part of him sighed when someone told them they were praying for him, and a part of his heart wasn't joined with Zachary in prayer now. Because from his point of view, all the prayers of family and friends and therapists hadn't accomplished one iota.

Chapter Seventeen

Thursday, May 12, 2011
12:40 p.m.

AFTER HIS MEETING with Jenn White, Jackson drove home and had a quick lunch of leftover hamburgers. Plural. His body needed energy. He was starting demo on the upstairs today, with the ultimate goal of turning two bedrooms into one massive bedroom/office. He hoped some mindless work would give his brain a chance to sort and solve, and hoped a couple of hamburgers would give it the fuel it needed. Because the truth was, he didn't have much else to go on in finding Connor.

He changed into an old pair of jeans and a 2003 Orange Bowl T-shirt and hauled an assortment of tools, most of them gifts from his parents over the years, up to the second floor. At the top of the stairs, a door opened to a small bedroom over the garage. To the left, a short hallway provided access to the bathroom on the left and the second bedroom at the end of the hall. It too was over the garage, the backside of it, in this small split-level house. The wall between the rooms was coming down, and the back bedroom's closet was going to be extended to include a washer and dryer. The end of the hallway would be extended and turned into a linen closet, with the door that currently led to the back bedroom providing access to it while the joint bedroom/office would be serviced by the current front bedroom's door. At least that was the plan. He'd already upgraded the bathroom and had some plans to at least patch up the downstairs, if not downright remodel it. But for now, his focus was on his sleeping quarters.

First order of business was taking down the wall. Actually, he realized just before swinging his hammer, the first order of business was moving items in his bedroom away from the wall. The front bedroom was vacant and undecorated, but his bedroom had all his furniture—"all" consisting of a bed, a nightstand, and a dresser. In theory, he should have moved everything out before starting. But there was no way to get the dresser down the stairs by himself, and it had been such a hassle getting it and the bed up in the first place. So he grunted the dresser away from the wall and to the bed and decided to get back to it.

With hammers in each hand, Jackson assaulted the wall like a mountaineer slipping down the face of Mount Everest. In no time, chunks of drywall littered the floor and a haze of dust hung in the air. Jackson coughed a few times and spat in the corner, then resumed. Getting the drywall off was easy. It was the nails and tiny pieces of drywall stuck to the studs that was time-consuming.

Unfortunately, Jackson found that too much physical exertion—or exertion that required the level of attention that tearing down a wall required—left his brain little power left to solve a case. Especially when it started to wander, mulling such problems as what was Jackson going to do with all the debris? So far, he'd just put out extra loads of garbage each week, but this was a little more substantial. He had an excuse, however. His mind had been preoccupied.

He'd ripped most of the drywall off the front bedroom wall, and poked a hole between a couple of studs into the back bedroom, when he heard a knocking sound. At first he thought it was something demolition related, a reverberation running through the house or pipes reacting to the stress. Then he realized it was the front door, and that his doorbell didn't work.

"Yeah!" he hollered. Hailey was working, which meant it was likely Connie interested in a post-"date" recap, and that didn't merit a trip downstairs to get the door.

"Jack?"

It was Grant.

"Up here."

"You decent?" his brother asked as he climbed the steps.

"No, but I summoned you up anyhow," Jackson said, taking another swing with his hammer, claw first. He hooked one of the remaining sections of the wall and yanked it backward.

"What's all the . . . noise?"

"Demo day," Jackson said, turning to his brother. He was not alone. Hillary had come too.

Jackson still had to wonder how Grant had done it. He was decent enough looking—tall, muscular (more so because of all the working out he did), tanned skin, short brown hair with a dab of product to give it that preppy look, blue eyes a shade darker than Jackson's. And while he could be a little overbearing, especially for a younger brother, and a little bit of a choirboy, he was a nice enough guy, a perfect gentleman. But it was still a mystery how he had ever won Hillary's heart.

She was the most beautiful woman Jackson had ever seen—in person, on TV or in the movies, or even in his dreams. Hillary too was tall, six-foot, with a perfect figure she didn't flaunt but didn't hide either. Her skin was creamy and flawless, her eyes a frosty blue. Her golden hair was like the train of a goddess descending from Mount Olympus as it swaddled her cherubic face. That was a bit misleading, because Hillary's personality was more of a match with her eyes—icy. At least where Jackson was concerned. The rest of the Douglas family, most importantly Grant, were smitten with her. Jackson was still coming to terms with the reality that she would be his sister-in-law come August.

Hillary wore white Bermuda shorts and a charcoal gray V-neck top. Her hair, sadly, was pinned back in a low ponytail. Their differences aside, and until she and Grant officially tied the knot, Jackson deemed it wasn't inappropriate for him to enjoy her marvelous tresses.

Grant, for his part, wore khaki shorts and a powder blue T-shirt with "UCLA" in yellow script across the chest. The color looked almost as ridiculous on him, a grown man of nearly twenty-seven, as it did on a football team. Like Hillary, he wore a pair of flip-flops.

"I take it you didn't come to help," Jackson said, nodding at them. "Hey, Hill."

A flicker of irritation passed over her face at the nickname, but she let it slide. "Jackson."

"We're going tux shopping," Grant said. "You didn't answer your phone."

"I didn't hear it ring."

Grant shrugged. "We thought we'd swing by and see if maybe you'd like to join us, as best man and all."

"We?" Jackson asked.

Grant nodded. "It was actually Hillary's idea."

"Thanks, but I've got my hands full."

"Where are you going with all this?" Hillary asked, entering the room and being careful not to step on small pieces of drywall.

"To be determined. Keegan doesn't happen to have a trailer to go with that SUV of his, does he?"

"He and Heather broke up."

"Oh."

"I told you about that," Grant said.

Jackson shrugged.

Grant stepped forward and took hold of a stud. "Is this load-bearing?"

"We should know by dinnertime."

"Jack, you can't just rip down a wall. The whole house could come down."

"Not to mention you don't have a permit," Hillary said.

"You're hired if the city sues me." He swung again, the sound of metal tearing through drywall interrupting Grant. Last month, a contractor Jackson sort of knew from church had stopped by and confirmed the wall wasn't load bearing. But his casual attitude got under Grant's skin so much that he liked to egg him on now and again.

Jackson tossed a chunk of drywall to the corner, then turned to Hillary. "Pick a matron of honor yet?"

"Maid of honor, since they're not married, and no, I'm not picking between my sisters."

"Going third-party?"

"They'll both be maids of honor."

"Co-maid of honors? Is that—or is it maids of honor? Is that legal?" She sighed.

"It's actually pretty common these days," Grant said.

"And you know this, how, from watching *The Wedding Planner* with Karli Manning?" He turned back to Hillary before words could escape

Grant's open mouth. "Okay, so you hedge your bets. But who gets top billing?"

"You mean the honor of dancing with you?" she asked snidely.

He shrugged and began prying nails from a stud. "If it comes to dancing, I pick Holly."

"Oh?" Grant asked.

"Can it, Cupid. It's only because Heather would probably try to trip me or something. But seriously, who stands closer to you? Who walks down the aisle last?"

"Well, whoever gets the honor also has to walk back out with you, so it will be an easy sell to the loser."

He stuck out his tongue, which was about as close as he and Hillary came to civil repartee, then dropped a handful of nails in the corner.

"There's actually something else we wanted to ask you," Grant said.

"I will behave with my toast."

"Oh my goodness, he gets an open mic," Hillary said with nothing but dread in her eyes.

"Don't worry, Mom will write something for him," Grant said. "And it's actually about this weekend."

"What is?"

"What we wanted to ask you."

"So ask."

"Can Hillary ride with you to San Diego on Saturday?"

Jackson frowned. "How come?"

"Because I have an all-day seminar in San Diego on Friday, and Hillary has depositions scheduled until mid-afternoon Saturday. Mom said you weren't coming down till Saturday anyhow—"

"That isn't really set in stone."

It was—he'd decided a week ago to go down Saturday, but was suddenly feeling flexible.

"So instead of taking three cars or me making two trips, I figured you two could carpool."

"Three."

Grant frowned.

"Grandpa."

"He's coming?"

"Mom said he was invited along. I haven't heard if he's coming or not, but he isn't taking the Vespa if so."

"Okay. Well, the three of you then?"

Jackson looked back and forth between them. "That's it?"

"What do you mean?"

"No secret agenda?"

"Like what?"

"I don't know, but this seems like a personal favor instead of a practical request, and I know you're not suddenly ultra-concerned about the ozone."

"No tricks, Jack."

"A seminar? Since when do cops go to seminars?"

"We're trying to stay up to speed on dealing with immigration, customs and border crossings, deportations, etcetera."

"Let me guess, Appeasing Aliens 101?"

"How sensitive," Hillary said.

"And what's with depositions on a Saturday?"

"It's when all the parties are available. We've got a big trial that starts next week."

"So what do you say, Jack?" Grant asked.

He shrugged. "I guess."

"Great."

"You pick some shirred collared dueling blouse as part of my tux, the deal's off."

"You could always come along . . ."

From somewhere, Jackson's cell phone began ringing. He felt for his pockets, then ducked between studs and into the other bedroom. The phone was on his bed, and he opened it and accepted the call just before it went to voicemail.

"Yeah?"

"Jackson, it's Hailey."

"Oh, hey," he said, eyeing Grant and Hillary. "What's up?"

"Just wondering if you found anything this morning."

"No, not really. I couldn't get a read on Jenn. Well, I mean, I could, but . . ."

"I know what you mean." She paused. "So what's next?"

"I'm still mulling. And I've got another idea."

"Oh?"

"What time did you say you get off?"

"Not until ten."

"Give me a call when you're free. I'll let you know if I find anything else."

"Okay. Thanks, Jackson."

"Sure thing. Bye."

He clapped the phone shut and looked up at Grant and Hillary. Grant raised his eyebrows inquisitively. "Who's Jenn?"

"Pouty single woman with a frivolous claim but great legs?" Hillary guessed.

"Blind date?" Grant said with less—but not entirely without—derision.

"She's actually a member of the None of Your Business Club."

"How original," Hillary said. She looked to Grant. "Maybe he's planning a surprise birthday party for himself."

"Yeah," Jackson said, "and we have an opening for a clown. Interested?"

"Sounds more like when he used to play secret agent with *Kensie* Manning."

Hillary frowned.

"No, it's not a euphemism," Grant said. "They re-enacted *Mission: Impossible* episodes."

"When we were little kids," Jackson added.

"Funny you feel the need to clarify that," Hillary responded.

"Seriously, Jack, now you've got me curious."

"Terrible place to be, isn't it?"

Grant sighed.

So did Jackson. "Can you guys keep a secret?"

"Don't tell us, she's your fiancée," Hillary said.

"No, fiancée's sister," Grant said.

Jackson sighed again. "I was talking to a client."

Hillary huffed. "I was actually right?"

"No. I don't work for Bauer & Bauer anymore."

"What?"

"I quit a few weeks ago."

"You what?" Hillary asked.

"Jack, wha—"

"Stow the panic. I've got another job."

"And she's your client?"

He nodded.

"Let me guess," Hillary said, "you run a dating service for young, beautiful, buxom actresses."

"No, although not because it's a terrible idea."

"Come on, Jack. Out with it."

"I'm a private investigator."

Hillary laughed. A high-pitched giggle turned belly laugh that bordered on a snort that hedged on uncontrollable. It was the least dignified she had ever been.

"You serious?" Grant asked with shock more than skepticism on his face.

"Yes, I'm serious. That was my first client."

Hillary managed to compose herself. "You are a private eye?"

He nodded. "You can't tell Mom and Dad."

"Jack, they'll find out."

"I'm going to tell them. Saturday. I just want it to come from me. Please," he said, looking between them, "don't say anything."

"I couldn't keep a straight face anyhow," Hillary said.

"I won't say anything," Grant said.

"No hints, no suggestive phrases, no 'accidentally' calling me Magnu—er—Jack at dinner."

"I promise," Grant said. "So what brought this on? I know you mentioned it a few years ago, but—"

"He mentioned this to you?" Hillary asked. "And you didn't discourage him?"

"I'm sorry, Hill, I didn't think to clear my career with you."

"Come on, Jackson, a P.I.? I'm surprised you didn't just declare yourself a mysterious international man of leisure and print up business cards to hand to single women."

"As much as I'd love to spend the day being the butt of your jokes, I do have a wall to knock over, and then work to get to."

"'Work,'" Hillary said with air quotes.

"Go defend a rapist or something, Miss Noble Profession."

"Jack."

"Go. I'll fill you in Saturday."

"Come on, Grant," Hillary said. "If we don't do what he says, he'll send his new underworld friends after us."

"Ha, ha."

Grant extended his hand as he turned to leave.

"What's that for."

"Congratulations."

Jackson stared at the hand. "Uh-huh. Congratulate me when you can get your better half in sync."

Grant raised his hand and gave Jackson a friendly slap to the shoulder instead. "Sure you don't want to join us?"

"Only if you include a blindfold and a cigarette."

"I'll see you Saturday," Grant said.

"Yeah."

"Bye, Jackson," Hillary teased from the top of the stairs. "I'll text you about Saturday."

"Would you please?"

"So you know when and where to pick me up."

"Right. You know, with this new job, the remodel, I've got so much on my mind. I sure hope I don't forget and slip down the coast without you."

Hillary looked at Grant, who in turn looked at Jackson.

"I will play chauffeur. Now go. Somebody has to follow her around a haberdashery and say 'Yes, your highness' every few minutes."

Grant pointed at the ceiling as he turned to go. "Be careful. I'd hate to see the roof collapse on you."

"Same to you, buddy. Same to you."

Chapter Eighteen

Tuesday, June 18, 2013
2:07 p.m.

JACKSON HAD DRIVEN through it many times before, but had only visited Fort Rosecrans National Cemetery once, when he was seven or eight. His dad had brought him to the seventy-seven-acre cemetery on Point Loma back before Naval Station Point Loma had been established. On a majestic summer morning, they had watched the sunrise over the bay while wandering through the dew-covered grass. Young Jackson had marveled at row upon row upon row of brilliant white grave markers, each commemorating the final resting place of United States service members (many of whom had died in service of their country) and their spouses and families. Somber and serene as it had been, Jackson knew now the experience didn't have the impression David Douglas intended, what with his being so young. But he'd never forgotten it—he could still smell the grass, feel the morning breeze and the first rays of the sun as they dappled the Pacific Ocean with light—and the impression had intensified and solidified over time.

Now tombstones and monuments had an entirely different connotation, and as Jackson parked along the road dividing the park, he had no idea why he was here. But one didn't question an admiral's instructions.

The rain had stopped, but the air was still cool and raw, with a steady wind blowing in off the Pacific. The cemetery was situated atop a ridge on the protuberant Point Loma, with tombstones seemingly rolling down the hills to the ocean on the west and the bay on the east. Fastidiously clipped grass, along with stately palm, pine, and cypress trees, helped isolate the cemetery, and the surrounding vistas might as well have been vignettes.

Jackson stood staring down the hill, to the bay, to Naval Base Coronado, to the San Diego skyline. This city had once been home. The Navy had been a part of life, but distantly. David's first stint with ONI had taken place when Jackson was largely too young, frankly, to care. The second, in the final few years before his death, had been while Jackson was busy making his own way in Los Angeles. He had always had the utmost respect for the military, for his dad, for his family's history of service to its country. He still felt it, but now the Navy carried with it a negative connotation that made him want to run from it all. But he couldn't.

The whine of wheels on pavement turned Jackson's head. A black Cadillac SUV parked a few spaces down. It continued to idle while the rear passenger door opened and a petty officer stepped out. He was followed by Admiral Francis Sullivan.

Even in his service khaki uniform, complemented by a navy blue windbreaker, the admiral was regal and imposing. He stood six-three or six-four, tall enough to carry his two hundred twenty pounds without appearing heavy. His windbreaker was partially unzipped, revealing a bevy of medals above his left breast pocket, the accumulation of a lifetime of service. From what David had told his family, Admiral Sullivan had earned every one of them, first aboard the USS *Midway* in the latter stages of the Vietnam War, then in the Persian Gulf during Operations Desert Shield and Desert Storm, and in various capacities, including with the Office of Naval Intelligence, of late.

Sullivan's hair was brown turning to white. His face was firm and dour, but he was capable of warm smiles when meeting spouses and children. Jackson had only met him once or twice, but the admiral's reputation as a hard but fair C.O. had been well-known and often spoken of at the Douglas home. Even more renowned was his ardent love for his country and his fellow citizens. Rarely effusive, David had praised Admiral Sullivan, looking up to him as a father figure. It was one of the many reasons Jackson held the man in high regard, and why he had spent the last hour reminding himself to follow Dr. Zachary's advice to tread carefully.

"Jackson," the admiral said in a voice like an earthquake. He extended a large, powerful hand to Jackson.

"Sir. Thank you for making time for me."

Admiral Sullivan surveyed the grounds without taking his focus off Jackson. "Walk with me?"

"Of course."

"This place always gets me," Sullivan said a few paces down the side of the road. His aide had remained beside the Cadillac, which continued to idle noiselessly. "We speak so often in numbers—X number of service men and women, Y number of troops deployed to a particular theater, Z number of casualties. This," he said with a pause, looking around, "translates the numbers to something personal. Everyone here, whether they gave their life in defense of freedom, whether they served for a lifetime or for a single tour, whether they remained behind and supported a husband or wife, father or mother—every one of them—sacrificed for something greater than themselves. Every one of them put country ahead of self, put the welfare of their neighbor ahead of their own." His eyes roamed to the horizon, where a tanker ship was steaming toward the entrance to San Diego Bay. "It's a quality in increasingly lesser supply these days, I'm afraid. It's why I appreciate those who make that commitment, who make that sacrifice—and particularly those who make the ultimate sacrifice," he said with a spreading of his hands, "all the more." He looked at Jackson.

"Yes, sir."

The admiral turned his eyes back to the rows of headstones. With his right hand, he made a slight turn of the Naval Academy class ring on his left hand. It took the place of a wedding band. As far as Jackson knew, Sullivan was a lifelong bachelor.

"But you didn't call to hear an old man wax poetic, did you?"

"Uh, no, sir."

"You have questions about your parents' and brother's deaths?"

"Yes, sir. I visited NCIS this morning. I met with Special Agents Nicks and Dobraska, and also spoke via Skype with Special Agent Webb at Camp Lejeune. They informed me that NCIS's investigation into Mom, Dad, and Grant's death was basically a dead end, but that they were also advised, in Special Agent Webb's words, 'not to pursue the investigation any further.'" Jackson made eye contact with Admiral Sullivan, who had stopped walking. "Sir, he said the 'stand down' order came from you."

The admiral raised his chin slightly, pursing his lips. He then licked them. "And you want to know why?"

"Yes, sir, I do."

Admiral Sullivan nodded, then turned and resumed walking. Jackson kept pace for almost a minute, listening to the wind. The admiral's eyes were just slits, perhaps squinting against the wind. His expression was stone-like, but a stone that had fractured.

He swallowed, then spoke. "Jackson, there are details I cannot divulge. That's not me giving you the runaround or hiding behind regulations. But there are some things I absolutely cannot tell you. When I tell you it's a matter of national security, that's an understatement."

Jackson nodded, unsure where the admiral was going.

"I asked NCIS to stand down—and it was just that, a request. I don't have the authority to command them to do so—because I knew they were barking up the wrong tree."

"Sir?"

"Your parents and Grant weren't killed because of anything that falls under purview of the Navy. And NCIS wasn't going to find anything to prove otherwise."

Jackson stopped, feeling as if he'd been dealt a haymaker by a heavyweight boxer. He was standing, but dazed.

"Admiral . . . are you telling me you know why my family was killed?"

Sullivan's gray-brown eyes looked straight into Jackson's. "I'm telling you I know why they weren't."

Jackson turned, his eyes but not his focus settling on One American Plaza in downtown. Slowly, he turned back. "But you're saying they were killed, that it wasn't an accident?"

"I can't confirm that."

"Can't confirm it? You mean you don't know or you can't go on the record?"

"I can't confirm it."

Jackson sighed. Had the admiral not been one of his late father's closest confidants or had he not been a highly-decorated war hero—heck, had he not been both—Jackson would have slugged him. He got protecting national security and confidentiality and all that. But Sullivan knew something and was purposefully being vague.

Jackson sighed again, forcing himself to be civil and respectful. "With all due respect, Admiral, it feels like you are giving me the runaround."

Sullivan nodded. "I know. And I'm sorry. But I really can't tell you more."

Another sigh.

"Jackson, you trusted your father, and he trusted me. Please, trust me also."

The admiral's eyes and face had softened. They looked pained. Yet not half as much as Jackson's were as he nodded slowly.

Admiral Sullivan turned and the duo began walking back up the hill, toward their vehicles a hundred yards away.

"What about Joaquín Padilla?" Jackson asked.

"What about him?"

"He just got released from Kern Valley for turning state's evidence on some gang killings."

"I hadn't heard."

"Well, did you know that the testimony that put him at Petty Officer Grabel's apartment twelve minutes after the explosion killed my family has been refuted?"

The admiral's pace slackened, then he stopped. He turned to Jackson. "How's that?"

"At the time, one of Petty Officer Grabel's neighbors testified that he saw Padilla arrive at 7:23 p.m. His ex-wife now testifies that her husband was mistaken and has dyslexia. She testifies that the time was actually 7:32. Meaning Padilla could have been at the restaurant at 7:11 to trigger the explosion and at Grabel's apartment in time to assault her."

Admiral Sullivan licked his lips. "Have you spoken to the ex-wife?"

"Not personally."

He nodded and resumed walking.

"Admiral."

"Hmm?"

"Who's Joaquín Padilla?"

"From what I understand, a two-bit, repeat offender. A real mess."

"I mean, how does he fit in all this?"

"I don't follow."

"Did he kill my parents?"

The admiral stopped again. He looked at Jackson for several seconds. "The timeline always suggested he didn't."

"But now the timeline works."

Sullivan nodded, pursed his lips again. "If the ex-wife's telling the truth, if she's trustworthy . . . he looks good for it."

Jackson stood as Sullivan turned back up the hill. "What's that mean?" he asked, catching up to him. "Admiral, do you know who killed them?"

"No."

"So it could have been Padilla?"

Hesitantly, it seemed, he nodded.

They walked back to their vehicles, Jackson trying to make sense of what Admiral Sullivan had said—and what he hadn't.

"Is there anything else you can tell me?" Jackson asked as they stood behind the Granada. The aide hadn't moved from beside the admiral's SUV.

"I'm afraid not, son. I'm sorry."

Jackson forced his hand out. "Thank you, sir."

Sullivan shook the hand, patting Jackson's shoulder with his other hand. He nodded. "You take care."

Jackson could only nod as the admiral turned and retreated to the Cadillac, followed by the petty officer. Jackson watched the vehicle back out of the stall and drive away. He leaned back against the trunk of the Granada, mulling as the breeze turned to a mist.

Too much of this didn't make any sense. Visiting NCIS and now speaking with Admiral Sullivan hadn't cleared up anything—it had only muddied the water. Something was going on, something enigmatic, something the Navy—or at least the admiral—didn't want coming to light.

Had that been the reason Sullivan had suggested meeting at Fort Rosecrans? Had he wanted Jackson to see all the grave markers and think about all the lives given in service of their country? Had he given that little speech about numbers and the meaning behind the sacrifice as a message to Jackson to put his country's welfare ahead of his own? Or had the admiral really just been waxing poetic?

That was a question and a matter for another time, Jackson concluded. Because for all the secrecy, all the mystery, all the uncertainty, one thing was crystalizing in his mind.

Joaquín Padilla—for whatever reason—had killed his mom, dad, and brother.

Chapter Nineteen

Thursday, May 12, 2011
6:06 p.m.

FROM JACKSON'S HOUSE in Pacific Palisades, going almost anywhere meant taking a right on Sunset, then a left on Chautauqua, and following that to the PCH, which could take him west to Malibu or south and east to most of L.A. via the 10 or the 405. Since it was such a common route, he didn't think much of the tan sedan that followed him, other than that tan was a pretty stupid color for a car. Nor did the car's following him as the PCH veered inland at the Santa Monica Pier and turned into I-10 mean anything. And yet, he found it odd. Not that the car was taking the same route, but the way it seemed to mimic him in traffic. Jackson's 1976 Granada, bequeathed to him by his Grandpa Leroy after the passing of his wife Marsha, was still in tip-top shape. But she was showing a few signs of age, such as the inability to do more than about sixty-five on the open highway. So Jackson was used to cars zipping around him like a rock in a fast-moving stream. But as he journeyed east and the Santa Monica Freeway expanded to four lanes in each direction, the ugly, tan sedan remained a few hundred yards behind him in the right lane.

It was a newer model, maybe a Malibu or Impala. Jackson was not a car guy, and, frankly, they were all starting to look alike. Its windows were dark enough that he couldn't see anything through them, and traffic was moving at a good clip, but was a little too frenetic for him to try to read a license plate several cars behind him in a mirror. Besides, what would he do with it? He didn't have a Rick to his Magnum to call Icepick and run it down. Connie, his neighbor, worked for the DMV. But it was closed, and even if she had some remote access, Jackson wasn't wild about bartering favors with her. Somehow, he had a feeling he would end up regretting it.

So he decided to test his paranoia. Instead of continuing east on I-10, he took the ramp south on the 405.

The sedan followed.

No biggie. It could be headed to LAX, Long Beach, Orange County, or San Diego. But to be sure, Jackson took the Venice Boulevard exit, which actually required going over Venice Boulevard, exiting, and jogging back north.

The sedan followed.

Jackson turned right on Venice and then right on Sepulveda, just under the 405 overpass. When the sedan followed, Jackson realized that he had yet to make an "unnatural" turn, a turn the sedan wouldn't make unless it was following him. So he turned back west on Washington, under the 405 again, and when the sedan followed, he knew he was being tailed.

Magnum had one of two methods for dealing with a tail. Either he'd make some sharp, speedy maneuvers with the Ferrari to lose the tail (not happening with the Granada), or he'd stop and confront the pursuers. Jackson wasn't up for that either, what with his gun locked in his safe back at home. But he also didn't want to be late, so playing hide-and-seek across Los Angeles wasn't a viable alternative.

So he pulled a Jim Rockford instead. As he turned north on Sawtelle, completing the square, he called the police. He told them he was headed east on Venice and spotted an erratic driver in a tan, four-door sedan. He was weaving in and out of traffic, speeding up to pass everybody—and even veering into oncoming lanes—then slowing down and creeping along in the right lane. He was drunk, or stoned, or both. He told the dispatcher he was just passing under the 405, and was about to lose the sedan in traffic. License plate? He strained in the mirror as he stopped at the light at Venice. He could make out a couple digits, and read them back.

He disconnected the call and turned right, driving normally on Venice. He drove steadily for about a dozen blocks, and was just passing a Ralph's at the corner of Venice and Midway when he saw flashing red and blue lights in his rearview mirror. He smiled as he coasted through the light at Overland, while in the rearview mirror he saw the sedan pull into the parking lot of a California Pizza Kitchen, the police cruiser behind it.

Jackson's smile vanished as he contemplated who might be following him, and why. Whoever it was, they had picked him up right as he left home. Had someone been surveilling him? And who? The people responsible for Connor's disappearance? Were they concerned that Jackson was onto them? Was it the mayor, sending his professional goons to snoop on Jackson's progress? This was L.A.—was it just some crazy person with a thing for old, red cars?

With no way of knowing, and keeping a slightly guarded eye out for any other signs of a pursuer, Jackson reached for his phone again and dialed a number he had recently memorized.

"Hello?"

"Maggie, it's Jackson. Sorry, but I'm running a little late."

"As in get a table or you're about to ask for a rain check as your way of canceling?"

"As in get a table and order us some wings. I'll be there in fifteen or twenty minutes, as soon as I can figure out how the heck to get to BHCP from Venice Boulevard."

"What are you doing on Venice Boulevard?"

"Took in some juggling this afternoon. I'll explain when I get there."

"Okay. What's your poison?"

"Lady's choice, but I am a fan of boneless. Gnawing on bones like a lion in the Serengeti isn't my thing."

"Boneless it is. See you soon."

"Yeah."

He clapped his phone shut and smiled again. There was something about Maggie, about her nonchalant banter, about the way she flirted without being a flirt, about her authenticity that appealed to him. It was part of the reason he'd called her that afternoon and asked about going over some of her past articles and research. It was a long shot, but he was hoping to figure out why Connor had selected Maggie of all possible reporters, and in so doing, figure out what trouble or situation had led to Connor's disappearance. With nothing much else to go on, he figured he owed it to Hailey to turn over every rock. And while he was happy to have another excuse to see Maggie, it was a legitimate investigative move, he reasoned. Suggesting they meet for wings and hockey instead of just poring over old articles—that was directly attributed to Maggie's personality.

He arrived ten minutes late, not bad considering, and found a parking spot next to a Yamaha "crotch rocket." Taking a quick glance in his rearview mirror, he concluded he looked fine, and hurried inside. He quickly spotted Maggie at a bistro table with a view of several TV screens. Most prominent was one featuring a Rangers-Bruins hockey game. Two longneck bottles of Coors sat on the table, on either side of a basket of orange-tinged chicken wings.

"Hey," Jackson said as he pulled out a chair.

"Hey," Maggie said, without looking. Her eyes were glued to the TV, and Jackson turned to watch a quick sequence of frenzied action around the Rangers' goal. It ended with a sprawling save and cover by the goalie, and the customary pushing and shoving of several players in front of him.

"Sorry," Maggie said, looking down. "Long penalty kill."

"I feel the same way when Ted Lilly gets into a bases loaded jam."

She smiled. Her wavy hair was pulled back in a schoolgirl ponytail. It would make eating wings easier, and did nothing to diminish her allure. She wore a faded blue tank top with "New York" stenciled across the chest in faded white letters, and "Rangers" beneath and partially overlapping it in faded red.

"Why the Rangers?" Jackson asked as she took a swig of her beer.

"I'm from New York originally. They stuck with me. Yankees too."

"And the New York football Giants?" he asked, imitating famed broadcaster Howard Cosell.

"Bills."

"Hmm."

Her eyes went back to the final thirty seconds of the Boston power play. Hockey rules dictated that rules infractions, instead of being punished by free throws for the opposing team or yards marked off on the field, were enforced by taking a player away from one team, giving the opponent a man advantage, or power play. They generally lasted two minutes, but Jackson caught enough commentary to learn that this had been a "double-minor," meaning New York was shorthanded for four minutes.

When they survived it unscathed thanks to another great save by their goalie, Maggie sat back. The game went to commercials, and she reached for a wing. "Hmm what?"

"New York, New York, or just New York State?"

"Why?"

"I'm wondering why the Bills and not the Jets or Giants, or why not the Sabres instead of the Rangers?"

"Super Bowl XXV," she said.

"What about it?"

"I felt terrible for that kicker."

"Scott Something."

"Norwood."

"Looks like Randy Travis."

She frowned. "Okay, sure." She shrugged. "I started cheering for Buffalo, you know, hoping they'd get the next one."

"That didn't go so well."

"No. But I became a fan."

"Fair enough."

She nodded at the basket on the table. "I ordered boneless wings."

"I see that."

"Plain, old buffalo sauce," she said, shoving the basket his way. "Took a chance on a beer too."

"Thanks, but I don't drink."

"You don't?"

"Nary a sip," he said, reaching for a wing.

"You're not a Mormon, are you?"

"You not like Mormons?"

"The shirt-and-tie salesman stigma is kind of hard to shake."

"Lucky for you, I spilled buffalo sauce on my tie the last time I met a lady reporter for wings and hockey." He took a bite. "Mmm, good."

"Kicks a little, so you may want to reconsider that beer."

"I'll be fine," Jackson said in a falsetto.

Maggie's eyes returned to the TV, and Jackson took the opportunity to scan the menu. When he found something that appealed to him, he looked around, taking in some of the other action. A couple of baseball games—A's at Rangers, Red Sox at Orioles—highlights of some or other golf tournament, and a documentary on some MMA fighter all failed to hold Jackson's interest, so he watched the hockey with Maggie until their waitress came.

"So I'm not too up on the Stanley Cup Playoffs," Jackson said when she was gone. "What's at stake here?"

"At least you know enough to call them the Stanley Cup Playoffs?"

"I didn't just come in on a bus."

"Game six of the Eastern Conference semis," Maggie said. "Three-two Rangers."

"How are my Kings doing?"

"Bowed out in the first round."

"Really more of a baseball and basketball town anyhow."

"Uh-huh."

A couple of minutes of up-and-down action resulted in a few good scoring chances but no goals, and the first period ended in a scoreless tie. Maggie leaned her elbows on the table. "Okay, so what's up? You didn't give me much on the phone."

"My investigation into Connor's disappearance has stalled."

"No leads?"

"Not really. But I keep asking myself, why you?"

"You don't think it was just random?"

"Maybe. A guy wants to talk to a reporter, so he opens the newspaper and contacts the first name he sees? Sure, that could be it. Or, and don't take this the wrong way, but he liked your picture, liked the way you looked. That could be it too."

"How would I take that the wrong way?"

"I don't know. If you're one of those feminists who gets offended if a guy opens the door for them or thinks any compliment of a woman's appearance is equivalent to saying 'take off your socks and get into the kitchen and make me something to eat.'"

"You meet a lot of such women?"

"Can't say as that I do."

"Well, I'm ambivalent as to who opens the door, I have no problem being complimented on my appearance, and if you tell me to make you something to eat, I'm probably ordering a pizza."

"It's kismet."

Maggie grabbed a wing. "So if it's not random?"

"Then Connor targeted you for a reason. Since we don't know why he's missing or what happened to him, I'm hoping we can find something in your writing history that would suggest why he'd call you."

"Something such as?"

Jackson shrugged. "You said the other day you weren't yet famous. But are you the *Times'* go-to reporter for celebrity scandal or gang violence or anything?"

"Nope. I'm the *Times'* go-to reporter for whatever the more accomplished journalists don't want to write about."

"Were you able to bring a compilation of articles you've written?"

"Yeah." She reached into a shoulder bag hanging over the back of her chair. She retrieved a laptop and set it on the table.

"I'm going to feel silly if you tell me to go to latimes.com."

"No, but I'm not exactly the newspaper-clipping scrapbooking type. I've got final drafts of everything saved on here."

"I don't want to get buffalo sauce on your keyboard."

"I'll drive. Scoot over."

He slid his chair around so he was right beside her, which also provided him a better view of the Rangers-Bruins game, currently still at intermission. He looked at the screen as the laptop came alive. Maggie's wallpaper showed a gigantic wave crashing against dark cliffs and engulfing the base of a stubby lighthouse. It was half covered in icons, and Maggie clicked open a folder, then browsed to a subfolder entitled "LA Times." Nestled in that folder were more folders with year designations, dating back to 2006.

"That when you started?" Jackson asked.

"Uh-huh. Start at the beginning?"

"Might as well."

They spent ten minutes reading file names, which corresponded with headlines and article names. Maggie, with almost perfect recall, was able to give him a short synopsis of each story. She'd written about celebrity scandals and gang violence, as well as industrial accidents, trade talks, zoning battles, and several "personal interest" stories—a wide gamut of types of articles, none of which jumped out at him. When their dinners came, and since the Bruins and Rangers had resumed, they closed the laptop and set it aside.

"So why were you late?" Maggie asked as they ate and watched hockey.

"I was followed."

"What?"

He explained about the tan sedan, his maneuvers to determine it was indeed following him, and his method of eluding it.

"You know it's against the law to make a false 9-1-1 call, don't you?"

"I fudged a few details, but they were driving erratically."

"To keep up with you."

"Like I said, details."

"Who do you think it was?"

"I don't know. You don't happen to have access to license plate records, do you? I'm still cultivating sources."

"Sorry."

The Rangers gave up a pair of goals in the span of five minutes, and Maggie lost interest in hockey. Game seven would be back in New York, she said, so her Rangers were still in good shape. Jackson asked if she had managed to convince herself yet, and she backhanded him in the shoulder.

"So we made it through 2007," Jackson said as they continued eating. "What about after that? Anything relating to math, statistics, algorithms."

"Math and algorithms?" Maggie asked.

"Connor's a math guy. You happen to interview an SC professor who discovered cold fusion or some mathletes who finally beat China in a competition?"

"Can't say as that I did."

"Anything about dating services, online dating?"

She shook her head.

He finished a bite of his bacon cheeseburger. "Dating, relationships?"

"I interviewed a runner-up on *The Bachelor*."

"What was the angle?"

"She was from Buena Park."

"Anything unusual about her?"

"Not really."

"Hmm. Worth looking into, I guess. She cute?"

Maggie smirked at him. "How is that relevant to Connor's disappearance?"

"Just covering all bases."

"Uh-huh."

He ate a handful of fries and washed them down with some iced tea. "Anything about city councils, mayoral politics, that sort of thing?"

Maggie shook her head. "No. Well, there was one story. An assemblymember from upstate was busted for using his political clout and his business partnership in an employment agency to take advantage of his constituents."

"Take advantage how?"

"He used info gathered on employment applications or submitted to various agencies to blackmail and extort them. A real piece of work."

"Upstate?"

"San Jose."

"How'd a good-looking lady reporter from the *Times* end up covering it?"

"He was originally from L.A., and there were some sordid details that made it bigger than your average political scandal."

"Such as?"

"A whistleblower died under potentially suspicious circumstances, a female intern was taken advantage of, that sort of thing."

"Actually sounds quite a bit like the average political scandal."

Maggie shrugged.

"How'd you draw the story?"

"I was covering for our political reporter while he was skiing in the Canadian Rockies. And it was a slow news cycle, so I pursued it because of the local connection. Then the story kind of took off."

"A big break?"

"Not really. I didn't break much news, and certainly didn't uncover it. I just reported it."

Jackson nodded and cleaned up his plate while the Rangers shot blanks on a power play. Maggie sighed. "They've been great with the man advantage all year, and now they couldn't hit an open net."

"So are you like a diehard, face-painting, glass-banging Rangers fan?"

She shrugged again. "A typical Thursday in February, not so much. But when the Cup is in view . . ."

"You grow up with a bunch of brothers who played on frozen ponds?"

"No," she said softly.

He nodded.

"I like the physicality of hockey. And I don't mean because I get to watch cute guys running into each other or something."

"I've never seen a cute hockey player."

"I mean the physical nature of the game itself."

"Yeah, I like women's beach volleyball for the same reason," he deadpanned.

"Shut up."

"What else have you written? Any exposés? Any reason Connor would think you're the one to call if he wanted to shine a light on somebody doing something underhanded?"

"Aside from a story about PEDs in the NFL, not really."

"You wrote a story about PEDs in the NFL?"

"Why is that surprising?"

"I'd think that'd fall to the sports guys—Plaschke or Adande or somebody."

"You at least read the sports section, huh?"

"I watch *Around the Horn*."

At the second intermission, with New York trailing 2-0, Jackson and Maggie pushed aside their empty plates and leaned in to look at her laptop again. They spent about ten minutes scanning more headlines, with Maggie outlining stories and Jackson mulling any potential connection to Connor's disappearance. Once again, nothing grabbed his attention.

"Now what?" Maggie asked.

"I guess it depends how much you're enjoying my company."

"You want to read each article?"

"I'm thinking something grabbed him. And maybe it wasn't a headline or a topic but something you said."

"Okay, but how are you going to pick up on it?"

"I don't know. I might not. But it's worth a shot."

She eyed him bemusedly.

"What?"

"Just trying to figure out if you're really thorough or if you're looking for an excuse to prolong a date."

"Is this a date?"

"I meant in your mind."

"I see. Well, I am being thorough. But I'm also not in a hurry to head home."

Maggie nodded. "What would you say to heading someplace a little more conducive to your research?"

"Like what, Dave & Buster's?"

She grinned. "I was thinking like my apartment. A couch beats a barstool, plus it's quieter."

Jackson heard a very faint dinging sound, like a distant alarm bell. He ignored it. There was no reason to think Maggie was suggesting anything other than better seating and a quieter environment. If she excused herself to "slip into something more comfortable" when they got to her apartment, he'd reevaluate his assessment.

"Sure. But won't you miss the third period?"

"It's on the DVR. And the way it's going, there won't be anything to miss."

"Okay then. Dessert to go?"

"You like brownies?"

"That's like asking if I enjoy breathing."

"I have brownies. Made 'em just last night."

"Brownies on a Wednesday. Book club?"

"Hunger. You want to go or make jokes all night?"

"Check please."

Chapter Twenty

8:56 p.m.

IT WAS HARD to tell who was more excited. After a flurry of shots, saves, whiffs, blocks, pokes, and an assortment of mad scrambles and dives, the Rangers' centerman had put a rebounded, rolling puck into the back of the net, tying the game at 2-2 with less than thirty seconds to play. Maggie had leapt off the loveseat in her living room, then stood looking incredulously at Jackson as he lowered his eyes and attention back to her laptop screen instead of partying with her.

After following Maggie back to her apartment in Park La Brea, he'd settled down with her laptop while she'd queued up the Rangers game and set a plate of brownies on the table. She'd then joined him, adding a little commentary and rooting on New York's comeback while he read.

Since it was the only story with any promise, Jackson had begun by reading Maggie's article on the assemblymember from San Jose. Joseph Murtaugh had been a two-term assemblymember in the California 25th when he'd been arrested in January of 2008. He'd been charged and convicted with a host of crimes, and in all had taken almost $200,000 from his victims. But it wasn't Assemblymember Murtaugh's scheme, nor Maggie's story—which was very well-written—that kept his attention off the action on the ice.

In addition to flagrantly breaking the eighth commandment by bilking clients and constituents out of their life's savings and nest eggs, Murtaugh had also violated the seventh commandment. He'd had an affair with a young intern in his office, no more than a girl, who had fallen hard for the politician and become duplicitous in his schemes. According to Maggie's article, this intern had been a victim, fooled by Murtaugh as much as his clients had been. She made for a very sympathetic figure, both to the authorities in San Jose and to Maggie's readers.

"Come on, Jack," Maggie said, slapping his shoulder. "I know hockey's not your thing, but unless you're from Bahstan, that had to stoke your fire."

"Yeah. No, it was great. You have anything more on this Murtaugh case? Research that didn't make your article, photos, follow-ups?"

"Yeah," Maggie said, turning back to the TV for the final seconds of regulation. "Why?"

"The intern, the young girl in Murtaugh's office."

"You want to know if she's cute too?"

"No. Well, I mean, sure, but no. You got a picture?"

Maggie watched a Bruin slap shot from near center ice sail wide as the horn sounded before nodding. "Yeah. I'm not a scrapbooker, but I do keep copies of all the editions that contain my articles. Big box under my bed."

"Nothing to be ashamed of," he said in reply to a grimace on her face.

"I don't know, it seems sort of cat ladyish to me."

"Would you mind terribly?"

"Give me a minute."

She disappeared into the bedroom and Jackson ate another brownie. They were delicious, but then again, it didn't take a gourmet to mix up a box of brownies.

"January 2008, right?" Maggie asked when she returned.

"Yep."

She set down several full newspapers, minus the ads and inserts. "You got a date?"

"Um, January 28."

"Okay, here we go," she said, pulling it from the stack. She opened it to the appropriate page and folded it back for him. "Wipe your hands."

"Yeah, right." He wiped them on a napkin, then his pants for good measure. He took the paper from her and quickly ran his eyes down the page. Halfway down the second column were two pictures, one of Murtaugh and one of the intern. He brought it close to his face.

"Need your bifocals there, gramps?"

"Else your newspaper could invest in a digital camera. Kind of grainy," he said, tipping it toward her.

"Gonna bet you that wasn't a photo we took. What are you looking for anyhow?"

"Homemade facial rec. This hair looks brown."

"It was."

"I know her as a blonde."

"Who?"

"Jenn White."

"You mean Jennifer Winters?"

"You say po-ta-to. I think Assemblymember Murtaugh's intern-slash-mistress is Mayor Kendrick's girlfriend-slash-stock advisor."

"What?"

"May I?" he asked, gesturing at her computer.

"Sure."

He pulled up MatchStick's website, which was graced with photos that resembled those on the wall in the office—smiling, happy, beautiful young couples.

"If you didn't want a second date, just say so," Maggie said.

"Clever." He clicked on the About tab and then a short introductory video. In it, Jenn White practically seduced the camera while walking along the beach in a fluttering sundress. She managed to flirt and flaunt while still coming off as professional, and in the process explained in clear, concise terms how MatchStick would arrange matches that stuck.

"Kitschy."

Jackson nodded. "Yeah. I mean, seriously, just ask a girl out for wings and hockey and oh could you also bring your life's work, preferably not in a scrapbook."

"Why are we watching this?"

"Because Jenn White, founder of MatchStick, is Jennifer Winters, tragic victim of Assemblymember Murtaugh's seductions."

Maggie studied the frozen image of her on the screen, then the newspaper picture. Back and forth. Then she shook her head.

"No?" he asked.

"No, I'm stupid. And vain."

"Oh?"

"The story's probably archived online, with a better photo." She took back the laptop, still shaking her head. "And instead I troll for accolades by talking about my stash of newspapers."

"That's okay. That cat lady crack was funny."

Maggie smiled crookedly as she searched the *Times* website. It only took a minute to call up the article. "Ha," she said, spinning the screen to Jackson. It showed a much clearer photograph of Jennifer Winters. The hair was definitely brown, shorter and straighter, and her eyes were the wrong color. But it was her. He was ninety-five-percent sure. Ninety at least.

"What do you think?" he asked.

Maggie leaned over. She'd taken her hair out of her ponytail, and it hung against Jackson's shoulder.

"Looks like a match," she said.

"Yeah. Put in some colored contact lenses, or take some out . . ."

Maggie sat up straight. "So what does that mean?"

"My guess, Connor found out and wanted to talk to you. Maybe he was hoping you'd expose her or maybe he just wanted info, to confirm a hunch."

"So why didn't he show up at the meeting? You think somebody grabbed him?"

"Or he got cold feet, got scared off. You mentioned a whistleblower in the Murtaugh case. I didn't see much in the article."

"Yeah," Maggie said, again taking the computer. After half a minute of clicks, she handed it to him. "My rough notes on the article. Includes what made it into the story and what didn't. It's everything I know."

He read while she fast-forwarded through intermission. As overtime started, Jackson balanced his attention between Maggie's facts and a riveting but scoreless period of hockey. It reached another intermission, and Maggie caught up to real-time before the second overtime period.

"What'd you find?"

"Parry Bilas," Jackson said.

"Right. The whistleblower."

"From what I can tell, he was a software programmer who was going to testify against Murtaugh."

"But then his car ran off the Dumbarton Bridge and he died."

"Ruled an accident despite several reports that he appeared to have been run off the road."

"But they never found the vehicle that supposedly did it," Maggie said.

"Here's the best part," Jackson said. "Parry Bilas wrote the software that Murtaugh's employment agency—technically, the agency he had part ownership in—used to screen applicants. Which to me seems remarkably similar to the role Connor played in MatchStick, designing an algorithm that would match prospective singles to each other. And now he's missing."

"Was Jenn part of this employment agency?"

"It doesn't say. But she was seeing Murtaugh and now she's seeing Kendrick."

"Does he have any interest in MatchStick?"

"No. Not that I know of."

"So what exactly is your theory?"

"I don't know," he said with a sigh. "But this has got to be it, what Connor wanted to see you about. Maybe he knew something more. Or maybe, like I said, he wanted to pick your brain." He sat back, staring at the ceiling.

"So now what?"

"I don't know," he said, turning to look at her. "I'm still new at this. Somehow, I've got to figure out what Connor could have known."

"Have you talked to Jenn?"

"Yeah. She was coy. I doubt asking if she happened to be the same Jennifer who had an affair with a crooked assemblymember will get her to divulge any more information."

"Not likely, no."

"Is there anything else you can remember about the ordeal, anything that isn't in your notes?"

Maggie shook her head. "No. Well, one thing I remember hearing that was odd."

"What?"

"They never found the money."

"What?"

"They found about fifteen grand in a business account Murtaugh co-owned, for the employment agency. But the rest they never located. Figured it was transferred from offshore bank to offshore bank to—"

"Co-owned with who?"

"What?"

"Who co-owned the account? Jenn?"

"No. His business partner."

"Hmm. What's his name?"

"I don't remember. He wasn't involved in the investigation much. Another victim."

"Well, I guess I have research to do. Although, I'm not sure it helps me find Connor. Either . . ."

"Either what?"

"The sedan that was following me."

Maggie furrowed her brow.

"Let's assume that all these connections mean something hinky's going down, that Jenn Winters-White—the link between the two cases—is dirty as a coalminer's pants. If she kidnapped or killed Connor to shut him up, why would she be following me?"

"Who said she was?"

"Who else?"

Maggie shrugged.

"Following me means risking me noticing I'm being followed."

"New at this as you are."

"Right," he said, acknowledging her smirk with one of his own. "I notice I'm being followed, I might confront my followers or call the cops on them or something, which could expose them and thus whoever hired them. It could also suggest to me that I was onto something, because why follow somebody barking up the wrong tree?"

"Okay."

"So if Jenn is up to no good and if she did bump off Connor or has him stashed in a warehouse or something, she'd want to lay low, so to speak, more than she'd want to keep tabs on me. At least, I figure."

"Makes sense."

"But if she doesn't have Connor, if he's in hiding, then she might want to follow me so that I could lead her to him."

"So that's good news, right? He's not a victim of foul play?"

"If my figuring is worth anything. I am a novice."

"Seems solid to me."

"So less important than proving Jenn's guilt is finding Connor and seeing what info he has that could maybe provide proof of criminal activity on her part, as right now all we have is conjecture and circumstantial evidence."

"All right, how do you do that?"

He sighed. "I don't know. I have to think."

"Well, want to watch a little hockey while you think?"

"Do I get another brownie?"

"Sure, eat me out of house and home."

"I'll return the favor sometime. I make killer chocolate chip cookies."

"I'll hold you to that."

"Yes, I'll watch another period. I'm waiting for Hailey to call anyhow."

"Your good-looking lady client?"

"Better than good-looking, and yes."

"Yes, but will she let you eat all her brownies?"

"And lick the batter out of the bowl too."

Chapter Twenty-One

Tuesday, June 18, 2013
4:27 p.m.

MELANIE GWYNN DID not fit Jackson's expectations for a parole officer. She was short, with brown eyes behind thin, square-framed glasses, and dark brown hair pulled into a sloppy but trendy ponytail. She wore a three-quarter-sleeve blazer over a print blouse, Capri pants, and slides. She was younger than he expected—maybe thirty—and cute-ish.

Her desk was a mess, with stacks of paper, uncapped pens, a brown apple core, several flavored Tootsie Roll wrappers, a tall mug of tea, two books turned upside down and propped open, and a laptop. The cubicle wall beside her was tacked full of photos of a woman who could have been a sister, and dogs of various sizes. They were the same color and breed, and Jackson concluded they could have been the same dog over different stages of life. A calendar of peaceful beaches hung crookedly in the midst of them. It was still set to May. Of 2011. Jackson frowned when he saw it, thinking it was the sort of thing one would see in a dream. Or nightmare.

"Please excuse the mess," Gwynn said, nodding at a chair on the opposite side of her desk. "What can I do for you, Mr. Douglas?"

He'd introduced himself on the phone and had already showed her his ID, so he got down to business.

"What can you tell me about Joaquín Padilla?"

Gwynn sighed. "I try to keep a positive attitude, or this business will eat you up. You have to see the good in people, see their potential, or what are you doing here?" she asked, extending her hands. She then folded them in her lap as she sighed again. "I'm also a realist. And unfortunately, Joaquín Padilla is one of those guys who makes it hard to stay positive."

"How so?"

"Because this is the what, fourth time—fifth if you count juvie—that he's been released from prison? And he's a perfect four-for-four at going back." She tipped her head to the side. "You never say never, but . . ."

Jackson nodded. "He got out a week ago?"

"June 12."

"Has he checked in with you yet?"

"Yes, the next day. He's required to check in by phone every day for the first month. So far, he hasn't missed."

"Any issues, any signs of trouble?"

"Not since he got out. But I only met him in person once, and it is admittedly a small sample size. He's due to check in again in person on Thursday."

"What else do you know about him?"

Gwynn narrowed her eyes at Jackson. He tried to figure out if her glasses were cosmetic or not.

"Why don't you tell me what you want to know," she said, "and if I can give you answers, I will."

"Fair enough." He explained his interest in Padilla, his suspicions, the new timeline. He felt like it was the hundredth time he'd recapped it for someone, and found himself doing rote recitation. When he was finished, Gwynn nodded. Then fidgeted with her ponytail. The result was a loose strand she swiped behind her ear.

"You want to know if he killed your family."

"I do."

"I'm not a psychologist, Mr. Douglas."

"I appreciate that, Officer Gwynn, but you also work with ex-cons. You're an admitted realist. You see some of them reform, you see some of them fall back into old habits. You have to be a good judge of character."

She pursed her lips. Then scooted forward to lean her elbows on the table. "Okay, here's the deal. I don't know any of the specifics of the explosion, other than what you told me, so it wouldn't be fair for me to guess whether Padilla was involved or not. And you know the timeline, so my telling you 'it could fit' won't help. But here's what I can tell you. Joaquín Padilla is a bad person. He's kept his nose clean for the last few days, and he's kept his nose clean for longer periods of time before. But there has never been any sign of remorse, aside from what was necessary to con a parole board or meet some requirement of the state. He's unconscionable. With the list of crimes, convictions, and charges on his record, nothing would surprise me. Yes, Padilla could be your guy. But I have no hard evidence to suggest that, nor do I have any evidence to suggest otherwise."

Jackson nodded. "From what you know, what does your gut tell you?"

She pursed her lips again.

"I'm sorry, I'm putting you in a hard position."

"No, I get it. I've seen people where you are, Mr. Douglas." She sighed and paused, as if searching for words. "Don't quote me on this. Don't base your decisions on this. But with what I know of Joaquín Padilla, if he's a suspect in a crime of any sort—as much as I hate to say it—my gut tells me he's probably guilty."

Jackson nodded again.

"I wish I could give you something more concrete, one way or the other."

"I appreciate what you can give me."

She sat back.

"Is Padilla living here in San Diego?"

"As a peace officer for the County of San Diego, I'm not allowed to divulge that information."

Jackson met Gwynn's brown eyes, sending the message back to her. Understood.

"Before his arrest, he had an apartment in South Park, correct?"

"That's what I read in his file, yes."

"Do you know what happened to the place while he was in prison?"

"Yes," she said, reaching for her laptop. She tapped at the keys for a minute. "Padilla was actually being evicted from his apartment at the end of the month, and had moved in with his sister."

"He has a sister?"

"Jacinta. She moved to Phoenix this past winter."

"She leave a forwarding address?"

"She did."

"But you can't tell it to me."

"I'm sorry."

"Don't be."

"His possessions were moved to a storage facility here in San Diego, paid for by his sister. He was going to reclaim them after he met with me last week."

Jackson nodded.

"Jacinta. Her last name Padilla as well?"

Gwynn looked down. "No."

"Let me guess," Jackson said with a flat grin. "You can't reveal it to me."

"I shouldn't have even given you her first name. I'm sorry."

"I get it." He sighed. "Padilla have a job?"

"He was supposed to report on that at our next meeting. I gave him lines on a couple possibilities. I can't—"

"Tell me where. Okay." He took a breath. "Thank you for your time."

Her head slightly to the side, Gwynn probed her cheek with her tongue. Then she said, "Would you like a cup of coffee?"

Jackson looked at her, wondering how exactly she meant that.

"I ask because I need to reheat my tea," she said, reaching for her mug. "I'm supposed to lock my computer and remove all files from my desk and have them secured if I leave to go to the bathroom or get a cup of coffee, but it only takes two minutes, so I usually just dart off and save myself the hassle." Her eyes went to her laptop, then to Jackson.

He nodded.

"Coffee? I can answer any additional questions when I get back?"

"Sure, that would be great. Black."

She smiled as she stood, then edged around the desk and disappeared from the cubicle.

Jackson waited a moment, looked around to see if anyone else was watching, and glanced at the ceiling to see if he spied a hidden camera. He didn't, and he got up and walked around her desk.

The laptop was open to Joaquín Padilla's personnel file, showing his demographic info, his lengthy criminal record, and his past and present places of residence. According to the file, Padilla's current residence was a dive motel out by the airport. Jackson memorized the address, then quickly scanned the file for anything else. He found the full name of Padilla's sister, Jacinta Alomar, and a phone number. Then he ducked back around and was in his seat when Gwynn returned with a steaming mug of coffee.

"Thank you, Officer Gwynn," he said, and they again made eye contact for a moment.

Then she sat back down and jostled the teabag in her mug. "Anything else I can do for you, Mr. Douglas?"

"You said Padilla has to check in with you daily?"

"Yes, by phone."

"What's that entail?"

"Not much," she said, taking a drink. "I ask if he's left the county, if he's sober and clean—part of his deal—if he's broken any of the terms of his parole. He tells me no, which proves nothing but satisfies the state. He agrees to call back, and that's it."

"Do you trace the calls?"

"We can, but we don't, not unless there's a reason to."

Jackson nodded. He tested the coffee. It was hot and bitter, so typical coffee.

"Thursday he's due to appear in my office by five. I ask a few more questions then, but other than his being here to prove he's not in trouble at that moment, it doesn't give us any real assurances that he isn't falling back into a life of crime."

"I see." He took a final drink of his coffee, then set the two-thirds-empty mug on a rare open section of Gwynn's desk. He handed her a business card. "If you think of anything else, would you give me a call?"

She took the card and nodded. "I will. I wish you the best, Mr. Douglas."

They stood and shook hands. "Thanks again, Officer Gwynn." He winked. "Especially for the coffee."

Gwynn smiled and nodded, and Jackson exited the Probation and Parole Office to more rain.

Chapter Twenty-Two

Friday, May 13, 2011
8:06 a.m.

JACKSON HAD NO qualms about showing up at his grandpa's so early, because to Leroy Douglas, it wasn't early. It was to Jackson, who had stayed at Maggie's apartment until the Rangers triumphed on a triple overtime power play goal. During that time, he'd played phone tag with Hailey, and he owed her a call yet this morning, updating her on his and Maggie's discovery—namely, that he thought Connor had discovered a connection between Jenn White and the Assemblymember Murtaugh scandal in San Jose in 2008 and something related to MatchStick or Mayor Kendrick or both now. What that something was, and where Connor had gone or been taken, were part of the reason Jackson was swinging by to see his grandpa. In addition to being his oldest pal, Leroy was also a sounding board whenever Jackson had issues in life, and he concluded cases as a private investigator were part of that.

With a small box of donuts from Krispy Kreme in his hand, Jackson left the Granada at the end of Bora Bora Way in Marina del Rey. After his wife's death, Leroy had sold his house and bought an old houseboat, which he'd then named *Marsha* in her honor. It was more house than boat, docked at the southern end of the marina, providing Leroy the solitude from which to fish and think and, Jackson noted with a wince, listen to opera music.

It was a familiar number, and not from Saturday morning cartoons. But Jackson couldn't place it, and he gave up trying. He hesitated for a moment before boarding at the stern. Something about the way the boat rocked ever so slightly in the water and against the rubber dock bumpers bugged him. No, not bugged him, but sent some chain of thoughts rampaging through his brain. The problem was, they were moving too fast for him to catch them, and he didn't know what they were even about. It happened sometimes—an experience similar to déjà vu. Every once in a while it was his subconscious connecting dots for him. More often than not, it was an irrelevant connection of dots he didn't know or care existed.

Shrugging it off, Jackson stepped onto the boat and rapped on the screen door. Leroy was in the kitchen, oblivious to Jackson's presence, as he hovered over his range. At seventy-four, Leroy looked a decade younger. He was still in good shape, still had a nearly full head of mostly brown hair, still had all his faculties. He wore a plain gray T-shirt and faded blue jeans, which was his wardrobe for everything but church and weddings. A retired pastor, he'd seen his share of both.

"Don't tell me you're just eating breakfast," Jackson said as he walked through the boat's living room. Small, it was comfortable in a rustic way, and if not for the water out the windows, gave no indications it wasn't permanently attached to something.

Leroy spun around, then exhaled heavily. "Good ga-rief," he said, making it two syllables. "You trying to give me a heart attack?"

"I knocked, but what with somebody butchering hogs next door, I can understand why you didn't hear it."

"That's cute." Leroy reached for a remote control, the extent of his technological aptitude, and muted the opera.

"A happy ending for a change," Jackson said.

"Even cuter. You want some eggs?"

"You're just getting to breakfast now?"

"I've been having sciatica pain lately. Can't sleep."

Jackson frowned as he set the donuts on the counter. He straddled a stool. "So how does that make you late?"

"Because when I finally do get to sleep, I need a few extra hours. Plus, it's all I can do to get myself out of bed. What are these?"

"Long johns."

"Beats toast," Leroy said, twisting shut an open bag of bread. He bound it with a rubber band—his quirk—and heaved it to the corner of the counter. "No on the eggs?"

"If you can spare a couple."

Leroy turned back and cracked two more eggs into the skillet. His method was to cook at high heat under glass, stopping when the bottom was just short of burned. It left the eggs brown and crispy. And delicious.

"What's new, kiddo?"

"Can you keep a secret?"

"I haven't let slip your parents are getting you the *Magnum, P.I.* box set for your birthday, have I?"

"Now who's cute?"

"What's your secret?"

"And I have the entire box set, by the way."

"The secret?"

"I'm a private investigator."

Leroy cast a cockeyed glance at his grandson. "For real?"

"Quit at Bauer & Bauer a couple weeks ago and got my license last week. I'm official."

"You are serious."

"Even got my first case."

"Oh?"

Jackson started explaining, but stopped to grab forks and juice from the refrigerator as Leroy plated the eggs.

"You sure you should be telling me this?" Leroy asked as Jackson sat down. Leroy stood, saying simply, "Sciatica," when Jackson looked his way. "Don't you have client-investigator confidence or something?"

"Hmm. Yeah, I suppose so. But you're an associate."

"That a paying gig?"

"This job's on the house, so no."

Leroy nodded as he cut into his first egg. Given the crispy nature, it took some doing. "So it's a girl client then, huh?"

"Did I say that?"

"I doubt you're doing charity work for some dude."

He sighed. "Yeah." He took a bite of his eggs and resumed explaining. He concluded by running his theory that Connor had wanted to confirm a suspicion about Jenn, and thus contacted Maggie, but something had caused him to rabbit before getting the chance.

"Rabbit?"

"Run, make a break for it."

"Hmm."

"You think not?"

Leroy shrugged. "Beats me. I'm just an old man who can't bend."

"You should see a doctor."

Leroy waved. "I've been putting heat on it. I've had it before, just never quite this bad." He winced as he wandered around the counter to turn off the range. So his faculties were waning slightly.

"So where'd this guy bunny off to then?"

"Rabbit, and that's the question."

Leroy consumed half a donut in one bite, then nearly died from a coughing fit.

"Maybe shove the whole thing in next time."

"Why would I need a doctor when I have you?"

"Just want my grandpa to make it to my thirtieth birthday."

"Speaking of, I don't think I'm going to be able to make it tomorrow, seeing as how I can't sit."

"You could lay down in the backseat. But, I'm roped into taking Hillary now, so count your blessings."

"You're taking Hillary?"

"Long story," Jackson said with a wave and a scoop of eggs.

"You'd better make nice with her, kiddo. She's not going anywhere."

"Yeah, don't remind me."

"She has her rough edges, but she's also got some very good qualities. Focus on those instead."

"Yeah," Jackson said, absent any conviction. He used a bite of donut (just a quarter) to change gears. "I can call Mom. Maybe they can come up here instead."

"Don't bother. I'll make it next time. These bouts never last more than a few days or so."

"I'll save you some cake."

"Counting on it. Where are you eating anyhow?"

"Some place called Carl's or Carol's. Apparently has the best Mexican food in the county."

Leroy held his stomach. "Maybe it's for the better anyhow."

"Hey, yeah, how do you, uh, you know if you can't bend?"

"Yeah, well, we haven't gotten to that point yet."

They both finished, and before Jackson could clear his plate, Leroy had swiped it and taken it to the sink. He rinsed their plates and forks, then set them aside to wash later. "So what's on your docket today?"

"Seeing if I can track down Connor." He frowned. "Where would you hide if you thought some evil black widow was after you?"

"A spider?"

"No, a woman taking advantage of her man, in this case the mayor."

"Hmm. I suppose I'd hide right here."

"Right here?"

"No one's going to find me."

"Yeah, unless you keep blaring Brünnhilde all day."

"Do you need a straight man for this P.I. thing?"

"You'd never qualify. Where do you think I got my sass from?"

"And your mother will never let me live it down."

They chatted for another half hour, then Jackson said goodbye to his grandpa and left the houseboat, un-paused opera music serenading him as he walked to the Granada. He turned back with a shake of the head and a smile, feeling a little sad that Leroy wouldn't be joining the family for Jackson's birthday dinner the next day. And serving as a catalyst for the two-hour ride down with Hillary. In a way, Jackson envied his grandpa— sciatica or not aside, he was old enough that he could get away playing the solitude card and just hanging out and avoiding situations or people on his houseboat.

Jackson stopped with his hand on the door handle.

Houseboat.

He nearly dropped his cell phone as he dug it out of his pocket, and his fingers shook as he dialed the number.

"This is Hailey," her voice said after several rings. He sighed, knowing he'd gotten her voicemail for the third time since she'd left him one last night. Her call had come during a furious, frenetic finish to the second overtime, and a guy couldn't answer the phone during that.

Her greeting ended, followed by a beep, and Jackson spoke. "Hailey, it's Jackson. Call me as soon as you get this. I think I know where Connor might be."

*   *   *

4:10 p.m.

"WHERE IS he?"

"Get in."

Hailey practically dove into the passenger seat of the Granada. "What about my car?"

"Leave it."

"Jackson, what's going on?"

He watched her door close, then accelerated. "There's a tan sedan parked about three back," he said as he eased into traffic.

"So?"

"So, it followed me from my house last night. Now it's back."

"Who is it?"

"If I had to guess, one of Jenn's minions."

"What? Jackson, you're not making sense. You're still not making sense."

He sighed. He'd left her two more messages that morning, neither of which had been terribly coherent. The fact was, he was nervous. This was his first case, possibly his first break in a case, and he had spent the morning second-guessing his hunch. It was just a hunch, one based on deductive reasoning, but a hunch nonetheless. Hunches were great for Magnum when it was ten to and the episode had to wrap, but in real life, they were very susceptible to crapping out. And as much as Jackson wanted to be right for his own ego, he really wanted to be right for Hailey's sake. The thought of buoying her hopes only to have them dashed made him nauseous.

Hailey had called back at noon, explaining that she had been forced due to a coworker's illness to follow up her Thursday night shift with an 8-4 on Friday. She had explained this to Jackson's voicemail, as he had been in the bathroom at the time. Instead of playing more phone tag, he had opted to meet her after work, as she had suggested. Seeing the sedan had changed his plans, and his primary focus now was on losing the tail, again.

"Give me a minute," Jackson said.

Hailey turned around in her seat, looking out the rear window.

"You may want to buckle up."

"Huh?"

"Seatbelt."

She fastened it, and no sooner had she than Jackson made a hard left turn, toward the ocean. He racked his brain, trying to think of ways his P.I. heroes had dodged tails without using the high-powered engine under the hood of their sports car.

He made another left, and Hailey braced herself against the door. "Why would Jenn have someone following us?"

"Because she wants to find Connor too."

"She does?"

"Hang on!" Glancing both ways, Jackson gunned the engine through a red light. It earned him a shrill blast on the horn, but did the trick. The tan sedan was forced to stop, not by the light, but by traffic.

Hailey took several deep breaths. "Jackson."

"Hang on," he said again, making a pair of quick turns, now heading back the way they had come.

"Where are we going?"

"Back to O'Bannon's."

"What?"

"We stand out like a sore thumb in this car. Plus, it's the last place they'll look. We bought ourselves a little time, but if we keep heading south and east, there's a good chance they'll spot us." He looked at her purse, in her lap. "Get your keys."

"What? Oh, right."

A minute later, they were back at O'Bannon's, a small bistro on 5th Street. It had a side parking lot with room for maybe a dozen cars. Hailey's BMW was in the back, and Jackson pulled in and parked beside it, shielded partially from the road by a new-model Jeep.

"If it's okay with you, I'll drive."

She handed him the keys, and they got out. He locked the Granada with one hand, beeping open the Beemer with the other. They quickly got in, and with looks all around, Jackson turned north on 5th. A few blocks later, he turned east on California, and not seeing any signs of the tan sedan, began to relax.

"Are we clear?"

"I think so. They'd have to think to double back, have to see the Granada and conclude we're in your car, and then find your car. We should be where we're going by then."

"Where are we going?"

He looked at her. "That depends. Where does Christine's new husband keep his boat?"

Chapter Twenty-Three

SAN DIEGO BAY had been turned into a choppy, roiling cauldron by high winds and driving rain. The gray waters were speckled with white heads of foam that exploded as they crashed against the jetty. And that was inside the marina, sheltered from the bay proper by the obviously named Shelter Island, a sandbank built up into solid ground with fill dredged from the bay. Hundreds of sailboats, sport fishers, pleasure cruisers, and mid-sized yachts rolled and danced back and forth, their mooring lines playing a game of tug of war with the docks, which creaked and groaned in protest, the noise caught up in the maelstrom.

Jackson watched it all from the parking lot of a small apartment building on the marina's north shore. Nightfall was still a few hours away, but already the gloom was taking over the city, its skyline barely visible behind him. His eyes ran up the hill in front of him, the massive promontory known as Point Loma. His thoughts went to the cemetery perched atop its ridge, then to another cemetery on another dreary day.

Finally, he forced himself out of the car. He was drenched in no time, but made no extra haste in reaching the overhanging canopy of the nearest of two apartment buildings. He paused for a moment under the overhang of the stairway leading to the second floor, then climbed the stairs. He hesitated again before knocking on door A14. No one answered, and he cut his eyes to the apartment's sole window, a large triple casement job facing east. Vertical blinds were drawn but not closed, enabling him to see inside, in theory. The lights were off, and even with the storm, it was brighter outside than inside, and he couldn't see much.

He hated apartments, mostly due to their transient nature. He had no idea when someone was working, sleeping, had moved out, or was inside burning tree and didn't want to be disturbed. He shrugged, figuring if she could ignore one knock, she could ignore two. He banged on the door again and gave it another minute. Then he turned to go.

"Can I help you?"

He turned over his shoulder to see that a woman had just climbed the steps at the other end of the corridor. His eyebrows went up. She was soaked, from her blond-brown hair in two stubby ponytails to her ASICS. She wore a black sports bra and matching shorts, and she was breathing deeply but not gasping.

"What, you never see a woman in Spandex?" she asked.

"Not when it's practically snowing."

She huffed. "Californians are such wimps. What do you want?"

"I'm looking for Mira Austin."

"You found her. Now what?"

Jackson reached for his wallet and his license. "My name's Jackson Douglas. I'm a private investigator. Wondering if I could ask you a few questions."

"A P.I.?"

"That's right."

Mira shook her head. "If it's about the boat, it's not for sale anymore. I've paid all my bills, so you're not here to serve me. And if this is about my ex, he's got a place up in Pacific Beach. Try the phone book."

"Well, Blake Shelton, it's not about any of that. I was hoping to ask you about the incident with Petty Officer Grabel a few years back."

Mira sighed like a jet on takeoff at nearby North Island. She studied Jackson with dark brown eyes for a few seconds. "Wait here," she said, leaving him little choice as she punched a code into her door and promptly closed it behind her. She returned two minutes later, her hair free from the ponies and now a thatched mess, a towel over her shoulder, and a plastic bottle of blue liquid in her hand.

"You training for a triathlon or just the mad at the world type?" Jackson asked.

"You butter up everybody you want to ask questions to like this?"

"Sorry, I just didn't expect to find anybody jogging in this weather."

"I wasn't jogging," she said with disdain, dabbing her face with the towel. It may have been a shirt. "I was running. And I'm going to be on *American Ninja Warrior*."

"I'll have to tune in."

She eyed him as she swigged her electrolytes. Then she set the bottle on the railing, dabbed her arms and stomach, and then slipped the towel/shirt over her head and arms. A shirt then, long-sleeved, with some faded corporate logo on the chest.

"What about Grabel?" she asked.

"I understand you spoke with Ike and Juliet Haywood about her sexual assault."

"Yep."

"They're old friends of mine, and gave me a heads up."

"Why'd they do that?"

"Because the man who assaulted Petty Officer Grabel, Joaquín Padilla, is a suspect in the murder of my parents and brother."

Mira's eyes widened. "You're serious?"

"I am."

She took another swig. "I'm sorry."

"Thanks."

Then she shook her head. "What do you want from me?"

"I was hoping you could spare a few minutes to tell me everything you told them—everything about that night." He shrugged. "I'd rather have it firsthand."

Mira sighed as she turned and leaned against the railing. "There isn't much to tell. I was working out and listening to the Pads get their clocks cleaned, and I took my buds out after the first inning," she said, gesturing at her ears. "I went to the fridge to get something to drink, and when I came back to my stair-climber, I see this black pickup whip into the lot on two wheels." She shrugged. "I didn't think anything of it; there's always some hotshot driving like he's in Monoco around here. Then the cops came maybe forty-five minutes later and started asking questions. My wonderful husband, who was tarring his lungs when the truck arrived, spoke with them."

"And he gave them the wrong time?"

"Tim can't read. Dyslexia. And a little bit of being stupid too."

"He said it was 7:23 when Padilla arrived. And you said 7:32?"

"Ballpark. I know the inning ended at the bottom of the hour, because I looked up to see how long the shelling had taken. It was a minute or two later when I saw the truck. If Tim said 7:23, I figure it must have been 7:32."

"Any idea why he noted the time?"

She shrugged. "Better question is why the jack-wad didn't get an analog watch since he can't read numbers."

Jackson nodded. "Did you see anything else, other than Padilla's truck arrive?"

"No. I didn't know it was his truck until I heard the cops ask about it. I took a shower shortly after it arrived and didn't see anything else."

"If you don't mind my asking, why didn't you speak up and correct your husband, especially at Padilla's trial?"

Mira set her jaw. "I didn't say anything at the trial because I figured Padilla was guilty as sin and I didn't want Tim's testimony that established his presence to come into question. What difference did it make when the turd arrived? He raped that lady. Or tried to. From what I understand, she about split his lip." She paused to laugh under her breath at the thought. "The other reason is that my dear husband was an overbearing, domineering jerk. I'd learned long ago not to cross him."

"You don't seem like the type to take a backseat to anyone. *American Ninja Warrior* and all that."

"Yeah well, I'd finally had enough, like that J. Lo movie. So one day when he was giving me crap, I reared back and broke his jaw, then told him we were getting divorced. He tried to sue me for assault, but when I showed the judge all the pictures of bruises from the times he'd roughed me up, they laughed him out of court. I got everything—apartment, car, boat. Last I heard, Tim's working the nightshift at some chemical factory. Serves the bum right."

"Yeah, I guess so."

"Is there anything else? I should do some cooldown."

"Not unless you have anything else to add."

"No. Like I said, I was in the shower and don't know anything else but this Padilla's truck arrived at 7:30, give or take a couple minutes."

"Thanks for your time."

He turned to go.

"Hey. What's all this got to do with your family?"

He faced her again. "That same night, there was an explosion at the restaurant where my family was eating. Padilla seemed good for it, but there's no way he could have been there and been here in time to assault Petty Officer Grabel."

"Unless he didn't get here until later than originally thought."

"Right."

Mira nodded. "Well, the guy's a piece of garbage. I hope you nail him to the wall."

Jackson nodded in reply as he started to turn back toward the stairs. "I intend to."

Chapter Twenty-Four

Friday, May 13, 2011
5:50 p.m.

LONG BEACH'S SHORELINE Marina was located just south of downtown Long Beach, right on the open ocean, and across the mouth of the Los Angeles River from the hustle and bustle of the port. Close to Shoreline Park, the Aquarium of the Pacific, the convention center, and dozens of shops and eateries, it was the perfect place to dock a boat. With slips for more than 1,700 recreational craft, it would also make a pretty good place to hide out.

Jackson had explained as much to Hailey on the drive across town, which thanks to traffic had taken the better part of an hour. There was nothing to indicate they had been followed in her BMW.

"So let me get this straight," Hailey had said. "Your grandpa, who lives on a houseboat, says if he ever has to hide from somebody, he'd hide out by staying at home on his boat, and you conclude that's what Connor did?"

"It wasn't just that. I also remembered the photo at his place, at his mom's wedding. You said it was one of the best days of your life. Seeing as how you both have the photo, I figured he might have thought so too."

"That's it?"

"It is a hunch. Worth checking, don't you think?"

"Yeah, I suppose."

"And I'm working off the theory that he wasn't kidnapped, meaning his disappearance was his idea. He's not answering his phone, which means he wants to be off the grid. Not much more off the grid than a boat amongst a thousand others."

She'd chewed on that for a while. "Okay," she'd said after several minutes, while they were bogged in traffic on the 405, "why wasn't he kidnapped?"

"Because if somebody had taken him, why are they following me?"

"You think someone is using you to find Connor?"

"I do."

"And you think it's Jenn?"

"It fits," he said, going through all the details about San Jose, Assemblymember Murtaugh, Parry Bilas the whistleblower, the photo of "Jennifer Winters," and the casualness with which she and the mayor were searching for Connor.

"Wait. You don't think my dad's involved in this, do you?"

"No. Not intentionally."

"What does that mean?"

"I think this is what Jenn does—uses influential men to get what she wants."

"And what does she want?"

"That I don't know. But I'm guessing Connor might."

Hailey shook her head. "I thought Jenn White was the victim in San Jose."

"She was, or so it looked. But I'm guessing that was all part of her plan. Set Murtaugh up, play the innocent, victimized intern, and skate with most of two hundred large. Dye her hair, change her last name, and run it again here."

"Run what?"

"I don't know. I can guess, but that's all it is."

"Guess."

He looked at her.

"We're playing a hunch, right? Play it out."

He sighed. "Murtaugh's scam involved an employment agency that compiled all sorts of data on people—complex personal profiles—and then used that info to blackmail them, extort them, rip them off."

"And now Jenn run's a dating service that compiles the same information."

"You're pretty good at this," he said.

"Why Dad?"

"He has influence. She can use him to grease the wheels, direct favors. And, I'm guessing, she can dump this all in his lap and play the unsuspecting girlfriend who was taken advantage of again."

"I'm going to be sick."

"It's just a guess."

Hailey mulled for another minute. "But it's also possible he's complicit, isn't it?"

Jackson didn't answer.

"It's possible Jenn and Murtaugh were partners and she left him high and dry, and now she's got a new partner."

Jackson nodded. "Yeah, that's possible. In theory. I don't know your dad very well, but if you say he's innocent, I'm inclined to take your word for it."

"He is," Hailey said, but absent much conviction.

After the briefest of internal debates, Jackson concluded it wouldn't be out of bounds to reach for her hand, and did so. He gave it a quick squeeze. "We'll get to the bottom of this, okay? No need to worry about what might be."

She forced a smile, and he withdrew his hand.

"Thank you, Jackson."

They'd driven the rest of the way in silence, parking on the breakwater that formed the south and west edges of the marina. Before they got out, Jackson reached into the waistband of his pants and pulled out his new Glock 19 pistol.

"What is that for?" Hailey asked.

"Caution. And to earn Connor's trust."

She frowned. "What? How?"

"Think about it, Hailey. Why didn't he call you? You two are close, and yet he ran and never contacted you, never left you any sort of message. The only reason he wouldn't do that is because he wasn't sure he could trust you."

"No, that's crazy. He would never think that."

"Maybe not normally. But if he feared his boss—who is also his stepfather's girlfriend—enough to go into hiding, he might not be thinking clearly. Paranoia can do strange things to people."

"He'll trust me, Jackson."

"This will make sure."

"How?"

"Because I'll show it to him, letting him know that if I wanted to hurt him, I could."

She shook her head.

"It's a last resort."

"You won't need it. And maybe he never contacted me because he didn't want me caught up in whatever's going on."

"Yeah, that could be too."

"Now can we go?"

"Yeah."

Jackson returned the gun to his waistband and got out, squinting against the late afternoon sun that reflected off the mouth of the river and cast the starboard side of the *Queen Mary*—permanently moored across the channel—in shadow. On the other side of the Beemer, Hailey fastened her hair into a makeshift ponytail. She was still dressed as an O'Bannon's hostess, which meant a black, knee-length skirt and a purple, cap-sleeved blouse. And heels, which she left in the car.

"This way," she said, leading the way barefoot down the sidewalk and onto one of three docks extending east from the breakwater.

"Does Connor have a gun?"

"What? No, he's scared of them."

"What about Shane, on his boat?"

"No, I don't think so."

Jackson nodded and followed a pace behind Hailey. He swept his eyes over the marina and the parking lot, even though he was sure they hadn't been followed. A few boats were making their way in or out of the marina, and across the numerous docks, a handful of other people were taking advantage of a gorgeous day to clean, tidy up, or prepare for a voyage. But the immediate vicinity was quiet.

Twelve slips along, Hailey stopped and faced a thirty-foot sloop. A chrome railing rimmed a clean white hull, and a single mast jutted from its sleek surface into the sky. Blue cursive letters identified the boat as *Hey Baby*, and Jackson immediately deduced that Shane Stoeckl was in his forties and still trying to be in his twenties. Else a Gwen Stefani fan. So in his forties and still trying to be in his twenties.

Jackson and Hailey walked between *Hey Baby* and a slightly larger boat beside it, stopping by a small platform at the stern. Water lapping against the hull and the squawking of gulls and distant ship's horns were the only sounds.

"Connor," Hailey called without any prompting from Jackson. "Connor, it's Hailey. Are you here?"

Nothing.

She reached for Jackson's hand and used it to steady herself as she climbed aboard *Hey Baby*. Jackson followed her.

"Connor," she called again. She stepped around the boom. "We know what's going on. You're safe with us."

There was a thump from inside the cabin, then the door opened and a head peeked out.

It was Connor, Jackson knew from the photo above his desk, but barely. The hair was a frazzled mess, going in every direction. His face was long and gray, covered in the beginning of a scraggly beard. His eyes were bloodshot as they latched first onto Jackson.

"Who are you?"

"He's with me," Hailey said. "Connor, are you okay?"

He didn't answer, instead darting his eyes left and right, squinting and turning away as they felt the full force of the sun. "How—how did you find me?"

"We've been looking for you. We were scared to death." She embraced him as he stood atop the cabin stairs, his eyes still on Jackson. He pushed her back.

"Who's he?"

"A private investigator."

"No," Connor said, shaking his head. "No, you shouldn't have come here."

"Connor, relax. We know about Jenn."

"What? How . . ."

"When you didn't show up for work, I hired Jackson to find you. Well, I didn't hire him. He's doing it for free. But he figured out where you were."

"I found Maggie's name at your apartment," Jackson said.

"Who's Maggie?"

"Sorry, Anne Magstadt. I spoke with her, looked at the different stories she'd written, and saw the one about Assemblymember Murtaugh and Jenn White—then Jennifer Winters. I put two and two together."

Connor's eyes flitted all around. They settled back on Hailey. "How do you know you can trust him?"

"I told you I hired him."

"No, you said he's working for free. Why?"

"Because he's new in the business."

"So what, you feel sorry for him?"

"No, he . . . offered to help."

Connor shook his head, his eyes wide. "No. Hailey—"

Jackson drew his gun, then quickly ejected the magazine. He tossed the magazine to Connor, who caught it reflexively. "If I was going to hurt you, I would have." He extended the gun to Hailey, then sat on the gunwale of the boat. "I know you're scared, and I get it. What can I do to set your mind at ease?"

Connor looked down at the magazine in his hand.

"Connor, please," Hailey said. "We want to help."

He breathed deeply, then leaned back against the doorpost. "You can't."

"Why not?" Jackson asked.

"Because I have no proof."

"Proof of what?" Hailey asked.

Connor's eyes darted between them. "Jenn is ripping off MatchStick clients."

"How so?"

"I don't know exactly. That's sort of the problem."

Hailey sat down on the bench at the stern. "Tell us."

Connor sighed, then sat opposite Jackson on the starboard gunwale. He squinted into the sun, then dipped his head out of its rays.

"Friday night I was doing some standard adjustments on the algorithm MatchStick uses to match clients based on a variety of profile questions. Aside from the mathematical component, that also includes analyzing profile responses in relation to successful or unsuccessful matches. Jenn provides me that data, sanitized so I don't know actual names, social security numbers, addresses, that sort of thing. And Destiny and Meredith, the matchmakers, also analyze it and give me their feedback. So Friday, I'm going through all this, and the numbers weren't coming out."

"Weren't coming out how?" Hailey asked.

"Percentages. I tallied all clients—successful matches, unsuccessful matches, pending matches, clients yet to be matched. And they weren't coming out. I looked at them half a dozen times, then asked Jenn to resend me the data. I assumed somehow a portion of it hadn't been copied the first time. But when she sent it to me Friday night, it still wasn't adding up. I was missing five to seven percent of the data, which threw off all the percentages, which would totally mess up my algorithm."

Jackson nodded. So far, Connor's story matched what he'd been told by others, including Jenn.

"Saturday morning, I was still stymied. I figured somehow Jenn had sent me insufficient data, maybe by accident, but maybe on purpose too. I thought it was possible she was cooking the data so that failed matches weren't included."

"Why would she do that?" Hailey asked. "Wouldn't that throw off your algorithm and mess with their success rate?"

"Ultimately, yeah. But it was just a thought. Anyhow, there's usually nobody in the office on the weekends, so I went in and accessed the data myself."

"Off the server?" Jackson asked.

"Yeah. I patched in a hacker buddy of mine so that I could see the raw data, no redaction. And that's when I found my hunch was correct. Approximately six percent of the data had been excluded from what Jenn sent me, and all of them were in the Fail category—matches that hadn't worked out. I mean every one, from all different demographics." For the first time during his tale, he made eye contact with Jackson. "There's no way that could be an accident. That means someone had to have excluded the data—either Jenn, Destiny, or Meredith."

"I still don't get why," Hailey said. "I mean, sure, you'd want to hide that from the public maybe, but not you. Else your algorithm would be based off an inaccurate sample and would be skewed."

"I know, it didn't make sense. But we downloaded the full set of data so I could analyze it. I didn't dare go to Jenn because I thought she was most likely the one responsible, and I wanted to analyze it and see what was going on before I did anything."

"What time was this on Saturday?" Jackson asked.

"Mid-morning. Ten, eleven."

That fit with the time his neighbor had seen his car leave the apartment parking lot.

"The more I thought about it, I realized that if this data had been excluded for any period of time, my algorithm was already off. MatchStick had been defrauding its clientele. I mean, this was criminal activity, not just unethical."

"Did you find anything in the data?"

"Yeah. I spent the afternoon analyzing it and found that all of these 'fail' responses hadn't just experienced a bad match. They had crashed and burned. They reported all sorts of disasters, from dates who stole their wallet or purse to seemingly promising relationships that ended when they realized their life savings had been cleaned out. At first I thought they had been excluded because of their spectacularly bad experiences. But story after story was the same—every one of them had been ripped off or swindled in some way. And then I saw another similarity—they had dated a lot of the same people."

"You mean each other?" Hailey asked.

"No. Others from the system. That happens now and again," he said to Jackson, "where one match doesn't work, and we pair somebody with someone else in the database. But I found a small handful of clients who had been matched with eight, nine, ten of these 'fail' responses." He ran a hand through his hair, which, given its current condition, didn't do much to mess it up. "I knew then something was up—some sort of racket or something—and it was worse than I'd thought."

He stood up and paced. "I was panicked. I'd stumbled on something bad. That's when I remembered a story I'd read in the paper a few years back." He looked at Jackson. "I've got a pretty good memory. Stuff sticks."

"Me too."

"I looked back and found the article, written by Anne Magstadt, about a San Jose assemblymember who took advantage of clients in an employment agency in much the same way. I knew it wasn't a coincidence when I reread the story and saw he had an intern named Jennifer, and she looked just like Jenn but with darker hair. And then I read about the guy who died—the 'accident.'" He shook his head. "I panicked. I didn't know what to do. I called Anne, hoping she could give me more details—confirm my suspicions or show me I was wrong."

"Why didn't you meet with her?" Hailey asked.

"She was busy that day, and I was scared. Jenn had seemed suspicious when she sent me the data the second time, and she'd already called me a few times to check in. I thought maybe my phone was bugged or something. We agreed to meet Sunday morning, but I was going crazy. So I went back to the office Saturday night, looking for more evidence."

"What kind of evidence?" Jackson asked.

"I didn't know. I patched my hacker friend in again. I thought maybe he could check logs or something and see who was responsible. But when we logged in, the data was gone."

"What?" Hailey asked.

"It had been wiped. All the failed responses—that six percent. They were gone."

"Jenn."

"I didn't know yet. I had my guy trace the login that wiped the data, and he traced the IP back to Arnie's office."

"Dad?"

He nodded, biting his lip.

Hailey's mouth opened but nothing came out but a stammer.

"I was really freaked," Connor said.

"Dad?" she managed again.

"I didn't know what to think. Was he behind it all and using Jenn? Was she using him? I didn't know what to do, but knew I had the only copy of evidence on my flash drive." He sighed. "I left in a dither, and then saw somebody following me on the way home."

Jackson sat forward. "Who?"

"I don't know."

"What kind of car?"

"I couldn't tell. Just headlights that stuck with me. I got on the freeway and lost them in traffic, but my hands were shaking so bad I could hardly drive." He sat back down, rubbing his hands together. "When I got back to my apartment, I was so worked up I decided to go for a walk to try to clear my mind. I was gone maybe fifteen minutes, and when I got back, there were two guys going through my place."

"Going through?" Jackson asked.

"They were tossing it. And one of them was Danny."

"Who's Danny?"

"He works for Jenn. Security or something. I've seen him around a few times. I slammed the door on the other guy and made a break for it. I had just enough of a head start, apparently."

"What time was this?" Jackson interrupted.

"Nine-thirty?"

He nodded.

"I ran until I couldn't run, then walked maybe five or six more blocks. I caught a taxi at Lincoln Boulevard and took it to LAX and then another from there to here. I didn't know where else to go."

"It was quick thinking," Hailey said.

"How'd you get in?"

"I know Shane's code."

Jackson nodded again.

"I didn't know who I could trust. I didn't know if your dad was somehow involved. I didn't know if Jenn had power over him, or could use him or you to find me. I didn't know if Anne had turned me in. And I had no proof."

"The flash drive?"

"I plugged it into the computer before going on a walk." He sighed. "If I tried going to the cops, it would be my word against hers." He sighed and shook his head, almost on the verge of tears. "It still is. I have nothing."

Hailey got up and sat next to him, her arm around his shoulders. She raised her head to look at Jackson. "He's right. We have no proof."

Jackson wanted to correct her, to point out Jenn's area of vulnerability or devise some clever way to expose her actions. But instead he nodded, having to admit that Hailey was right. They had nothing but conjecture on his part and the testimony of a paranoid man who'd spent the last five days hiding in the cabin of his mom's third husband's sloop.

Chapter Twenty-Five

Wednesday, June 19, 2013
7:24 p.m.

SAN DIEGO WAS in danger of sinking into the ocean. Rain overnight and throughout the morning had given way to a muggy, overcast afternoon that had bred more showers and thunderstorms Wednesday night. Jackson sat in his Granada, looking through rain-streaked windows at a motel just off Rosecrans Street that was, according to the file he had viewed on Melanie Gwynn's computer, Padilla's current residence.

It was a real fleabag, eight rooms in a row at the end of a lobby, a style famous in the '50s or '60s along the open highways. Now most of them were in disrepair, reserved for cheap affairs, folks on the run, and ex-cons trying to get clean. Or whatever Padilla was supposedly up to.

Jackson had staked it out for twenty-four hours, since leaving Mira Austin's apartment complex the night before. He'd arrived in time to see a man matching Padilla's description leave his room around 7:30. Jackson had watched from the parking lot of a slightly less repulsive hotel across the street, as Padilla walked a block to the bus station and boarded a metro bus a few minutes later. Jackson had followed the bus across town to National City, where he'd watched Padilla get off and set out on foot. Not wanting to be too conspicuous, Jackson had found a parking place down the street and waited for close to an hour. When Padilla hadn't returned, Jackson had gone for some fast food before returning to the parking lot across from the dive motel to wait. He'd been in and out of sleep all night, and had happened to be half-awake when he'd spied Padilla shuffling up the block and back to his room around eight a.m.

He hadn't left since, nor had Jackson, except once to quickly pee at a nearby McDonald's. Now his bladder was starting to tingle again, even though he hadn't had anything to drink except the melted ice from last night's soda. For that matter, his stomach was also growling, but he wanted to see if Padilla would leave at the same time again. Jackson had a hunch, and he wanted to test it.

Shortly after seven-thirty, Padilla exited his room and again shuffled down toward the bus stop. He really did shuffle too, with a bit of a swagger, his hood up to protect against the steady rain. It was the walk of a guy who didn't care—about much of anything.

Jackson craned his neck and saw Padilla take shelter in the bus stop, and was able to see him board it five minutes later. He started the car and waited to exit the lot until the bus began moving. He followed it for a couple of blocks, then took a chance. He peeled off and took an alternate route to National City, arriving earlier than the bus had last night. He turned down the same street Padilla had walked down the night before and found a parking spot along the side of the road, two blocks down.

Padilla's eyes hadn't deviated from the ground in front of him as he'd walked to or from the bus stop, so Jackson doubted he could make the Granada. The rain helped provide a cloak—Padilla wouldn't see him through the windows unless he was looking for him, and even then, while a manned car parked in front of a closed ethnic grocery store at 8:10 p.m. was unusual, it wasn't that unusual.

The bus was on time, and again Padilla exited and started walking down the sidewalk, oblivious it seemed to the rain or the rumbles of thunder. He swagger-shuffled right past Jackson, his hood still up, his eyes straight ahead and down. He continued for another block, then entered a hole-in-the-wall Mexican joint named *El Pequeño*. Jackson's hunch was correct. Padilla had spent a lifetime in restaurants and in bars, working at several and committing most of his crimes in or outside them. Now, a week out of the joint, it only made sense that he'd be found working the graveyard shift at some greasy spoon.

Content that he had the next several hours free, Jackson found a slightly better neighborhood to empty his more-than-tingling bladder and fill it and his stomach with some food and drink. Then he drove back to Padilla's motel again. It was dark and secluded, and the only people he imagined running into were drunks, gangsters, or illicit lovers. So he parked across the street and took the direct method, picking the lock on Padilla's room.

It was a pigsty, with clothes on the unmade bed, hanging over the dresser, spilling out of a duffel in the corner, and on the floor. They were joined by empty fast food containers and by some not-so-empty ones. Several porn magazines sat on the end table next to an alarm clock and a half-empty bottle of tequila. A box in the corner contained a handful of personal items—a couple books, a statue of the Virgin Mary, a rabbit's foot, a few hip-hop CDs, some playing cards, a few other odds and ends, and a framed photo of two ugly people, a man and a woman. The man was Padilla, and Jackson guessed the wolfhound beside him was Jacinta. Holding it with his sleeves so as not to leave prints, Jackson broke the frame over his knee and tossed it back into the box.

He scoured the bathroom, seeing nothing—including any indication that Padilla had showered that day. It would explain the smell, a combination of liquor, body odor, expired Mexican food, and the dreck of humanity.

He returned to the main room and spotted a laptop open on the table in the corner, behind the door. Jackson kicked back a chair and sat down. He used a knuckle to press the power button, then got up while it booted and retrieved a couple of sheets of toilet paper. He draped one over the mouse, enabling him to use it without leaving prints.

The screen blipped and came to life, showing a mostly naked woman mid-gyration. Jackson quickly opened an internet browser to cover it, then sat in dread waiting to see what Padilla's homepage was. Yahoo, and the only things filthy on it were a headline story about some senate subcommittee investigation into a senator's misappropriation of funds (perhaps what the pundit on the news program with Maggie had referenced) and a Saudi prince found murdered at a gay night club in Bahrain. Wary of leaving a trail, Jackson carefully scanned Padilla's internet history and clicked through his Documents folder. He found nothing, other than more evidence Padilla was a real perv.

Instead of searching every folder and file location, Jackson pulled out his phone and called Mouse. He hoped his friend wasn't at work or too busy killing virtual terrorists to answer the phone.

"Yeah?" Mouse said after two rings.

"Hey, Mouse, it's me."

"Dude, where have you been?"

"Why?"

"I haven't heard from you in weeks."

"Yeah, sorry. Say, I need a favor."

"Yeah?"

"Can I send the entire contents of a computer to you?"

"Well, yeah, in theory."

"What do you mean in theory?"

"Depends on your connection, the size of the hard drive. Why don't you just bring it over?"

"It's not my computer."

"Whose is it?"

"Long story."

"What do you want with it?"

"I don't know. I was hoping you could search it and let me know what you find."

"Search it for what?"

"Whatever, Mouse. Anything. I can read you in later, but I need to get you everything first."

"We could try FTPing it, but it's not ideal."

"Yeah, neither is the Wi-Fi here," Jackson said, clicking to check his connection. He was actually piggybacking on a nearby bar's network, as the motel didn't have its own, and he was alternating between one and two bars. "Is there any other way?"

"What kind of computer is it?"

"Laptop."

"I mean HP, Dell?"

"Uh . . . HP Pavilion."

"You could jack the hard drive."

"Won't that be kind of obvious?"

"Depends on how astute of a guy we're talking. But not as obvious as a missing laptop."

"Okay, walk me through it."

Fortunately, the set of lock picks Jackson routinely carried also included a miniature screwdriver. With Mouse directing him, he removed the back panel of the laptop and disconnected the hard drive, being careful not to leave or to wipe away any fingerprints. He closed the computer back up, pocketed the hard drive, and double-checked to make sure he hadn't left any evidence behind. Content that he hadn't, he left the room, wiping down the doorknob as he exited. Ten minutes later, he was on I-5 headed north toward L.A., Joaquín Padilla's hard drive on the seat beside him.

Chapter Twenty-Six

"I WANT TO hire you, Jackson."

"You already did."

"No, you took the case *pro bono*. And you solved it. You found Connor. Now I want to hire you again, and this time I'll pay."

"That's not necessary, Hailey. As far as I'm concerned, this is the same case."

She leaned back slightly and frowned.

"Besides, I want to see justice done here. That's payment enough."

Her frown intensified as a grin broke out on his face. "What?" she asked.

"Sorry, but I think I just lifted that from ¡*Three Amigos!*"

They were interrupted by a waiter who brought three drinks and asked if they were ready to order. Jackson asked for a few more minutes.

"Okay, how do we see justice done?" Hailey asked. "It's like Connor said, it's her word against his."

Jackson leaned back into the booth at Cameron's. They were in the downstairs of the beachside bar and bistro owned by Jackson's good friend, Reggie Cameron. It had taken some doing, but he had convinced Connor it would be safe. Not just because of his friendship with Reggie, or the fact that the owner was built like The Hulk. Cameron's was a public place, hopping on a Friday night, and no one knew where they were anyhow.

Connor had quickly packed up, and the trio had driven back from Long Beach. All the while, Jackson had contemplated Connor's story. He saw no holes in it; everything Hailey's stepbrother said checked out with what Jackson had learned from other sources. Unfortunately, it left Connor in a dicey place, knowing Jenn was using MatchStick to scam clients, but not having any proof.

"I have a couple ideas," Jackson said.

"Like what?" Hailey asked, then scooted over as Connor returned from the restroom. He still looked haggard and worn, but had at least regained a little color and vibrancy.

"Let's order and get that out of the way, then we can talk."

Five minutes later, Jackson took a drink of his iced tea, set it aside, and leaned forward on the table. "Connor, you said you walked in and Jenn's guys were tossing your place, right?"

"Yeah."

"You mean pillows and couch cushions all over ransacking, or just going through drawers?"

"Um, a little of each."

"Why?" Hailey asked.

"We found it Tuesday and everything looked normal."

"You think I'm lying?"

"No. No, I believe you. But you interrupted them, and they chased you, right?"

"Yeah."

"Wednesday morning, when we met with your dad, Hailey, his guy Luke said they searched Connor's place before us and found it sterile."

"Yeah, so?"

"So, maybe they put it back together."

"Why?"

"I don't know. Just theorizing. Connor, you said your hacker guy traced access to MatchStick's server back to Mayor Kendrick's office, right?"

He nodded.

"But maybe it wasn't the mayor who used the computer."

"Of course it wasn't," Hailey said. "Jenn practically has the run of the place."

"Another possibility is she has one of your dad's people working for her."

"Luke?"

"Or that other guy, the silent one."

"Vince?"

Jackson shrugged. "Just theorizing, again."

Connor sighed. "How does any of this help us?"

"I don't know yet." He took another drink. "You said you downloaded everything to a flash drive?"

"Yeah."

"And you left it in your computer?"

"Yeah."

"The one on the desk in the living room?"

"It's the only one I have."

Hailey's eyes widened. "It was still there Tuesday night." She turned to Connor. "The evidence could still be there."

Jackson shook his head. "There was no flash drive in it. They must have grabbed it."

"I'm so stupid," Connor said. "I shouldn't have left it. I should have kept it on me. And I should have backed it up to the cloud."

"It's okay," Hailey said, patting and rubbing his shoulder. "Jackson will think of something."

So he wasn't the only one falling into predictable, '80s TV private investigator tropes. Hailey, the beautiful client, now believed the smooth-talking, somewhat handsome P.I. could work miracles.

"Look, Mr. Douglas, I—"

"Jackson."

"Jackson," Connor said with a nod, "I want to thank you for helping Hailey. But I think it's best if I just disappear again."

"And what," Hailey asked, "hide out on Shane's boat forever? They are going to come back from Spain, you know?"

"I know, I know. I've thought about that. I've got a plan. I've got a cousin who lives in Provo. I thought I could maybe—"

"Idaho?" Hailey nearly shouted.

"Utah," Jackson said quietly.

"You want to move to Utah?"

"No, but I don't know what else to do. I can't go home, I can't afford a hotel long-term, I can't live on Shane's boat forever."

"You can stay at my place."

"Hailey, it's the first place they'd look."

"Well, you're not moving to Idaho—or Utah," she said with a quick glance at Jackson, "or anywhere."

"Let's think about this for a minute," Jackson said. "I get that you're scared, Connor, and with good reason. But you said it yourself, you have nothing on Jenn—no tangible proof."

"So?"

"So, it would just be your word against hers, and her word— particularly backed by the mayor, who trusts her implicitly—trumps yours."

Hailey shook her head. "Meaning?"

"Meaning, it won't do any good for Connor to accuse her. And she has to know that. She's kept cool and composed when we've talked to her, she hasn't run and abandoned her scam. My guess is she's been laying groundwork to throw suspicion on Connor if he came back at her."

"What do you mean?" Connor asked.

"When we met with the mayor and when I met with Jenn, they were very dismissive of your disappearance, almost as if there was nothing to be alarmed with. She hinted that something was off with you, that you were fidgety or nervous about something."

"Not until Friday when I found the discrepancy in the data."

Jackson nodded. "Right. And now that we know what happened in San Jose, her comments make sense. She was setting you up. If you came after her, she'd burn you. She wiped the evidence, her guys took your flash drive. If anything, they're ready to hit you with false evidence if you come after her."

Connor sagged back and dropped his head against the backrest of the booth.

"The good news for us is, she has a lucrative criminal enterprise going, so she won't want to start any trouble. If you keep your mouth shut, she's not going to harm you."

"She killed that guy in San Jose," Hailey said.

"Parry Bilas."

"We don't know that," Jackson said. "And he was preparing to testify against Murtaugh. Connor's not. But if she were to come after him, if he were to die, it would bring an investigation down, and she wants to avoid that, believe me."

"What about the guys who followed us?" Hailey asked.

Connor sat up. "What?"

"I had a tail the other night."

"And today," she said.

"What? You were followed?" His eyes and head began darting around the downstairs dining room. "They could be here!"

"We lost them," Jackson said.

"You could have brought them right to me."

"We lost them," Jackson said again. "Connor, you're safe right now."

"But why was she following you, if she isn't going to hurt Connor?"

"To keep tabs on me and the investigation. And, because she probably did want to find Connor first, to see what he knew. Which is why we have to think of a story for where he's been and what he does know. We have to convince her that he doesn't know all that he does— that he doesn't suspect her. She knows he doesn't have evidence, and once he reappears from wherever we pretend he's been and once he doesn't start making accusations, she'll have no reason to come after him and open up this can of worms."

"I don't know, Jackson."

Truth was, neither did he. It sounded plausible. And he didn't think Jenn was the type to whack a guy and drop him in the river to keep him from potentially talking. But if it was him, would he take that chance?

"I think I'm better in Utah," Connor said.

"We're still going to need a cover story," Jackson said.

"Say I stole the data and ran."

"That'd be a felony and they could send the authorities after you."

"Oh, great."

"Unless . . ."

"Unless what, Jackson?"

He looked at Hailey to answer, but their meals came first. All three ignored them, and when the waiter was gone, Hailey repeated her question.

"Unless we plant the idea that he took the data but for a different reason."

"What's that?"

Jackson looked to Connor with something of a grin on his face. "Do you have a girlfriend?"

"What? No."

"Recently?"

Connor sighed. "No."

"Okay. Connor was lonely, wanted a female companion, and decided to use his position with MatchStick to find himself a girl. He was studying the data himself, then suspected Jenn was onto him, and ran."

"How does that change anything?" Hailey asked.

"Because if they buy it, it would still explain Connor's paranoid actions while also convincing Jenn he isn't a threat to her."

"Why'd he call Anne then? They know about her."

Jackson shrugged. "To ask her out."

"Really? The woman who wrote the *Times* piece on Murtaugh."

"Okay, so it's not the perfect cover. But worth a try."

"I'm still for Utah."

"That might not be a bad idea," Jackson said, picking up a pair of fries. "Play it that you're so ashamed that you run away to be with your cousin. And the other upside is," he said, pausing to bite the tops off the fries, "if we convince them you stole the data because you were lovesick, it makes you more sympathetic. Hailey can puppy-eye her dad into persuading Jenn not to call the cops, and you're in the clear."

"And living in Utah," Hailey said. "This isn't a viable plan, Jackson."

"It's only temporary."

"Temporary?"

"Until we take down Jenn."

"And how are we going to do that? We have no evidence, remember?"

He picked up his club sandwich, a favorite at Cameron's. "We have to get it."

"What if we smear her?" Hailey asked. "Pull out the San Jose story, the pictures."

"It's all circumstantial. Even if we connect her, there's no proof she did anything wrong in San Jose. She was the victim, remember?"

Hailey's eyes fell.

"And she had to know that was a possibility, which is probably why she's so close to your dad, so she could set him up for the fall if things went south. Now with Connor finding what he did, she's probably set to play it all off on him. Or both of them."

"Great."

"Yeah, we can't blow the whistle, because we don't have the goods."

"She doesn't know that, does she? Connor could have made a copy. Maybe that's why she wanted to find him. We can blackmail her."

"It's risky. I have a little experience with blackmail, and you'd better be sure you have more on them than they have on you."

"We do."

"And you'd better actually have it. If she calls, we're laying down a junk hand."

Connor sat forward. "Okay, so how do we get a better hand? How do we get evidence? Let's say we go along with this plan and say I was taking advantage of my role with MatchStick to find a girl. How do we ever get the goods on Jenn so I can come home and come clean?"

"Your hacker friend," Hailey said. "Could he get it?"

"Won't work," Jackson said before Connor could answer.

"Why not?"

"Inadmissible in court."

"But we could blackmail her."

"With what?"

"The evidence."

"I mean, what's our play? We have illegally-obtained evidence. What are we going to do with it?"

"I don't know, give it to Anne or Maggie or whats-her-name."

"She won't use it because it's—"

"Inadmissible," Connor muttered.

"Right. And I'm guessing Jenn's covered her tracks. And even so, even if we hack in and find everything Connor found, it isn't proof that she's ripping off clients—not the kind of proof that will sink her ship. To do that, we need to catch her in the act."

"In the act?"

"Yeah. We need her to expose herself, her operation. Plus, that's the best way to find out who all's involved and to what degree."

"You mean my dad?"

"I do. Hailey, my gut tells me he's not involved—that she's using him as a pawn to set him up for a fall, same as with Murtaugh. Now if this hacker guy is really good—"

"He is."

"Then maybe he could even hack bank accounts and transactions and discover any connections that way. But if the feds couldn't pin the San Jose job on her, I doubt he will be able to pin this on her, and it would still be—"

"Inadmissible," Hailey singsonged.

Jackson nodded. He ate a few more fries. "But, if we can uncover the entire operation, and especially if we can catch a couple of her racketeers in the act too, we can get them to start talking and hopefully expose everybody involved—and everybody not involved too."

Hailey shook her head. "How? You're talking a massive investigation. No offense, but isn't this over your head?"

"Yeah."

"So we're sunk."

"Not necessarily. I have an idea. I just need to think it through a little more."

"Well, what is it?"

"We need to make love."

"Excuse me?"

"Bad expression," he said, putting his hands up. "Blame the hippies. What I meant was, we have to do a little matchmaking of our own."

Chapter Twenty-Seven

Wednesday, June 19, 2013
11:22 p.m.

A BLEARY-EYED, OVERWEIGHT, naturally cranky woman opened the door. Her "blond" hair was pinned and twisted and held in various clumps around her puffy cheeks. They matched the eyes. She wore a pink spaghetti-strap tank top that didn't conceal enough of anything, shorts with flowers on them, and fuzzy slippers. Her breath smelled of alcohol, although Jackson wasn't familiar enough with booze to know which type. With a sigh that was more a moan and a curse, she asked what Jackson wanted.

"Hi, Pam. I need to see Mouse."

She sighed again, running her brown eyes over him. "It's like eleven-thirty."

"He's up."

"You're soaked."

"It's raining. Can I come in?"

Another sigh and a, "Whatever." But she backed up and admitted Jackson to the duplex she shared with her brother Kyle, a.k.a. "Mouse." Jackson didn't actually know where the nickname had come from, but it fit. In addition to being a whiz with a computer, Mouse had the diminutive personality to fit the moniker.

Pam didn't shout for Mouse, didn't offer to get him, didn't offer Jackson a drink or a towel. Instead, she swung the door closed and padded in her slippers down the hall to her bedroom, leaving Jackson to fend for himself. It was okay; he knew the drill.

Mouse was in his bedroom, which, save for the bed, more closely resembled a CIA substation. A massive corner desk housed three wide-screen monitors, at least one standalone laptop, keyboards, mice, joysticks, other videogame controllers, subwoofers, and more flash drives, CDs, and DVDs than could possibly be kept ordered, had Mouse made the effort. He hadn't, spending most of his waking hours in a cushy chair at the desk, cruising through pirated games or hacking around the internet for kicks. He was deep in code when Jackson rapped on the door and let himself in, and with the quick press of a key, two of Mouse's screens went dark.

"H-hey, dude."

He wore dark jeans and a black hoodie. His hair was a shaggy brown mess, minimizing an already drawn face and covering, Jackson knew, a scar on his forehead. Mouse and Pam's late father had been a piece of garbage, which accounted in no small way for Mouse's withdrawn personality. And his bleak outlook on life.

"Hey, Mouse. Sorry I'm so late."

"What time is it?"

"Eleven-thirty."

Mouse waved.

"Pam seemed to think it was late," Jackson said, dropping onto the corner of the bed.

Mouse spun to face him. "She's in a funk. She broke up."

"With Clark?"

"No, Gary, the rancher from San Jacinto or San Bernardino or Somewhere," he said with another wave. He leaned forward and actually snickered. "Dumped her for a cowgirl from Boise."

"That's too bad."

"Yeah, a crying shame. You get the hard drive?"

Jackson reached into his pocket and withdrew the small but heavy metal and ceramic device.

"And you're not going to tell me where you got this?"

"You going to tell me what was on the screen when I walked in?"

Mouse bit down on his tongue. He turned and opened a cabinet door in the side of his desk. He pulled out an old, nicked and scratched laptop. "Pavilion G-series. Should work."

"Great."

"You want to tell me what I'm looking for?"

Jackson looked down. He sighed. "The guy who owns this . . . He killed my parents. And Grant."

"What?"

"At least I think so. He's a repeat felon with a rap sheet like a novel. I need to find anything on here that could tie him to the explosion. Bank records showing large deposits around the time, receipts for accelerants, did he Google delayed timers, was he corresponding with somebody on e-mail or Facebook or whatever. Anything, and I mean anything, that could possibly be relevant, I want to know it."

"Y-yeah. Yeah, sure. I'll see what I can find."

"He's been in prison at Kern Valley for two years, so there won't be much new on here, except porn."

"P-p-prison? Is he dangerous?"

"Yeah. But he's working an overnight shift at a dive in National City, and he has no idea I took this or brought it to you."

"Okay."

"I have got to go home and crash. I haven't had a good night's sleep in . . . I've gotta crash. Call me when you find something."

"Yeah. It'll take a little while to pick it clean, but I'll record everything I find."

"Thanks, Mouse. I owe you."

"No, we're good, man. I'll call you."

Jackson nodded and let himself out. It was a twenty-minute drive back to his house, and the steady rain kept him focused and awake. He felt like a guest in his own home as he climbed the steps to bed. He peeled off his wet shirt and kicked his shoes to the corner and dropped into bed.

Exhausted as he was, sleep wouldn't come. He kept tossing and turning, running facts and timelines through his head. Finally his body succumbed and he drifted into unconsciousness, dreaming about a fiery ball of flame that chased him through a cavernous, empty, restaurant.

*   *   *

Friday, May 13, 2011
9:14 p.m.

"HIS NAME'S Mouse?" Reggie asked from the driver's seat of his black Hummer H3. It'd been his gift to himself when Cameron's had made it big a few years ago, and it was kind of ridiculous. Or at least, would have been for anyone else.

"Nickname," Jackson said with a shrug.

"Wasn't that dude in *The Matrix* named Mouse?"

"Never seen it."

Reggie nodded and turned onto Lawler Street in Culver City. It was not one of L.A.'s nicer neighborhoods, and after dark, Jackson was glad to have Reggie along.

"And this Mouse guy's a hacker who's going to help you bring down this chick with the dating site?"

"Yeah."

"You sure you know what you're doing, J?"

Jackson turned to look at his pal. "Kind of playing it by ear."

Reggie nodded again and pulled to the curb, leaning down to see the address. "This is it."

"Lights are off," Jackson said, reaching for his seatbelt.

"Didn't you call ahead?"

"No answer."

"Well, at least this ain't a wild goose chase."

It had taken all of dinner for Jackson to sell Hailey and Connor on his burgeoning plan. He had then enlisted Reggie as a wingman, mostly because he wanted a wingman, while Hailey and Connor had taken her BMW to a hotel for the night. Connor was still on edge, still talking about going to Utah. They were going to call when they got settled, which apparently wasn't yet.

"That him?" Reggie asked as he reached for his door. Up ahead, a thin man shuffled hurriedly down the sidewalk. He clutched a backpack under his arm, and a mop of sweaty, shaggy hair followed behind him.

"I don't know," Jackson said.

"There's more," Reggie said, and Jackson squinted into the darkness to see three more figures walking just as quickly after the first. He was almost to the sidewalk leading to the duplex when one of them grabbed him.

Jackson opened his door and jumped down. The three pursuers had clustered around the first guy. One held his shirt while the other grabbed his backpack.

"There a problem here?" Jackson asked.

The guy nearest him turned. "This don't concern you, man. Move out."

He might have been Hispanic—it was too dark to tell, and his accent, if any, was minimal. He, like the other three, was dressed in black. One had a hood up. Another wore a stocking cap. No noticeable gang colors, and they looked young.

Jackson took another step. "Thing is, I'm already concerned."

The guy in the middle, the one who had grabbed the backpack, dropped it and stepped forward. "Maybe you didn't hear, esé. Take a walk."

Jackson heard a switchblade flick open. Before he could turn, he heard another sound, the breaking of cartilage. He looked just in time to see Reggie's well-packed, meaty fist withdraw from the first guy's nose, leaving a stream of blood gushing over his mouth and chin.

"Man asked you a question," Reggie said, looking at the guy in the middle. He took two steps back, then turned and ran. The third guy followed, while the one whose nose Reggie had just broken stumbled as he turned around, looking back once as he took off after them.

"W-wh-wh-who are y-you guys?"

"Are you Mouse?" Jackson asked, pleased that he didn't stutter. His heart had been thudding in his chest ever since he got out of the Hummer, and it wasn't showing any signs of letting up.

"Y-y-yeah."

"It's all right, man, you're safe," Reggie said. He picked up the backpack and extended it to Mouse.

"Th-thanks."

"We're friends of Connor Novak's," Jackson said, stretching the meaning of "friend" just a little. "He said you helped him out with something last week. I was hoping you could help us too."

Mouse's eyes darted back and forth, then once down the sidewalk where the trio had vanished. "I, uh . . . You know Connor?"

"My name's Jackson. The guy with the brass knuckles is Reggie. I'm a private investigator. Connor's sister hired me to find him when he disappeared over the weekend. It's kind of a long story. Do you have a few minutes?"

"Y-y-yeah, I, uh . . . I guess. You wanna . . . You wanna come in?"

"Yeah, thanks."

"Man, who were those guys?" Reggie asked as they followed Mouse up the walk.

"I don't know. They followed me from the bus station."

"Wannabe 'bangers," Jackson said.

Mouse reached into his backpack for some keys, which he nearly dropped, then fumbled with as he tried to open the door. He finally got it, swinging it inward and reaching for a light.

A woman screamed. More like gasped and swallowed a pocket of air. A girl Jackson sort of liked at college had talked him into going to some performing arts deal full of bad, wannabe stage actors. This sounded like one of their death scenes.

The noise was accompanied by a blur of blond and brown hair and a flailing arm that nearly knocked over the lamp. There was another blur, this of gray, and a thud as something—or someone—rolled off the couch and into a cheap coffee table.

The woman screamed again, this time forming several four-letter words, among them "Kyle." She stood, nearly lost her balance, and braced herself against the arm of the couch. She madly swiped hair out of her face. "I thought you worked till ten."

"Got off early. I'd have called but I didn't know you guys had a make-out session scheduled."

She swore again as a form emerged from between the coffee table and the couch. It was a pear-shaped man in khaki pants and a gray pullover. "Are you all right?" she asked.

"I think so."

"Who are these guys?"

"Uh, what were your names again?"

"Jackson."

"Reggie."

"Right. Some guys just tried to mug me."

"And you brought them inside?"

The guy felt his lip, then his elbow. He looked as confused as Jackson felt.

"They saved me. Y-you want some ice?"

"No, man, I'm good."

"Uh, this is my sister, Pam. Her better half, Clark."

He waved awkwardly.

"We can, um, we can talk in my room," Mouse said, pointing to the hall. He led Jackson and Reggie to the second door on the left, which opened to a small bedroom made even smaller by the presence of a huge computer desk in one corner. Mouse closed the door behind them, then tossed his backpack across the bed. "Sorry. They usually keep the crap to a minimum when I'm around."

"Don't sweat it, man."

"And thanks for out there. I don't know what that was about."

"You have trouble in this neighborhood before?"

"Not really." Mouse exhaled and collapsed into his chair. "So what's this about Connor being missing and you needing my help?"

Jackson gave him the short version, which still took several minutes. "Connor said you hacked MatchStick's server. I'm wondering if you can do it again?"

"I didn't hack it. I connected through a shared terminal session after he logged on."

"Which you couldn't do if he wasn't there to initiate it, right?" Reggie asked.

"Since when are you Steve Jobs?" Jackson asked.

"Had to do it with a couple of vendors before."

"So could you hack it?" Jackson asked.

"Y-yeah, I g-guess so. Probably."

"I wouldn't ask if Jenn wasn't guilty of everything from fraud to extortion."

"He's got a sliding scale of justification," Reggie said.

"And if Connor wasn't in a pickle," Jackson added.

"I can do it," Mouse said. "I just don't know what you want me to find."

"Two things. One, proof Jenn's guilty."

"I thought you knew she was."

"I do, but I want rock solid proof. A memo to one of her minions, financial records, anything."

"Hacked evidence won't hold up in court," Reggie said.

"It's not for court. It's for my peace of mind."

"Okay," Mouse said. "What's two?"

"I need you to help me make a couple of killer MatchStick profiles. We're talking A-rated super-dates."

Mouse frowned, then look at Reggie. "Is he serious?"

"Oh, I'm afraid he is."

Jackson only grinned in reply.

*   *   *

Thursday, June 20, 2013
10:50 a.m.

THE SURF rock riff of the James Bond theme song broke into the famous ba-da-BA-DA melody. From his bed, where he lay staring at the ceiling, Jackson reached for his phone. He had no idea what time it was, nor how long he'd been awake. Only that he'd slept fitfully through the night and that the morning light coming in through the blinds was subdued.

"Yeah," Jackson said, putting his phone to his ear.

"Dude, you need to get over here," Mouse said.

"Why?" He sat up. "What is it?"

"You need to see it."

"I'm on my way."

Jackson skipped the shower, taking only a few minutes to dress and douse himself with body spray. Not that Mouse would care, or smell any better. As he backed out of his driveway, he spotted a gray two-door with tinted windows parked a few houses down, partially around the curve. He didn't think much of it, other than that it normally wasn't there. But it made no move to follow him, and he quickly forgot about it as he speculated as to what Mouse might have found on Padilla's hard drive.

He drove five over the limit, reaching Mouse's house in just under twenty minutes. He knocked and let himself in, which earned a startled exclamation from Pam in the kitchen. He nodded in passing and similarly entered Mouse's room.

"That was fast," Mouse said from the computer desk.

"What have you got?"

Mouse tapped a key on the Pavilion laptop on the desk and the screen came to life. "You were right. Lots of porn and crap. But I found this folder hidden in a really weird place on his C: drive."

"DCD," Jackson read.

"Hadn't been opened in two years, since it was created."

"Exactly?"

"May 10, 2011."

"What's in it?"

"See for yourself," Mouse said, tapping to open the file. It contained several dozen images, sorted in list view so that Jackson could see the names. IMG001, IMG002, and so forth. He double-tapped the first one and a photograph filled the screen. He frowned, then leaned in. It showed a parking lot, one Jackson couldn't identify, and all or part of ten or twelve cars.

"What is this?"

"Keep going."

He clicked to the next photo, which had zoomed in on one particular car, a silver four-door Dodge Stratus with a Navy parking sticker.

"That's . . . that's Dad's car."

Mouse looked at him but said nothing.

The next photo showed David getting into the car. Two more followed it in traffic. A third showed it pulling into the driveway of the

Douglas family home in the Tierrasanta neighborhood of San Diego. Jackson's heart simultaneously threatened to burst out of his chest and to stop.

Managing the saliva to swallow, he continued. The next ten shots showed David Douglas at a variety of locations—getting the mail from the curb, on a morning jog, in the drive-thru at Dairy Queen, and chatting with the guard at the base's main gate. The last two photos showed David and Hannah dressed for dinner, walking along the Embarcadero in San Diego.

Jackson looked through them twice, then collapsed back onto Mouse's bed. "Is that it?" he asked.

"Yeah. I looked everywhere—there's nothing else. Photos, links, anything."

"He did it. He targeted my dad. He killed them."

Chapter Twenty-Eight

Thursday, June 20, 2013
3:47 p.m.

TRUE TO HER secretary's words, Jackson found District Attorney Daniella Moreno as she was exiting the county courthouse on West Broadway. He quickly climbed a half dozen steps to the small terrace shielded from the wind. It was not shielded from rain, which had let up but threatened to commence again at any moment.

Moreno wore a black skirt and matching blazer, albeit one cut short around the waist, with a white blouse and a red, scarf-like belt. All that was missing was the sombrero on her back and a guitarrón. Her heels clicked on the pavement as she strode briskly toward the sidewalk and the U.S. District Court across the street and a block down. She was due at four, according to her secretary.

"D.A. Moreno," Jackson called as she moved past him, the breeze coming around the corner to lift her raven hair off her shoulders. The mariachi look worked on her, but Jackson didn't dwell on it.

"D.A. Moreno," he called again as she slowed and turned over her shoulder. Her eyes narrowed slightly.

"Mr. Douglas."

"Nicole told me I might find you here."

"I'm sorry, but I'm in a bit of a time crunch."

"I can appreciate that," Jackson said, following her down the steps. "She also said your schedule is packed for the next few days."

"It is."

"Could I buy you dinner?"

She stopped. The wind, now fully in their faces, whipped her hair around her jaw as she looked his way.

"No tricks, just dinner. I'd just like a few minutes, and I thought dinner might make it worth your time."

Moreno resumed walking. "I have quite a bit of trial prep to get to tonight."

"I understand."

"But I do have to eat. A quick dinner?"

"You can leave after the appetizer if you want."

She nodded as they waited briefly for the light to turn at Union Street. "You like Italian?"

"I like whatever you like."

"Okay, how about de'Medici in the Gaslamp District? Fifth and F. Five-thirty."

"I'll be there. Thank you, Ms. Moreno."

"Give them my name," she said, then marched on down the street, leaving Jackson a little over ninety minutes to kill. He thought about bumming over to the old neighborhood, where he'd lived with his parents and Grant for so many years. But he wasn't in the mood for bumming. Instead, as raindrops started to splotch down around him, he returned to his car and spent half an hour looking at the images Mouse had pulled from Padilla's hard drive. Jackson had printed them off before making the tedious, traffic-laden drive down the coast again.

He'd made little of them, other than that Padilla had been following David Douglas. But had he been alone? Several of the shots showed David at the Naval Base San Diego, meaning whoever took them either had access or a very powerful lens. It could have been Padilla with a telephoto, or he could have sneaked onto the base. Or he could have had an accomplice, which threw a wrench into the works and called all deductions into question. That was part of the reason Jackson wanted to talk to Moreno.

As far as determining when the pictures had been taken, he'd made little headway. Obviously, they had been taken before the May 10 date on the folder on Padilla's hard drive. But how much before? And for what purpose? They didn't seem to show David in any strategic way—that is, showing a particular vulnerability that an assassin could take advantage of. And why blow up a restaurant when Padilla could have killed him at any time by trading the lens on his camera for the scope on a rifle? Or was there more to it?

Dozens of theories floated through Jackson's head, everything from Padilla being hired by terrorists to him connecting David's work at ONI to some middleman in his own criminal enterprises and wanting to pay David back for any part he'd played in getting Padilla arrested. It was all theory and conjecture.

Shortly after five, Jackson set out for de'Medici. It was still a little early for the festive Gaslamp District to be in full swing, but as work let out, the streets began to crowd. Jackson found parking just down the street and shuffled through intermittent sprinkles to the green awning spanning de'Medici's small patio and front entrance. He announced to a sharply dressed host that he was meeting D.A. Moreno for dinner, and the host guided him through pungent Italian aromas to a table set for two in the back.

Jackson had put on a button-down shirt before leaving for San Diego, mostly so he'd appear a little more professional to Moreno. Now, as he sat on a leather chair at a candlelit table with fine linens, he was glad to meet the minimum possible requirement for attire. At least he hoped.

He perused a menu while he waited, wondering how often Moreno frequented de'Medici, and whether it was most often for business or pleasure. Given her good looks and successful career stature, he doubted Moreno lacked male companions. But he also got the vibe she was too busy climbing the ladder to spend much time in romantic dalliances. Not that it really mattered.

She was ten minutes late, and when the host directed her to the table and pulled back her chair, she offered Jackson a thin smile. "Sorry. You know how it goes."

"I do."

As soon as the host disappeared, a waiter took his place. He introduced himself and offered greetings, then listed the evening's specials. "Will you need a few moments?"

"I'm actually ready if you are," Moreno said to Jackson.

He extended a hand to tell her to go ahead.

"Tortellini alla Romana and a glass of de'Medici Pinot Noir."

"Very good. Sir?"

"Uh, the same, hold the wine."

The waiter jabbed his pen into his pad, slipping the former into a breast pocket and tucking the latter under his arm to collect their menus. With a smile, he departed, and Jackson reached for his ice water. He took a sip, then leaned forward. "Ms. Moreno, thank you very much for making time for me. I know you're busy, so I'll get right to it."

She shrugged. "We have time. Just know I'm a light eater and won't be hanging around for an after-dinner coffee or dessert. Like I said, trial prep."

"I understand."

Jackson reached under the table and lifted a folder off his lap. He set it on the table in front of Moreno.

"What's this?"

"Photos, taken by Joaquín Padilla."

She lifted her eyes from the unopened folder to him. "How'd you get them?"

"I plead the Fifth."

Her face froze for a moment. Then she opened the folder. She sorted through the first half dozen images, then looked up. "What is this?"

"Recon. These are photos of my father, taken shortly before his death. As you can see, everything from him at work to getting the mail to enjoying a night out with my mom. Padilla was casing."

"Do you know that?"

"What else would you call it?"

"I don't mean that harshly, but as a prosecutor, I'm always thinking like a defense attorney. Do you know for a fact that Joaquín Padilla took these photographs?"

"I didn't see him snap the pictures, if that's what you mean. But he owned them. Even if he didn't shoot them himself, somebody did it for him."

She studied them for another minute, until a steward came with her wine. She took a sip and then set it aside. "And you're not going to tell me where you got these?"

"No."

"Nor how?"

"No."

She shook her head. "Then they won't hold up in court. Even if they did, if they were admissible, they don't prove anything, unfortunately."

"By themselves, no. But after we spoke the other day, I talked to Agent Kilpatrick. Then the NCIS agent in charge of the investigation. Then Admiral Sullivan, my dad's C.O. Yesterday I talked to Mira Austin, the ex-wife of the witness who put Padilla at Petty Officer Grabel's apartment at 7:23 p.m. She confirmed it was after 7:30, like she told Ike and Juliet Haywood. I talked to Padilla's parole officer. I've talked to everybody but Petty Officer Grabel, who last I heard had moved to Mississippi. And everybody tells me the same thing—even you: the evidence is stacked against Padilla."

Moreno listened carefully and nodded. "Jackson, I agree with you. I think the odds are better than not that Padilla's the guy—that he killed your family. But 'better than not' is not the burden of proof. Conviction requires proof beyond a reasonable doubt, as you know. And even you would have to admit that doubt exists."

"Define reasonable."

"Lacking conclusive proof. And even with the photos, Jackson, we don't have it. I'm sorry, I really am."

He sighed.

She took another drink of wine.

"Can I ask you something?" he asked.

"Of course."

"What do you do when you know somebody's guilty, I mean know it in your gut, but you don't have the evidence?"

"We do whatever we can to make the case."

"What's that mean, 'whatever we can'?"

"We go over the evidence again, we check stories, re-interview witnesses, spin and brainstorm. We question the investigators, make sure they didn't miss anything, make sure we didn't overlook something. We look to see if there's someone else who can be pressured into providing testimony, like we're doing with Padilla now. Is there a statute we've missed or a loophole we can use to get a just conviction? Anything."

"And when that fails?"

She sighed. "Sometimes, I'm sad to say, we have to admit defeat."

"All due respect, Ms. Moreno, but when it's personal, that's not an option. My brother," he said with a sigh, "before he died, he was engaged to a defense attorney. A real bulldog, worked for one of the big firms in L.A. Still does. And she and I used to go 'round and 'round. I couldn't understand how she could subvert justice for the sake of her client."

"A legal defense is a constitutional right."

"That's what she said, and I get it. But when a defense attorney knows somebody's guilty, and still tries to get them off . . ."

Moreno narrowed her eyes and sat forward. "What are you looking for, Jackson?"

"Excuse me?"

"What do you want out of this?"

"I want the man who killed my family to pay. I want justice."

"Justice or revenge?"

"Same end in this case."

"Maybe, but the path is drastically different."

He frowned.

"I've stood beside families who have watched the man who ruined their life be sentenced to life in prison, no parole. I've been with them when justice was done. For some, I could see that the weight had gone off their shoulders. For others, it was like the life had been sucked out of them."

He frowned some more.

"Both scenarios, justice was done."

"So what's the difference?"

"The difference is," she said, leaning closer over the table, "is one group wanted justice—they wanted a fair verdict. They got it, and in their eyes, the scales were balanced. Their pain still existed, but justice had been restored. The other group—they wanted to see someone pay. They wanted to be made whole by having the missing part in them taken from someone else." She shook her head. "But it doesn't work. You can't be made whole again by taking what you lost out of somebody else—a pound of flesh won't satisfy you."

She sat back, just as their entrees arrived, steaming plates of cheese-stuffed pasta in cream sauce, with peas and mushrooms.

"The point is," Moreno continued, "if you're crusading for justice, you may or may not get it, but even the pursuit can be fulfilling. But if you're out for revenge, it's a lost cause, because even if you get it, you'll still be left empty and hurting. And if you don't . . ." She shook her head while unwrapping the silverware from her napkin. "It will gnaw at you even worse."

Chapter Twenty-Nine

Saturday, May 14, 2011
8:10 a.m.

AFTER HALF A day of backbreaking labor, Hannah Douglas had finally expelled her eight-pound, six-ounce firstborn into the world shortly after one in the morning—five days past her due date. That meant that by the time Jackson woke up from a too-short night of sleep, he was already twenty-nine. He'd long ago learned that birthdays didn't change much of anything—not from one day to the next. But they did usually provide a good chance to spend quality time with family, something that even at twenty-nine, Jackson still relished. He also usually got some pretty good merch.

But that was secondary on his mind as he quickly showered and dressed. Instead, his thoughts were on Hailey and Connor and Jenn White/Jennifer Winters. The plan he'd hatched last night was still a go, assuming Connor's pal Mouse could come through for him. And assuming the other players in his ensemble cast were willing and able.

His first call of the morning went to Mouse, who he hoped had been able to pull everything he needed. The line rang and rang, then went to a generic voicemail greeting. Instead of leaving a message, Jackson waited two minutes and called back.

"Yeah?"

It was a female. Pam?

"Hi, is Mouse there?"

"Who?"

"Uh, sorry. Kyle."

"Hold on."

Jackson wandered onto his deck as he waited. It was a beautiful sunny morning, absent any marine layer. Only a hint of breeze carried a salty tang onshore. He took several deep breaths, enjoying one of life's simple pleasures.

"Ky-le!" he heard her scream through the phone. Next came a banging, then a repeated two-syllable shout. Followed by another minute of dead air. Then, finally, Mouse came on the line.

"Yeah?"

"Hey, you awake?"

A groan. "I am now. Jackson?"

"Yeah. Sorry to wake you up."

"Yeah, no, it's fine."

"Were you able to get everything?"

"Uh . . . huh," Mouse answered through what sounded like a yawn. "At least, I think so. I was up till two."

"Oh man, I'm sorry."

"Forget it. That's usual."

"Sorry to call so early then."

"Yeah, well. I'll send you a zip file."

"Sure." Jackson gave Mouse his e-mail address and thanked him again. Then he went upstairs to get his laptop, which he had stashed somewhere in preparation for his remodeling job. In theory, he should have finished that project before taking on clients. But what was done was done.

He sat down in front of his TV, tuning in to the morning *SportsCenter*. He opened up his e-mail and unzipped the file Mouse had sent, containing the criteria MatchStick used to pair matches. The algorithms Connor designed handled most of that, but from talking with Hailey, Connor, and Jenn, Jackson knew there was also a personal component. So he needed both the cold, hard numbers and the human input to help him understand how MatchStick made matches, and in particular, how they targeted potential victims.

Mouse had provided everything, and to his credit, had sorted and parsed it for Jackson. But there was still a problem in that the "Fail" responses Connor had discovered—the ones who had been victimized—had been removed by someone on Saturday. And they were still missing. Without them, Jackson would be guessing at what would constitute a profile that grabbed Jenn's attention as ripe for the picking.

He called Mouse again, and again got Pam's courteous greeting.

"Hey, is Mou-Kyle there?"

"Again?"

"Yeah, again."

"Hold on."

When Mouse came on a minute later, he sounded again as if he'd been sleeping. "Yeah, dude?"

"Hey. Sorry to bug you again, but last week when you and Connor were on MatchStick's server and found that somebody had wiped all the failure responses, did you look around for them?"

"No, not really. Connor was in a hurry."

"Any chance you can hack back in? I'm guessing Jenn didn't have everything completely removed."

"You think she hid it somewhere else?"

"Yeah."

"She could have exported a partial backup or something. I'll check."

"Thanks, Mouse. I appreciate it."

"I'll call you back. Give me an hour."

"Sure."

Jackson closed his phone, then thought better of it. Ideally, he'd wait until he heard back from Mouse. But he had no Plan B, so even if Mouse couldn't recover the "deleted" data, he intended to go through with his idea. And to that end, he dialed another number.

"Go for Haywood."

"Ike, it's Jackson Douglas. We met the other day at the Santa Monica CoC social."

"Yeah, I remember you. The P.I. What's up, man?"

"You and Juliet happen to be free this morning? I've got a proposition for you."

"We are actually just getting set to meet a client. Does this afternoon work?"

"Maybe. What time?"

"Jules, four hours?" Ike asked.

Her reply was clear. "We're walking. Might be closer to five."

"We've got a nine o'clock tee time," Ike said. "Jules says five hours. Shower, grab a bite to eat. Say three-ish?"

Jackson did quick math in his head. "That should work. You take clients golfing? Man, you do run a high-end service."

Ike chuckled. "He's a member at Riviera. Tough work, but somebody's got to do it, right?"

"Yeah, right. You got a preference where we meet?"

"After a day on the course, someplace with cold drinks."

"How about Cameron's, on the beach, just west of the Incline."

"Yeah, I know it. Hey, Jack, we gotta go. No cell phones in the clubhouse."

"All right."

"Three. I'll give you a buzz if we're off schedule."

"Sounds good. Thanks."

Ike disconnected, and Jackson clapped his phone shut. He had several more calls to make, but decided to make them en route to breakfast. Besides, he could use his wingman.

After stopping at Mouse's the night before, Reggie had driven Jackson back to O'Bannon's, where he'd picked up his Granada. Now he got in and headed for the coast, following the usual route along Sunset to Chautauqua. No gold sedan followed him. As he drove, he tapped in Hailey's number.

"Jackson, what's up?"

He quickly briefed her. "How's Connor?"

"Wound tight. He's convinced Jenn is still coming for him." She paused. "Jackson, he's going to Utah. He bought a ticket this morning. He's flying out of John Wayne at noon."

"What's he telling work, your dad, his mom?"

"He's going with your story, that he took the data to find a girl. I don't know about work. But he's more worried about Jenn pressing charges."

"We'll sell your dad on it, play on his sympathies."

"We have to. And we have to pin this on Jenn, Jackson. This has to be temporary."

"It will be. Connor need a ride to the airport?"

"I'm driving him."

"Before you do, have him write a statement, giving the true account of what happened. I'll sign it too for verification. I'm not sure what good it will do, but it's something."

"Okay."

"I'm meeting the Haywoods at three. You want to come?"

"Yeah, sure."

"Okay. I'll call you later."

"Okay."

Jackson made his last call as he turned into Cameron's parking lot. Hillary didn't pick up, probably busy deposing.

"Hey, Hill, it's Jackson. I'm not sure when you'll be done, but I've now got a three o'clock. Shouldn't take long, so I can pick you up by four. Maybe four-thirty. Depends where I'm picking you up, I guess. Did we talk about that Thursday? Anyhow, call me. Bye."

He parked and finally closed his phone, then got out and headed inside. Split into two levels—an upstairs fine-dining bistro and a downstairs casual bar and grill—Cameron's served everybody, and all three meals. Only the lower level was open for breakfast, and Jackson flirted briefly with the hostess Katie to procure a table. He'd just started looking over the menu when Reggie slid into the booth opposite him. He wore a bright green polo shirt, which constituted dressy for him.

"How's it goin', man?"

"I've got first-sting nerves."

"That's natural."

Jackson nodded. "Wait, natural because it's a first sting or natural because my plan's dicey?"

Reggie wiggled his hand back and forth. "Ah, fifty-fifty." He grinned. "So what are you doing here?"

"Treating myself to breakfast."

"What's the occasion, expected success?"

"My birthday."

"This your birthday? May 14?"

"Yeah."

"Man, that's my grandma's birthday. She's got to be almost eighty."

"Live around here?"

"Nebraska."

Jackson nodded.

"So this Mouse guy come through?"

"Mostly. Still waiting on one thing."

"And you get a hold of these other P.I.s?"

"Sort of. They're golfing at Riviera right now."

"For real?"

Jackson shrugged.

"Well you need something, J, you let me know."

"Thanks."

"I mean it. I've never run a sting before."

"Me either. Well, unless you count Leila. Or that time with Walker."

"Who's Walker?"

"Long story. But that was different. That was just us. We didn't have a client depending on us." He looked into Reggie's dark brown eyes. "It weighs on you, man."

"I believe it, brother."

"Anyhow, I figure some pancakes will take my mind off it for a while."

"It's on the house today, man. Whatever you want."

"In that case, tell your cook to get cracking on the bacon. The thicker the better."

"Whatever you say, bro." Reggie stood, clapped Jackson on the shoulder, and left him to ordering. He settled on the Big Herbie, named after Reggie's alma mater's mascot, Herbie Husker. It contained everything—bacon, sausage, eggs, hash browns, and pancakes. One of the many benefits of Cameron's was the quick service, and Jackson's food had just arrived when Mouse called back, informing Jackson that he'd found the deleted data. He'd copied it and sent it to Jackson's e-mail in another zipped file. It was still inadmissible in court, but it would provide the recipe Jackson needed.

He was halfway through his breakfast when his phone rang again. He scooped it from his pocket and answered without looking at the display. "Yeah?"

"Jackson, it's Hillary. Did you not get my texts?"

"I don't text."

She sighed audibly. "We should be done by two or two-thirty at the latest. Can you move your meeting up?"

"Afraid not."

Another sigh.

"What's the big deal? Run home, slip into your 'happy birthday, Jackson' outfit, and meet me at my place."

"I rode with a coworker so I didn't have to leave my car in the garage all weekend."

"Garage?"

"At the office. It's where we're working."

"Oh."

"I figured it made sense, seeing as how you'll be picking me up."

"Wow, deposition going poorly?"

"Jackson."

"Calm down, Hill. I'll be there as soon as I can, all right?"

"Call me if anything changes."

"I will," he said to no one as she disconnected the call. He sighed.

"Trouble?" Katie asked as she approached the table. In her hand she held a cupcake—frosted, with a candle sticking out of it.

"My brother's fiancée. She's a piece of work. What's that?"

"Reggie said it was your birthday."

"It's not even ten a.m."

"I can take it back," she said, turning.

"No, no. Just didn't think you served dessert this early."

She set it down. "Twenty . . . six?"

"Nine."

"Hmm. You look young."

"I've lived well."

"Enjoy."

"Thanks, Katie."

She smiled and left, and he spent a moment comparing Katie with Hillary. Katie had been nice enough to bring him a cupcake, just because. Hillary—soon to be family—hadn't even wished him a happy birthday when prompted. Then again, for her last birthday, he'd gotten her a desktop penholder.

He didn't dwell on it, choosing instead to enjoy his cupcake.

Chapter Thirty

Friday, June 21, 2013
10:06 a.m.

HILLARY MCKENZIE STRODE across the courtroom floor, her red heels clicking with each measured step. They drew attention to her long, slender legs while also offsetting the navy blue skirt and blazer she wore with a white V-neck blouse. The V was just high enough to maintain reasonable standards of modesty, but low enough to leave room for a pendant necklace, one Jackson had never seen her wear before. Hillary's golden hair was curled but drawn into a very loose, low-pinned ponytail, with several strands left loose to fall around her face. Somehow, she managed the harried, on the go look while still coming off as professional.

By comparison, the woman in the witness stand was ugly. She was middle-aged, short brown hair, faint makeup, dressed like a soccer mom. Her face was a little red, from nerves or the bright lights shining on her, whereas her hands were white from being squeezed so tightly together.

"To be clear," Hillary asked, "you were in the passenger seat at the time of the accident, correct?"

"That's right," the woman said.

"Which way were you looking?"

"Excuse me?"

"Which way were you looking?"

"I was . . ."

"Do you not remember?"

"I was looking out the window."

"Which window?"

"My window."

"You mean the front passenger window? To your right?"

"Yes."

"What were you looking at?"

"I'm sorry?"

"What was to the right out the front passenger window that you were looking at?"

"The sun. It was setting. It was a beautiful sunset."

Hillary smiled perfunctorily. The woman had the look of a deer in the headlights. From where he sat at the back of the small courtroom, Jackson couldn't blame her. He'd observed Hillary in action before, and she was in full whirring cobra mode.

"How long did you watch the sunset?"

"Excuse me?"

"How long did you w—"

"Objection," a dark-haired man on the opposite side of the courtroom called out. "Your honor, are we really talking about sunsets?"

Hillary said nothing, but looked at the judge, a scowling man with saggy jowls.

"Overruled."

She turned back. "How long did you watch the sunset?"

"I don't know. Only a few seconds."

"And why did you stop?"

"It was—the accident."

"Why did the accident make you stop watching the sunset?"

"I turned to look at it instead."

"And why did you do that?"

"I heard a crash. I wanted to see what was going on."

"So you didn't actually see the crash take place?"

"Objection," the same man said, rising again. "Even the defense isn't disputing the accident occurred. There's no need to badger Mrs. Pendleton about whether or not she saw the impact."

"There seemed to be reason when the prosecution called her to the stand this morning to testify about the accident."

"Overruled," the judge said a moment later.

"Thank you. Mrs. Pendleton, you didn't actually see the crash take place, did you?"

"W-well, no."

"So you have no way of knowing who caused the accident?"

"Objection! LAPD's forensic experts—whom Miss McKenzie agreed to be competent—testified that Mr. Darrow's car had caused the accident."

"Same reply, your honor."

"Overruled."

Hillary looked to Mrs. Pendleton.

"No."

"Then you also, by your presence at the site, don't have any idea why the accident occurred, do you?"

No objection this time, just a very quiet, "No," from the witness.

"How bright was this sunset?"

"Excuse me?"

"How bright was the sunset you were watching?"

She frowned. "Very. It lit up the whole sky."

The prosecutor dropped his head.

"Were you wearing sunglasses?"

"No."

"Did you squint or shield your eyes?"

"I put my hand up, like this," she said, holding her flattened hand above her eyes, as if saluting.

"One last question, Mrs. Pendleton. In your opinion, having witnessed the sunset from a moving vehicle, was it so bright that an oncoming driver—had he not been wearing sunglasses or taking one hand off the wheel to shield his eyes as you just demonstrated—might have temporarily been blinded by it and unable to see a stoplight above an intersection?"

"Objection!" the prosecutor practically screamed.

"Withdrawn," Hillary said in a clipped tone. She turned back toward her desk, her eye catching Jackson's for just a fraction of a second. Her face showed nothing to indicate it had even registered. "No further questions, your honor."

Jackson watched Hillary's back for two minutes while the prosecutor tried to pick up the pieces. Jackson had ducked in just in time to see him finish his examination, and had to draw upon what he'd seen to piece together the case. His guess was a DUI, because he doubted a simple running of a red light would lead to a major court case, and not one that merited the notorious Conway, Davenport & Rankin to provide counsel for the defense.

"You may step down," the judge said to the witness. "We'll be in recess till ten-forty-five."

He rapped his gavel and everyone stood. Jackson had found a seat by the aisle, but Hillary didn't even look his way as she exited the courtroom. When he filed out, however, she was standing just to the side next to a young, short stiff in a gray suit, and she turned to Jackson. "What are you doing here?" she asked. Her breath smelled like cinnamon.

"I need to talk to you. Do you have a few minutes?"

She sighed.

"Else I can wait for lunch."

"I have a working lunch." She turned to the guy beside her, a CD&R lackey, Jackson guessed. "Tom, call Fitch for me, update him on where things stand. Tell him I'll call him at lunch or the afternoon break. Then keep Randy company until I get there."

"Will do, Miss McKenzie."

He left, and Hillary motioned for Jackson to follow her. They walked through the crowd, down an empty hallway, and into a small office labeled "Counsel Lounge." It contained an arrangement of chairs and couches around an unlit fireplace. Hillary set her briefcase on an end table and unbuttoned her blazer. She turned around. "What's going on?"

"It's been a while since I've seen you cross examine someone," he said. "Someone other than me. I thought you were going to make that lady cry."

"She testified as a witness to an accident she didn't witness. She should cry."

"What'd your guy do, anyhow?"

Hillary's eyes blazed. "Why do you care?"

"You know me, I'm always curious."

"Too much so."

He shrugged.

"My client was accused of an aggravated DUI."

"And you bully a lady who was watching a sunset to get him off?"

"If you came all the way down here to badger me about my job, thanks, but I do have things to do."

"No, sorry. Old habit. I'm sorry."

She turned and sat down on a loveseat, crossing her legs. "I am pressed for time, Jackson. What do you want?"

He sat in a chair opposite her. "It's about Mom and Dad and Grant."

"What about them?"

"I think they were murdered, Hill. And I know who did it."

Her blue eyes narrowed. "What are you talking about?"

He spent ten minutes catching her up, from his meeting with the Haywoods to the photos on Padilla's hard drive to his conversations with everyone, including D.A. Moreno. Through it all, Hillary stared blankly, stoically, taking it all in. Finally, she licked her lips.

"You broke into Padilla's motel room and stole his personal property?"

"Seriously, that's the part of this you're getting hung up on?"

"That's a felony, Jackson."

"I know a good lawyer. Hill, this guy killed them. He killed your fiancé."

She looked away. "You can't prove it," she said softly.

"What?"

"You can't prove it." She turned back. "It's all circumstantial, and your strongest piece of evidence is inadmissible and now, thanks to you, forever tainted. Even if he's guilty, there's no proof."

"Come on, Hill. He's guilty as sin."

"That may be."

"You don't see it?"

"I see suspicion, yes. But I also know the FBI and the San Diego Police Department investigated the explosion two years ago and found nothing. No link to Padilla. No proof even that it wasn't an accident."

"So that's it, you're going to play lawyer with me?"

"I'm not playing, Jackson. I'm telling you, there's no way to make anything stick to Padilla. And it hurts too much to dig it all up again for nothing. I don't want to go through that and I don't want to see it happen to you either."

"It's not nothing."

"It is. Legally, D.A. Moreno was right, you're not even close. Jackson, if I were Padilla's lawyer and some prosecutor brought the case with what you have, I'd have to take a pay cut if I even let it get to a trial."

He sighed, rubbing his head with his hand. "Well, thanks for nothing."

"What did you want me to do?"

"I don't know. You specialize in finding loopholes to get defendants off, to crack airtight cases. I thought maybe you could see something I'm missing, find a way to get this guy."

"I'm sorry, Jackson. But unless you're holding out something, there is no legal way to get this guy."

"Well, then. I guess we'll have to find another way."

"What's that mean?"

"It means that sometimes the legal system, virtuous beacon of society that it is, fails. And it falls on somebody else to see justice done."

She shook her head. "I don't like what I'm hearing."

He shrugged.

Her look and her voice softened. "Jack, you can't let this eat at you."

"The guy who murdered my parents and brother? I can't let that eat at me?"

"You're obsessed."

"You think?"

"Jackson," she said, reaching to put her hand on his arm. "I know we've never been close, and I know this is going to be hard for you to believe, but I do care about you—about what happens to you. I don't want to see you fall apart. I know what a fixation like this can do to someone. Please, don't do something you'll regret."

His eyes went from her insistent look down to her fingers, wrapped loosely around his wrist. To one finger in particular, and to the glittering, silver-swaddled diamond she wore around it. He looked back up. "You're engaged."

She nodded. "Just a few weeks ago."

He withdrew his hand. "Is that . . . is that why you're giving up?"

"What?"

"Is that why you don't care?"

"What do you mean I don't care?"

He stood. "That's why you're so calm about this, why it doesn't seem to bother you, why you can just tell me to let it go. You replaced your loss."

"Jackson."

"What happened to just taking things slow?"

She stood too. "Jackson, I get that you're upset. But don't try to paint this like Grant didn't mean anything to me. I loved him, and I am still broken inside that I don't get to spend the rest of my life with him."

"Yes, I can just see how it tears at you."

She didn't stoop to respond. "But I also know that I had to move on with my life. And for the first time since he died, I am starting to feel whole again. So don't you dare stand there and insinuate that I don't care. I'm just able to see reality, and as much as I want to see whoever's responsible punished, you don't have the evidence. You're not close."

She bored her eyes into him until he broke away.

"You know what, go, get married, have a happy life with Ryan or Brian or whatever his name is. I just hope you're not haunted by how easily you swept the first love of your life under the rug."

He expected a blistering reply from Hillary, or at least a look that could melt steel. Instead, he got a look of pity. She retrieved her briefcase and brushed past him to the door. She stopped. "Goodbye, Jackson. I hope you can find a way to be at peace."

He said nothing as the door closed behind her.

Chapter Thirty-One

10:52 a.m.

HAVING TAKEN A few minutes alone in the lounge to compose himself, Jackson walked calmly out of the courthouse and two blocks to his Granada. The sky was a bland white, somewhere between sunny and overcast, and thoroughly blah. At least it was dry.

He got into the car and reached for his phone, flipping it open to see he had a voicemail. Leaning back into his seat, he put it to his ear.

"Mr. Douglas, it's Melanie Gwynn with the U.S. Probation and Parole Office in San Diego. Would you please give me a call when you get this message? It's in regard to Joaquín Padilla." She left her number, and Jackson quickly memorized it, then dialed it back into his phone. The line rang and rang, then went to voicemail, and he pounded his wheel in frustration. Then, instead of sitting there any longer, he headed for home.

It had been a week since Ike and Juliet Haywood had called and broken the news about Padilla. He'd made three trips to San Diego and back, questioned everyone he could—but Petty Officer Grabel—and found concrete evidence that Padilla had been targeting his father. And yet, he was no closer to justice than he had been a week ago, when his life was just miserable instead of torturous.

Speaking of Petty Officer Grabel, he'd thought long and hard about asking the Haywoods for her number in Mississippi. Although she wasn't likely to have had an epiphany regarding the time of Padilla's arrival at her apartment, it was possible she might remember something—some tiny tidbit that had yet to come to light that would prove his guilt. But Jackson had no idea what that something might be, and he was hesitant to force her to relive the worst night of her life on a long shot that, even were it to hit, probably wouldn't change Padilla's legal vulnerability.

His phone rang, and Jackson reached over to the seat to grab it. "Yeah?"

"Mr. Douglas? It's Melanie Gwynn."

"Hi."

"Sorry I missed your call."

"No worries. What's up?"

"I don't know if this is relevant or not, but I thought you should know. Padilla missed our in-person check-in yesterday, and I haven't heard from him since Wednesday evening."

"Wednesday evening?"

"That's right. He called around seven, said everything was fine."

"Did he mention a job?"

"No. I expected to discuss it yesterday."

"So what now?" Jackson asked.

"In some cases, we would give the parolee twenty-four hours. Given Padilla's history, when he hadn't contacted me by this morning, he officially violated his parole and I put out a BOLO."

"Anything?"

"No. Police went to the motel where he was staying and found it cleaned out. He was gone."

Jackson took a moment to consider how much to tell Gwynn. Remembering she'd gone out on a limb for him, he reciprocated. "I, um, I followed him the other night. Twice actually. Tuesday and Wednesday nights. He went to a dive Mexican joint in National City. Named *El Pequeño*."

Now Gwynn hesitated. "Did you follow him inside?"

"No. But he was there a while. I'm guessing he might be working nights there, but you could send SDPD to check it out, see if he's there."

"*El Pequeño*," she repeated. "It doesn't ring a bell. Look, Mr. Douglas, there's something else."

"What's that?"

"When Padilla didn't show, I contacted a couple of informants, just to see if they happened to know his whereabouts. They didn't, but one had heard a rumor that Padilla had gotten in trouble with the L Street Gang."

"Trouble how?"

"I don't know, and it was just the scuttlebutt off the street. My experience is such rumors are about fifty-fifty."

Jackson nodded. "Okay. Thanks for letting me know."

"I'll let you know if he turns up."

"Thank you."

He closed the phone and growled. Had he spooked Padilla? Had he come home from a long night of work, flipped open his laptop to look at some smut, and found the hard drive gone? And could that, the realization that someone had found him and broken into his place, have made a repeat felon bolt? Especially if he was in trouble with a San Diego gang?

When Jackson got home, he booted up his laptop and began making phone calls. The first was to Dick Davis, a chain-smoking throwback of a P.I. Jackson knew from his days at MTR Investigative Services in San Diego. Dick was a walking cliché for a '70s detective, which meant he was the type of guy with his ear to the ground. They shot the breeze for a minute, and then Jackson asked about Padilla. Dick had heard nothing, but promised to make some calls.

Next Jackson called Greg Cole, a police academy buddy of Grant's who had transferred to San Diego when his mom got breast cancer a year after he joined the force. Jackson hadn't seen him since the Douglas family's funeral, at which time Greg had still been with SDPD. He didn't pick up, so Jackson left him a voicemail and asked for any scoop on Padilla's whereabouts or involvement with gangs.

Not knowing anyone else to call, Jackson sat down at his computer and Googled the L Street Gang. He didn't find much, other than the meaning for their name—kind of obvious—and the fact that the majority of its members were Latino. Everything else was sketchy at best.

With nothing else to do, he paced the house, running his conversations with Hillary and D.A. Moreno over in his mind. Were they right? Was this the end of the line? Was there no way to make Padilla pay?

No, there was a way. Two of them, actually.

But in order to execute either one, he'd need to find Padilla again. He thought about driving down to San Diego and checking out his motel and *El Pequeño* himself, but realized it wasn't worth it. If SDPD couldn't find him, Jackson wasn't going to.

So with nothing to do but wait to hear back from Dick, Greg, or Gwynn, Jackson did what he'd done for so many months—he tried to escape in the virtual world inside his Xbox. As had been the case for so many months, he succeeded, but only somewhat.

*   *   *

3:44 p.m.

JACKSON'S PHONE rang as he was mopping up against Washington State. He paused his Xbox and practically tore the cover off his phone in an effort to answer it. "Yeah?"

"Jackson, it's Greg Cole."

"Hey, what's up?"

"I put out some feelers and I just heard back from a guy I know."

"Yeah?"

"Word is, Padilla went to Rey Cartagena."

Jackson froze. "Rey Cartagena?"

"You know the name?"

"Yeah. Yeah, I know him."

"He runs the Cartagena Family," Cole said, "the Mexican version of the mob. They make some of these street gangs down here look like cookie-hawking Girl Scouts, man."

"Why Cartagena?" Jackson asked.

"If your intel is right, that Padilla's in trouble with the L Street Gang, he might be looking for protection. The L's and the Cartagenas don't exactly see eye-to-eye."

"Oh?"

"Nothing much has ever come of it, because the L's are smart enough not to start anything. But there's bad blood."

"Okay, thanks. Hey, you happen to know where Cartagena hangs out these days?"

"Jack, man, you're not thinking of going after him, are you?"

"No."

Cole paused. "I honestly don't know. He's like a shadow."

"All right, thanks, Greg."

"Sure thing. Jack, whatever you're into here, be careful, man."

"I will. Thanks."

He clapped the phone shut and sighed. Rey Cartagena?

Seven years ago, Jackson had been an assistant at MTR, when late one night a big, scary black dude had rolled into the parking lot, looking desperately for a P.I. to help him prove the woman blackmailing him didn't have what she claimed. That guy was Reggie, and the woman was his very recently ex-wife's sister, Leila Mann. On a Friday, no associates had been available, and Jackson, for some reason moved by the big man's plight, had offered to look into things. He'd discovered that Leila had owed gambling debts to Rey Cartagena, the brutal then-next in line in the Cartagena crime family. He'd also discovered that she had paid back Rey by borrowing, unbeknownst to him, from his little brother Angel. Jackson had turned the tables on Leila, threating to reveal to Rey where she had gotten the money if she didn't back off her false claims against Reggie. She had capitulated, Reggie had opened his new restaurant without any hassle or strings attached, and a new friendship had been born.

And Jackson had avoided any retaliation from the Cartagenas—or any association with them whatsoever.

Now, that was apparently past.

He took ten minutes on the internet to learn that Rey had indeed become head of the family. Seven years ago, he'd kept a clean profile, in part by strictly punishing his own family and crew if they stepped out of line. From what Jackson could tell, Rey was still untouchable by the authorities.

Jackson quickly packed an overnight bag while trying to put the pieces together. Padilla, fresh out of the joint, living in a dive motel and working an overnight shift, had tried to make a "better" go of things by working for the L Street Gang and had botched a job, incurring their wrath. Or maybe he had worked for another crew, maybe even the Cartagenas, and interfered in the L's operations. But that didn't make sense, because Rey wasn't the type to hire a multiple screw-up like Padilla. But there were plenty of gangs in San Diego, so swap out the Cartagenas for some other bunch—Padilla still could have offended the L's and run to Rey because he was the one guy the L's were scared of.

Or was it possible Padilla was working the other side? He had cut a deal with Moreno in exchange for testifying against a killer with ties to the Logan Heights Gang? Had he been working for the white hats again and, in the process, ticked off the L Street Gang?

Packed, Jackson got into his Granada and headed south again. The weather hadn't changed since the morning, with the exception that the air seemed loaded with intensity. There had been so much gray and gloom that Jackson hadn't bothered to check a forecast recently, but he gathered a storm was brewing. How apropos.

As he drove, he made more phone calls. The first was to D.A. Moreno, to see if she was aware of any work Padilla might be doing as an informant. He doubted she would hold out on him, given their talks, but didn't put it past her either. He got her secretary, asked for a call back at Moreno's convenience, and moved on.

He also called Special Agent Collier, who had first informed him about the nature of Padilla's testimony that led to his early release from Kern Valley. Collier knew nothing of Padilla's current whereabouts or activity, but promised to ask a few sources.

Jackson then called Dick Davis, who answered amidst a coughing fit.

"Dick, it's Jackson."

"Hey, probie," he said, coughing again. He called everyone his junior "probie."

"Hey. You find anything about Padilla and the L's?"

"Not per se. But I did hear the L's have a hit out for some flunky."

"But not who that flunky is?"

"No."

"You know why?"

"Word is, this mark botched a deal, got one of their own shot."

"What are the odds it's not Padilla?"

"With these guys . . ."

"What do you hear about Rey Cartagena lately?"

"Rey Cartagena? What do you want with him?"

"I've heard from other sources that Padilla went to Rey."

"Where you hear that?"

"One of my brother's old buddies with SDPD."

Dick harrumphed, either because he wasn't wild about police sources or because he was regurgitating his lunch.

"So, any idea where I can find Rey Cartagena?"

"Wouldn't advise trying, probie."

"Suppose I need to find him?"

Dick sighed. "He moves around."

"So I hear."

"Yeah, well, the feds have nothing concrete on him, but—"

"Feds?"

"And local LEOs. Everybody wants him. Including other gangs. His brother, Angel, is next in line, and he's got about half the brains of his brother. You take out Rey, the Cartagena Family's suddenly not so tough. Which is why Rey moves around, because somebody's always looking for him."

"So who do I call to find out where he is?"

Dick sighed again. "You're serious about this?"

"Dead serious."

"Yeah, maybe so."

Jackson waited.

"Let me make some calls."

"I appreciate it, Dick."

"Yeah, we'll see."

Jackson closed his phone and focused on driving. Back in high school, he'd gone on a ski trip with the youth group from his church. He'd gone snowboarding, because skiing was for dorks, according to teenage Jackson. It'd been just his second time, and he'd been getting used to his rental board. But a couple of the youth group's better looking girls

253

had been watching, so he'd opted for one of the intermediate runs. He'd been fine, at first, but had struggled to control his speed. He remembered the moment, just before he crashed, when he'd realized he was going too fast—where the slope was going by him faster than he could process it and make decisions. Fortunately, his head over heels wipeout had left him with nothing more than a face-full of snow and a shaken psyche.

Now, Jackson felt the same way. He was acting one step faster than he was thinking, on his way to roust the most powerful gangster in San Diego in an effort to find a two-bit thug. And for what? What exactly was Jackson going to do when he found him? Shoot him? Pistol-whip him into confessing? Drive him over to the L Street Gang's headquarters?

It was a long way to San Diego, which gave him plenty of time to think.

And to remember the sensation of flipping end-over-end down a mountain.

Chapter Thirty-Two

Saturday, May 14, 2011
2:47 p.m.

HAILEY WORE A pink baby doll blouse and white Capri pants. Her hair was down and wavy, the blond catching every ray of SoCal sunshine while the brown added contrast and texture. She'd gone simple with jewelry, just medium-sized silver hoop earrings, a heart-shaped necklace, and a few rings on her fingers. Simple for her, at least. Her already cute face was enhanced by a carefree smile, one Jackson hadn't seen on her yet. He didn't need MatchStick to know that he and Hailey weren't compatible long-term as a couple, but a small part of him wished that instead of driving to San Diego to meet his family, he was taking her to dinner for his birthday.

She had dropped Connor at John Wayne Airport late that morning and seen him board a flight to Las Vegas, then to Salt Lake City, where his cousin was waiting. He'd seemed relieved, she said, which in turn made her relieved. But also, she expressed to Jackson as they drove from her place toward the coast, a little pensive about how everything would play out. If they couldn't convince the mayor, and thus Jenn, not to press charges against Connor, and if they couldn't ultimately prove Jenn's guilt in the MatchStick scam, Connor's future was muddy. It was somewhat muddy anyhow, what with him leaving his job and his apartment and everything he knew to run away, but Hailey was covering his rent and was going to go and explain things to his boss, J.H. Hahn, on Monday.

"Mouse hacked MatchStick's server," Jackson said as they drove.

"And?"

"He found the wiped data, the 'Fail' responses."

"He found it? Where?"

"Hidden folder somewhere."

"So what does that mean?"

"Judges kind of frown on hacking, so it won't do us any good in court. But it proves Connor right, and also gives us a template for what kind of marks Jenn's looking for."

"So you can create a . . . what did you call it?"

"Honeypot."

Hailey nodded. "You think this will work?"

"Honestly?"

"Yes, don't sugarcoat it."

"Honestly, I think it has a good chance. Too many variables to say if it will or won't."

She nodded again. "And if not?"

"Then we come clean with the truth. Tell your dad, tell Maggie so she can write a spirited exposé, let the San Jose authorities know in case they want to reopen their investigation up there, and . . ."

"And what?"

"I'm just thinking."

"About?"

"Connor logged onto the server and found the Fail responses. I don't think he broke any laws in doing so."

"What difference does it make? That data was removed."

"No, it was copied and hidden. Mouse hacked it, so we have it again."

"But you said it was inadmissible."

"It's inadmissible if it was hacked. But since Connor legally procured the same data anyhow . . ."

She shook her head. "I don't think a judge would allow that."

"Well, we could cut out all the middleman stuff. Make the judge—and Jenn—think Connor had saved the data elsewhere and **voila**."

Hailey raised an eyebrow.

"Just a thought. But it's Plan B. Let's focus on Plan A first."

They pulled into Cameron's parking lot five minutes before three. Juliet had called about two-thirty, saying they were having a quick bite to eat and should make it by three-fifteen at the latest. Jackson had not called

Hillary to update her, mostly because he was in a good mood and didn't want it tarnished.

Katie was working the hostess desk when they entered Cameron's. Jackson combined a frown with a smile. "You're still working?"

"Somebody's always calling in sick," she said with a smile. "Just two of you?" she asked with an added twinkle.

"We're meeting another couple," Jackson said. "Ike and Juliet Haywood."

"Up or down?"

"Down's fine."

Katie nodded. "Sit where you like, and I'll send them to you when they come."

"Thanks."

"Ex?" Hailey asked as they took the steps down.

"No, just a friend. I frequent the place."

"I see."

Mid-afternoon on a Saturday, the downstairs at Cameron's was half full of walk-ins off the beach and tourists taking a break or a late lunch. Jackson scoped out a booth in the corner, and he and Hailey ordered drinks from an unfamiliar waiter.

"Oh, I have this," Hailey said, reaching into her purse when the waiter was gone. She handed Jackson an envelope, and he opened it to find a four-page, handwritten statement from Connor, detailing the events of the past week. He'd signed it, dated it, and left a place for a witness.

Jackson quickly scrawled his name and the date underneath Connor's, then excused himself to make a copy in Reggie's office. Reggie was absent, but Jackson knew the code, and two minutes later, he slid back into the booth. "Copy for you," he said, handing the original to Hailey. He pocketed the actual copy. "Just in case."

She smiled, rather sweetly. "So what's next?" she asked, bending the straw on her fruit drink to take a sip.

"How so?"

"I mean, after you wrap this case. How do you attract more clients?"

"I've got a moderate advertising plan. I'm attending a few more meet-and-greets in the hopes of making contacts. And there's always word of mouth."

"Well, you have my endorsement, but my circle doesn't find a lot of need for a private investigator."

"I figure it will take a little while to get the ball rolling," he said. "But this feels right. Not to get all schmaltzy on you, but I feel this is what God wants me doing. I haven't felt that before, so . . ."

"That's good then, right?"

"I think so." He took a swig of his tea. "What's next for you? You have long-term career plans, family?"

She shrugged. "I don't know. I like O'Bannon's but I don't want to still be seating people ten years from now. I don't know," she repeated.

"There may be a moderately successful dating service that needs new management soon."

"I'll pass."

Jackson's phone chirped, and he excused himself to take the call. "Yeah?"

"It's Hillary."

"Depositions will drag on into the night and you have to cancel?"

"You wish. They dragged, but I'm finally done."

"Okay. My three o'clock has become a three-fifteen, so hang tight." She sighed.

"Else call a cab. You can afford it. I'm at Camer—"

"Just get here as fast as you can."

"Right. Where am I picking you up again?"

Her sigh this time was more of a growl.

"Relax, Hill."

"Hillary."

"I'll call when I'm on my way."

She hung up on him again.

"Trouble?" Hailey asked.

"Yeah, unfortunately." He didn't get a chance to explain, as Katie appeared at the bottom of the stairs, pointing him out to Ike and Juliet.

"They're here," Jackson said, and stood as the Haywoods approached the booth.

They were still dressed for golf, even though they had supposedly showered afterward. Ike wore a light green polo, white pants, a copper bracelet on his wrist (they were still a thing, apparently) and loafers instead of golf spikes. Juliet had changed into flip-flops, but wore a white skirt, a bright blue sleeveless collared top, and had her hair pulled through a white visor into a ponytail. Mr. and Mrs. Country Club.

Jackson shook hands and introduced the Haywoods to Hailey and vice versa as all four sat around the corner booth. The same waiter quickly came with menus, but Ike waved him off and ordered two Arnold Palmers.

"Excuse me, sir?"

"Half iced tea, half lemonade."

"I see. We can do that."

"Great. Plenty of ice."

"Yes, sir."

"Who's Arnold Palmer?" Hailey asked.

Ike shot Jackson a "She serious?" look.

"The King," Jackson answered.

"Of where?"

Ike just shook his head.

"Thanks for meeting us on short notice," Jackson said.

"Of course," Juliet replied. "What's up?"

It took Jackson the better part of fifteen minutes to explain all the details of meeting Hailey at the same event where he'd met the Haywoods, his search for Connor, and Connor's discovery of Jenn's MatchStick scam. Ike and Juliet listened quietly, and by the time he was finished, their drinks were half gone.

"So you're stuck?" Ike asked.

"Ish. But I have a plan, and that's where you two come in. Hopefully."

Ike nodded for him to continue.

"The only way we can take Jenn down and expose not only what she's doing but whoever else may be involved, is to catch her in the act."

"'Whoever else'?" Juliet asked.

"He means my dad," Hailey said.

"The mayor of Santa Monica?"

She nodded.

"I meant more associates," Jackson said. "This isn't a one-man operation."

"One-woman," Juliet said.

"Touché. Plus, the way we figure it, she's probably guilty of everything from extortion to potentially homicide up in San Jose, whereas Assemblymember Murtaugh might be guilty of nothing more than being a gullible dupe. I'm hoping if we blow the lid off what she's doing here, it might have reverberations up the coast and enable the authorities there to make sure justice was served."

Juliet nodded.

"What do you mean 'catch her in the act'?" Ike said.

"You don't know where he's going?" Juliet asked.

"I have a suspicion, but I want to hear it from the horse's mouth." He turned to Jackson. "No offense."

"None taken. Juliet's right. We need someone to go undercover, so to speak, with MatchStick. Create bait profiles that will look ripe for the picking to Jenn and her cronies. Then, when they start to run their scam—blackmail, extortion, simple theft, grand theft, embezzlement, whatever—we turn the tables on them. If you do it right, it will provide the authorities actionable evidence that at the very least will take down Jenn's coconspirators, and they should squeal like a stuck hog."

"How colorful," Juliet said.

"Grandpa lingo, sorry."

Ike sat back. "It could work."

"I'd do it, but I'm blown. Jenn knows me. Same with Hailey, obviously, and Maggie."

"Maggie?"

"The reporter. She'd be a go for it otherwise, I have a feeling."

Ike raised an eyebrow, then turned to Juliet. "What do you think, Jules?"

"I agree, it could work. But how do we know she'll bite?"

"The marks Connor found had a number of profile traits in common. We duplicate enough of them, add a zero here and there to your bank accounts, and she won't be able to resist."

"And you've got all this profile info?"

Jackson reached into his pocket and withdrew a USB drive, which he set on the table. "All on there. Don't ask where it came from, but suffice to say, it won't hold up in court."

Ike nodded.

"If you're up for it, I'll pass this off to you. I'll still help in any way I can, but I'm not going to micromanage. You run this however you see fit."

"And I'm covering all expenses," Hailey said. "Plus whatever your rate is. If we can put Jenn out of business, save my father from getting deeper into her web, and restore Connor's life to normal, it will be worth it."

Ike nodded again.

"How much are you paying Jackson?" Juliet asked.

"Nothing. He gave me his 'grand opening' discount."

Ike shot Jackson another glance, a check, if he read it right, to see if Jackson had fallen for a pretty girl and compromised sound business principles. He looked back to Hailey, seemingly satisfied. "Then we'll match it."

"What?"

Juliet nodded.

"Only fair," Ike said, "since we're being brought in under the wing of his investigation. If anything, we should bill him."

"I'll still pay it."

"I'm only kidding. You cover any reasonable expenses, and we'll do it on the house. A 'reciprocal' discount."

Hailey beamed.

"On one condition," Ike said.

"Name it."

"Give us the weekend to look things over, make sure there's no hitches we're missing, do a standard background check, and if everything checks out, we'll take it from here."

"Works for me," Hailey said.

"Me too."

"We do have a standard contract," Juliet said. "Non-disclosure, terms of service, that sort of thing. We can shoot it to you Monday."

"Okay."

"We'll keep you in the loop, too," Ike said to Jackson. "And if we need any dirty work done, we're bouncing it back to you."

"That's fair."

"Now, if you don't mind, it was a long day."

"I hear the kikuyu grass at Riviera's a killer."

"Not half as bad as a chatty client who won't shut up while you're putting."

Juliet whacked his arm. "Like that was to blame for all those three-putts."

They exchanged contact info and said goodbyes, and after settling the small tab, Jackson and Hailey followed them out to the parking lot.

"So, you want to grab dinner or something?" Hailey asked. "As a thank you, especially since I was so hard on you at first."

"You weren't that hard," Jackson said, his mouth forming a smirk.

"What?"

"Nothing. And I would like dinner, but I'm actually meeting my family in San Diego for a little birthday dinner."

"Yours?"

He nodded.

"Happy birthday. Why didn't you say something?"

"I hate to beg for well-wishes."

"Another time then?"

"Sure. Once the Haywoods take Jenn down, we'll celebrate her prison sentence."

"They seem competent."

"Yeah, I think so too. If anybody can do this, it's them."

"I hope so."

They'd reached the Granada, and Jackson got her door for her. It was only a few minutes back to her apartment, and when they arrived, she reached out her hand and placed it on his. "Thank you, Jackson."

"You're welcome."

"I had my doubts, I'll admit, but I'm glad you talked me into it. If you hadn't . . . I don't know what would have happened to Connor."

"He'd have given Shane a shock when he decided on a day cruise to Catalina."

Hailey laughed, then leaned over and pecked him on the cheek. She smiled, pausing a few inches from him, and for a second, he thought she was going to kiss him for real. When she didn't, withdrawing instead with another smile, he was both relieved and disappointed.

"Bye, Jackson. I'll call you about dinner."

"I look forward to it."

She got out and closed the door behind her, and Jackson watched her bound up the steps to her building's front door. Then he laughed, realizing what a ridiculous parody he was of all those TV detectives who always fell for their clients.

Chapter Thirty-Three

Friday, June 21, 2013
6:12 p.m.

THROUGH A PAIR of binoculars, Jackson watched a low-riding Chevrolet Corvette turn into the gravel parking lot outside a square box of a building. It drove around to the side and parked several yards from a door a few shades darker brown than the building's beat-up siding. It was still in better shape than the roof, with shingles worn and curled. Situated on a spit of land projecting out from a bushy overgrowth of trees, with salt ponds on one side and the brackish backwater of San Diego Bay on the other, and with just a weed-infested parking lot on two sides, it resembled an old quarry office or a temporary construction headquarters. It was neither.

Two men got out of the Corvette. The passenger was big and tall, probably six-four and well over two bills. He wore a suit coat over a T-shirt, with wraparound sunglasses covering his eyes even though it was heavily overcast with distant rumbles of thunder hinting at rain. The driver was thin, with light brown skin and slick, short, very black hair. He wore a collared shirt untucked over what might have been leather pants. Jackson had no difficulty, even after seven years, recognizing the head of the Cartagena Family.

The passenger tapped digits on a keypad beside the door, but Jackson was too far away to make them out. The two men slipped inside and the lot was quiet. A dozen cars were parked in various places, half in the side lot next to Rey Cartagena's Corvette, half in the main lot around the front. Aside from a small porchlight beside the door Rey and his passenger had entered, the only other light hung from a pole in the far corner of the lot.

Even on the longest day of the year, and several hours before sunset, the lights were on, fighting the gloom.

Jackson waited.

He'd had an eventful ride down to San Diego. Melanie Gwynn had called back, confirming that Padilla's whereabouts were unknown. His motel room was clean, and he hadn't shown up for work the night before at *El Pequeño* in National City. Law enforcement was looking for him, but she feared he had gone underground or left the area.

Dick Davis had called with a couple of names, people who might know Rey's whereabouts. The first had been a former cop turned "private contractor" who had come up empty when Jackson called him. He'd been interrupted before calling the second name by a call from Hillary that he had let go to voicemail. She'd tried to smooth over their meeting that morning, saying she understood Jackson's frustration, but pleaded with him not to do anything reckless. He'd deleted the message.

Dick's second source, an ex-con named Rodriguez who now ran a downtown city mission, had told Jackson that Rey lived in a "fortress" in Lynwood Hills, and also had a couple of other residences. He would spend a weekend at one or a night at the other every once in a while, just to mix things up. Wherever he was, he would be well secured. Being the head of San Diego's biggest crime family was apparently a dangerous business.

He proved just as elusive in his everyday movements, Rodriguez had said. Best way to pin him down in a hurry, call his brother Angel, who served as a screen for all potential meetings. It had been a long shot, but Jackson had called Angel, disguising his voice on the off chance Angel remembered him from seven years ago. He'd claimed to be a cop with info that Rey would want to know about. Angel had blown him off, and Jackson had waited, playing a hunch.

Thirty minutes later, Angel had called back. Six-thirty, the Saltwater Room in Chula Vista. Ask for Cayenne. Jackson wasn't sure if that was the name of some foreign waitress, a rarely ordered sauce, or a random code. And he didn't much care, because he had no intention of meeting Rey, especially after asking Mouse to look up the Saltwater Room online.

It had taken a few more calls, to Greg Cole and Connie, to verify the vehicle Rey drove. Then Jackson had navigated to Chula Vista and parked just down the road from the old, tan building and waited. Now, having seen Rey and his bodyguard enter the building, Jackson started the Granada and drove into the parking lot, backing into a space between cars on the side of the building, a few dozen feet from Rey's Corvette. He remained in the car, studying the building. He'd seen no security cameras with his binoculars, and spotted nothing up close either.

He killed the engine, pocketed the keys, and waited. Another fifteen minutes until the scheduled meeting. He pegged Rey to give him ten to fifteen before blowing him off. Then, it was all about timing. Rey's passenger would complicate matters, but Jackson had expected it after talking with Rodriguez. And he'd have the element of surprise. Hopefully.

At six-thirty, Jackson withdrew his gun from his waistband. It'd been a long time since he'd used his Glock 19. In fact, the last time he'd used it, he hadn't used it. He'd drawn it on New Year's Eve, after being summoned to the Woodlawn Cemetery and attacked. With memories of too many shootings in his mind, he'd been unable to pull the trigger, and it had cost him a bullet to the shoulder. He hadn't made the same mistake two nights later, when he'd saved a young actress from being raped by her stalker, Jackson's shooter. He'd used his SPAS-12 shotgun then, obliterating the stalker's head.

Verifying a round was in the chamber, Jackson set the Glock on the seat beside him, keeping his hand on it. He'd changed since New Year's Eve. He was more resolute. More determined. He wouldn't hesitate again.

He wasn't sure if that was a good thing or not.

The minutes ticked by, and repeated thunderclaps announced the onset of rain. It started as huge sprinkles, then turned into a heavy shower. At ten till seven, Jackson began to fidget. At five till, he checked his phone, even though it hadn't rung or vibrated. At seven, he began reconsidering.

Rey had to suspect that he'd been stood up or duped. Either way, why was he still here? A couple more cars had come in and parked around front. Sooner or later, another would arrive in what Jackson deemed was the employee lot, and likely notice a candy apple red antique. There was no telling how long until Rey came out. On one hand, Jackson knew he had to come out, and could wait him out indefinitely. On the other, he was getting twitchy, and twitchy wasn't good. Silencing multiple internal warnings, at ten after seven, Jackson got out, taking with him a flathead screwdriver from his car's emergency kit. Having wiped it carefully to remove prints, he crouched down beside the Corvette and wedged the screwdriver at a forty-five-degree angle against the tire, even kicking it with his foot so that it wouldn't budge—until the car was put into reverse and the tire popped itself.

Then he stood and headed around to the front entrance.

Jackson had never been to a strip joint before, and all he knew was what he'd seen when Magnum or MacGyver's investigations had led them to such a place. Turned out, TV had hit the nail on the head, at least as far as the Saltwater Room was concerned. Low lighting in the form of an odd mix of red, purple, and blue. Loud, aggressive music. Absence of eye contact from the bouncer, bartender, a reasonably-clad waitress, or any of the clients. And of course, women with no self-respect who were willing to flaunt themselves in front of perverts for cash.

Jackson had heard a "testimony" once from a former pole-dancer turned praise and worship artist, who had bemoaned the stereotype so many Christians put on strippers and exotic dancers. Having been transformed, she didn't condone their behavior. But they weren't all immoral pagans, plunging headlong into debauchery for the sake of profit. They were strapped college students and struggling single moms and runaways and orphans just trying to make ends meet. She'd pled with tears for her new brothers and sisters to welcome these "outcasts" with open arms, understanding their point of view.

It was a load of crap. If he had to hear one more jackwagon justify sinful behavior with the excuse that Jesus had eaten with tax collectors and sinners, he was going to lose it. And while he understood the impoverished state some people found themselves in and was well aware of the instability in the economy, it wasn't like it was impossible to find honest work. Nobody's only alternative was to work a pole in some seedy, smoky pit.

And yet, here he was, Mr. High and Mighty, setting aside his morals in pursuit of the head of the Mexican Mafia to make him rat on a killer. At least he didn't dawdle.

He swept his eyes over the darkened main room, keeping his focus on the far walls and corners. He identified the kitchen entrance, and a private hallway that could lead to dressing rooms, offices, restrooms, or only the devil could imagine what else. Another doorway opened to the right, the same direction as the side entrance. With a few looks over his shoulder to make sure no one was monitoring him, Jackson ducked through it and into a hallway.

Flickering fluorescent lights lit the hallway in shades of green. The music was reduced to a driving bass beat that shook the walls. What sort of slimy cockroaches crawled out from this place? And what was Rey Cartagena, successful thug that he was, doing here? Jackson knew little of San Diego's exotic club scene, but had to believe there were "higher end" joints than this one.

The hallway ended in a door that Jackson concluded led to the parking lot. There was what looked like a break room or lounge on the left, along with two unisex bathrooms and a janitor's closet. Three more doors opened to the right, each labeled. Office, Assistant Manager, Manager. Jackson walked to the last, labeled "Manager," and stood with his ear to the closed door. The reverberating music was too loud for him to hear anything else.

He hadn't spotted Rey in the main room, and doubted he had used the employee entrance to come watch a striptease. So Jackson took a deep breath, then rapped on the door. He figured one of two things would happen. Either Rey's muscle would open the door, in which case Jackson would stick the Glock in his face, or he would ask who was there.

"Yeah?" a voice came from inside, close to the door it sounded.

Jackson mumbled something incoherent.

"Huh? Speak up?"

He mumbled again and stood back.

The door cracked open, and as it did, Jackson lunged forward, kicking the door open. It cracked and recoiled, and Jackson drove into it with his shoulder. He righted himself and quickly took stock of the room.

It was dark, with two windows both with blinds drawn, and light coming from a desk lamp and a TV on the wall in the corner. It was a standard office, with a couple filing cabinets, a small table and chairs, and a private bathroom off to one side. More important than the layout was the location of Rey Cartagena, seated behind his desk with stacks of money on it in front of him, and the muscle, who had fallen back into a small couch against the wall when Jackson drove the door into him.

He held a bloody hand to his nose and stood, ready to come at Jackson. He didn't give him the chance, chopping at his forehead with the barrel of the gun. The blow spun the man around, and Jackson drove the butt of the gun down into his nape. He crumpled into a ball.

Just that quickly, Jackson spun around, aiming the gun at Rey, who had just started to reach a hand for a desk drawer. "You so much as blink, I put a bullet in each button of that shirt," Jackson said, easing the door shut with his free hand. He threw a quick glance at Muscles, who wasn't moving.

"Hands up," Jackson said to Rey, who complied.

"Who are you?"

"A dirty cop. Interlock your fingers on your head."

Rey obeyed, and Jackson came around the desk. He jerked him back in his chair, just in case he had any panic buttons under the desk or accessible by foot. Jackson lifted him by the collar, at the same time jabbing the barrel of the gun into the back of his head. He dragged him around the end of the desk and shoved him onto the couch, where he could see both him and Muscles. Still comatose.

"What do you want?"

"I'm asking the questions. You answer them, you stay alive to keep corrupting this city. But if you try anything, I start plugging joints."

"That's twice you have threatened to shoot me." Rey's eyes narrowed. "Most of the people who make threats, make them because they don't have the guts to carry them out."

Jackson pushed the gun into Rey's nose, stopping short of breaking cartilage. "You know, maybe I should just do America's Finest City a favor and blow you away."

"Keep talking, tough guy."

Jackson scowled as he removed the gun. Rey flashed an evil smile. Before he could open his mouth, Jackson knocked the smile off by cracking him in the jaw with the gun.

Rey swore a blue streak, spitting blood into a garbage can at the end of the desk.

"Shut up," Jackson said, repeating his command when Rey kept swearing. "You like pirates?" he asked.

"What?" Rey spat.

"Pirates. They had a saying: Dead men tell no tales. And that is why you are alive."

He spat again. "What do you want?"

"Where is Joaquín Padilla?"

Rey huffed. "I have no idea."

Jackson kicked the inside of Rey's kneecap as hard as he could. Rey winced, but kept silent.

"I know he came to you, looking for protection after getting in trouble with the L's. Tell me where he is."

"I don't know."

"You up to code, Rey?"

"What?"

"Smoke detectors," Jackson said. He reached for a stack of bills off the desk, twenties and fifties. "Sprinklers." He tossed them in the metal garbage can at the end of the desk. "Awfully old building," he said, grabbing a lighter next to a pack of cigarettes on the corner of the desk.

Rey glared.

Jackson shrugged and tossed another stack into the bin, then flicked the lighter.

"Wait."

He clanged it shut. "You remember something?"

"I don't know where Padilla is," Rey said. "He came to me, like you said, but I've got no interest in starting anything with the L's. I told him to get lost."

"Keep talking."

"That's all."

"Nice try," Jackson said. He ignited the lighter again, then tossed it into the can with the money.

"You're crazy!" Rey said, leaping off the couch.

Jackson sat him back down with the gun. "Where is Padilla?"

"Okay, okay, I'll tell you, just put that out."

"Talk first."

"He came to me, like I said, and I didn't want to start anything, like I said. I had no use for him. He was frantic, said he was a dead man if he couldn't get protection or disappear."

"What'd he do?"

"What?"

"What'd he do to upset them so much?"

"He got one of their boys killed on a job gone bad. I told him if he wanted to disappear, I knew a guy."

"Who?"

"Husband of a girl I used to know. Keisha. I don't know his name."

"Keisha?" Jackson said with a frown. "Keisha Lawrence?"

He'd made a mistake. He'd lost focus. Muscles had started to stir, and Jackson hadn't noticed until he was on his feet. He turned the gun toward him, but that meant taking it off Rey, who lunged and tackled Jackson backward. He lost the gun and fell beneath one hundred eighty pounds of angry Mexican. Rey reached for Jackson's neck, but overextended himself. Jackson rammed his knee into Rey's groin, and felt it connect with soft tissue. The life went out of Rey with a soft moan.

Jackson shoved him to the side and rolled over him, then kept rolling under the desk. It was a tight fit, but the right move, as Muscles had come to and charged for the place where Jackson would have been.

Popping up on the opposite side of the desk, Jackson saw Muscles reach inside his suitcoat, presumably for a gun. Jackson reached for the first thing available, a half-empty glass of tequila on the desk, next to the money. In one motion, he grabbed it, lifted it, and flung it at Muscles. He ducked to the side, so the glass only made a glancing blow, but the alcohol splattered his face, including several cuts made by the glass. His wince was audible as he recoiled, for a moment pulling his hand away from his gun.

It was all Jackson needed. He dropped to the floor and scrambled to the end of the desk. He grabbed the garbage can, now crackling with the flame of Rey's likely illegal money. Jackson stood and flung the fiery contents of the garbage can at Muscles, again getting him just before he reached the gun. The fire fed off the alcohol, and Muscles spun away with a scream of pain.

Jackson didn't wait around. He picked up his gun off the floor and beat a hasty retreat. There was no one else in the hallway, and Jackson quickly ducked out the entrance through which Rey and Muscles had entered earlier. He half jumped, half scrambled across the hood of the Corvette, reaching for his keys as he ran to the Granada. He finagled them out and forced himself to focus on the simple act of opening his door. He set the Glock on the seat, started the car, slammed the gearshift into drive, and spun wheels on the gravel as he tore out of the lot.

He was sweating profusely as he balanced his eyes between the road ahead and the rearview mirror. He'd seen no signs of anyone coming after him, either out the side door of the Saltwater Room or on the roads leading back to the interstate. When he merged with northbound traffic on I-5 a few minutes later, Jackson finally started breathing normally again. His shirt was soaked with sweat and his head was pounding. That had been foolish. And sordid.

But it had worked. He had a name.

He just didn't like what it meant.

Chapter Thirty-Four

Saturday, May 14, 2011
4:21 p.m.

THE OFFICES OF Conway, Davenport & Rankin, Attorneys at Law, were located in southern downtown L.A., with a pretty good view of the city skyline and the San Gabriel Mountains in the distance. Or so Jackson assumed. He'd never actually been in their offices, just the lobby. Since it was a beautiful day, even in the concrete jungle, he didn't go that far, instead calling Hillary from his parking spot in front of the building. She said she'd be right down and once again ended the call on him. He tuned the radio.

The Dodgers were in Arizona, so the first pitch wasn't for a couple of hours. He hopped from station to station and, finding nothing, turned off the radio when he saw a shadow appear outside the car. He looked over as Hillary placed a small overnight bag in the backseat, then laid a blazer over it before getting in beside Jackson.

"I thought maybe you'd gone without me."

"Sorely tempted. How were depositions?"

"They've been over so long I can't remember." She reached for her seatbelt, buckled it, then lifted the lacy attached scarf on her sleeveless blouse over the shoulder strap. The blouse was bright green—Boston Celtics green—complemented by a knee-length, form-fitting black skirt. Her pumps were also black. She wore her hair down, resplendent as ever, with silver jewelry to match the darn engagement ring, and a hint of citrusy perfume. The most beautiful woman he'd ever seen, let alone met, was in his car, but he'd just as soon it be, say, Maggie in jeans and a

273

Rangers tee—and not because Maggie was on the market and Hillary wasn't.

"I told you, I had a meeting," Jackson said as he edged into traffic.

"What, some nerdy P.I. club? Do you have buttons?"

"Is there anything I can do that won't earn your disdain?"

"Time will tell," she said. "Where are you going?"

"The 110."

"The 5 is quicker."

He shrugged. "Deuce a piece."

"What?"

"What's your all-fire hurry, anyhow? You make Mom seem like a Brazilian."

Hillary shook her head. "What in the world are you talking about?"

"Brazilians. They're notoriously laidback, have no concept of time."

"You're basing this on your vast experience with people from Brazil? Let me guess, some hot Amazonian 'chick' in your dorm at SC?"

"There was a girl from Brazil in my building, but she looked like Rafa Nadal's heavy sister. My point is, what's your hurry? You miss Grant that bad?"

"It's your birthday, and I didn't want to be late. I was being nice."

"No, for real."

She made a pained smile.

"We won't be late. It's less than two hours."

"There's traffic."

"It's Saturday."

"You know what, whatever."

They were silent until Jackson had caught the flow of traffic on Interstate 110 south. "I think I solved my first case."

Hillary rolled her head, resting in her hand, his way. "You solved the case?"

"Well, I know I did that. I found the guy yesterday. Very clever of me," he said with a wink. "But now we're running a sting to take down his corrupt boss."

"You're running a sting?"

"Maybe we should put the windows back down. There seems to be an echo in here."

"Forgive me, I'm just having trouble believing you could solve a cereal box mystery with the free decoder ring."

"I actually put the pieces together pretty well. And this sting involves taking down a beautiful blond woman who manipulates her way into a relationship with unsuspecting, semi-powerful men only to take advantage of them and use them for her evil schemes."

He looked at Hillary. She glared back. "What are you trying to say?"

"Nothing. You're the one apparently drawing comparisons."

"Why are you telling me all this?"

"I don't know, because I'm excited. It's my birthday, I get to have dinner with the people I love—and you—it's a beautiful day and I live here and not the panhandle of Texas or Oklahoma, or really any panhandle for that matter. And I just solved my first case and earned a kiss on the cheek from my rather attractive client."

"And there it is."

"There what is?"

"This is all buildup to tell me that some needy, clingy Valley Girl was so taken by her knight in shining armor that she kissed you. I'm surprised your shirt didn't rip the way your chest puffed up."

"Not needy, not clingy, not a Valley Girl although I did have my suspicions, and I find her kissing me kind of funny and prosaic, albeit not unpleasant. But the reason I'm telling you all this is because I am trying to have a normal conversation with my future sister-in-law."

She looked at him for several seconds. "No, for real."

"You know, I wonder something," he said as he moved into the right lane.

"I'll bite."

"I wonder if in about ten years, when you and Grant have a couple of adorable and somewhat snotty children, if our constant feuding will turn into a respectful, good-natured sparring, very Niles and Roz."

"Or?"

"Or if some Christmas morning when we're all together one of us won't wake up and the other will be feverishly hiding the arsenic in the back of the spice cabinet."

"Neither," Hillary said. "You'll fall for some client with an accent and 'great hair' and have a shotgun wedding, then follow her across the Southwest in support of her all-girl rock band. Where are we going?" she asked as Jackson exited at West Martin Luther King Jr. Boulevard, just past the USC campus and the iconic, historic Los Angeles Memorial Coliseum.

"Huh?"

"Where are we going?"

"Right, sorry. Just thinking about that all-girl rock band idea. I have a stop to make."

"You're not going to pray at a statue of Reggie Bush or something, are you?"

"No, I think they took all those down. It'll be quick, I promise."

Hillary sighed and dropped her head into her hand against the window.

Jackson decided not to leave his dinner plate unattended in her presence.

*   *   *

Friday, June 21, 2013
10:04 p.m.

EVEN WITH stopping for gas and a very late supper, Jackson made good time back to Los Angeles. He'd thought about calling ahead, but some things just had to be done in person. And he already hated himself for what he was going to do.

When he inquired at the hostess desk, he was told Reggie had been pressed into service in the kitchen. It wasn't that unusual, seeing how his official role was owner, part-time chef, part-time server, and occasional glad-hander. So Jackson let himself into Reggie's office, flipped on the

TV, and mindlessly watched some CNN talking heads debate something about a developing scandal regarding some paramilitary CIA operations or something along those lines. No German words were involved, but he gathered it was the same thing Maggie and the other panelists had been debating a week ago. None of the talking heads was a knockout brunette with whom he'd previously had a semi-romantic relationship, so Jackson didn't pay real close attention.

It was maybe half an hour before Reggie entered the office, surprise playing out in a quick raise of his eyebrows. When you were six-three, two-fifty, you didn't startle.

"Hey man, make yourself at home, come on in." He stopped. "Man, you look like crap."

"Comes from raking my hand through my hair for two hours."

Reggie came around the desk and sat on the couch. "They're still talking about this?" he asked, muting the TV. "What's up, J?"

"I've got to ask you something, and I hate to ask it, and if you want to say no you can—I really understand and won't be—"

"Ask."

"There's a little preamble."

"Should we order?"

"No, I'm good." He sighed, catching Reggie up on where things stood with his investigation into Joaquín Padilla. It had been such a crazy week, he couldn't remember who he'd told what or updated when. When he mentioned Rey Cartagena, Reggie's face clouded. Then his eyes widened.

"You what?"

"I kicked down his door and forced him to tell me where I could find Padilla."

"Let me get this straight, J. You dummy-call his brother, pretending to be a dirty cop, then walk into his strip club and, what, shove a gun in his face?"

"Well, I never told Angel I was a *dirty* cop, and I pistol-whipped his henchman before shoving the gun in his face, but that's the gist of it."

"So did he know something?"

"I think so."

"You think?"

"I had to burn some of his dirty cash first, which kind of made him mad."

"I'd figure."

Jackson looked down. He sighed again. "He told me a girl he used to know had married a guy who could help somebody disappear, which is what Padilla apparently wanted."

Reggie exhaled. "Leila?"

"Worse."

"Keisha?"

Jackson nodded.

Reggie sighed again. "You see her?"

"No. That was about the time his thug came to and I had to fight my way out of there. I drove straight here. Reg . . . I was hoping you . . . I can't even ask it." He took a quick breath. "I was hoping you could call Keisha and see if she'd talk to me."

Reggie nodded slowly.

"My only other option is to kick in her door and stick a gun in her face, and bad blood aside, I hate to do that to your ex. And frankly, I think I might be pressing my luck as it is. I'm hoping you can catch a fly with honey."

"More like a wasp, J."

"I'm sorry. I don't know what else to do. I'm at that point where I'm no longer leaning on my friends but becoming a nuisance."

"You ain't a nuisance, man. Believe me, I'd tell you if you were." Reggie stood and paced, rubbing his hand all over his head. "I'll call her. It's fifty-fifty she takes it, and far less she'll hear me out, much less meet me. But I'll try."

Jackson closed his eyes. "Thanks, Reg."

The big man exhaled. "I didn't even know she'd remarried."

"You haven't been in touch at all?"

"I wrote her a long letter, Christmas of '06. I explained where I was, what had happened in my life. I apologized for . . . everything. It wasn't a take-me-back sort of a deal, just a peace offering." He shook his head. "She never replied. No call, no text. I haven't heard from her since."

"I left Rey singing falsetto, but I wouldn't be surprised if he called her and tipped her off right after I left. This might be a total waste of time, and I hate to dredge all this up for nothing."

"J, quit apologizing, man. I'm a grown man. I can handle this."

Jackson nodded.

"It's late. I'll call her in the morning. In the meantime, you should get some sleep."

"Yeah, right."

Reggie frowned.

"I don't really sleep anymore, Hoss. I just stare at the ceiling while my brain runs laps inside my skull."

"You seen your shrink lately?"

"Really, play the crazy card right away?"

"If the shoe fits . . ."

Jackson managed a grin. "Talked to him Tuesday. Thing is, I don't think this is the sort of thing that can be talked away. Wheels have been spun, events set in motion. There's only one way this ends, and that's with me bringing Joaquín Padilla to justice, by hook or by crook."

Chapter Thirty-Five

Saturday, June 22, 2013
6:52 p.m.

COVERING TWELVE HUNDRED acres of prime San Diego real estate just northeast of downtown, Balboa Park was as rich in history as in recreational beauty. With over a dozen museums and gardens, outdoor pavilions and amphitheaters, golf courses and ball fields, tennis courts and a swimming pool, walking trails through groves of rare trees, and the famed San Diego Zoo all within its boundaries, the park had something for everyone.

Jackson had been there a number of times growing up and while living in San Diego—all the flowers and art made it a great place to take dates. He had always loved the Spanish Colonial Revival architecture of so many of the museums and buildings, including the California Bell Tower and Casa de Balboa. To him, such architectural style always carried with it an ambiance of tropical adventure (probably due to a pirate fascination as a child). It was especially so in the late afternoon or early evening, when golden sunlight ornamented the stucco exteriors and red clay shingled roofs, and the buildings' towers and spires cast long shadows across the grounds.

Normally.

But as Jackson and Reggie walked along the pedestrian-only section of El Prado, the main east-west thoroughfare through the park, low clouds blocked all sunlight and potential shadows and covered the historic buildings, arched porticos, and diverse palm trees in a bland pallor. They and the unseasonably cool temperatures also kept crowds to a minimum, especially since the museums and visitors center had closed for the day.

"I never asked," Jackson said. "She pick this place or you?"

"She did," Reggie said. He had called his ex-wife, Keisha, that morning, prevailing on her to meet with him and a friend. He'd said it was important. He'd said it wasn't for him but for his friend. He'd promised he'd never contact her again if she agreed, and that seemed to have sealed the deal.

Jackson nodded and turned his eyes to the shadows of a portico on his right.

"We had our first kiss by the reflecting pool," Reggie said.

Jackson looked at him. "You think she's strangely sentimental?"

"No, I think she's vindictive and is trying to tear open an old wound."

His eyes going back to the shadows, Jackson turned the few details he knew of Reggie's pre-divorced life over in his head. As a football player at the University of Nebraska, Reggie had met Keisha Lawrence while on some sort of summer break trip. She was from San Diego originally, which made his signing a free-agent contract with the Chargers out of college—and just before their wedding—seem like a fairy tale. Three years in, they had made the choice to abort a pregnancy—or rather, Keisha had made the choice. Reggie had been unable to live with the decision, which had been the wedge that divided an already splintered marriage. Jackson had come into the picture shortly thereafter, just after Reggie had hit rock-bottom and found Jesus waiting there for him, as he liked to say. He'd also found Jackson, who had helped him get out from under Leila's blackmail scheme. A sordid affair, it had turned out all right for all parties concerned. At least, all parties Jackson was concerned about.

"What you looking at?" Reggie asked, knocking Jackson's shoulder. "This way."

"I don't know. I can't help feeling like there's a sniper watching us or something."

Reggie laughed. "Keisha wouldn't use a sniper, man. She'd kill you with her own bare hands."

"How comforting."

They had turned toward the reflecting pool—technically the Lily Pond and Lagoon—in front of the giant Botanical Building. Made out of lath for the 1915-1916 Panama-California Exposition, it reminded Jackson of a Quonset hut mixed with a Budapest train station. Others viewed it more whimsically and flocked to see the myriad of permanent plants inside it.

Jackson had spent the day making calls. Neither Melanie Gwynn nor Greg Cole had any updates on Padilla's whereabouts, which meant SDPD didn't either. Dick Davis had heard no further "word on the street" about him. Rodriguez, the ex-con rescue worker, had heard nothing new either. D.A. Moreno knew nothing of Padilla's failure to contact his parole officer, nor did she have any clue where he might be. Mouse used his web savvy to search the wire and police scanners for any signs of Padilla or report of a dust-up at a Chula Vista strip club the night before. All negative.

That meant Keisha was Jackson's last chance of tracking down Padilla. He'd been within his grasp a few nights ago, but that was before he had definitive proof he was responsible for his family's death. Never mind if Moreno or Hillary or a judge thought it was definitive—having seen the photos from Padilla's hard drive, Jackson no longer had a doubt, reasonable or otherwise.

The pool was maybe one hundred fifty feet long, spanned three-quarters of the way to the Botanical Building by a footbridge. As they approached it, Jackson kept an eye out for a woman who looked as if she'd just been told there were no more vowels to buy on *Wheel of Fortune*. There was a middle-aged couple walking hand in hand off the bridge, an Asian family talking in some Oriental language as they looked at fish in the pool, and two men in Arab garb either discussing where to have tea or plotting to blow up the Coronado Bridge—it was hard to tell these days. But no angry black women.

For the third time that day, Jackson asked, "You think she'll actually show?"

For the third time that day, Reggie shrugged and said, "Yeah," with as little conviction as possible.

They walked to the middle of the bridge and leaned against the thick, concrete railing, their backs to the Botanical Building. A few more people came and went. Then, almost as if appearing out of the mist like a femme fatale of film noir, Keisha stepped onto the bridge from Jackson's left.

She wore red high heels that were a mile from the bottom of her tight-fitting red dress, which in turn wasn't nearly as far from the top of it. On second thought, it might not have been so much a dress as a very bright tattoo, seeing as how snugly it fit her ample curves. Well, it didn't really fit all of them, which was sort of the point Jackson deduced as she sauntered toward them. He kept his attention on her face, which was attractive if not beautiful. Aside from the eyes, that is. They were like burning coals. Her hair hung in loose curls to her shoulders, giving way to large hoop earrings. She wore abundant lipstick on pouty lips, which she seemed to thrust at Reggie as she stopped in front of him.

Keisha didn't speak, forcing Reggie to make the first move. He stood, and spoke softly. "Hello, Keisha."

"Reggie." She flicked the burning coals at Jackson.

"This is Jackson, the friend I told you about. J, my ex-wife Keisha."

"Pleasure to meet you," Jackson gagged, extending a hand.

"Let's skip the lies," Keisha said. "No friend of Reggie's would possibly consider it a pleasure to meet me."

"It's not like that, K," Reggie said.

"My name isn't K, either," she said. She sighed as she shifted a purse on her shoulder. "I have somewhere to be. What's this about?"

"Jack asked me to arrange the meeting," Reggie said. "I'll let him explain."

"Still passing the buck, huh?"

He said nothing, and she eventually turned to Jackson. "So explain."

"I work as a private investigator," he said. "I'm looking for a man named Joaquín Padilla," he continued before she could huff or make a snide comment about his profession. "Various intel led me to inquire of Rey Cartagena as to his whereabouts. Cartagena told me Padilla had come to him and that he had referred him to you."

Keisha laughed menacingly. "You expect me to believe Rey Cartagena told you anything?" Her eyes went to Reggie. "What is this, a setup?"

"No setup."

"I can be very persuasive," Jackson said. "Rey said Padilla wanted to disappear. He said your husband could make that happen."

Keisha's eyes narrowed, and possibly grew darker. "And what else did Rey tell you?"

Jackson shook his head. "Nothing. He more or less forced me to leave after that."

She smirked. "Assuming it's true that my husband can make people disappear, and assuming I know this Padilla person, what would possibly make you think I'd ever tell either of you where to find him?"

"Because he's the worst of the worst—a thief, a rapist, and a murderer. And if we don't find him now, he may do it again."

"Well then," she said, taking several steps toward Jackson, "I guess you're in a real pickle, aren't you?"

"Keisha, please."

"Please what?" she said, snapping her head toward Reggie. "Please help the man who ruined my life, who wasn't there to support me when I needed him most, who was busy running around being a big football star, chasing cheerleaders like some small-town high school jock? I wouldn't stop to spit on you if you were on fire."

She turned to go but Reggie grabbed her arm.

"Let go of me!"

He released her as quickly as he had taken hold of her. "I know you hate me. Don't do it for me. Do it for J."

"And if not for me, for Padilla's victims."

"Padilla's 'victims' can do what everybody else does and go to the police. As for you, I don't know you and I don't care about your problems. But I'll give you some free advice anyhow. He," she said, aiming her polished thumb at Reggie, "isn't going to help you solve them. He's just going to cause more of them."

She turned her head back to him. "Don't ever call me again."

They both watched her march off in the direction she had come. Jackson searched for the words to tell his friend he didn't care what Keisha said about him, didn't believe what she said about him. But they wouldn't come.

"Come on, J," Reggie said, tapping his arm. "Let's get out of here."

They retraced their path, heading back to the parking lot where El Prado went from a two-lane entrance to the park to a walkway. Reggie strode with purpose, not with the hunched shoulders and stooped posture of a man who'd just been eviscerated by the woman he'd once pledged his love to.

The air had been muggy and hinted at rain, but instead the clouds seemed to envelope the park. Jackson felt like he was on a mountain as the clouds rolled in, but was barely above sea level. "June Gloom" was common in San Diego, and seemed to fit the mood.

"You all right, Hoss?" Jackson asked when they were inside Reggie's H3.

He paused before turning the key. "I'm fine. But I deserved that, and worse. She's right, you know. I wasn't there for her."

"Hold on a sec, man. She's the one who wanted the abortion, not you. And she's the one who walked away from the marriage. You told me you weren't cheating on her like she claimed."

"All true, but I also wasn't the man I should have been. Wasn't the husband I should have been. It never should have gotten to the point it did, and that's on me as much as her. More so. As the husband, I'm supposed to be the leader, and I wasn't no leader, man. I did have an eye for other women, even if I didn't act on it. I was too focused on football and making my life." He nodded. "I deserved that."

"Seven years ago, maybe. But that's not you anymore."

"Yeah, well, she doesn't see that." Reggie finally started the car. "Sorry you didn't get any answers."

"That may not be a total loss," Jackson said, reaching into his pocket. "Oh?"

"I don't mean to insult your lovely ex-wife, but I didn't trust her any farther than I can throw you. I had a feeling she might show up and give us nothing just out of spite, so I had Mouse whip something up."

"What, like that iridescent spray they use in spy movies?"

"No, like a cheap listening device," he said, removing an old Nokia cell phone from his pocket. It had been converted to a receiver, and he powered it on. "I'm hoping she'll call Padilla to warn him we're onto him or call her husband or something we can use."

"Listening device, huh? Where'd you put it?"

"Dropped it in her purse when she turned to give you the business."

"You'll have to be more specific."

"Yeah. It was when she was standing so close that other, ahem, features of her anatomy would have blocked her peripheral vision."

"That's my ex-wife you're talking about, J."

"I didn't pick out her clothes," he said, thumbing his way to the "app" Mouse had created that would record and stream any sounds it picked up from inside Keisha's purse. "She always dress like that?"

"Naw. Just when she wanted to make a statement."

"Like, 'Hey, look at what you're missing, big man?'"

"Your sassy black lady accent needs work, but something like that," Reggie said as they passed under the first of two arches in the figurative shadow of the California Building, which housed the San Diego Museum of Man. With its colorful dome and the sightline-grabbing California Bell Tower, it was another iconic structure in Balboa Park.

"You getting anything?" Reggie asked.

"It's not picking up a real strong signal. These arches, or maybe the fog," Jackson said. It had gotten thicker in just a few minutes, so that as they crossed over I-5 on the multiple-arched Cabrillo Bridge, it felt like they were driving through some *Jurassic Park* setting and not urban San Diego.

"Yeah, it might be something else," Reggie said.

"Causing a weak signal? Like what?"

Reggie dropped his left hand under his right and tossed Jackson his cell phone. He looked at the big man with a frown.

"Tracking device."

"What?"

"When I grabbed her arm, I pressed a micro-tracker to the back of her forearm."

"That's very *Mission: Impossible*. Ethan Hunt would be proud."

"Yeah, well, I don't trust her any farther than you can throw me either. There's an app on the home screen."

Jackson navigated on Reggie's phone. "Where'd you get a micro-tracker?"

"That guy I set you up with to get the earbuds last summer. He's still in business."

"That couldn't have been cheap," Jackson said, looking over at Reggie.

"What's a few bills between friends?"

The app opened and displayed a zoomed out map of the entire U.S. It blipped a few times, then triangulated and zoomed in on the park. It jumped to the south side of the park, and a red dot began to flash. It was moving south on Park Boulevard.

"Where we going, J?"

"South, toward downtown."

"Not getting on I-5?"

"Not yet. How'd you stick this thing on her anyhow, tuck it under her sleeve?"

"I'm not that slick. Just attached it to the fabric. Which means we've got until she changes clothes or starts bumping and grinding on the dance floor and loses it."

"Still better than nothing. You know, if the restaurant business ever fails, we can go into business as the reincarnation of *I Spy*. You're a little heavy for Bill Cosby, but still."

"And you'd never pull off a Robert Culp straight man."

"True." He looked down again at Reggie's phone. "She passed the turn for I-5 east. She's headed to downtown."

Reggie nodded just in time to hang a left on 6th Avenue, which formed the western boundary of Balboa Park, and also led to eastern downtown. "Let's see where the bird dog points."

Chapter Thirty-Six

Saturday, May 14, 2011
5:04 p.m.

"WHAT, YOU NEEDED a fix of wings before dinner?" Hillary asked as Jackson returned to the car. She sat with her arm out the window, dangling her fingers in the breeze, her head lazily reclined against the seatback. All that was missing was her feet on the dash.

"No, I needed a . . . shoot. You have a pen?"

"What?"

"In your purse, a pen?"

She sat up and reached for her purse and withdrew a ballpoint pen with CD&R's name, logo, and contact information on the side. "What are you doing?"

"Had to stop and get a gift for a friend," he said, opening an envelope. It contained a much smaller envelope, itself containing a Buffalo Wild Wings gift card he'd purchased for Maggie.

"What, right now?"

"Yes, and I need to find a mailbox, but let me think a minute."

Hillary sighed. "Where did you get the envelope?"

"I asked a somewhat cute redhead hostess if she could spare one."

"Should have asked for a stamp too, genius."

"Shoot."

"Who are you sending a gift card to anyhow?"

"A friend."

"What's her name?"

"Who said it was a her?"

"Well, I doubt the famous 'Jackson Douglas Dude Code' permits one guy mailing a gift card to another."

"Fair point. Can you see where the nearest post office is on your phone?"

"It's after five on a Saturday."

"Okay, then a stamp machine or something."

"Now what's your hurry?"

"I just want to get this in the mail, okay?"

She retrieved her phone while leaning over to read his note. "'The Final is on me'? Final what?"

"Snoop much?"

"Final what?" she asked, holding her cell phone teasingly.

"The Stanley Cup Final. Hockey. It's their World Series."

"Then shouldn't it be finals, plural?"

"You'd think so, but it's a Canadian thing. Now can you find a place that sells stamps?"

"Might also want to consider phoning in your dinner order."

"We'll be fine," he said, quickly scribbling his address and Maggie's name on the outer envelope. He couldn't remember her address from the one trip to her apartment, so he addressed it to the *L.A. Times*, and asked Hillary to quickly look up the address too.

"When are you going to get with the times and get a real phone?"

"If it bothers you so, I have a birthday coming up in about . . . now."

"Clever." She tipped the phone so he could see the *Times'* address, then announced the Albertson's just across the parking lot sold books of stamps. He was out the door before she finished, and back in the car with the gift card in the mail in just over five.

"There. Next stop, artery-clogging, intestine-bloating Mexican food on Mom and Dad's dime."

"That being the key part."

"Yeah, well, when you do *pro bono* work, you have to take a few freebies if you can get them."

"*Pro bono*," Hillary said with a laugh and a shake of her head. "So, are you going to tell me why you're sending a Buffalo Wild Wings gift card to a woman who works at the *L.A. Times*?"

Jackson sighed. "She helped me out on the case."

"And your professional courtesy is to urgently send her a gift card to a sports bar?"

He sighed again as he made a couple of quick turns onto Crenshaw Boulevard and began the process of getting back to the interstate. "We met there to watch hockey and go over evidence. I know she likes B-Dubs, I know she likes hockey . . ." He shrugged. "I thought it might be a way of securing a second date."

"That's stupid."

"Yeah, well, sorry it doesn't meet your lofty approval. I suppose I should have sent her an engraved invitation by private steward?"

"Or called her up and asked her out, Mr. Dude."

"Yeah, there's nuances to our . . . relationship."

"I see. Like going to watch hockey and calling it work. Does your 'super-cute' client know about this?"

"What are you, like spying on me? And I never called her 'super cute.'"

"If you took her case 'pro bono' I figured she had to be."

"You know what, Hill," he said, emphasizing the nickname he'd given her, "mock me all you want. The fact is, my client is super cute, and nice, and I just found her missing brother for her. And in the process, I met a girl I kind of like who might kind of like me, and so I'm putting out a feeler, which is how dudes sometimes do it when they want to be casual about it. And to top it off, it's my birthday and I get to pig out and enjoy a good time with my family and guest," he added, looking her way. "So scoff and chide me all you want, but nothing is ruining this day."

*   *   *

Saturday, June 22, 2013
7:34 p.m.

JACKSON AND Reggie trailed Keisha to the East Village neighborhood of downtown San Diego, at which point the tracking app on Reggie's phone indicated she had entered an upscale restaurant a few blocks from Petco Park, the home of the Padres. They found a parking spot and waited, utilizing the software Mouse had rigged for Jackson to listen in. Hastily dropped in her purse, it picked up only muffled sounds, particularly when Keisha had been driving. Now, they heard strains of conversation, but couldn't tell if it was with a waiter or a dinner companion. The clamor of the restaurant didn't help matters, nor did occasional interference, similar to that incurred when listening to a baseball game on the radio during a thunderstorm. Interference, they concluded, from Reggie's device.

"Ask you something, J?" Reggie asked.

"Sure."

"What's your end game?"

"Huh?"

"You find Padilla, find out where he is. Then what?"

Jackson looked out the window. It was almost a minute before he turned back to look into Reggie's penetrating eyes. "I'm going to bring him to justice."

"Justice," he said with a nod. "Whose justice?"

"It's a pretty standardized term."

"J, I'm with you, man. From everything you've told me, this guy Padilla killed your family. He deserves to go down for it."

"Then we're in agreement."

"The question is, who gets to put him down?"

Jackson just looked at him.

"You and I have the same compass, J. And it tells us both he should pay. But it also tells us who should make him pay."

"This another 'vengeance is mine,' speech?"

"Nope. God clearly gave that authority to people."

"Okay then."

"But not all people, not anyone at anytime."

"Ordained authorities, I get it. But what happens when they whiff? What happens when they don't have the means and resources? Is true justice letting a killer get away because the ordained authorities are incapable or is true justice the good people of this or any country stepping up and seeing justice served?"

"Vigilante justice."

"Call it what you like, Hoss. But it's not just that. Padilla's the lousiest piece of crap to ever walk the earth. A killer, a rapist, he's beat people half to death, torched buildings, he drinks and drives. He's a cancer on the backside of society, a repeat offender who's blown second, third, and tenth chances. He deserves to go down."

Reggie nodded. "Who imposes justice on the vigilantes? Who makes sure they're administering actual justice and not revenge?"

"Other vigilantes, I guess."

"Makes for kind of a he-who-shoots-last-wins sort of world, doesn't it?"

"What's the alternative?"

Reggie shrugged.

"Look, man, I don't have all the answers. And I know I can't just go gunning down anybody the law can't touch. But that's not my plan."

"Then what is, man? I saw you pack your Glock."

"And I saw you pack your SIG."

"I've got to watch your back, don't I?"

Jackson sighed.

"So what is your plan, then?"

"The law can't touch Padilla, right? They don't have the evidence. The D.A. here in San Diego and my favorite defense attorney agree, that short of much more damning evidence, he skates."

"So you want to get more evidence?"

"No, I want to get a confession."

"That's what you're after?"

Jackson nodded.

"How you gonna get him to confess, man?"

"I haven't decided. Either con him or give him an injection."

"What, Mouse cook you up some truth serum too?"

"No," Jackson said. "A lead injection. Say, that would render him incapable of ever raping a petty officer again."

The muffled static that had been transmitting through the Nokia suddenly crackled and then cleared. "I'll be right back," Keisha's voice said as clearly as if she was in the backseat of the Hummer.

"She on the move?" Reggie said, glancing over at the app on his phone.

"No. Not discernably."

They heard the usual background noises of a restaurant—the din of multiple conversations, clatter of utensils, background music—all slightly muffled. Then a change in frequency and only the background music.

"Bathroom?" Reggie guessed.

"Hope she doesn't start checking out her elbows in the mirror."

"Three years of marriage, can't say I ever saw her do that."

A stall door clanged shut, followed by a sequence of beeps. Silence, then Keisha's voice.

"It's me. There's been a change in schedule."

Jackson and Reggie looked at each other. "Phone," Jackson mouthed.

"You've got people looking for you," Keisha said. "No, not them. Some P.I. . . . I don't know and it doesn't matter, because after tonight you'll be gone. . . . That's right. Same place, same protocol, but ten o'clock tonight. . . . Yeah, I'm sure. He's had it set for days. . . . You can't. I'll call you. Ten o'clock."

The toilet flushed, and when that sound died away, they heard more running water. Then Keisha returning to the restaurant's dining room. Maybe it was a change in where the listening device was inside her purse, or maybe where she'd placed her purse, but Jackson and Reggie could now hear her conversation with more clarity and regularity. She and a man were discussing everyday life, plans for the rest of the weekend, upcoming work projects.

"If I didn't know better, I'd say we're hearing a staged conversation," Jackson said.

"Do you know better?"

"Fair point."

"I'm serious. What if Keisha's been playing us all along?"

"You serious?"

Reggie shrugged.

"She's your ex, but I don't think so. The only way she could know anything is if Cartagena tipped her off and she knew we were listening to her, and if she did, she didn't give us enough to know anything."

"Unless she knows we're following her too."

"Awfully complicated ruse. If she was leading us into a trap, she'd be leading us a lot more directly."

"Yeah, probably," Reggie said.

"Bigger question is why'd she take it into the bathroom to make the call?"

"Easier to hear."

"Into a stall? She wanted privacy, and it wasn't like she was calling out a hit. That was pretty nondescript language."

Reggie shrugged.

"And why's she making arrangements? Rey said it was her husband."

"Maybe they tag team."

"Yeah, maybe. Or maybe . . ."

"What?"

"Maybe Cartagena gave me bad intel. Maybe she's the one with underworld connections."

"Well, she's got the soul for it, but it's a long ways from the circles she ran in when I knew her."

"And yet she knows Cartagena, and he knows her well enough to know she or this husband of hers could help Padilla."

"True."

"At any rate, we've got till ten o'clock tonight to figure out where and how she's making him disappear. Or her husband is. Or whoever."

"We can follow her."

"Assuming she doesn't change clothes."

"Almost eight," Reggie said, glancing at his watch. "Still time to get home, change into smuggling apparel."

"And spot the device and know she's blown." He sighed. "You know what kind of car she drives?"

"I knew seven years ago."

"All right, I'm calling Mouse. He can maybe find out. And get me the skinny on this husband of hers. Maybe he works at the docks or something."

"Don't think Keisha'd go for a stevedore, man."

"In a supervisorial role, perhaps."

"I see."

"Worth a shot," he said, retrieving his phone. He dialed and gave Mouse the scoop on what he needed. He promised to call back soon.

"Maybe we're looking at this wrong," Reggie said.

"How so?"

"Maybe Keisha's not going to actually make him disappear, like smuggle him to Panama on a freighter."

"Okay?"

"Maybe she or her husband can give him new ID, new papers. Maybe he's a plastic surgeon gonna give him a nose job or something."

"I'll give him a nose job," Jackson said, then sighed, running his hands over his head. "We're running blind."

Reggie too swiped his palm over his face. "I'm racking my brain, J, trying to think what Keisha would be doing in all this. She was a secretary and administrative assistant—no sort of connection to making 'bangers and killers disappear, in any sense of the word."

"Been seven years, Hoss. You were just an enterprising restauranteur back then, not a wingman for a P.I. with a vendetta."

"True that."

They listened to a few more minutes of dinner conversation. It was the typical banal stuff of a couple on a Saturday night. No coded communications about an upcoming smuggling operation or rehashing covert plans.

"Ask you something?" Jackson said.

"Man, after all these years, why we keep asking each other if we can ask questions?"

"Don't know."

"Ask away."

"I want an honest answer."

"I ever give you anything but?"

Jackson nodded. "Tell me you don't call me J because you used to call Keisha K."

"For real?"

"For real."

"What you want me to call you, J.D.? J-Dawg? Jackie D?"

"J's fine. Just a little weird you use the same nicknaming nomenclature for your wife as for your boy."

"Nomenclature?"

295

Jackson shrugged.

"Man, you never cease to amaze me with the crazy things going through your head."

Jackson shrugged again as he looked down.

"What?" Reggie asked.

"No more delightful Sam and Callen banter. She's on the move."

Chapter Thirty-Seven

Saturday, May 14, 2011
6:31 p.m.

JACKSON AND HILLARY said virtually nothing to each other as they made their way through the sprawl of Los Angeles and Orange County. He focused on navigating steady and at times heavy traffic and tuning the radio while she flipped through a couple of bridal magazines. Just past San Juan Capistrano, the city made famous by migratory birds, I-5 rejoined the coast. As the final few suburbs gave way to Camp Pendleton Marine Corps Base, traffic thinned just a little. Hillary had closed her second magazine and Jackson, unable to find anything consistently good on the radio, turned it off.

"How are plans coming?"

"Excuse me?" she asked.

"For the wedding."

She stared at him until he asked, "What?"

"Just trying to figure out your angle."

"My angle?"

"For pretending to care about the wedding."

"Hill, remem—Hillary," he corrected seeing her downturned look at him. "Remember what you said to me Christmas Day, just after Grant proposed?"

"What?"

"You said that this—you and Grant, you being part of the family—was my life now and I should deal with it." He shrugged. "So I'm trying to deal."

"Since when?"

"It's incremental."

A smile tugged at the corner of her mouth, but couldn't budge her flawless lips. "Plans are coming along just fine."

He nodded.

She looked at him for a long time, finally breaking off her gaze to the ocean out her window.

"What?" Jackson asked.

"What what?"

"That look. What was that about?"

"Nothing," Hillary said.

"No, it was something."

"I thought you were gearing up for the speech where you tell me you're just looking out for your brother."

"Heck no. He made this bed. He can sleep in it."

"I should have known better."

Jackson grinned and looked away. "Besides, he's been looking over my shoulder his whole life."

"And you don't want to repay the favor?"

"What, now you want me to vet you for him? I just figure if he's so concerned that my house is in order, he'd better make sure there's no plank in his eye first."

"Nice mixed metaphor. You're something else, you know that?"

He shrugged.

"The reason Grant looks over your shoulder is because he cares about you so much."

"Right. He micromanages everything from my birthday presents for Mom to my house remodeling because he cares about me so much. That must have been why he had to remind me to wear the most ridiculous-looking bike helmet to ride half a block down the street or send me a toothbrush and floss care package when I went to summer camp. He treats his older brother like a little kid who needs their hand held at the zoo because he cares for me so much. How could I not have seen it?"

"I didn't say he was perfect or had never crossed the line as a kid. But I know where his concern springs from."

"You know?"

"Yeah."

"How?"

She said nothing.

"How?"

"Because he's told me."

"He told you?"

"That echo's back," she said with a thin smile.

Jackson did not reciprocate. "Told you what? What exactly has he told you?"

Before she could answer, his phone began playing a stirring organ rendition of "How Great Thou Art," Hannah's favorite hymn. He leaned back to make it easier to reach into his pocket, then flipped it open. "Yeah, Mom?"

"Hi, Honey. Are you and Hillary almost to San Diego?"

"Yeah, we're not far."

"You are going to make it by seven, aren't you?"

Jackson rolled his eyes, looking at Hillary and mouthing the word, "Mom."

"We have reserva—"

"We'll be there."

"Okay. I'll see you in a little while. I love you, Jack."

"I love you too, Mom." He shook his head and closed his phone. He turned to Hillary. "Where's your phone?"

"In my purse."

"Better get it out. Mom Jr. will probably be calling you to check on our progress." He stuffed his back into his pocket. "Now, what has he told you about me?"

"You're making a big deal out of nothing."

"Spill, Hill."

She exhaled. "The reason he keeps such close tabs on what you do and how you do it is because your life is so . . . unsettled."

"Unsettled? I've done all right."

"Have you? You've had more jobs than I can count. You have no career plans or ambitions, unless you count this private investigator thing."

He glared at her condescension.

"You've dropped out of college twice and washed out of the Army. You haven't had a steady girlfriend as long as I've known you, and whenever anyone talks about it or brings it up, you get a stupid look on your face and make some cavalier remark about Penelope Cruz or that lady from *Lost*."

"Evangeline Lilly."

"You've bounced from apartment to apartment to your parents' house to now some crack house you'll never be able to afford or maintain. And through it all, you never seem to recognize any concerns of your own or heed any advice from anyone else. You just make a smart-aleck crack and talk about looking at the ocean and flash a cheesy grin."

She paused, then looked down. "The reason he treats you like a kid is because at almost thirty years old, you still kind of act like a kid."

They drove in silence for half a mile.

"I'm sorry if—"

"No, it's fine," he said. "At least I know where you both stand. I guess I should be thankful a screw-up like me has a couple of successful people who've figured it all out to make sure I don't crash and burn."

"That's not—"

"Also funny how, for all his mothering when we were growing up, it's intensified since he started dating you. Almost makes a guy wonder if it's Grant who really thinks it or his fiancée putting thoughts in his head."

"Jackson—"

"But you know what, I really don't care one way or the other. And you're not spoiling this day, my new house, my job, or my life. I'm happy. So I don't care what either of you think."

"Clearly."

He let her have the last word, content not to speak to her again until they got to the restaurant. Or, for that matter, ever.

*   *   *

Saturday, June 22, 2013
9:22 p.m.

KEISHA HAD left the restaurant and driven east to Broadway Heights. Reggie and Jackson had followed a block behind, then used the app on Reggie's phone to pinpoint her exact house. Their arrival had corresponded with Mouse's return phone call. In addition to confirming her address, he had provided them with the name of her husband, Jayron Watts. Jayron ran his own import/export company, Watts Industries, Inc. Keisha, in addition to working part-time in a local insurance company's HR department, was also a secretary and assistant at Watts Industries. The pieces were falling into place.

Having driven past her house, Reggie had circled back and parked on the opposite side of the street, six houses down, far enough away to avoid detection but close enough to see if anyone came or went. He'd speculated that she'd changed into something far less constrictive than the form-hugging dress and was relaxing with a glass of wine. Seven-to-ten years ago, it had been her M.O.

"I wonder if it was Jayron she had dinner with," Jackson said.

"Who else?"

He shrugged.

"Why you doubt it was him?"

"You two often drive separately to dinner when you were married?"

"When one of us had a clandestine meeting with an ex and his white sidekick."

"Good point. I just keep wondering why, if Rey said Jayron was the guy who could make Padilla disappear, Keisha's the one handling all the transactions."

"Don't know, but we got movement."

Jackson reached for binoculars and trained them on the Watts' house. He hated the stupid things. He could never get the picture totally clear, and he always saw double. He didn't know if it was an inventor's defect or if he had goofy eyes.

"Here," he said, handing them to Reggie. "You see anything?"

"Forget the glasses, man. He's on the move."

"He?"

"Too big to be Keisha."

Jackson watched as the lights of a Buick Encore in the driveway flashed on. A moment later, the car backed out of the driveway.

"Stay with the car or with Keisha?" Reggie asked.

"Can you tail him without being seen?"

"We'll find out."

"Do it."

Reggie waited until the Encore signaled a right turn at the end of the block, then pulled away from the curb. He turned on his lights halfway down the block, and made a right turn just in time to catch tail lights in the distance.

He closed the gap as they exited the small subdivision and headed west on Federal Boulevard, and even more so when they joined traffic on Highway 94. The driver of the Encore, presumably Jayron, cruised contentedly along at sixty miles per hour, which made tailing him easy. They crossed the 805 and Highway 15, then over I-5 into downtown on F Street.

"Hang on," Reggie said as the Encore made a right turn onto 16th Street. "I think he's headed for the 5."

A moment later, his guess was proven correct when the Encore hung another right, onto a twisting onramp to I-5.

"Border?" Jackson asked.

Reggie shrugged.

"Watch, we'll be busted as the first people in history trying to cross the border *into* Mexico."

To their right, the lights of downtown dissipated in the damp marine layer that blanketed the city, even forcing Reggie to use his wipers a time or two.

They followed for less than a mile before the Encore signaled for a right-hand exit ramp.

"We gotta follow," Jackson said.

"He sees us, he diverts, we don't find Padilla."

"We lose him, we don't find him either."

Reggie waited until the last second before flipping on his blinker too. The ramp turned and opened into a street running toward the bay. New,

302

upscale apartment buildings quickly gave way to warehouses and scrapyards with barbed wire running their perimeters. After several blocks, they crossed three sets of railroad tracks and stopped directly behind the Encore as it waited to make a left turn onto Harbor Drive, a four-lane road that circled the bay all the way past the airport to the north, and past the naval base and shipping yards south.

"You think he's onto us?" Jackson asked.

"Can't be a lot of cars that take this route at this time of night. But who knows, man, he may be so consumed with thoughts of whatever he's got cooking at ten that he's not even thinking about traffic."

The Encore caught a break in traffic and turned. Reggie had to wait half a minute, by which time the Encore was already making a right off Harbor Drive and onto a road paralleling the Coronado Bridge some fifty feet above.

"Next right," Jackson said when Reggie finally pulled onto Harbor Drive.

"I see him."

Reggie turned onto Caesar E. Chavez Parkway, which took them past the BNSF Railway building and more fenced in properties before crossing another set of tracks. They didn't make it that far, because the crossing gate was already closing, forcing Reggie to stop short.

"Dangit!"

"Ain't too many places he can go from here, J."

"Yeah, but unless he leaves bread crumbs, we'll never find him."

A single green and black Burlington Northern locomotive crossed backward in front of them, pulling a string of boxcars. When it passed and the gate lifted, Reggie accelerated. The road curved to the right, with the BNSF freight yard on the right and a small waterfront park on the left. Both were fenced in, as was the marine terminal beyond them. Access was also barred by a gate, forcing Reggie to turn around.

Jackson slammed his fist against the side of the door, his growl this time so furious it consumed any words.

*   *   *

Saturday, May 14, 2011
6:59 p.m.

"I TOLD you we'd be late," Hillary said.

"Only because of this," Jackson said, gesturing toward bumper-to-bumper traffic that was inching south on I-5 through Del Mar. Backup from an accident, a mad rush to get to a Padres game, or just inexplicable congestion—Jackson didn't much care. Nor was he bothered by what Hillary had said earlier, about Grant constantly looking out for him because he was such a kid that he needed it. He'd tuned the radio to tune her out, and had stumbled upon U2's "Beautiful Day." It was just that, and the song had put him back in a good mood, as it usually did.

"Yeah, well, I warned you about this too," Hillary said.

"Seriously, when we get there, you might want to take a few minutes to get the bunch out of your shorts."

"It's rude to be late."

"Not to your own party, and we're almost to the Ted. We'll be like ten minutes late. That's still fashionable. Now do you mind, this is the best part," he said, giving the volume knob on the radio a twist. Bono filled the Granada, singing about China and tuna fishermen and Bedouins and oilfields and rainbows. Jackson hummed along, drumming his fingers on the steering wheel.

Hillary sighed and sat back. Traffic picked up, almost to full speed, then bogged down again just past the Del Mar racetrack. Hillary sighed again, and Jackson smiled as U2 was followed by Bon Jovi. When "Lost Highway" came to an end, Jackson reached into his pocket and withdrew his phone.

"What are you doing?"

"I'm calling my mother."

Hillary smiled smugly. "See?"

"See nothing. I just want to make sure they don't get impatient and order an appetizer without us."

Hillary rolled her eyes while Hannah's cell phone clicked to voicemail.

"Hey, Mom, it's Jack. We got held up in some traffic, but we're just getting off I-5 now. We'll be there in five. Oh, and Hillary's . . ."

"What?" she asked.

He looked at it. "Battery's dead." He clapped his phone shut and resumed fiddling with the radio.

"Hillary's what?"

"Hmm?"

"You were going to say Hillary's what?"

"Uh, looking lovely and gracious as ever, of course."

"Mm-hmm."

He caught the intro to "Stars" and cranked it, to the point that Hillary winced. He didn't care. She then rolled down her window, likely to let the sound dissipate. He didn't care about that either, because traffic was creeping along again and the sign above announced Carmel Valley Road. He gunned the Granada into the exit lane and accelerated down the off-ramp before coasting to a stop at a yellow light. It gave him a chance to survey the rugged countryside—where it hadn't been developed—while tapping his fingers on the wheel.

"Arrow," Hillary announced, and he turned his attention back to the road and accelerated. The two-lane Carmel Valley Road, after a somewhat unique interchange with I-5 and El Camino Real, had turned into the Ted Williams Parkway. They cruised along with sleek commercial buildings and swanky suburban neighborhoods to their left and rolling, tree- and shrub-covered wilderness to their right. Geographically, San Diego was a terrible place to build a city, as it was nothing more than one ridge and ravine after another. They were in something of a gulley on the parkway, albeit a dry one. The ridge to their right was not yet high enough to block the sun, but its various rims and swales were colored in alternating forms of deep, dark green and bright, golden yellow. And, of course, the sky above was the same magnificent powder blue it had been all week.

"What's the name of this place again?" Jackson asked.

Hillary reached over to adjust the volume of Switchfoot. "Curly's," she said.

"A Mexican place named Curly's?"

She shrugged.

"You know how far it is once we get off the freeway?"

"Seriously, how do you dress yourself in the morning? Not far. I'm guessing it's the only Mexican place . . ."

"What?"

"Did you hear that?"

"Hear what?"

She turned around.

"What?"

"I thought maybe you ran over something. Else your car is breaking down."

"I didn't hear anything."

"Your ears are probably still ringing from the music."

"Hill, you can't listen to 'Stars' pianissimo."

"Nor can you probably spell pianissimo."

A couple miles east, Jackson exited onto Carmel Country Road, which cut through the ridge and eventually led to neighborhoods of cookie cutter mansions. Curly's was before all that, an old supper club turned Mexican joint in the wilderness. Jackson had glimpsed a Yelp review that had put it a little more poetically. He still didn't know why his Mom hadn't picked some seafood or surf and turf place by the bay or ocean, but who was he to question Hannah's generosity?

The road curved around a ridge, and as it did, a thick plume of black smoke appeared over the crest of the ridge.

"Wow, that's black," Hillary said.

"Very 'the others are com . . . ing.' Is that . . . Hill?"

Fifty yards ahead of them, a gravel driveway led just as far into a small dale formed by the curve of the ridge. Half a dozen cars sprinkled a gravelly, weed-infested lot set against a copse of trees that climbed the side of the ridge. Standing on the south side of the lot, between it and a small, stagnant pond, was a sprawling, rambling, dirt-streaked building.

Or rather, part of a building. Approximately the back third had been engulfed by a ball of flames that shot up higher than the trees, proliferating the sky with the blackest, thickest smoke Jackson had ever seen.

He didn't finish his question. He didn't need to. Beside the gravel driveway was a rusted, crooked sign. The white letters on the blue background had long since faded, but not so much that Jackson couldn't read them.

Curly's.

Chapter Thirty-Eight

"HANG TIGHT, J," Reggie said as he drove away from the marine terminal on the short access road.

"We lost him, Reg."

"We lost him. Not Padilla."

"We don't even have Padilla. Jayron's our only link."

As the road curved back toward Harbor Drive, Reggie made a right instead, onto a stub of a road leading along the south edge of the park across from the freight yard. It also led to a dock several hundred yards down. But Reggie only drove a short ways before making a tight U-turn and parking on the side of the street. He cut the lights but kept the engine idling.

"Now what?" Jackson asked.

"Now we wait. One way in, one way out. If Padilla's meeting Jayron here as part of some exfil operation, money says he comes right down this road."

"Or hops a fence or hobos his way on the back of a freight car or gets dropped at the rear entrance."

"Well, then Plan B. Jayron drove in this way; he'll drive out this way."

"And what, we tail him back home and tuck him in?"

"I was thinking grab him and shoot him in front of Keisha or her in front of him to make one of them talk."

Jackson turned his head. "You just saying that for my benefit or is the green-eyed monster raising his head?"

"Maybe a little of each. Either way, we're not out of plays yet."

"Yeah, I hope you're right." He sighed and sat back. On the other side of a fence—everything down here was fenced in—was a parking lot, leading to what looked like a factory in the shadow of the Coronado Bridge. Maybe two dozen cars were parked around the lot, but there were no signs of life. Three or four cars lined the street, so that Reggie's H3 didn't look out of place—any more than ever.

They waited. Keisha had told whoever she'd called from the restaurant bathroom to use the same place and protocol at ten. But what did that mean? Was Jayron going to stuff Padilla in a boxcar bound for Tijuana? Take the money they were presumably charging, bash him in the head with a wrench, and dump him in a tanker car full of acid to have his bones discovered by some unfortunate soul down the line? Simply use the freight yard as a meeting place to provide Padilla a fake ID and credit card? Or had Keisha, as Reggie claimed she was wont to do, slipped into something more comfortable with a bottle of wine and in the process seen a small "micro-tracker" attached to the sleeve of her dress and dispatched her husband to lead potential pursuers on a dead-end chase?

"Where'd Mouse say Watts Industries was located?" Reggie asked.

"Not here. Morena, out by the interstate."

"Okay. But do they lease a loading dock or something?"

Jackson raised his eyebrows and lifted his phone to call Mouse. Before he could, Reggie whacked his knee. Jackson looked up and saw headlights approaching. A car made the turn and headed between the park and the freight yard, toward the marine terminal. As it passed, just enough ambient light fell on its side to mark it as a City-Wide taxicab.

"Don't imagine they get a lot of fares down here," Reggie said.

"You got the glasses?"

Reggie lifted the binoculars from the center console and handed them to Jackson. He peered through them after the taxi, and was just able to see around the trees at the edge of the park as it pulled to the curb.

"Odd place for a drop-off," Jackson said.

"Yeah," Reggie said, his head craned to look through his window.

"Two people," Jackson said as heads popped out the rear passenger door. "Keisha."

"Keisha?"

"And an ugly Mexican with a bald spot. Padilla."

"She picked him up. I'll say this, they run a quality smuggling service."

The cab made a U-turn and headed back their way.

"What they doing?" Reggie asked.

"Standing."

"You sure it's Padilla?"

"I'd recognize that horse's butt of a face anywhere."

Reggie put the still idling Hummer into gear.

"Hang on, Hoss. This still doesn't make any sense."

The cab passed them and headed back toward Harbor Drive, crossing the railroad tracks just before the red lights began flashing and the crossing gates lowered. "They're just . . . no, now they're moving."

"Going?"

"Just down the sidewalk. Wait. They stopped. I can't see where they went."

"What do you mean you can't see?"

"There's a little tree there and . . . Inch forward."

Reggie did, changing Jackson's angle. "Anything?"

"No."

"What, did they drop down a manhole cover?"

"There was no gate in that fence."

"Not till the end of the road."

Jackson panned again. Keisha and Padilla had disappeared. He lowered the binoculars. "Let's go, Hoss."

Reggie accelerated and turned sharply onto Crosby Road. With his lights off, he coasted to the curb in the same vicinity where the cab had just dropped the duo off. He cut the engine, and they got out.

A sidewalk and a dirt slope the same width as it were all that stood between the street and a six-foot-high slat fence topped with barbed wire. A few small trees and more than a few weeds poked out of the otherwise barren ground, as did a telephone pole a hundred feet behind them. On it was mounted a streetlight, and it cast just enough light on the fence for Jackson to note a discrepancy, a shadow in the slats that was a little too big.

"Reg."

He jogged toward the shadow, the big man on his tail. He stopped and climbed the dirt slope, crouching to see that a two-foot by two-foot square section of the slat fence had been scored. The reinforcing chain-link wire had also been cut.

"A door," Reggie breathed.

Jackson nodded, running his eyes over it until he spotted the pin and knuckles of recessed hinges on the right side of the square. Unless a guard—or a wretched, bitter, divorced-and-remarried black woman with a Hispanic thug—was looking specifically for them, they would never be spotted between the slats. There was no handle, so Jackson looped his finger inside a section of chain-link fence and pulled. The makeshift door opened with only a marginal squeak.

"Age before beauty," Jackson said.

"It's fifty-fifty I make it through that. You'd hate for me to plug the hole and Padilla get away, wouldn't you?"

"I hate it when you make sense."

Jackson dropped to his knees and peeked his head through the opening. He was looking at a mostly vacant parking lot, void of human presence. He quickly scampered through, then turned to watch Reggie squeeze through the opening.

"I told you to lay off the bacon."

"I made it, didn't I?" He brushed dust off his pants. "What are we looking at?"

"Don't know. Employee lot? Police impound? Come on."

The lot was bound by fence on three sides—east, south, and west. Concluding Keisha and Padilla hadn't climbed through a secret hole in a fence to go hang out by another fence, Jackson led the way north, moving quickly, keeping his eyes peeled. Several railroad tracks ran parallel to the east fence, a string of tanker cars sitting on one of them blocking the view in that direction. Ahead, at the north end of the lot, several concrete retaining walls held scrap metal and other debris. Beside them, railroad ties were stacked in a makeshift pile. To the left of the crude storage dump, a narrow drive provided egress from the parking lot, and Jackson led the way out of the lot, stopping on the other side of the westernmost concrete wall.

A hundred yards left was the guardhouse for the marine terminal. Straight ahead, across more debris piles and a couple of rusted out flatbed cars on an overgrown siding, was a trio of round oil storage tanks, and well beyond them, the tall silos of a grain elevator. They were connected by long feeder pipes to a waterside loading dock that ran parallel to the harbor and was flanked by rows and rows of warehouses.

"They could be anywhere," Reggie said.

Jackson looked to his right, across a couple more dilapidated sidings, to where the quartet of tracks that crossed the road had split and switched into nearly a dozen parallel tracks. Railroad cars of various size and shape appeared to have been randomly scattered across the yard. Some were coupled in long strings, trains lacking only means of propulsion. Other sidings contained only a small chain of cars. Others were completely empty. The bright beam of a locomotive's headlight pierced the foggy darkness as it maneuvered cars around the yard. Even from a distance, it caused the ground beneath Jackson and Reggie to rumble.

"J!"

Jackson turned and followed Reggie's outstretched arm. Between the freight yard and the oil tanks, silos, and piles of junk near the harbor was another chain-link fence, this one with a gate across the tracks that meandered past the oil tanks to the silos. On the opposite side of the fence, just about to disappear into the shadow of a long, narrow trailer, were two humans, walking briskly to the north. Jackson didn't have the binoculars to verify it was Keisha and Padilla, but how many human smuggling operations could be going down at once?

Without a word, Jackson and Reggie took off running. This fence wasn't topped with barbed wire, and they quickly hopped it, then continued north. They were almost to the trailer when Jackson spotted movement off to his right. Keisha and Padilla had veered from the fence and across a vacant siding before passing out of sight behind a string of tankers. Jackson didn't hesitate in going after them, pausing only when he reached the tankers.

His hand on one of the cars, he peeked around its rear end. On the next track over, stationary boxcars and covered hopper cars stretched as far as he could see to the north. With Reggie on his rear, Jackson crept around the back of the tanker. Back south, the string of cars on the next track broke after two cars.

"They couldn't have made it to the end that way," Jackson said, pointing north. "We were closing ground."

Reggie nodded, breathing heavily but no more so than Jackson. They turned south, jogging to the southernmost car in the chain, a reddish-brown boxcar covered in gang graffiti. Jackson again peeked around the end of a car.

On the next track east, a train was slowly rolling south, the wheels of the cars in tow steadily clacking and creaking as they wobbled along. It passed in less than a minute and, when it did, revealed another series of graffiti-marked boxcars on the next track. Jackson started forward, then stopped before coming around the boxcar immediately to his left.

Up ahead and to his left, the fourth boxcar in the string had its sliding door open. Standing beneath it, their heads barely to the floor of the boxcar, were three people—two men and a woman. Even with the fog, the distant yard lights illuminated them enough for Jackson to recognize them as Jayron, Keisha, and Padilla. They were talking in low tones that failed to carry beyond a garble to where Jackson and Reggie stood.

"How we play this, J?"

"About to ask you the same thing."

They looked at each other for a moment.

"Wait here," Jackson said. "I'm going to circle back north and squeeze between cars to come at them from the other side."

"And then what?"

"Make a citizen's arrest and hope Padilla goes for a piece."

"Citizen's arrest?"

"That's right."

"On what charge?"

"We'll figure it out, but I'm guessing we're not interrupting a sale of Boy Scout popcorn."

"Your show," Reggie said.

"Give me two minutes."

"One fifty-nine," Reggie said, and Jackson turned back and headed north along the west side of the string of cars. It was a dangerous game, running around a freight yard. It was easy to get disoriented, or run over by a train coming from nowhere. Cars were always being moved and shuffled around. It was even more dangerous when you were so focused on something else that you were only paying the trains minimal attention, giving them the same focus as walls in a shooting gallery.

Jackson counted cars, and between the fourth and fifth, sneaked between them, climbing over the coupler. He'd heard horror stories about brakemen getting hands pinched or feet jammed in between the coupler or in the brakes. Limbs could easily be mangled. But these cars weren't moving, and he peeked out the other side unscathed.

The coast was clear—no trains coming in either direction. And the trio was still outside the boxcar, only they were moving. Padilla had reached up for the boxcar, with Jayron giving him an assist. It hadn't yet been two minutes, but it was now or never, and Jackson hoped Reggie would follow his lead.

Gun drawn, he darted from concealment. Hoping for an excuse to squeeze the trigger, he shouted, "Don't move."

They of course moved. Jayron spun to see who had shouted, in the process letting go of Padilla. He grasped a handle with one hand, but lost his footing and twisted around, banging against the side of the boxcar. Keisha just turned and ran.

"Freeze!" Reggie shouted from Jackson's right.

That's when red and blue lights started flashing, the sharp whine of a siren pierced the darkness, and all chaos broke loose.

Chapter Thirty-Nine

Saturday, May 14, 2011
7:15 p.m.

THE NEXT FIVE minutes of Jackson's life were absolute chaos.

He skidded the Granada to a stop in the gravel, bounding from it almost before it stopped. He was vaguely aware that Hillary had reached for her phone, likely to call 9-1-1.

People streamed from various doors of the restaurant like cockroaches running from a suddenly lit room. Some looked about frantically. Some just ran. Some turned and watched the fire.

It was like nothing Jackson had ever seen, the intense ball of orange trying to consume the billowing tufts of smoke it generated. Even across the parking lot, the heat was blistering.

The fire was stiff competition for Jackson's eyes, but he forced them to look at the faces emerging from the restaurant. Methodically, almost robotically, he moved from one body to the next, checking them off.

He heard a siren in the distance. It was accompanied by shouts and screams, people calling names of other people, and calling God's name in a variety of ways. Both sounds were largely obscured by the insatiable roar of the fire.

"Jackson."

He whipped his head at the calling of his name, recognizing Hillary's voice before he turned to see her beside him.

"Do you see them?" he asked.

For once, it took her mouth a moment to form words.

"Do you see them!"

"No."

He turned toward a man in white, rushing his way. "Is anyone else inside?"

"I-I-I . . . d-d-d-don-don-don't . . ."

Jackson darted to his left, around to the side of the restaurant, where a number of exhaust vents in the roof suggested the kitchen was. He'd seen several people exit that way, farthest from the fire.

Hillary shouted his name again, but he ignored her. He raced toward the door, stopping just short of it. There was no exterior handle. A fire door, openable only from the inside.

He spotted a window, high up, to the right of the door, and looked for something with which to break it. No debris outside, no tree limbs big enough. He looked to a dumpster beside the pond, but gave up, figuring it would take too much time. He turned back toward the front of the restaurant.

The sirens were louder.

Hillary materialized from the crowd of people, nearly twenty, most of whom were holding or clinging to each other as they watched the fireball skyrocket.

She said something, but the noise carried it away.

"What?"

"Their car." She pointed. "Your parents' car is here."

He followed her outstretched hand to where he spotted David's silver Dodge Stratus. It was not a unique make and model, but he recognized the plate number, not to mention the Navy parking tag.

"Where are you going?" Hillary asked as he turned. She tugged his arm back.

"They're in there."

"Jack, you can't."

"They're still inside, Hillary!" He broke free and dashed for the front entrance, throwing off the arm of someone else who tried to deter him.

He was almost to the front door when an explosion shook the ground, shattering glass and blowing whole panes from their jambs. A ball of flame shot out the window Jackson had been scouting just a minute previously.

With an almost stoic detachment, he reached for the front door handle. He was stopped by a hand on his shoulder.

"Jackson!" Hillary shouted.

"Let me go."

She reached with her other arm and tugged him back. They stumbled and fell into the gravel as flames knifed out a front window and shot upward.

Jackson sat up and tried to push himself up, but before he could, Hillary tackled him sideways. Her arms wrapped around his chest, and she hugged him to her on the ground.

"You can't! It's suicide."

"Let me go!"

More hands grabbed him by the shoulder, and he was lifted and dragged back, as was Hillary. He saw two other shapes, both clad in yellow and black, going toward the front door.

He saw the reflection of blinking lights, then heard a baritone horn. He turned to see a fire tanker truck crunch over the gravel and stop almost where they had been.

The hands holding him let go, and two more firefighters rushed forward.

A voice shouted to step back, and he did as a ladder truck barreled in front of him, blocking his view of the door and the majority of the fire, filling his vision instead with strobing lights against the darkness of the ever-pluming smoke.

*   *   *

Saturday, June 22, 2013
10:10 p.m.

TO JACKSON, the flashing lights seemed magnified as they reflected off the rows of boxcars. The same was true of the sirens, their sound reverberating off the walls of steel. Both were mere context to Jackson as he watched his target.

His first impulse was to squeeze the trigger. But he realized anyone doing shooting might get popped by a police officer, and justly so. Instead, he lowered and holstered his Glock. Glancing to his side to see Reggie doing the same, he made a run toward Jayron and Padilla.

Keisha had darted south and ducked between cars. Jayron followed her, leaving Padilla twisting as he hung onto the side of the boxcar. He made two quick efforts to swing himself up into the car. When he realized it was pointless, he dropped to the ground. Jackson was closing in, and instead of running after Jayron and Keisha, Padilla dropped to all fours and rolled under the boxcar.

Again, Jackson resisted an impulse, this time to follow him. Seeing several police cars jouncing down the chute between strings of boxcars, Jackson turned the other way. He saw two cars parked, lights strobing, as uniformed officers came his way. He also saw Reggie make a flying leap, taking down Jayron as he tried to dart between boxcars.

Figuring Jayron had no chance against his wife's ex, even if they were thoroughly estranged, Jackson didn't hesitate in sidestepping them and following Keisha's path between the cars.

He found himself facing a row of long, black, grimy tanker cars, stretching as far as he could see in either direction. He saw Keisha running north between them and the row of boxcars, and was about to give chase when he spotted a shoe disappear under a tanker. Padilla, executing the same maneuver again.

Jackson gritted his teeth as he ran to the nearest break in tankers and leaped over the coupling. His momentum nearly cost him his life, as he had to reach for the side of a car to slow his progress before he hurtled in front of an orange, yellow, and black BNSF locomotive backing southward, a string of cars in tow. Falling to his knees, Jackson whirled around and out of the way of the locomotive, raising his eyes just in time to see Padilla dart across the tracks in front of it.

Jackson bit off the curse that tried to escape his lips as he saw the length of the slow-moving train. With a growl of frustration and determination, he stood and ran south, along with the train. There wasn't much room between the locomotive and the row of tankers, and one false step could send him under the wheels of the huge diesel locomotive. Even at such a slow pace, it was deafening as it chugged beside him, shaking the ground like a six-point quake.

Sprinting on the hard-packed gravel ground, Jackson took a hundred yards to outdistance the locomotive, but sprinted another fifty before he had enough room to safely cross the tracks. Even so, one misstep, such as tripping over one of the rails or ties, would be fatal.

He made it and stood clear as the train rumbled and clacked past him. Three more sets of tracks separated him from a fenced-in parking lot. Only the farthest set had any cars, what looked like sleeping cars from an era gone by. Swiveling his head right and left, Jackson pleaded with his eyes to spot Padilla. They didn't.

Nor did they see any more police cars or officers, although the sirens echoed across the yard and the red and blue lights bounced off the foggy atmosphere.

Movement caught his attention by the sleeping cars, and he took several steps in that direction. More movement, then a figure emerging from the darkness. Jackson quickened his pace, and the figure did too, running north, along the chain-link fence.

Jackson ran with fuel he didn't know existed, aiming to cut the corner. The figure was slow, and Jackson was almost close enough to reach out and grab him when something slammed into his shoulder. He took one step and lost his balance, crashing into the chain-link fence hard enough to make it clatter and quiver. He turned his head in time to see Padilla take a quick look back, then keep running.

Turning the other way, Jackson saw what had collided with him. A woman, in blue jeans and a leather jacket, who herself had rolled into the fence. Keisha.

She was getting to her feet and, in the process, reaching for a gun. Jackson didn't give her the chance, launching himself up and at her, driving her back into the fence. It shook and rattled again, and they both tumbled to the ground in a heap of arms and legs and spat epithets. She came up clawing at his eyes, and he turned his head away, then found her chin with the heel of his hand and gave it a shove. She fell back into the fence, his full weight and fury grinding her head into the chain-link. It threatened to break when she somehow got a fist free to jab in his ribs. It backed him up just enough that she could regain her balance and deliver a spinning kick to the head that sent him reeling.

He wasn't sure what it was—blinding anger, just plain stupidity, or the fact that her gun wasn't loaded—but instead of drawing her gun and shooting him, Keisha stripped off her leather jacket, under which she wore a black tank top. Arms flexed like a karate fighter, she circled, then advanced.

He knew why it was he didn't go for his gun. He couldn't bring himself to kill Reggie's ex-wife. And she was on him too fast. He blocked the first kick, but the second in the combo caught him off guard, rattling his head and driving him back against the fence. Fortunately, he kept his balance, which enabled him to block a pair of tandem punches. Then he struck.

He had no interest in a long, choreographed, spinning and twirling fight sequence, especially if Keisha knew half as much martial arts as it appeared. Instead, he punched at her throat, a short little jab that connected. It stopped her cold, and her eyes bulged, one hand reflexively going to her neck.

Jackson had qualms about shooting Keisha, but not about decking her. While she was still off balance, he jabbed with his other fist, flush on the nose. Blood spurted out and she rocked backwards, opening up her chin for an uppercut that dropped her as if she was a marionette whose strings had just been cut.

Leaving Keisha for the cops or the night watchman or the 3:10 to Yuma, Jackson took off running north, along the fence. He saw no sign of Padilla ahead of him, just a switch branching off one of the lines to form another siding that was lined with boxcars, stretching from a hundred yards in front of him all the way to the Harbor Drive overpass. Several vacant—at least for several hundred yards—tracks ran between them and the next chain of cars. It left an open chute, in which Jackson should have spotted Padilla had he run that far.

Had he ducked under another train? If so, preferably a moving one. Had he hopped the fence while Jackson was tangled with Keisha? Or had he veered left or right, behind one of the strings of cars in the middle of the yard or the boxcars on the right?

Jackson doubted Padilla would run back into the yard and toward the police. So he veered to the right side of the boxcars. All the running and jumping over couplings and his fight with Keisha had sucked his energy, and even his determination to catch Padilla couldn't push him to full speed. He reached the boxcars and covered a couple hundred yards without spotting Padilla or an obvious exit from the yard. But he could have climbed the fence at any point.

Realizing further pursuit was pointless, Jackson turned back and just controlled himself from punching one of the steel-sided cars. He instead walked between them, then waited as another train thundered past. For late on a Saturday, the yard sure was hopping.

When the train passed, Jackson saw two police officers crossing the yard, their flashlight beams cutting a swath through the thick air. A third man was with them, his arms behind his back in handcuffs.

The flashlights found Jackson at the same time he identified the third man as Reggie. Jackson stopped walking and raised his hands. The police officers quickened their pace.

"Why is he in handcuffs?" he shouted, realizing a third officer was walking with Reggie.

"Sir, don't move."

"I'm a private investigator. License is in my rear pocket with my wallet."

"Are you armed?" a female officer asked.

"Glock 19 in my back waistband. What's going on?"

"Was hoping you could tell us that," her partner said. His shield identified him as Officer Kalganov. "You're trespassing on private property, and we found him brawling with another man."

"Brawling. You win?"

Reggie tsked.

"Sir?"

"Who called you?" Jackson asked.

321

"He's clean," the woman said, having removed his gun and frisked him while the man covered him. The third officer kept an eye on Reggie. Jackson hoped someone kept an eye out for freight trains. "Here's the license. It looks legit."

"It is, and he's with me," Jackson said, nodding at Reggie.

"Afraid that's not good enough."

"We were following a man we believe is part of a smuggling operation," Jackson said, never minding that wasn't even close to their motives.

"How'd you get in here?"

"Same way he did, through a hole in the southern fence. By the way, he was with a woman. Last I saw her, she was sawing lumber over by the fence."

He gestured while the officers frowned. Reggie joined them. "Keisha?"

"Sorry, Hoss, but she threw down."

"You know the suspect?" Kalganov asked.

"His ex-wife. The guy I'm guessing he knocked into next week is her husband."

"Then who were you chasing?"

"The man they were smuggling."

"Smuggling. Into the U.S.?"

"Out of the U.S."

"Who is he?"

"A pile of dog mess named Joaquín Padilla, convicted of a handful of crimes and guilty of a lot more."

"Where is he?"

"I don't know. He got away while I was going to the middle rounds with Keisha."

The officers looked at him.

"That's it, honest. You mind telling me how you all showed up when and where you did?"

"We've been aware of some smuggling operations for a while, and tonight we got a tip to check a freight car for illegally obtained electronics and weapons being smuggled into Mexico."

"And you just happened to show up at the exact car?"

"All RFID tagged and tracked by the railway."

"Were they there?"

"Oh yeah. Bound for Mexico City."

"Jayron smuggles guns and cheap DVD players to Mexico and gives Padilla a spot in his boxcar. Not bad."

"Only where's Padilla now?" Reggie asked.

"Same place he was twenty-four hours ago—Who knows?"

*　　　　　*　　　　　*

Saturday, May 14, 2011
7:54 p.m.

THE SIRENS had long since silenced, but the flashing lights of half a dozen fire trucks still lit up the sky as they battled the blaze. It had consumed almost the entire restaurant, and the firefighters had been able to do little more than protect the surrounding cars and trees in an effort to keep the blaze from turning into a raging wildfire.

Several ambulances and police cruisers had also joined the scene, and Curly's parking lot was now almost full, a mess of survivors, families who had come to the scene to verify their loved ones' wellbeing, cops and paramedics and firefighters—all tripping over hoses running from trucks to the pond to a hydrant to the fire, which still raged. Back on the road, several local news crews had set up, their TV lights adding to the glow in pre-sunset gloom.

Jackson and Hillary stood against David's Stratus in the far corner of the lot, waiting, praying, desperately hoping. His phone battery was dead, and hers was low from calling cell phones—Grant's, David's, Hannah's. None answered. Grant had texted her at 7:02. Hannah had left a voicemail at 7:07, checking where they were. Another missed call, this one from Grant, at 7:09. That was the last of them.

A police officer dressed in black distinguished himself from the crowd, walking without ambiguity toward them. Jackson stood upright, as did Hillary when she saw him approaching.

"Are you Jackson Douglas?"

Jackson swallowed hard, eyeing the officer. "I am."

A cloud passed over the officer's blue eyes, and Jackson's heart sank. Plummeted. A visceral growl—a death wail—rose up from within him, but he bit it off, clamping his teeth into his bottom lip. His throat constricted in a gulp, and he blinked the moisture from his eyes.

"I understand your parents and brother were inside," the officer said.

Jackson was unable to answer, barely able to nod.

The officer swallowed. "We spoke to a number of witnesses, and . . . I'm very sorry to have to tell you this . . ."

Beside him, Hillary mouthed a quiet, "No . . ."

Jackson's heartbeats were like pile drivers. His teeth nearly drew blood as he waited for the sentence, one he hoped against hope wasn't coming.

"But your family . . ."

"No," Hillary moaned again, a little louder.

"They didn't make it out," the officer said. He opened his mouth once, closed it, then opened it again. "Mr. Douglas, I'm sorry, but I'm afraid they're dead."

His last words came in slow motion as Jackson's legs gave out. He collapsed to his knees, oblivious to the smoke and flashing lights and voices all around him—oblivious even to the officer's crisp pant legs in front of him or Hillary in her heels at his side. He was consumed by an ache so sudden and so powerful that nothing else existed.

Chapter Forty

THE GOOD NEWS was that Jackson and Reggie had not been arrested or detained by SDPD. After questioning them a second time—and quite thoroughly—the officers had taken their contact information and escorted them off BNSF property. Beyond that, it was pretty much all bad news.

Jayron Watts had lawyered up. That wasn't a surprise, and neither Jackson nor Reggie cared what happened to him, unless he decided to file a civil suit against Reggie for assault and battery. He had a case, Reggie said with a wink, because he had most definitely assaulted and battered him. He'd also said it had nothing to do with Jayron being with Reggie's ex-wife, estranged or otherwise. The jury was out on that.

Keisha had disappeared. She and her leather jacket had both been gone when Jackson had led the officers to the spot where he'd fought with her. A few drops of blood seemed to back Jackson's story, but other than taking a description of Keisha, SDPD didn't seem all that interested in her.

They hadn't divulged any more details about the tip that had brought them to the freight yard—whether or not they knew who the tipster was, whether or not it had come out of the blue or in conjunction with an active investigation, or whether or not they believed there to be any ties between Jayron's smuggling operation and Keisha helping Padilla make a run for the border.

And Joaquín Padilla was in the wind.

"Sorry, J," Reggie said as they climbed back into his Hummer, parked just off Crosby Road.

325

"I had him, Reg. I was steps away from grabbing that piece of garbage, when the lovely Mrs. Cameron-Watts had to go all Eric Weddle on me."

"Sorry, J," he said again.

"And I can't figure it out. We show up at the boxcar, she splits. Sorry, Joaquín. Sorry, Jay-baby. KayKay has to look out for herself."

"You're falling into that sassy black lady accent again."

"So why does she pull the every smuggler for herself routine, then suddenly come to Padilla's rescue five minutes later?"

"I don't know. She's hard to figure, in a lot of ways."

"Unless . . ."

"Should I be going somewhere while you ruminate?"

"No, hang here."

"Cops might be watching."

"Okay, then take us to Coronado and back."

Reggie looked at him.

"I've got an idea, but I need to give Five-0 time to get out of here."

"You're the boss." He put the Hummer into drive. "Unless what?"

"What if Keisha's the tipster?"

"What?"

"Think about it. An anonymous tip had to come from somebody, but we don't know any other parties in this."

"Don't mean they don't exist. And we also don't know, for the record, that she was having dinner with Jayron. Could have been the fourth party."

"Okay, but even so, that could be the deal. She calls the cops to blow Jayron's smuggling deal. It would explain why she ran."

"Why would she do that?"

"I don't know. Maybe marriage just isn't her thing. Or maybe he was crowding her side operation, or her side operation was growing enough to take over his main operation."

"Her side operation? Smuggling criminals to Mexico?"

"Right."

"I thought Rey said that was her husband's business."

"Right, 'cause he'd never lie."

"You're grasping at straws here, J. And even if it's true, it doesn't explain why she'd come take you out to let Padilla escape."

"Try to take me out, and because she didn't want to hang a paying client out to dry."

"Then why'd she run and leave him at the boxcar?"

Jackson exhaled and sat back. "I don't know."

"Why'd she show up at all, if she was the one who alerted the cops? Wouldn't that blow her side operation?"

"I don't know that either."

They were headed back toward I-5 on Caesar Chavez Parkway, but before reaching the interstate, Reggie hung a right on a ramp that would take them up onto the Coronado Bridge, headed for Coronado Island.

"We could ask her," Reggie said.

"Ask her?"

"We'd probably have to be a little more assertive than last time."

"I would have had Padilla and she let him get away. Your ex-wife or not, I'll be assertive. In fact, I was rather assertive to her nose already."

"You didn't?"

"She was fixing to go all Kitana on me, so I had to."

Reggie actually grinned. "She had a nose job first year we were married. Real uptight about it."

"Then I hope it's broken. Problem is, I doubt she just goes home to something more comfortable and a bottle of wine. She's either all broke-up because her hubby got pinched or she's the one who pinched him and is on her way to a new life in Dallas."

"Guessing you're wrong on both counts."

"You have a lead?"

"If she had to crash and lay low, I'm thinking there's a first choice in San Diego."

"Leila?"

Reggie nodded as they made the sweeping curve north on the bridge.

"Yeah, but Jayron would know that too."

"He's a little occupied."

Jackson exhaled. "That's Plan B, if Plan A doesn't work."

"Man, I think we a lot further down the alphabet than A and B."

"Touché."

When they reached Coronado Island—technically an isthmus extending around the bay—Reggie made a U-turn instead of passing through the naval base's checkpoint, and headed back onto the bridge.

"You wanna clue me in on this Plan A?"

Jackson reached into the door pocket and withdrew Grant's old LAPD shield that he'd brought along, just in case. He held it up for Reggie.

"Oh no, man."

"There's got to be a control tower or some kind of yard security. Maybe they can tell us how Padilla exited the yard."

"How would they do that?"

"Security cameras, remote sensors. Beats me."

"And then what? He's got an hour's head start."

"If he's on foot, maybe we see what direction he goes. Maybe he had somebody pick him up. If this was the movies, this is the scene where we'd all call something undignified holy because we saw Keisha's car pick him up while she looked furtively at the camera."

Reggie shook his head. "You remember what happened last time we played cops with that thing?"

"Yeah, I saved two LAPD detectives' lives and took down a gangbanger."

"After we got into a firefight with a bunch of 'bangers armed to the teeth and you went on a mad chase across L.A. And we were lucky we didn't get busted by the cops."

"Well, that was a warehouse full of them. This will just be a night security guard who's beyond sleepy."

"You have any idea where the sleepy night security guard hangs out?" Reggie asked with a sigh.

"No, but we have another stop first anyhow."

"I can't wait."

*   *   *

11:27 p.m.

IT TOOK a little doing to find an all-night coffee supplier—in the way of a McDonald's—and to find the BNSF Railway security offices. But the driving around gave them time to rehearse.

"If all else fails, just follow my lead," Jackson said as he and Reggie approached the front door.

"You mean cover your butt."

"That too."

Jackson opened the door and nodded at the solitary guard behind a counter. As predicted, he looked bored. "Evening," Jackson said before the guard could speak. He lifted his shirt to reveal Grant's badge clipped to his belt. "I'm Officer Douglas. This is Officer Switzer."

"Officers?" the guard asked.

"LAPD," Jackson said.

"You're a little out of your jurisdiction, aren't you?"

"A little," Jackson said with a grin. He tipped up his cup and winced. "Aw, man this is awful." He set it on the counter, then looked at the guard. "You like it strong? Black, I promise no spitback, and I'm not sick."

"No thanks."

"Take mine," Reggie said. "Haven't touched it, and if it's too strong for him, I know I'll hate it."

"I'm good, guys, really. What's LAPD doing down here? You working with that FBI sting?"

"FBI? No. I spoke to an Officer . . . What was his name, Bear? Kalashnikov, Kasparov?"

"It was something Russian."

"Right, with SDPD. He said they tagged a boxcar full of stolen electronics and weapons, but he didn't mention the FBI."

"Officer Kalganov," the guard said.

"That's it," Jackson said, snapping his fingers and hoping he'd passed the guard's test.

"Okay, so you still haven't told me what two LAPD officers are doing down here. And can I see that badge again?"

"Sure." Jackson unclipped it and tossed it on the counter.

"He got one?"

"He did until he tussled with Jep."

"Who?"

"Joaquín Enrique Padilla, biggest cocaine dealer in Orange County. Working with multiple cartels in Mexico, Latin America, Colombia. Plays all sides against the middle and makes out like a bandit. Or *bandito*, I guess." He chuckled. "Padilla started making forays into L.A. last summer, so LAPD put together a task force to try and stem the flow of coke coming across the border. Long story not quite so long, Bear and I here have been working undercover since Christmas, trying to infiltrate Padilla's operation. We'd just made headway when we heard the Reynosa Cartel put out a hit on him, and he was trying to get out of L.A. We tracked him down here, found out he was trying to get out of the U.S., maybe North America, maybe the entire Western Hemisphere. He'd be on the first plane to Mars if feasible."

"And we'd pay for a one-way ticket," Reggie chimed in.

Jackson pointed at him. "We followed him here tonight, and figured we'd better grab him while we had the chance, you know, instead of letting this op play out. Bear had his hands on him, but Padilla's slippery as an eel. We had a witness who saw him headed south along Harbor Drive, but that turned out to be a red herring. So we're back here hoping you've got some kind of security footage that shows Padilla leaving the yard and not hopping a freighter to Mexico."

"He'd never make it if he did," the guard said, "not unless he could get inside a car. And there's only one, maybe two trains a day that cross the border, all the way over in Calexico. He'd have to be really lucky or, even more, smart to grab the right car."

"Still, he could get a long way from here."

"Come on around," the guard said, tossing Jackson's badge back to him. They circled the end of the desk and found themselves looking at six black-and-white security screens, each showing different parts of the yard. "Four main lines in and out of the yard," he said, pointing at a map tacked to the wall. "Any train that goes in or out passes security cameras here, here, here, or here." He tapped the locations as he spoke. "So if he hopped a train, not only would we have it on camera, but it would have sounded an alert."

"You got good cameras."

"And better software. He didn't ride out of here hanging off the back of a boxcar."

"Good to know."

"We have dozens of cameras spaced throughout the yard and around the perimeter. SDPD took the footage from the smuggling op you spoke of, but we've got everything else. What's your time frame?"

"Ten . . . ten, fifteen?" Jackson asked, looking at Reggie.

"Just say ten."

"Yeah, ten till now."

"Where should I start, any particular location?"

Jackson pointed to where he and Keisha had fought. "We chased him north from here."

"Okay, we've got a camera there at the end of the parking lot. Let me call it up."

He did, then played it back at four-times speed, from ten o'clock.

"There!" Jackson said.

The guard backed up the footage and slowed it down. It was grainy and only caught him from the head up, but it showed Padilla running north.

"What's your next camera north of there?"

"On the overpass."

"Let's see it."

They started at the time stamped on the previous image, and five minutes later, Padilla passed by, moving more slowly as he crossed a pair of tracks under the overpass.

"Wait, what's that?" Reggie asked.

"Can you zoom in?"

With a couple key clicks, the guard zoomed the footage in, and it showed what at first appeared to be a blur after Padilla had passed to actually be a boot sticking out of a pant leg.

"He's climbing the fence," Reggie said.

"Looks like. What's there?" Jackson asked the guard.

"Just under the overpass . . . access to East Harbor Drive."

"Outside the grounds?"

"That's right."

"Any cameras that show that terrain."

"No, sir."

Jackson sighed. "He got away again."

They spent ten more minutes looking at other cameras in that general direction, in case Padilla had stayed close to the grounds and boarded a bus in view. He hadn't, at least that the cameras could see. Then again, they were trained on the freight yard, not to spot runaway murderers making their getaway. Jackson and Reggie thanked the guard and made a hasty retreat.

Reggie shook his head. "I don't believe it, man, I don't believe it."

"What, that he did it again?"

"No, that your little '80s detective con worked."

"Yeah, well, I had a great supporting cast."

"So where'd Bear come from?"

"I named you Officer Switzer. Bear, Barry."

"Thanks, by the way. Barry Switzer, really? He could have picked up on that."

"Not his generation, and you look nothing like The King."

Reggie exhaled. "So now what?"

"Now, you drop me at a motel and go back about your life."

"Why? What are you going to do?"

"Call Mouse, see if he can find a traffic camera. Hack bus cams or something."

"Bus cams?"

Jackson shrugged. "Pound every inch of pavement in the city. Possibly kidnap your ex-wife."

"I can stay."

"You've got a job and life back in L.A. I can't have you playing Doc Holiday all the time."

Reggie looked hard at him.

"Besides, I don't want your hands to get dirty."

"As opposed to the soapy and fragranty clean they are right now?"

"Seriously, Reg. I've lost him twice now. If I get him in my sights a third time . . . he ain't walking away."

Chapter Forty-One

REGGIE NEARLY BROKE the sound barrier, much more the speed limit, on the way back to L.A. He had persuaded Jackson to come back, sleep in his own bed, and not make a decision in the heat of the moment. The knowledge that Padilla could vanish at any time—vanish for good, that was—had made it a hard sell. Jackson didn't want to put a hundred miles between him and his prey, nor wait until morning to resume the chase. But his call to Mouse had pushed the decision. At ten till midnight, Mouse had been up, hunting aliens, and had agreed to pull an all-nighter trying to find a trace of Padilla. And it would likely be just that if he had to hack every camera in the vicinity of the freight yard.

They drove mostly in silence. There was little to say. They had pulled off a small coup to track down Padilla and have him in reach. Neither needed to say the obvious—getting an equally viable second chance at anything was rare. And technically, Jackson had had a chance previously to nab Padilla, making the near miss in the freight yard a second chance. Third chances were even rarer.

Jackson had also mulled Keisha's role in all of this some more, trying to figure out her motivations. He had seriously considered going to her house, Leila's house, their father's house—any house he could find—and going all bull in a china shop in pursuit of answers. Very Jack Bauer. His desire not to get Reggie in trouble, and the slim chance that any of them knew where Padilla was actually located, kept that plan at bay.

Mouse's Culver City neighborhood was eerily silent as Reggie rolled to the curb in front of his and Pam's duplex. At least there were no signs of hoodlums, like the first time they'd come.

"Nice driving, Hoss. Never gone Mach speed before."

"It's late, J. I'm hoping to get to bed sometime tonight."

"You can go. I'll take a cab home or crash here."

"Let's see what he's got first."

Jackson opened his door. The fog that had blanketed San Diego was more like a fine mist in L.A., and he shivered in the cool night air.

"We just ring the bell at one-thirty a.m.?" Reggie asked as he circled the Hummer.

"And wake Pam? Good call." Jackson reached for his phone. "I'll call him. You watch my six."

Mouse answered on the second ring.

"Hey, dude, we're here."

"So come in. It's unlocked."

"We're not going to wake Pam, are we?"

"She's spending the night at Clark's."

"Wait, what? Didn't she just break up with some rancher from Santa Fe?"

"Something like that."

Jackson shook his head. Whatever. "Okay, we're coming in." He clapped the phone shut and nodded for Reggie to follow him. The duplex was completely dark, except for a faint blue-green light emanating from down the hall. They followed it to Mouse's bedroom.

He sat at his station, a half-empty one-liter of Mountain Dew in his hand. A dead soldier lay on the floor. A bag of Gardetto's was open next to a rumpled bag of Cheetos. His focus was on two screens, with a third on a laptop sitting on his right. He wore a long-sleeve T-shirt with a software company logo on the chest and dark jeans. His hair was even shaggier than usual, a result of running his hands through it again and again. He repeated the movement, then used his hand to turn the laptop screen toward Jackson.

"Downloading all the footage to this, so you have it."

"You find anything?"

Mouse swiveled in his chair, flicking his eyes up at Reggie. "Hey."

Reggie nodded.

"You said you saw him hop a fence here?" Mouse asked, pointing to a satellite map—Google or Bing or something—on one of his screens.

"Yeah."

"I've been working my way out, checking traffic cameras on Harbor Drive. No good." He reached for a handful of Gardetto's, crunching on them as he continued. "Then I started working my way around the area, various businesses. A lot of them have closed circuit feeds, which I can't hack. But I did get this from the parking garage of the Hilton just to the northwest of the seaport."

He pointed to the other screen, and Jackson leaned in to look. Focused on the parking garage, the camera also captured, through an opening in the garage wall, the sidewalk outside it, along Harbor Drive. It was a long-distance shot, and typically grainy, but it showed a man walking northwest while wearing jeans and a hoodie, as had Padilla.

"That him?" Mouse asked.

"Yeah." Jackson looked at Reggie, who nodded. "When was this?"

"Ten-twenty-four."

"Just a freeze-frame, or you have motion?"

"Parts of a few freeze-frames. He's moving past the window."

"You got him after this?"

"This is as far as I am."

"What? After almost two hours?"

"Hey, man, you try hacking all these servers. It's not just logging onto your bank or something."

Jackson sighed. "Sorry, man."

"Yeah, yeah." He reached for more Gardetto's.

"Mouse, man, how can you eat Cheetos while working on a computer? How are your keys not all orange, man?"

"Easy," Mouse said, turning in his chair so Reggie could see. The denim covering his thighs was stained orange. "I wipe my hands like a civilized human."

Reggie grinned at Jackson as Mouse spun back around.

"So this is what you've got so far?" Jackson asked, picking up the laptop.

"I didn't spot your guy on any of those cams, but I still pulled about ten to fifteen minutes of footage from the time he went over the fence." He shrugged. "If it was like TV, you'll see some car go by that will match a car you saw at the freight yard or something."

Jackson raised his eyebrows. "That's not bad, Mouse. Worth having anyhow."

He shrugged again, pounded a swig of Dew, and resumed hacking.

"I'm calling it a night, J. Let me take you home. You can come back in the morning."

"No, I want to be here if he finds anything. I can get a cab."

"And if he does find something, what you gonna do at three in the morning?"

"Get your butt out of bed to take me back down to San Diego."

"Yeah, that's what I was afraid of. You sure, man?"

"I'm sure, Hoss. Thanks for everything."

They slapped hands, and Reggie exchanged a "See ya" with Mouse as he headed for the door.

"I'm like five minutes from being into the convention center," Mouse said a short while later. Jackson had just started watching the footage on the laptop.

"Okay."

"He was going that way, and if we can see him there, we have a pattern."

Jackson nodded.

"Of course, he could have taken the footbridge over to the stadium, disappeared in downtown."

"We'll find him sooner or later."

"Or holed up at the Hilton for the night."

"Not likely. He wants to keep a low profile, and the Hilton's going to have lots of cameras, lots of security inside."

"That's what I figured. It's why I went for the convention center first." He downed more soda. "So you really chased this guy around a freight yard?"

"We did," Jackson said, recapping their adventure. By the time he finished, Mouse had access to the San Diego Convention Center's security cameras. Spanning several city blocks between downtown and the marina, the convention center ran parallel to Harbor Drive. If Padilla had continued walking northwest, he would show on one of the cameras on the building's northeast side.

He didn't.

Mouse checked them twice, and pulled all of the footage from every entrance or any camera that might possibly show the exterior, and none of them showed a man in jeans or a hoodie.

Jackson dropped his head back against the wall. Mouse stood. "Need more fuel," he said, waving the empty Mountain Dew bottle.

"Can I move this?" Jackson asked, lifting the laptop.

"Yeah, it's on wireless."

Jackson carried it over to Mouse's bed and lay down on top of the bedspread. His body wanted to shut down. His brain wanted rest. He forced them both to keep going as he watched through the footage Mouse had pulled, hoping to spot something they had originally missed. Maybe a man without a hoodie, if Padilla had discarded it. Maybe a reflection in a window—that always happened on TV. Instead he saw nothing.

Mouse was working on hacking the security cameras at Petco Park, on the other side of the pedestrian bridge over Harbor Drive, when Jackson decided to shut his eyes for just five minutes.

He lay his head back, and the next thing he knew, he was dreaming about taking a tour of San Diego via a Golden Age-era passenger train with former Oklahoma football coach Barry Switzer.

*　　　　　*　　　　　*

4:41 a.m.

"DUDE!"

Jackson blinked his eyes into what could vaguely be categorized as consciousness.

"Dude, wake up."

His eyes focused on Mouse, standing over him, shaking his shoulder.

337

"Yeah?" Jackson asked. He looked around. The room was still dark. No bedside clock. "What time is it?"

"I don't know, four, five. I found him."

Jackson was suddenly alert. "What?"

"I found your guy."

Jackson sat up. "You found him? Where?"

"Now don't get too excited. But yeah," Mouse said, walking back to his desk. He sat down, and Jackson rubbed his eyes as he followed him and peered into the screen.

"Where is that?"

"Imperial Avenue."

"Imperial?"

"I figured he'd crossed Harbor, so I started moving up the street when I didn't spot him around Petco Park. Omni Hotel—which was a tough nut to crack—half a dozen restaurants, a few traffic cams. Nothing. So I figured maybe he hadn't crossed Harbor after all. And then I thought, maybe he expected somebody to be following him, since you'd tracked him to the freight yard and chased him around."

"Where are you going with this, Mouse?"

"He doubled back, to the east. I got him a few blocks from the stadium."

"On here?" Jackson asked with a nod at the screen.

"Yeah." Mouse pointed to the time stamp in the bottom corner. "This is the camera on a parking lot at the corner of 14th and Imperial. Ten-thirty-six. Wait for it."

They had to wait thirty seconds before a man matching the description of Padilla—which Jackson had given Mouse—walked by the camera, headed east.

"That him?" Mouse asked.

"That's him all right. Is this it?"

"No. Keep watching."

Three minutes passed, then he returned and stood on the corner, next to a portable toilet across the street at a construction site.

"What's he doing?" Jackson asked.

"Wait . . . He doesn't know he's on camera."

Padilla paced, looking nervously around, but never at the camera.

"What's he . . ."

A vehicle coasted to a stop in front of Padilla. It was a dark reddish color, a newer model sedan, thoroughly standard except for the taxi light on the top, identifying it as a cab.

Jackson turned to Mouse. "He called a cab."

"I did some Google-Earthing. There's a payphone half a block up the street. I think he went and called the cab, then came back to wait for it."

"Who uses a payphone anymore?"

"I know, right?"

Jackson squinted. "Can you enhance this, see what that sticker on the door says."

"Already did. Bayside Cab."

Jackson clapped his hands.

"I tried hacking into their dispatch, but didn't get anywhere."

"You got a phone number?"

"Yeah, but the bad news is, they're only open till midnight. Don't open again till six."

"What time is it?"

Mouse looked at the clock in the corner of his computer screen. "Quarter to five."

"Thanks, man. I owe you one."

"Does this mean I can get some sleep?"

"Yeah. Just let me use your phone first. I need to call myself a cab."

*   *   *

7:22 a.m.

JACKSON HADN'T intended to sleep upon returning from Mouse's so much as just rest his eyes and body. But before he knew it, he had slipped into unconsciousness. When he woke, full-blown light was streaming through his window.

He sat up on the couch, instantly alert, instantly aware of the events of the previous night. And still possessing in his pocket the phone number Mouse had found for Bayside Cab in San Diego. According to Mouse, they opened at six a.m.

Jackson stood and grabbed his phone off the coffee table. His battery indicator blinked, telling him he was almost out of juice. Making a note to charge it when he was through, Jackson dialed Bayside Cab while pacing into his kitchen. As the line rang, he looked out at the gray Pacific, churning beneath skies a lighter shade of the same color.

"Bayside Cab," said a female dispatcher.

"Uhhh . . . yeah, hi. I, uh . . . I took a cab last night—one of your cabs. I think I may have left my wallet inside."

"What is your name, sir?"

"Uh, Joaquín Padilla," Jackson said, hoping Padilla hadn't given a fake name. And hoping his attempt at dazed and hungover also passed for Hispanic.

"Last night?"

"Yeah."

"I don't see any record of that name last evening."

"Crap."

"Are you sure it was one of our cabs?"

"You're the third company I've called. I know the name had something to do with Bay. Bay City, Bayside . . ."

"Well, we haven't had a report of finding any wallet, but I can take a number if we do."

"Um, maybe . . . Maybe I lost it . . . I'm sorry, I'm not real clear on the details this morning. I'm afraid," he said with a chuckle, "I don't even know where the driver took me. I woke up at some woman's house, but I'm pretty sure that wasn't it."

"I'm sorry for your trouble, sir, but—"

"Is there any way you can see where I went?"

"Sir, we don't have record of your name."

"I was picked up a few blocks east of the park . . . uh, the baseball park, about ten-thirty. Emperor or Imperial Drive or something. Right by a big parking lot."

A pause. Then, "One moment, sir."

He heard fingers on a keyboard, background chatter. He put his odds at fifty-fifty.

One moment stretched into two.

"Sir, can you please describe your appearance?"

He gave the woman a rough description of Padilla, figuring she had activated in-cab footage to verify he was who he said he was. Else she had a Mouse in her office hacking traffic cams too.

"We show a fare from that location at ten-forty-one last night."

"That sounds right."

"A drop off at the Border View Inn in San Ysidro. The driver said you paid in cash. I don't know if that means you still had your wallet or not, sir."

"Thank you. I'll check the motel. Uh, thanks again."

"Of course, sir. Have a nice day."

He clapped the phone shut and forgot about charging it. There wasn't time. San Ysidro was just north of the Mexican border. Padilla was going to try crossing into Mexico on his own. If he succeeded, he would be gone forever.

Chapter Forty-Two

Thursday, May 19, 2011
8:08 p.m.

JACKSON DIDN'T BOTHER to turn to see who had just placed a hand on his shoulder. He didn't much care. It was one of dozens, most followed with some form of condolence or a "How ya holding up?" or "Hang in there." He did not need any more platitudes, well-intentioned as they may have been, from people who couldn't possibly be experiencing the grief he was.

Sure, others were sad. They'd lost a distant family member—a cousin, an uncle, a nephew, an in-law. Nothing even as close as a brother, much less both parents. Maybe Leroy—maybe he was on Jackson's scale. To lose a son, to lose Hannah who was like a daughter, to lose a grandson. And it was unnatural to have to bury one's offspring. Maybe Leroy could commiserate with Jackson, but he was busy conversing with rarely seen distant family members and old parishioners, and otherwise acting the host for the remnant of the Douglas family.

The aloneness of the moment was stifling. Even Reggie, his best friend, was so stuck in a mess at work that he couldn't be there. Not that he could have done much of anything anyhow. This was beyond what a pal could cure.

The hand moved from Jackson's shoulder, and he was aware of a blur of black and red to his right. He kept his eyes on the front of the large receiving room at the funeral parlor, where a small nursery's worth of flowers and wreaths had been positioned in front of a trio of ornate, wood caskets. With nothing better to do as afternoon dragged into evening, he'd read the cards identifying the flowers' senders: David and Hannah's church; the Navy; LAPD; Conway, Davenport & Rankin,

Attorneys at Law; several local charities; family members; and a number of other individuals. They were loving gestures, showing how many people held David, Hannah, and Grant in such high esteem. And all Jackson could think about was what he was going to do with all the dang flowers.

"Do you mind if I sit down?"

He shook his head and uttered a soft, "No," lifting a glass of brown liquid to his lips and admitting a small sip of the lukewarm fluid past them. Then he turned his eyes to see if his brain had properly matched the voice.

From the chair adjacent to his, Holly McKenzie offered a thin smile. Her bright, blond hair was swept back and held with a clip, drawing more attention to eyes that were at the same time mirthfully blue and tearfully red. She wore a short-sleeve burgundy blouse and a black skirt, as buttoned up as he'd ever seen Hillary's youngest sister. Fun, flirtatious, flamboyant—yet still a McKenzie—she was the one of the trio of sisters Jackson could manage to stomach. In fact, under different circumstances, were the age discrepancy a little less, the two of them could have been good friends.

"I didn't think you drank," she said.

"It's apple juice," he said, tipping the glass back for another gulp. "Stiffest drink they're offering."

Holly reached out her hand, cupping it over Jackson's free hand. "Are you okay?" She shook her head. "I know that's a stupid question, but . . . you've just been sitting here with a thousand-yard stare for a long time."

"Somehow the 'So what's new with you?' conversations with cousins don't appeal to me right now."

"It might help. I know that seems absurd, but they say—"

"Nothing's going to help, Holly. Right now . . . right now I'm just in a fog. And I'd really rather not do anything that might make that fog clear, because if it does, I know I won't like what I see."

She nodded, swallowed, it appeared holding back tears.

"Do you . . . do you want to be alone?"

He looked at her as a tear fell from her eye. He wanted nothing more than for everyone to leave him alone. At the same time, he was terrified of being by himself. Somehow, just her simple presence meant something he couldn't quantify.

"I . . . I don't know."

She squeezed his hand, then withdrew hers to wipe a tear.

"How's Hillary?" he asked.

"Oh she's just fine, on the outside. That famous McKenzie veneer won't let anything penetrate—always in control." She sniffed. "Inside . . . I'm afraid she's crumbling like a mummy in a sarcophagus."

"You should be with her."

"She has Mom and Dad, and Heather."

"And I don't."

"Jackson."

"It's okay, Holly. I have to get used to being alone now."

She bit her lip, trying unsuccessfully to stem more tears. They trickled down her cheeks, and a gasp-like cry escaped her mouth. Before he knew it, Jackson had extended an arm. Holly came and buried her face into his shoulder, half sitting beside him on and against the arm of the chair and half sitting on his lap. Several times, her body convulsed in quiet sobs, causing him to wonder, as he turned his eyes from her fragrant hair back to the flowers at the other end of the room, why he was the one consoling someone else in tears.

After a few minutes, Holly composed herself and sat up on the arm of the chair, wiping with the back of her hand at tears that came faster than she could clear them away.

"Jackson, I'm so, so sorry."

He nodded, unable to speak.

She reached for both of his hands, holding them between hers. "If you need anything . . . I don't know if I can possibly help in any way, but just know I'm here."

He nodded again, managing to utter a soft, "Thank you."

She stood, forcing that same thin smile she had greeted him with, then slipped back into the crowd.

He thought for a few minutes about seeking out his cousins. All he'd done so far was shake a few hands and receive a few hugs. But he just couldn't bring himself to smile and discuss past Fourth of July softball games or a trip to Yellowstone years ago, or tease each other over sports allegiances. So he sat and stared some more, doing his best to remain in a mental and emotional haze as the gathering of people slowly dwindled.

He lost track of time, and was almost in a trance when Leroy clapped his shoulder. "Hey, bud."

"Hey."

"Looks like things are winding down here. Sam and Stephanie have a suite over at the Four Points. They're inviting any family who wants to come hang out to do so. Donny's going to drive me over for a while."

Jackson nodded. Samuel Goldman was—had been—Hannah's younger brother. He and his wife Stephanie lived in Chicago, where he worked for Accenture and she was a flight attendant with United Airlines. Their kids, Steve and Shannon, were eight and ten years younger than Jackson, both students at Northwestern. He couldn't recall the last time he'd seen any of them. And Donny was Leroy's oldest—and now only— son.

"I know the last thing you want is to be around a bunch of people telling stories and trying to cheer you up," Leroy continued, "but they'd sure like to see you. And it's like the Lord said, it ain't good for a man to be alone."

"I don't think God said 'ain't,' Grandpa." He exhaled. "I'll think about it."

Leroy nodded, then cupped his hand around Jackson's cheek. "I love you, Jackson."

"Yeah. I love you too, Grandpa."

With another nod, Leroy wandered off. "Any family" likely included Hannah's sister Ruth's five kids. Jackson liked them all well enough, but they were each a little . . . zany was probably going too far. But unique was not, and he wasn't in the mood for his cousins tonight.

Or extended consciousness, for that matter.

No one seemed to be paying him any attention, so he got up and slipped out of the receiving room. He followed a hallway to the rear exit. The coast was clear as he pushed through the door and out into the rain.

*   *   *

Sunday, June 23, 2013
10:20 a.m.

JACKSON'S HEART began to pound as he took exit 1A off I-5 in San Ysidro—the last exit before Mexico. After talking with the dispatcher at Bayside Cab, he'd taken time only to stuff a fresh set of clothes into a duffel bag before hitting the road again. He'd had the better part of two and a half hours to think while driving that same stretch of highway he'd traveled so many times in the last week that he'd lost count. Now, as he turned off the interstate and onto Camino de la Plaza, within sight of the border wall between the U.S. and Mexico, he still hadn't answered the question to himself.

What would he do if he found Padilla?

There was still nothing any court could do. All the evidence that had convinced Jackson and others that Padilla was guilty of setting off the explosion at Curly's was circumstantial, illegally obtained, or both. Maybe Jayron Watts would testify that Padilla had been seeking to be smuggled into Mexico, but Jackson doubted it—that would only incriminate Watts further, and wouldn't do much to mitigate his sentence. Plus, why would SDPD care if some repeat offender was trying to leave the country? No, the legal route was out. A citizen's arrest would do no good.

Tossed in his duffel with a change of clothes was the Nokia that Mouse had rigged to be the receiving end of the listening device Jackson had planted on Keisha. By itself, it was just a phone. Maybe it had a record feature, and maybe he could do what he'd told Reggie, force Padilla to confess. He'd done that once before, in Las Vegas, by putting a gun to the kneecap of a U.S. Senator's wife to get the corrupt senator to indict himself. It had sort of worked, at least in setting the record straight, but it still haunted him. And confessions under coercion weren't admissible either.

There was always the Glock.

Despite his speeches about picking up the slack when the legal system failed, Jackson knew he couldn't justify—legally or morally—putting a bullet in Padilla's head. And yet, during the long drive down the coast, the image of him doing just that had continually presented itself at the forefront of his brain.

It hadn't been alone. He'd seen photos from Padilla's computer—photos of David Douglas, shot as a stalker might shoot his prey. He'd seen Special Agent Collier and D.A. Moreno and Mira Austin admitting they believed Padilla to be guilty, but untouchable. He'd seen Fort Rosecrans National Cemetery and Admiral Sullivan, mysteriously hinting that he knew more than he was telling, yet shaken at the revelation in the change of Padilla's timeline.

He'd seen his family, images of some of their last times together. Easter dinner with David and Hannah. Grant stopping by with Hillary to check in on him. He'd seen her face as she sat stoically at the funeral. And he'd seen his grandpa, breaking down as he tried to eulogize his son, daughter-in-law, and grandson—the only time Jackson could ever remember seeing Leroy moved so strongly.

Turning onto a side road, back away from the border and toward the interstate, Jackson set his jaw. Padilla wasn't getting away. Jackson could bait him, force Padilla into attacking first so that Jackson could shoot him in self-defense. Or he could find a way to frame him for some other crime. Or he could just beat the ever-loving crap out of him with his bare hands. But Padilla wasn't getting away.

Assuming he already hadn't.

The Border View Inn was technically a misnomer, but barely. It faced I-5, with two stories of yellowed siding under a black roof looking outdated and pathetic. The parking lot was grayed asphalt with faded white lines, and sat between the two "wings" of the inn. They were connected by a carport and lobby, and by access to the pool around back.

Jackson parked on the street. The rain and fog of the night before had lifted, but the sky was still overcast, with a wind off the ocean that was almost raw. Jackson paid it no attention as he crossed the road and the largely vacant parking lot and entered the lobby. It was needlessly air conditioned by a unit in the window, rattling on to block out the pop music playing from a hidden radio. Spartan, it was at least clean. And empty, save for a disinterested woman—little more than a girl—behind the counter. She had two-toned hair, dark eyes, and a tattoo of a snake or a dragon winding down from her shoulder under a plain gray T-shirt.

"Can I help you? Check-in's not till three if you need a room."

"I need information on a guest."

"Who are you?"

She didn't look bright enough to call the bluff, so he reached into his pocket and pulled out Grant's shield. He clunked it on the counter. "Special Agent Douglas, FBI," he said, swiping the shield before she could study it closely enough to identify it as belonging to LAPD. "We have reason to believe a member of a Mexican drug cartel is staying here."

"Here?"

"He would have arrived last night, around eleven or eleven-thirty, and used an alias."

She nodded. "Let me check the register." It was an actual register, and she traced it with her finger. "Yeah, only one single last night after ten. Name of Jesse Polanco, room 104."

"You know if he's still there?"

"He paid for two nights, but I don't know."

"You got a spare key?"

She reached under the counter and handed him a key on a small plastic dongle. "I'll need that back. It's a master."

"Of course."

"You want me to call backup or something?"

"No. If there's too much activity, it could spook him. I can handle it."

"Okay."

"Thanks."

Pocketing the key, he exited the lobby. Room 104 was on his right, halfway to the street. He followed the sidewalk instead of cutting across the lot, his heart pounding again, his brain still running options.

The blinds in the window of room 104 were drawn. Jackson stopped in front of the door, looking around. He saw nobody and banged on the door with his fist. His other hand hovered behind his back, ready to draw his Glock.

No one answered.

He pounded on the door again and, when he received no response, put his ear to the door. He didn't hear the TV, didn't hear water running. He heard nothing.

Removing his hand from his gun, he lifted the key from his pocket. Looking around again, he worked it in the lock. When he felt it give, he held the knob with his left hand while returning the key to his pocket and drawing his gun with his right. Then he swept the door open and leveled the Glock at an empty bed.

It was unmade, slept in. A glass sat on the end table in a puddle of condensation. Just water, judging by the lack of residue in the glass. He sniffed it to be sure. No odor.

Jackson quickly checked the bathroom. It was empty, a used towel and a washcloth tossed in the corner. The soap on the counter had been opened and used.

None of that was a surprise. Neither was Padilla's absence. The lady at the desk had said he'd booked for two nights, and Jackson could conjure up any number of places for him to have gone—a Denny's just down the street for an early lunch; a store to get a paper, a pack of smokes, or something stronger for his bedside glass; a stroll along the border wall to look for weak points. And yet, he had a sinking feeling as he searched the room more thoroughly that Padilla had eluded him again.

Chapter Forty-Three

12:40 p.m.

STAKEOUTS WERE ALWAYS fun on TV. Either a cute chick or a wisecracking buddy was there to help pass the time. There was usually food, or at least coffee, and without the typical stakeout-inhibiting side effects of eating and drinking. And they only ever lasted for about two minutes before something happened.

Jackson had been sitting alone, without food or drink, for almost two hours. He'd thought about calling Reggie, but didn't have much to tell him and didn't like what he guessed Reggie would tell him. Namely, don't murder Joaquín Padilla.

He'd also thought about calling one of his various potential contacts to see if there was any word on Padilla's location. He had yet to return to his room at the Border View Inn, and every minute he was gone lessened the chance that he was coming back. Brunch at Denny's or a liquor run didn't take two hours. So where was he?

Jackson had found nothing in the room to indicate where Padilla was or what his plans were. He'd thought about waiting in the room for him to return, but concluded sitting in his car across the street would be better. If Padilla happened to return with an entourage or a cranky black woman who knew passing judo, Jackson didn't want a confrontation he could possibly avoid. He'd returned the key to the clerk, asking her to call his cell phone if Padilla checked out or made contact with the front desk. Then he'd taken up a seat in the Granada and waited.

He saw movement in the mirror and glanced up. His heart sank. A San Diego Police cruiser had pulled to the curb behind him. He adjusted his shirt to make sure it covered the gun in his waistband, then waited with his hands on the steering wheel.

Two officers got out of the car. The passenger stood at the curb beside his open door. The driver slowly approached Jackson, who rolled down his window.

"Afternoon," the officer said. He was young, handsome, his face and features firm but not unpleasant.

"Officer."

"Do you mind if I ask what you're doing here?"

Jackson had half a mind to go all constitutional and tell him he had every right to park on an unmarked city street and so on, but decided some tact might be in his favor.

"I'm waiting for someone."

"Someone at the motel?"

"Someone not there, actually."

The officer nodded. "Do you have some identification?"

"Yeah," Jackson said and reached for his wallet. "Is there a problem?"

"We received a call from a nearby resident who spotted a man in a car sitting here for quite some time."

"I don't mean to be a jerk about it, but there's nothing against that, is there?"

"No, sir, but it is a little unusual. There is a school just back a few blocks, a playground up ahead."

Jackson nodded and decided to hand the officer his private investigator's license as well as his driver's license. The officer studied them for a minute. "You're a private investigator?"

"Yes, sir."

"Are you working on a case at the moment?"

"Uh, so to speak, yes."

"Well, Mr. Douglas, I can appreciate that. But I am going to have to ask you to move along and continue your waiting game elsewhere."

"You've got the badge," Jackson said. He took his IDs back from the officer. He tucked them back into his wallet, then started the car. Nothing more than an inconvenience, he figured. Drive around the block for fifteen minutes, then come back and park in the lot instead. He'd just have to hope Padilla didn't pick that time to return, check out, and catch a cab elsewhere.

Jackson bummed back toward Camino de la Plaza and followed it west, where it terminated in a north-south road that led into the desert to the left and back toward town to the right. Jackson hung a right, just as his phone buzzed in his pocket. He lifted it out, mindful that the battery was almost dead and he hadn't taken the time to charge it before leaving home.

"Hello."

"Special Agent Douglas?"

"Yes."

"This is Nina at the Border View Inn. You said to contact you if I heard anything from Mr. Polanco in room 104."

Jackson braked and veered onto the shoulder of the road. "Yes. Did he return?"

"No, sir. But he called a little while ago to inform us that he wouldn't be returning this evening, and left a forwarding number should he receive any calls. Well, not five minutes later he did. A man named Omar . . ."

"Hello? Nina?" Jackson looked down at his phone. It was dead.

He slammed it into the seat and then pounded his hand against the wheel. With a quick look for traffic—there was none—he whipped the Granada around and retraced his steps back to the Border View Inn. The cops were gone, and he wheeled into the lot and parked as close to the lobby as possible. It was empty.

He rang a bell on the desk, but nothing happened. Time ticked by in agonizing increments as his brain pondered why Padilla hadn't returned, what had changed his plans, who Omar was, why he had called for Padilla, and why he had known to call the motel.

The outside door opened and Nina, sullen-faced and snake-tattoo-entwined, entered. "Oh, hi."

"Hi. Sorry, my phone died."

"No problem. Yeah, a man named Omar called and said to have Mr. Polanco call him back."

"Did he call him Mr. Polanco?"

Nina nodded as she stepped back behind the desk.

"Did he give you a number?"

"No. I asked, but he said Mr. Polanco knew it."

"Okay. Anything else?"

"No, that was all."

"Did Polanco say anything else when he called? Where he was, why he wasn't coming back?"

"No, nothing."

"Okay. Thank you very much for calling."

"Uh, Special Agent Douglas?"

"Yeah."

"What should I do? Should I call Mr. Polanco?"

"Yeah, just tell him what Omar said. Leave me out of it, of course."

"Of course."

"Oh, do you have the number Polanco gave you, the forwarding number?"

"Yes." She wrote something down and handed it to Jackson.

"Thank you," he said, then exited the lobby again.

The chase continued.

*   *   *

2:24 p.m.

JACKSON PUT out a number of feelers while grabbing lunch at Denny's. Using the Nokia, he called Mouse and asked him to trace the number Padilla had given Nina. It came back, no surprise, as a burner. He called Dick Davis, Greg Cole, Dick's guy Rodriguez, and Melanie Gwynn, asking if they knew someone named Omar—someone likely with ties to San Diego's underworld, particularly in relation to human smuggling or forged identifications—or, in Melanie's case, if she happened to have heard word from Padilla. Then, because they were from the area, he called the Haywoods, leaving each of them voicemails on their cells.

Over time, he heard back from each of them. No word from Padilla. Nothing on anyone named Omar. No leads whatsoever.

He was getting desperate. Padilla was itchy to escape, whether it was over the wall or with a new face and identity. If he did escape, Jackson's chance for justice would be gone.

He thought about calling Keisha and begging for her help. He also thought about kicking down her door and putting a Glock to her neck until she told him everything. But he didn't. Instead, he sat at his table until long after his lunch had been consumed and his plate cleared away.

The Nokia chimed a generic chirp that was getting old. Jackson quickly took the call. "Yeah?"

"Jack, it's Juliet Haywood."

"Oh, hey. Ike already called back."

"Yeah, well, Ike should have checked with me first."

"Why? You know something about Omar?"

"Maybe. A few months ago, we helped a trio of Marines whose cars had all been boosted from outside a bar in Little Italy, a bar frequented by service personnel. We staked it out, set bait, kind of like we did with that dating service lady a few years ago."

"You just as successful?"

"We were. We busted a small-time thief named Carver, a young punk who admitted he was trying to earn his stripes for a hood named Omar."

"Omar?"

"Uh-huh. We turned him over to the cops, and he tried to plea down by testifying against Omar, but he didn't know enough to be worth anything. He's serving a nickel at Corcoran now."

"You know anything else about Omar?"

"Carver said he runs a huge chop shop over in El Cajon, Mexicali Automative. Mostly legal work, detailing and whatnot, and the cops can't prove anything illegal. Carver also said he imports a lot of stolen cars from Mexico, then breaks them down for parts here."

"Carver seems well informed."

"Sounded like Omar was something of an idol to him. Anyhow, none of that would probably warrant much interest to you, which is probably why Ike didn't think anything of it. But he forgot what else Carver told us, that word on the street was that Omar also used these cars to smuggle in heroin from Mexico. He said Omar made just as much on the side trafficking drugs as he did through the chop shop and his legitimate business deals. Seeing as how you're looking for an Omar who may or may not be able to help your guy Padilla disappear, I thought it worth mentioning."

"Yeah, thanks, Juliet."

"That's literally all I know about Omar. Once we caught Carver, he started rambling, trying to get us and the cops to go easy on him. But he didn't have more than rumors and scuttlebutt."

"It's more than I have."

"You need anything else, you let us know."

"I will. Thanks, Juliet."

He ended the call and held the phone to his chin, mulling. Then he made another call.

It took Mouse five minutes to find a Mexicali Automotive in El Cajon, a suburb of San Diego east on I-8. The owner was listed, although not publically, as Omar Núñez. Another five minutes of searching revealed that an Omar Núñez lived in nearby Bostonia, and had paid taxes as a Californian for the past decade.

Jackson paid the check, returned to the Granada, and headed north on the 805 toward El Cajon.

Chapter Forty-Four

Thursday, May 19, 2011
9:14 p.m.

"WHAT CAN I get you, mate?"

The bartender had an Australian accent, which seemed out of place in the dark, smoky bar. The TVs over the bar showed baseball and basketball highlights, not cricket or kangaroo races. Neon signs flashed American brews like Budweiser and Miller and Coors, not Foster's. The smattering of patrons looked like the typical bunch of losers one would expect at such a place, not red-faced blokes fresh off a walkabout. And yet, the bartender sounded just like that crocodile hunter who'd been killed by a stingray. Of all the ways to go . . .

Jackson slowly lifted his eyes to him. Water-drenched hair obscured his vision, and he shook it aside like a wet dog. "Something strong," he said.

"Bad day?"

"Bad life."

"Sorry to 'ear that, mate." He clunked a tumbler on the counter and turned toward rows of bottles on the shelf behind him.

"Make that two."

Jackson turned his head and saw Maggie settling onto the stool next to him. She wore a black blazer over a burnt orange blouse, black pants. Her hair was down, maybe a trace curlier than previously, thanks to the rain that was also evidenced on her shoulders. She looked at him with a blank face, perhaps emotionless or perhaps the result of sympathy for someone she barely knew.

He swallowed. "What are you doing here?"

"Somebody saw you duck out the back of the funeral home. I was heading back to my hotel and I happened to see you coming in here . . . and I didn't think you should be alone."

He nodded. "I meant, why are you even here, in San Diego?"

"I heard what happened. I felt like I should come."

Jackson nodded again as the bartender poured whiskey into two glasses. Jackson slowly reached for his and held it up, inspecting the brown liquid inside it. "You know something," he said, not breaking his gaze from the glass.

"What's that?"

"I've never had a drink of alcohol in my life."

"So you told me."

"Right."

"And yet here you are."

He raised his eyebrows. "Now seems like as good a time as any."

He started to raise the glass, but Maggie stopped him, placing a hand on his wrist. He looked over at her.

"You should wait."

"Wait?"

"Before you start drinking hard liquor, wait twenty-four hours."

"Twenty-four hours."

"It's not like things will suddenly be better, but your emotions will be a little less raw."

She let go of his wrist, and he set the glass back on the bar. He looked down. "Less raw? Tomorrow I have to sit through a funeral, after I stand in line and face a bunch of blubbering people who aren't a quarter as sad as I am." He released the glass. "I've been to funerals before. The family stands in line, backs aching, feet tired, hearts and minds burned out, but they've got one thing going for them. Each other." He looked her way. "I'm going to be up there all by myself."

That wasn't entirely true. Leroy would be there. Probably Hillary. But for all intents and purposes, it was true. Leroy was in his seventies, and while in ideal health, if a broken heart didn't kill him, time would catch up with him soon. And Hillary—she was young, beautiful, successful. She'd grieve, then move on. And it wasn't like she and Jackson were set up to be much of a support system to each other anyhow.

Maggie, to her credit, didn't try to counter Jackson's sorrow. She just sat there, beside him.

"You watch *M*A*S*H*?" he asked a minute later, after staring a hole through the whiskey.

"Yeah."

He licked his lips. "You ever see the one where Radar's all bummed because Hawkeye had to amputate some football player's leg, and he comes in to 'the swamp' and Hawkeye and B.J. pour him a drink? He takes a drink and makes a face and says he thought alcohol was supposed to make a guy feel better. And B.J. tells him it's actually supposed to make him feel nothing." He looked at Maggie. "That's me. I'm numb. I can't feel anything right now. And . . . I thought that was a good thing, I thought after so much anguish and agony over the last few days, feeling nothing would be nice. But I'm realizing something. This is kind of like being out in the cold. When you're numb, it's not that the pain goes away. It just hurts so bad it shuts off your brain's ability to process the pain. But it still hurts, it's still killing you, and deep down inside, you know it's killing you." He nudged the glass with the back of his hand. "So here I am, like Radar, hoping this will somehow make me feel better, because I figure I can't feel worse."

"Voice of experience, it won't," Maggie said.

"You know something about this?"

"I know about trying to find answers in the end of a bottle. There aren't any."

"Didn't figure you for a drunk."

"One time."

Jackson nodded.

"Come on, let's get out of here."

"Out of here? Where?"

She shrugged. "Somewhere warmer. Somewhere safer."

He shook his head. "Safer."

Maggie pulled some money out of her purse and set it on the counter, next to the whiskey glasses. "Come on," she said to Jackson again.

Robotically, and mostly because he was too tired to fight, he followed her to the door and out into the elements. They stood under a dripping awning that wasn't big enough for the two of them. "Where'd you park?" Maggie asked.

"At the funeral home."

She raised an eyebrow. "You walked?"

"Only a couple of blocks."

A rumble of thunder underscored her unspoken point. She reached for her purse. "We can take my car."

"Don't you drive a crotch rocket?"

"It's a rental. I flew down here."

"You flew?"

"I do drive a motorcycle, like you said, and the forecast called for rain. Besides, I have a deal with work," she said with a dismissive wave. "Come on."

"I'll be stuck at your hotel."

She shrugged. "I have unlimited mileage."

He sighed, then walked leisurely in the rain as she jogged to a small two-door parked a couple dozen yards down the street. The passenger door was unlocked by the time he got there. He opened it but didn't get in.

"What are you doing?" she asked from the driver's seat.

"I'll get your seat wet."

"It's a rental. Get in."

He did, and she started the car.

"So let me get this straight," he said. "You flew to San Diego, rented a car, drove to the funeral home, but didn't even say hello?"

"I didn't say hello because you were already gone. I was late. I saw you duck in the bar as I was driving off."

He nodded and reached for the heater. "Where you staying?"

"Sheraton by the airport."

"Long ride."

She shrugged.

"You didn't have to come all this way, Maggie."

"I know."

He glanced her way. She smiled thinly.

The ride took twenty minutes, and neither said much en route. Maggie stopped a few spaces away from a carport in front of the hotel and dropped the gearshift into park. "Do you want to come up?" she asked.

He turned her way. The rain drummed against the windows and bounced off the hood.

"I didn't mean like that." She shrugged. "I thought maybe you . . . would want somebody to talk to."

As much as Jackson had detested the idea of being with his family, with all those people wanting to talk, he also found himself craving company. And for whatever reason, craving Maggie's company.

"Yeah. I just need to make a call first."

They got out and hurried under the carport and into the hotel.

"You hungry?" she asked when they were in the air-conditioned lobby. "I can order room service."

"Now that you mention it, sort of. Club sandwich, a burger, whatever."

She nodded. "Room 612."

He repeated it back to her, then waited until she had entered the hallway leading to the elevators. As he left Leroy a voicemail to let him know he wouldn't be stopping by his cousin's suite, his brain practically screamed at him, asking what he was doing.

He told it to go pound sand, clapped his phone shut, and headed for the elevators.

*   *   *

Sunday, June 23, 2013
3:06 p.m.

MEXICALI AUTOMOTIVE in El Cajon lacked any aesthetic properties whatsoever. It was a hulking blue steel building, set back from the road about fifty feet. That area was all poured concrete, providing parking for several vehicles in front of a clearly marked office on the right, and access to three overhead garage doors in the center. A gated drive also led around back, where Mouse's satellite viewing had indicated there was room for maybe fifty to a hundred cars, depending on whether or not the semis that showed on satellite were parked there. The entire property was encircled by chain-link fence, topped with barbed wire. Jackson hoped there weren't dogs.

On a Sunday, he'd doubted the garage would be open for business—legitimate business, anyhow. But if Omar was prying cocaine from inside the rims of tires or hatching a plan to smuggle a killer into Mexico on one of his transporters, he might make exceptions to the traditional nine-to-five. It was also, Jackson reasoned, where Omar might keep records of illegal or quasi-legal activities. If Omar wasn't there, before Jackson went to his house and tortured him for info in front of his family, he'd prefer to try picking a filing cabinet or hacking a computer.

The lot was empty, save for a single car up close to the office door. It was a shiny red Mustang, an older model either kept in pristine condition for decades or masterfully restored. The latter, Jackson concluded as he drove past, noting the windows tinted almost black and the chrome scoops on the hood. Probably raced it for pinks on Saturday nights.

Jackson parked a block down and walked back. The sun was fighting to come out, but losing the battle. The muted glow added little warmth against a biting wind that made San Diego feel more like Chicago in March.

Seeing no signs of life in or around the Mustang, Jackson walked up to the office door. It used a numerical keypad instead of a traditional lock, so picking it was out. Jackson opted for the direct method and pounded on the glass with his fist. He was about to repeat the action when a face appeared in the window.

Dark skinned, Latino or maybe Arab, with a pencil-thin beard, mustache, and a Will Smith fade. He shook his head and hollered a muffled, "We're closed."

"I need some work done," Jackson answered. "Rush job."

"Sorry, man. Come back tomorrow."

Jackson had anticipated such a response, and reached into his pocket to pull out all the cash that had been in his wallet. He fanned it out, big bills facing out, and pushed it against the window.

The man inside shook his head. "Sorry."

"Me too," Jackson said. He stuffed the cash into his pocket and whipped around. At the same time, he pulled out his keys. He gouged them into the paint at the front of the Mustang's door, digging a channel forward toward the blinker.

The door clicked and opened and the man rushed out. Jackson spun back around, stopping him in his tracks with his Glock. "Inside," he said.

"You're *muy loco*," the man snarled, adding an epithet.

"*Muy*," Jackson said. "Inside."

The man turned around and tapped a code into the keypad, then opened the door.

"You alone?" Jackson asked, following him into a crude but clean office. A door led to the garage to the left. "Hey," he said, jabbing the gun into the man's back when he didn't answer. "You alone?"

"Yeah, I'm alone."

"On your knees."

"What?"

Jackson kicked the back of his knee, and he fell with a groan and a curse. He was wearing jeans and a black shirt, several gold chains around his neck and black and green tattoos up both arms. Talk about crazy.

"You Omar?"

"Who's asking?"

"Just answer the question, esé."

"Yeah, I'm Omar. And that's my car you just defaced. You're going to p—"

"Where's Joaquín Padilla?"

"Who?"

Jackson rapped him on the head with his pistol, and he fell to the ground with a shout of pain. He came up holding his head, looking for blood, and spouting curses.

"Where is Joaquín Padilla?" Jackson asked slowly, aiming the gun directly at Omar. "I'm not going to ask again."

"I don't know."

"When did you last talk to him?"

"I didn't—"

Jackson racked the slide on the Glock.

Omar licked his lips. He swore. "Man, this ain't worth it, man. This afternoon."

"What'd he want?"

"He wanted to disappear. Heard through the grapevine I could smuggle his sorry butt into Mexico."

"That true?"

"What are you, a cop?"

"Do I look like a cop to you? Would a cop key your pony out there, whack you over the head with his gun?"

"Then who are you?"

"Lady Justice's cranky little brother. What'd you tell Padilla?"

"Told him it wouldn't be easy, man. The border's hot right now, man. Feds busted a dozen cartel mules last week, then the cops took down some OG trying to smuggle weapons into Mexico last night. I told him to lay low."

"Yeah, what'd he say?"

"He was all panicked, man. I told him I might have another way."

Jackson nodded for him to continue.

"I said I knew a guy who could get him fake papers. Good, legit IDs—passport, driver's license, credit cards, whatever he wanted. Then lay low, head to Vegas or Phoenix and try again in a week or two."

"You arrange a meet?"

"Sort of."

"What's 'sort of' mean?"

"Means I've gotta call my boy yet. Sunday afternoon, he's probably playing eighteen."

"Your forger plays golf?"

"White collar business, man."

"When do you call Padilla back?"

"I don't. I set up the meet with him."

"When and where?"

"Torrey Pines Gliderport, eight tonight."

"The Gliderport?"

"Past it actually. Lot at the far end of the dirt road."

"Why there?"

"It's conveniently located for a third party. Now we done, man? You're making me nervous with that thing."

"Good. You haven't called your forger yet?"

"No."

"So he has no idea about Padilla."

"None, man."

"And Padilla's expecting you both at eight?"

"I said I'd be there with him. He was panicky, man."

"Yeah, well, unfortunately you're going to be detained at work."

"What are you talking about?"

"Up."

"What? You going to shoot me?"

"If you don't quit asking questions. Up."

Omar stood.

"Hands on your head, interlock your fingers."

Jackson marched him into the garage, then forced him to lie down on the concrete floor while Jackson found duct tape in a drawer against the wall. He used half a roll tying Omar's hands behind his back and securing his ankles tightly together. Then he walked/dragged him over to a flashy Dodge Charger parked on one of the garage's lifts. He opened the door and forced Omar into the passenger seat.

"What are you doing?"

"You married, Omar?"

"What?"

"Married. You got a wife, kids?"

"No. No, I'm not married."

"Okay. Then I guess I'll have to threaten *you*. You somehow get out of this before eight o'clock, somebody comes down here and finds you, you get amnesia, you got it?"

"And how am I supposed to explain being tied up?"

"I don't know, but it'll give you something to think about while you wait. But no matter what, you don't call your pal the forger and you don't call Padilla, you got that?"

"Yeah, I got it. You are *loco*, man."

Jackson tore off a length of tape and placed it over Omar's mouth. He patted his shoulder, closed the Charger's door, and found the button that controlled the lift. Thirty seconds later, Omar was six feet off the ground. Jackson tossed the duct tape toward the corner and turned to leave. He stopped at the door to the office, and turned back toward the Charger.

"Sorry about your car!"

Despite the duct tape over Omar's mouth, Jackson could still make out a muffled curse in reply.

Chapter Forty-Five

Thursday, May 19, 2011
9:46 p.m.

MAGGIE OPENED THE door minus her blazer, tousling her hair with a hotel towel. "Hey. Come on in."

Jackson stepped inside.

"I just called room service," she said, closing the door behind him. "They said about half an hour."

He nodded, feeling somewhat surreal, wondering what he was doing here. He should be at Uncle Sam and Aunt Susan's suite with the rest of the mourners. Or at his parents' house, sleeping in his old bed. But he couldn't bring himself to do that. Somehow, he knew, if he went back there, he'd stay up all night.

Maggie ducked into the bathroom and emerged with a towel, which she handed to Jackson. "You're soaked."

"Yeah, thanks." He blotted himself a few times, then paced over to the window, which overlooked the marina and, in the distance, downtown. Through the rain, he saw that familiar skyline, the distant lights of the city, and a jet on approach to San Diego International. He watched the light turn into two, then three, until finally a jet broke through the darkness. He caught Maggie's reflection beside him and turned to look at her.

She was beautiful, even rain-soaked with clumpy hair and sadness just below the surface on her otherwise carefree face. She looked at him with her gray-blue eyes, her straight mouth perhaps an indicator that she felt a tinge of awkwardness too.

"Thanks for coming, Maggie. You really didn't . . . I wouldn't have expected—"

"That's what friends are for."

He nodded. "Friends."

"At least."

He nodded again.

"Go ahead, have a seat," she said, turning from the window. "You must be tired."

He hadn't noticed until she said something, but he was. There was only one bed, a king, and he didn't want to sit on it while wet. Instead, he dropped onto a small couch beside the window. Maggie stepped out of her heels and sat on the edge of the bed, pulling one leg under her. It was several minutes before she spoke. "Jackson . . . I wish I knew something to say."

He turned his head. "I'm glad you don't." He shook his head. "I've heard it all today. All the same stuff. They mean well, but . . . I'm glad you don't have anything to say."

She formed a brief, wan smile.

"You know, the pastor said something," Jackson said, leaning back, "when it was just the family, before everyone else showed up. He said . . . he said this would be both a sad time and a happy time." He shook his head. "And I can't for the life of me figure out what the heck he was talking about." He focused on his hands, looking for words for what felt like minutes. "I know, I'm a thirty-year-old man—I'm supposed to be tough and a little cavalier, but my family is everything to me, Maggie, and I'm . . ." He looked up, seeing a tear in her eye. It was unmatched in his own. "I'm absolutely wrecked inside. I don't know how I am ever supposed to have a happy time again."

Maggie got off the bed and came and sat beside him. In that moment, something—the weight of his words and the meaning behind them, being removed from the death and funeral atmosphere, someone new to confide in—caused the dam to break. He doubled over and began sobbing uncontrollably, tears that hadn't emerged all week now bursting out of him.

Jackson wasn't a crier. Sadness manifested itself in anger, in brooding, not tears. He hadn't shed a single tear at any of his grandparents' funerals. He'd been perfectly sad, but just grieved in a different way. Or so he thought. Now, the full pressure was released like an unplugged fire hydrant.

He was distantly aware of Maggie's hand on his back, then her arm around his shoulders. Of a trace of fruity perfume. Of rain-dampened curls of hair on his neck. Of how warm it had become in the room. More than anything, he was aware of the gnawing emptiness inside him that he was coming to realize would never go away.

Jackson continued to cry. He was embarrassed, not because he was crying or crying in front of a girl, but because she was, practically, a stranger. And because it wasn't just tears flowing out of him, but every ounce of energy, every fiber of strength. He feared he might throw up. Or pass out.

Instead, he just kept crying, his entire body shaking, his stomach and throat both sore.

Maggie's hand held his neck, then crossed his back, as if trying to coax the grief out of him. She then slid off the couch, on her knees. She gently forced Jackson upright, then leaned into him. Resting her head against his chest, she wrapped her arms around him, holding him like he was a drunk going through the shakes.

Jackson wasn't through. He continued to cry—to bawl, his tears streaming off his face and into Maggie's hair, mixing with the dampness from the rain. She held him tight, until finally every drop had been discharged. Then all was quiet but for the distant hum of a light and their breathing as they continued to hold each other in a tight, wet embrace.

*   *   *

Sunday, June 23, 2013
7:15 p.m.

JACKSON SAT in the Granada, eating a tasteless burger and fries. His eyes drifted to the low, scuttling clouds framed against a few orange rays of sunlight, then back to the two-story charcoal gray house partway around the corner. The shutters had been repainted, blue instead of mauve. A flowerbed in front of the window had been reshaped and a couple of rose bushes outright removed. A black minivan sat in the driveway, evidence of kids, as was a multi-colored basketball in the grass next to the same hoop Jackson had used fifteen years earlier.

Selling the house had been more of a hassle than imagined, thanks in part to the Navy getting involved for reasons Jackson still didn't quite grasp. A local realtor from David and Hannah's church had made the actual transfer of ownership relatively painless. But cleaning it out, deciding what to keep and what to sell, proving that he was the one to make such a decision—that had been a bear. Not to mention every time he drove to the house he was tortured by memories. With every one of his dad's old sweaters or T-shirts, with each of his mom's cake pans and gardening tools, the pain came back like a branding iron. He should have let a company come in and handle it all, but he couldn't let all of their stuff go just like that, without some oversight.

As he ate and stared at the house, a thousand memories swirled around his brain, the most precious—and thus most painful—finding a way in: Sitting on the couch after a bath on Saturday night, reading Bible stories or The Berenstein Bears with his mom. Watching Kirk Gibson's epic homerun to beat the Athletics in the '88 World Series with his dad. Christmas morning, opening LEGO sets or baseball gloves with Grant while David and Hannah watched with mirthful smiles, while Christmas carols played in the background, and while fresh batches of cookies imbued the house with their warm aroma. Thanksgiving dinners around the table, followed by lighthearted (unless someone dove and got grass stains on their good pants) football games in the yard. Memorial Day games of catch, the sounds of a baseball popping into a mitt echoed by the crackle of burgers on the grill. School mornings when Hannah would have a hot breakfast for the boys—everything from bacon and eggs to waffles with her homemade custard. Donut runs in the morning and Dairy Queen on the deck with David on those rare occasions when Hannah was gone for the weekend. David's bedtime stories and Hannah's morning prayers. Covert missions to sneak candy from the pantry with Grant. Getting busted by Hannah for listening from the kitchen when Grant had his first "date" in the living room.

And on and on they came, like a flood tide, one after the other, each somehow more painful than the last.

His thoughts drifted to memories taken away—memories that would never happen. Future holidays, with late-night conversations about the serious and the silly. Bringing that special someone—should he ever find her—home to meet the folks. Special occasions and everyday moments with Grandpa David and Grandma Hannah. Sharing stories of solved cases and exciting P.I. adventures or commiserating and seeking solace after cases had petered out or proved unsolvable. Attending Dodger games on summer evenings, or watching Rose Bowls with an array of snacks and goodies. More than anything, knowing that he could *always* go home.

Sadness so raw—even after two years—that it gave way to agony overwhelmed him. His weeklong pursuit of the truth turned chase after Padilla had not so much renewed his grief as brought it coursing back to the surface. It was mingled with frustration at being unable to bring Padilla to justice, at being unable to bring his family back, at being unable to cope better with the grief. In truth, some of the frustration went heavenward. Where was the grace "sufficient for you," the "incomparably great power" of God? Where was the "Judge of all the earth" to administer almighty justice when you needed it?

Grief and frustration had bred anger that had turned to bitterness. It had been mixed with fear—of being alone, of the unknown, of the path he seemed to be hurtling down. Add in depression, doubt, and, lastly, desperation. Together, brought to a boiling point, they coalesced to form one, single, overriding emotion that had sprouted like a late-blooming weed to overshadow them all:

Rage.

If he was honest, it had been there for a while, churning and fomenting under the surface like lava ready to erupt out of a volcano. And now, it had an avenue toward the surface, a chute through which to exit the mountain and discharge with fiery wrath into the atmosphere.

Jackson turned the key in the ignition. He took one last look at the house, then accelerated away from the curb and toward his rendezvous with the man who had murdered his family.

Chapter Forty-Six

Friday, May 20, 2011
12:21 p.m.

A VOLLEY OF rifle blasts shattered the still air.

Jackson stood with eyes straight ahead, boring through three rented caskets. They were empty. Curly's had been so thoroughly decimated by fire that no bodies had been recovered, for any of the four victims. Only fragments of DNA, a tooth, one of Grant's sneakers, and half of Hannah's credit card had been present to confirm the deaths. Jackson had no idea why they still needed caskets, or why they were burying said caskets with no bodies. But it had been in David and Hannah's will, and all costs were being covered by the Navy.

The rain of the night before had ceased, replaced now by a steady drizzle that was just enough to coat everything—grass, trees, caskets, and mourners—with a wet sheen. Beside Jackson, Leroy shuddered. He wasn't sure if it was cold or grief that caused the seventy-four-year-old body to shake. For him, it was the former.

"Ready! . . . Aim! . . . Fire!"

A second trio of shots erupted in syncopation, shaking microscopic droplets of water from the leaves of two large oak trees that flanked the cemetery. The low, fog-like cloud absorbed the echo of the shots, and they died quickly to leave silence in their wake.

Jackson had left Maggie's hotel, taking a cab against her insistence that she could drive him, around one, long after the tears had dried up. They'd eaten and talked, or, in her case, mostly listened. Jackson had recounted family adventures and tender moments with his parents, baring his soul to Maggie over club sandwiches and fries. He'd finally called it a night, apologizing for staying so late. She'd shrugged it off and wrapped him in another long, tight hug before he left, one that had made doing so difficult on several levels. But he'd left with a sense of catharsis, until he'd stepped out into the rain again and realized nothing at all had changed.

Leroy had been asleep on the couch when Jackson had arrived at his parents' house. Jackson had reclined in David's old chair, watching the rain on the window until sleep had overtaken him. When morning had come, so had numbness.

"Ready! . . . Aim! . . . Fire!"

No, numbness wasn't the word. Numbness implied a loss of feeling, decreased sensation. Jackson felt it all, every stab of the scalpel, every slice of the knife. If anything, his sensation was heightened, to feel it all magnified as one unending, unmerciful, inescapable assault. It had dogged him as he'd showered and dressed, as he'd stood in the receiving line at the funeral until thirty minutes past the ten a.m. starting time. It had grown in intensity during the forty-five-minute service. Now, sitting graveside, he felt as if the entire world was pressing down on his shoulders, as if he was being crushed to death only in perpetuity.

Why have you forsaken me?

The third and final rifle volley concluded the salute, dying out as quickly as the first two. A call from the decorated non-commissioned officer to "Present arms!" gave way to a breathless calm over the seventy or so folks gathered around three fresh piles of earth and three freshly dug holes.

It should have been four. Jackson should have been there with them. He'd spent hours going over Saturday's schedule, wondering where he could have trimmed five minutes that would have also incinerated his body—and Hillary's—with David, Hannah, and Grant's. He could have driven faster to make up for lost time. He could have waited to buy Maggie some stupid gift card that was the equivalent of a "check yes or no" note passed in third grade. Or at least to mail it. He could have been more precise with his time with the Haywoods and Hailey, making sure to heed Hillary's warnings to be on time. But no. Casual, lackadaisical, carefree Jackson had waved a hand and said "close enough," and now he was looking at one too few caskets. Who knew, maybe had he been on time, events would have unfolded differently and nobody would have died at all. He might have been the one to smell a gas leak or see smoke or sense something was off, just in time to get everyone to safety.

The low, mournful strain of a bugle snapped Jackson's attention from his reverie. "Taps," each note warbling and floating away into the stillness of the dreary afternoon. The last note was particularly haunting, lingering as the mourners were seated and as the honor guard began to fold the United States flag that had draped David's casket. When it had been ceremoniously folded thirteen times, the NCO marched with it held between his palms and stopped directly in front of Jackson.

"On behalf of the President of the United States, the United States Navy, and a grateful Nation, please accept this flag as a symbol of our appreciation for your loved one's honorable and faithful service."

With trembling hands, Jackson reached out to accept the triangular United States flag. The NCO stood back, saluted, then marched back to the side where the rest of the honor guard stood.

Jackson clutched the flag, again staring straight ahead over the three caskets. He heard the preacher speaking again, and then his stare was broken by mourners offering their final condolences. He received them on autopilot, unable to muster more than a small nod in return, unaware of Leroy or Hillary's responses beside him, unaware even who was speaking to him. The final few notes of "Taps" continued to repeat in his head, as if the bugler was still playing.

Years ago, at some indeterminate time that didn't matter, Jackson had learned the actual words to the song, otherwise known as "Butterfield's Lullaby." Along with the tune, the final line kept repeating in his brain.

"God is nigh."

All evidence to the contrary.

*   *   *

Sunday, June 23, 2013
7:51 p.m.

A THIN line of orange just above the horizon represented the only break in the canvas of gray and white clouds as Jackson turned the Granada off North Torrey Pines Road just south of the famous golf course that was home to the PGA Tour annually, and to the U.S. Open just a few years back. He drove past several high-tech research facilities, and the terrain cleared, offering a panoramic view of the Pacific over the chaparral covered sandstone cliffs of Torrey Pines State Natural Reserve. Even on an overcast day with the sea a slate gray, it was beautiful.

But Jackson was not interested in beauty.

He drove past Torrey Pines Gliderport, the launching pad for hang gliders and paragliders whose vibrant chutes were mainstays over the cliffs and beach below. On an overcast day, and with dusk approaching, the sky was free of gliders, and the Gliderport's lot was almost void of cars.

Jackson continued north on a dirt road, with the Torrey Pines Golf Course impinging on the right. The road continued for another quarter mile, past the 12th green and 13th tee, to another, smaller parking area that provided access to more stunning vistas and Reserve hiking trails. The lot was empty, what with the park closing at sunset, and Jackson parked somewhere in the middle, just beyond a patch of chaparral that partially concealed him from anyone coming up the road.

Then he waited.

The orange line on the horizon grew, and several shafts of orange light shone down on the Pacific, turning the surface a sparkling golden color. Jackson checked the magazine on his Glock, setting it on the seat beside him. He looked over his shoulder, down the road, seeing nothing. He resisted the urge to check the Glock again and drummed his fingers on the steering wheel in an effort to drown out the voices in his head.

Voices saying Padilla wouldn't come, that he was on to Jackson or had been warned by Omar or had bailed on the meeting.

Voices saying the cops would be coming instead, having been called by someone who found Omar or by the chopper himself, had he managed freedom.

Voices questioning if Jackson was *one hundred percent* positive Padilla had murdered his family.

Voices shouting down the absurd doubts and reminding him of the proof of Padilla's guilt.

Voices warning him against taking justice—or worse, vengeance—into his own hands.

And voices of David, Hannah, and Grant.

No, not voices. They were actually starting to fade from his memory. All he had were words from his deceased parents and brother—remembrances of past expressions of love and camaraderie that would never again be given a voice.

Jackson saw movement out the corner of his eye. A taxi bounced over the uneven ground, kicking up a small cloud of dust as it stopped almost directly in front of the Granada. A minute passed. Jackson's heart threatened to burst from between his ribs as the rear door opened.

Joaquín Padilla got out.

He wore faded and torn jeans, a hoodie the same color as the ocean, unzipped over a white T-shirt. There was no mistaking the ugly, mean features of the face, the crooked nose, or the balding head, even though the scruffy beard had been reduced to a couple days' worth of shadow. It was him.

The cab didn't move. Jackson opened his door and got out, leaving the Glock on the passenger seat.

Padilla looked at him expectantly.

"Get rid of the cab," Jackson said with a nod.

"What?"

"Do it."

"You Omar's friend?"

Jackson nodded.

Padilla bent down, waited for the passenger window to lower, then handed some money through the opening. Jackson waited until the taxi accelerated into a U-turn. He slowly closed his door. The man who had murdered his family was thirty feet away.

"Where's Omar?" Padilla asked when the silence had grown awkward.

"Tied up at work."

Padilla nodded.

Jackson looked to see the cab rounding the corner, behind more scrub. He forced a congenial smile to his face and took several steps toward Padilla, who reciprocated.

"Jim," Jackson said, extending a hand. "No last name."

"Joaquín," Padilla said, reaching for Jackson's hand.

As they clasped, Jackson planted his left foot in the dirt. He looped his fingers around Padilla's thumb, clamping them over his wrist. He pulled the criminal toward him, at the same time raising his right knee. Before Padilla knew what was happening, much less had a chance to react, Jackson had thrust his right knee up and into the soft tissue of Padilla's groin.

With an exclamatory gasp, Padilla's body spasmed in response, his chin rising into the air. It made a perfect, easy target for Jackson as he released his grip on Padilla, formed a fist, and drilled the convict with everything he had.

Bone cracked against bone, and blood splattered from Padilla's mouth. Jackson's weight was thrown off balance, and he fell to one knee as Padilla thudded into the dust beside him.

In a fair fight, Padilla was big enough and mean enough to hold his own. But Jackson's surprise knee to the crotch had been a direct hit, and Padilla was defenseless. Jackson raised his right knee over Padilla, straddling his torso, and began flailing cross after cross at Padilla's head. Fueled by a visceral rage unlike anything he had ever known or felt, he continued to swing until the flurry of energy was exhausted. Off balance from his latest punch, Jackson half tumbled and half rolled to the side.

He came up on his knees, panting for breath, feeling pain in his knuckles. He sucked in a giant breath, spitting as he exhaled. Ten feet away, Padilla had rolled onto his stomach. He slowly propped himself on an elbow, then two, blood dripping from gashes on his cheek and from his nose and mouth and puddling in the dirt.

He made it to hands and knees and Jackson stepped forward. Raising his foot, he kicked down with the sole of his shoe, knocking Padilla over onto his back. His white shirt was spattered with blood, as was the unzipped hoodie that hung half off him. Pathetically, he rolled again and started to rise.

"You killed my parents," Jackson growled. He reared back with his right fist and belted Padilla in the face with another haymaker. He tumbled back like a ragdoll.

"You killed my brother," Jackson said, stalking toward him. He was unaware of anything in his surroundings—not the parking lot, not the split sky over the ocean, not the distant sounds of cars. All he saw was the blood-soaked murderer in front of him. But he wasn't sickened by the sight; he was invigorated, like the crowd at a bullfight. Padilla was finally getting the punishment he so richly deserved.

"You ruined my life," Jackson said.

Padilla scooted backwards, trying to lift his hands in front of his face. He wasn't in time, as Jackson dropped to his knees again and resumed wailing on the defenseless man.

Right.

Left.

Right.

Left.

Blood sprayed like lawn sprinkler, and the next right sent several teeth flying.

"Jack!"

He wailed some more, his punches getting faster and more powerful.

"JACK! Stop!"

Another right.

Another left.

"Jackson, stop! He didn't do it!"

Jackson paused. His arms were quivering. He was breathing so hard it hurt his stomach and throbbed in his head. Beneath him, Padilla was only semi-conscious.

Jackson sat back, resting his weight on his heels and Padilla's waist. His legs gave out, and he tumbled to the side, falling back in the dirt. His stomach heaving for air, he slowly turned his head to where a man stood not more than a dozen feet away from him.

The voice was raspier. The hair was a shade lighter, and longer than it had ever been. There was a beard, carrying a faint tinge of red to go with brown. The body was much thinner, and the face a touch more drawn. But although they seemed hollow and sunken compared to bright and cheery, there was still no mistaking the eyes.

His own eyes first pinched in disbelief, then widening in shock, Jackson pushed himself up with his palms and slowly stood on wobbly legs. For several seconds, he stared incredulously at the man in front of him as the world around him began to spin. He felt himself shaking, and expected to fall back into the dirt. But instead, the man rushed forward and took an arm in each hand to steady him.

Jackson blinked hard, then locked onto the man's dark blue eyes. Finally, his brain managed to send a signal to his lips. They trembled at first, as if unable to comprehend the message, before finally uttering the unthinkable.

"Grant?"

Acknowledgements

Thanks to the usual crew for their work proofing and editing the drafts of *Mine to Avenge*. Sierra, Mom, Dad, Mark, Tiffani, and Chris all lent their ears and eyes to the project, and I couldn't do it without them.

And thanks my faithful readers. I don't want to name names because I'll forget some, but you know who you are. I *greatly* appreciate you taking the time to read my books and share your thoughts with me. Keep it up!

www.ingramcontent.com/pod-product-compliance
Lightning Source LLC
Chambersburg PA
CBHW031923060726
47496CB00002BB/283